D B ROOK

Callus & Crow

The Wayward World Chronicles, Book 1

Of the gifts granted to me at birth, it is my imagination that fuels my soul the most. For those who have inspired, supported, shaped and shared this dream, I am truly grateful, for you have helped me stay well and fulfilled and you have helped to create a world that, I hope, will live on beyond its creator.
and to Lynsey and my angels, I thank you for the time you have allowed me to spend walking in this world and not our own. Without this generosity, the Wayward World would not exist.
DB Rook

Chapter 1

Ben Hoby

Hoby Ranch

Deep west

The season's drought had heightened the frustrations of the cattle, so much so that one desperate beast had butted its head through the wire fence, driven wild from the thirst. Pa had taken a real beating to release her and asked me to retie the wires good and tight while he dragged her inside to stop the bleeding and tend her wounds.

"Don't you be forgettin' gloves, boy. 'Man's work mendin' fences," he called after me; I sprang into action, gathering the tools needed from the house with the swagger of the man about the ranch. Brushing the back of Ma's empty chair as always, I ran to the back door, my gloves hanging from my back pocket the way Pa's did. The midday heat was choking, it hit me the moment I stepped outside, but I kept running, unfazed; I had man's work to do.

The hole was pretty big, but Pa had taught me how to gather the wires one by one and entwine them to seal the gap. I grabbed the first broken thread and immediately yanked my hand back.

"Damn it!" It burnt my finger; I stuck it in my mouth with a grimace and a metallic taste of baked-on cattle blood. Pa always knew best; the sun had cooked the blood stained fencing all morning. As I sucked and cooled away the pain, I looked up into the vast, sweltering desert surrounding the pen. A dark patch in the sky drew my gaze; it was darker than any cloud I'd ever seen and approaching months before the wet season. I watched as the dark

1

stain seeped across the sky and seemed to scatter in the desert haze. The black specks swirled around each other whilst continually advancing. I put my gloves on and grabbed the unruly fence wire, but never took my eyes from the mysterious black cluster floating on the horizon like peppercorns in a bubbling hot soup.

It was not until I had tied three wires that I noticed the smouldering figure below the approaching phenomenon. Like a flailing beetle in the shimmering heat, he trudged. Stooped and covered in black. Occasionally, he stumbled to one knee, then rose and continued toward our home, surrounded by mile upon mile of harsh, empty plains.

Almost without noticing, I had removed my gloves and began walking toward the stranger in the distance, my imagination clutching at explanations for what my eyes were telling me. As I closed the distance, my tongue seemed to clog my throat, and I stared at the sky in awe. The swarm of blackness I had watched eventually resolved into clarity as it neared. The staggering figure in black seemed to be hounded by a murder of crows; the cacophony of their calls became audible at the moment of my realisation. I stood dumbstruck. The circling birds acted not as scavengers but as chaperone to the broken character below them. They seemed to drive the stranger towards me.

By now I could see he wore a sand covered black greatcoat and a heavy cowl over his head and shoulders that completely shadowed his facial features.

At his stumbled approach, the crows silenced and dispersed to settle on our roof and fencing like a blanket of expectant black across the entire ranch.

"Won't you offer me shelter, son?" He said, his voice the desert floor rasping beneath cracked soles. Before I could think to answer, I was already helping him through the pen under the watchful eyes of the crows. Beneath his thick black clothing, I caught a smell of hanging meat, a fresh carcass, before Pa got to work on it in his brown leather apron, ma's room towards the end. The poor man was groaning in pain and an obvious thirst as I helped him over the threshold of our place. I remembered Ma in her final days, grey and sweating, pleading for more water that we didn't have. Suddenly Pa's booming voice smashed through my thoughts.

"What're you doin' boy?" He shouted, obviously startled as he emerged from the house, his tired eyes wide beneath unruly brows. He spat, then asked in a quieter voice, "Who is this?" his face creased with worry.

"Help me Pa, the man needs shelter." My voice cracked as I ushered him inside. It always sounded like a child's voice against Pa's.

Pa reluctantly helped me to settle the stranger into my bed. There was a creak of protesting timber, but it held, and we stood back in reflective silence. The man's hood had shifted slightly with our handling, revealing sharp cheekbones and the sunken craters beneath them. His skin looked a peculiar pale yellow, the likes of which I'd never seen before, though I realised the man was clearly sick. Again, my mind flashed back to recall Mother as she dry-retched into her chamber pot, her hands trembling.

"Shutters!" his urgent outburst startled me and Pa; we jumped into action and, window by window, blocked the sun's piercing beams from the room. The man sighed then, long and whistling through his dried-up throat.

"Thank you." He croaked; a twitch of a smile passed his bluish lips.

"What's your name, stranger?" Pa boomed, a little too loud. It made me jump again. In answer, the man's eyes suddenly flicked open. Huge black marbles in sunken sockets.

"They call me Callus." He said, staring straight at Pa.

"That's a funny name!" I interrupted before Pa could reply; he put his big hand on my shoulder as our visitor looked at me.

"I'm named after the tough bits on your father's hands." He said before coughing, dry and fruitless. Pa stared at the man sternly, his brows crushed together.

"Go on, Ben, go set the table for dinner." With a soft push, I was out the door, closing it behind me. I couldn't resist staying a few moments to listen before I went down the creaking stairs.

"You have the look of a tribesman." Pa was saying. From his tone, I imagined his hands were on his hips, thumbs in belt loops.

"Half breed," was the softly rattled reply. "Never been back. Reckon that's

3

for the..."

I couldn't linger any longer or Pa would catch me and I'd be for the strap; he didn't stand for bad manners.

I went downstairs and saw to my chores, all the time thinking of the mysterious crow man in my bed, his unusual face and how his lips hardly moved as he spoke. He fascinated me!

I prepared and cooked a stew that Ma would've been proud of. I left two bowls on the table and took one up for the crow man. Although it felt wrong, I crept up the stairs so I could catch the tail end of their conversation before I stepped into the darkened room.

"... was a long, long time ago." Crow man was saying. His voice sounded fuller somehow, still dry, but the rasp was lessening with rest. Pa seemed more comfortable as well; he straddled my chair, his thick arms resting on the back as I entered.

"I brought you some stew." Pa stood up immediately, as if I'd caught him telling secrets.

"Right then, set it down, Ben. Let's leave our guest to eat."

"Cal." said the crow man; "Call me Cal." Pa nodded and ushered me out of the room and down to the dinner table.

Pa was quiet during dinner; I caught him glancing at Ma's chair more than usual. At one point, as he was clearing the dishes, he put his hand on the worn chair-back and closed his eyes just for a second. Then, without a word, he put down the dishes in his other hand and went upstairs.

I finished up the dinner things and stood at the foot of the stairs. Pa and Cal were talking. I wanted so badly to creep up and listen, but I spotted Pa's leather strap over the fireplace and the idea vanished. I curled up on the thick hide rug in the sitting room and closed my eyes.

Chapter 2

Anonymous Author

Rhyme and Reason

The Communion was a world event that gave way to the fascinating epoch in which this story takes place.

The communion, a saturation of society and the greed that it incites, an evolution of connectedness that both exacerbated nature's decline and forced its evolution, it elevated its people to a state of God-like stature. A state of unnatural instability that could only end in cataclysm and could only be preceded by rebirth.

After the communion and during this rebirth, man's hunger for power finally cut a path through the giant, predatory fauna that, until then, had entirely ruled the seas.

The savage waters had kept civilisations apart, each of them ignorant of the others as they fed on the remnants of cultures long dead.

Thankful for what little guidance they could gather from a time before their entrapment and conscious of the cultural and historical lottery that each area provided, a small city found its way to technological superiority and ventured across the sea.

There was a clash of worlds, where previously isolated nations had grown and developed in vastly different directions. Remnants of technology, beliefs, creeds and history suddenly merged to create our great, dysfunctional planet. It was only the world wars that proceeded this fascinating era that finally constrained man's inclination towards a unified direction.

Ben Hoby
Hoby Ranch
Deep West

I dreamt of Cal and his crows. His black flock swirled around him as he arrived in the big city. People of all creeds looked on in wonder, just like I had earlier that day; only Cal wasn't sickly like when I'd first seen him staggering through the desert. He was tall and strong; his long black hair swung with each stride, and on his belt hung a hatchet made of metal. The folk dashed out of his way, tripping on the decked streets and shielding themselves from the swooping crows all around. As Cal made his way through the city, deeper into the maze of streets, one of his crows settled on his broad shoulder and seemed to point the way, eventually steering him to a brightly painted yellow door. He rapped three times and as his large hand lifted for a fourth; the door swung open. Ma and Pa were in the doorway; they were hugging and smiling and were so pleased to see Cal that Pa released Ma and wrapped his arms round Cal in an enormous bear hug. I could smell Ma's perfume as we all moved inside the house. It was the expensive stuff Pa only bought on her birthday; she looked so happy. Her hands didn't shake. They were long, pink and graceful.

Inside, the house was the same as our ranch, only there were no chairs at all. The three of them stood happily chatting and drinking tea; a deep red tea; mine tasted funny. I went in search of the chairs around the house as I sipped the tepid brew, but couldn't find any. I looked in every room; the chairs were all gone. I scratched my head for a moment, put down my empty cup and ran back to the kitchen where my family was still laughing and joking amiably. I quickly decided we didn't need chairs; I was just so happy to see everyone together and happy. I closed my eyes and grinned contentedly as I drifted off again to an even deeper sleep.

The next few days were unusually busy for me. I suspected Pa had given me most of his jobs so he could spend more time chatting with Cal. Initially, it annoyed me, but then I realised that since Ma was gone, Pa rarely got to speak to anyone but me.

One bright morning, whilst I was mucking out the pen beneath my window, I heard a clatter and a frustrated shout followed by Pa's unmistakable voice as he tried to pacify the stranger currently lodging in my room. I shifted my task closer and picked out Cal's voice as he retorted.

"...wasting time here! I'm ready to go now!" There was another crash, and I feared for Pa, but his muffled voice returned calmly. I moved away, then; worried Pa would see me slacking and somehow the tension in the room would shift to me. I didn't see Pa for a few hours and did not hear any further commotion as I slogged my way through the day's chores.

I ate alone and frequently looked up at Ma's chair, fighting the sting in my eyes. I had come to terms with her being gone from my world, though I missed her intensely, especially when Pa and I were at odds with each other. It was the injustice that haunted me. The unfairness of nature and life itself. Why would she fall ill just like that? Why was she unable to fight it off? She did not deserve to watch the grief build in her loved ones as they looked on and cared for her, their efforts ineffective against the raging disease in her weakening body. At times I was angry at Pa, and often I was angry at myself. Why did I not know how to help her, how to heal her?

"BEN!" Pa's voice made me jump. I quickly cuffed away a furious tear. "There's work to do." I followed him outside, relieved to leave my grief with my unfinished meal.

We approached a partial pit that Pa had obviously started. He threw me a shovel to help him finish while he tended something else. I got to work without a word, my thoughts moving back to Cal. I wondered how long he would stay; he was clearly wanting to move on. Where would he go next? I scanned the featureless horizon, wondering what had brought him our way. Pa approached behind me, he was dragging something heavy. I turned to help him and my heart sank. It was the beast that had got stuck in the fence a few days back. It had not survived, and Pa had been busy butchering its meat to store. I had been digging its grave.

With all my remaining strength, I hurled my shovel as far as I could and screamed out my rage, dislodging a handful of Cal's crows from the roof with the sudden noise. I suddenly wanted to destroy something, anything. If life could vanish so easily, why should I care to protect it? I stood shuddering as Pa's huge hand settled onto my shoulder. We stood in shared, pained silence for an age before he spoke.

"Save this." He said almost distantly, as if he was speaking to himself. "There'll be times when you can make a difference, when you can fight." I turned on him then, a little too fast, a little too accusatory.

"Not here." I said, glancing around at my small world. Cruel nature ruled over this place. If we were lucky, we could eat. If not, it fed us grief and hopelessness. I looked into his eyes, expecting another answer. He nodded once in agreement and patted my shoulder before walking away and back into the house.

I finished my chores and sought my bed as early as I could.

Chapter 3

Ben Hoby
  Hoby Ranch
  Deep West

That night, I awoke to a booming thud and a crack of splintering wood. I sat up disorientated and stared towards the foot of the stairs; my eyes unable to penetrate the gloom. Alarmed and confused, I fumbled for a match from the hearth as the booming continued, along with a grunting of effort.

"Ah, you're awake! Come help me, son." An unfamiliar voice sounded in the pitch dark; my breath would not come as fear squeezed my chest.

"Aint no need to be afraid." Another grunt of effort followed his inept reassurance, then a loud wooden creak. I struck a match on the hearth but still could only make out vague shapes until I found and lit a candle. As the soft light filled the room, one shape appeared before me. It was Cal; with a huge forced smile across his face. He looked different. His face was fuller and darker; his voice no longer rattled but clearly rang in my head.

"It's just me! Don't be afraid. I just need a little help and I'll explain everything." He patted my shoulder and turned away; I let out a breath, relieved, but still I did not know what was going on. Cal took a step away, then spun round, reaching into the pocket of his greatcoat.

"Here, drink this down. It'll help." He smiled again, this time less forced; he put something cold into my hand and stalked off back to the staircase. "Only a little mind." He called over his shoulder as I watched him; he was trying to drag what looked like Pa's wardrobe down the stairs; the banister protested every inch of movement. With each step came a rewarding *boom* as

9

it hit the next. It was only then that I realised I was probably still dreaming; I relaxed and took a deep breath as I raised the small metal hip flask in my hand. Embossed on the flat side were the words REV. W. J. BERKELEY. I unscrewed the top, careful not to snag my finger on a jagged seam that had uncurled in the metalwork.

"Stranger and stranger." I said to myself before I took a long swig of the thick tonic inside.

This time I *knew* I was awake; my head hurt like hell. An almost violent jostling had awoken me; I opened my eyes to a sparse, blurred landscape as it flew past. I was on a two-horse wagon, being driven at breakneck speed by a tense-looking Cal. He looked over and smiled.

"Good evening!" he called through the buffeting wind and his whipping hair. I took in my surroundings as my head slowly cleared. It was dark; I knew somehow, although I could plainly see the odd rock or cactus as it sped past. The horizon, though a strange grey-blue in colour, was still visible in the dark; random remains and crumbled foundations of pre-communion ruins were discernible despite the lack of light. It was a bizarre sensation.

"How you feelin'" Cal asked, the wind still whipping at his words.

"Okay, I guess. Where's Pa?" My headache had receded as soon as I opened my eyes and I felt pretty good, considering; I stretched my arms. They felt strong and quick.

"Just let me get you into town, son; sun'll be up in a couple hours. When we find a place to stay, I'll tell you everything. Just trust me for now, okay?" A panic surged through me.

"WHERE'S MY PA!" I screamed defiantly, fear and confusion suddenly seizing me. Cal leaned over and put a hand on my shoulder and looked me straight in the eye.

"Trust me for now, son, this is what your Pa wanted. I'm goin' take care of you." He patted me gently. "Just trust me." Strangely, I did trust him, but the panic at my missing Pa would not go away. Folding my arms, I frowned.

"I'm not your son." I muttered defiantly as we fled towards God knew where.

Eventually, a ridge we'd been following for miles dipped and spiralled gradually down into a massive bowl; right in the middle sat a town. Speckled dim lights peered out from wooden buildings, only faintly illuminating the criss-cross of familiar pen fencing. As we descended below the wind's reach, the night became quieter and Cal eased up on the horses.

"Made it before sunup." He said, obviously relieved. He didn't look at me.

"Where's my Pa?" I repeated, noticing the twitch of Cal's jaw as I spoke. He shook his head once, then turned towards me.

"I'm sorry… boy, your Pa's not comin'." He spoke hesitantly, unable to look me in the eye. "It's me and you now." He jeered on the horses as if that settled the matter.

"What do you mean?" my voice stumbled with its pitch and the movement of the cart; I couldn't believe what I was hearing. Cal shook his head regretfully again, but still couldn't look at me.

"Look, your Pa, he wasn't a well man. Just like," He paused, unsure if he should continue. "Like your Ma." He looked away as he spoke. "I'm sorry, boy, your Pa asked me to take care of you and here we are!"

"He didn't even say goodbye." I muttered as a tear streaked the road-dirt on my face. Cal hung his head, then looked up at the sky worriedly before he called to the horses.

"Wooah!" he pulled them to a stop and turned to me, one hand resting nervously near my shoulder. "I know this is hard for you, boy, but your Pa didn't want you to see him sick. You wouldn't want that, would you?" I shook my head silently as the tears came hot and fast. "He wanted you to have a new life with me." He shook my shoulder. "Have some adventure!" He smiled, but he knew he'd not convinced me. Then he looked at the sky again. A faint glimmer of sun was fighting through the clouds. "Come now, let's get into town and have a sleep. You'll feel much better; then we can have some fun!" He jeered up the horses. When we arrived at the town, I could barely see through the floods of tears.

Cal left me crying in a stable for what seemed like hours before he returned and ushered me into the back of the wagon. Inside was the enormous wardrobe Cal had been struggling with back at the ranch. He'd laid it vertically, with a bedroll and blanket beside it.

"Now," he said as he took out his hip flask and handed it to me. "We're both gonna get some shut-eye and nobody should come disturbin' us, okay?" He put both his hands on my shoulders and looked me in the eye. "Have a good swig now and I promise it will feel better by tomorrow." He ruffled my hair and climbed inside the wardrobe; suddenly he turned to me and raised his finger. "Do not open this door, understand?" I stared at him, confused and sniffling, the last of my tears still trickling.

"Okay." I sighed.

"If there's any trouble, you knock, okay?" He bent down to demonstrate with a knock on the heavy door. I nodded solemnly. With that, he climbed in and pulled the doors shut above him. I got down onto my bedroll, and with my mind spinning, I looked at the hip flask in my hand. The night had not been a dream; embossed on the small metal bottle was the name REV. W. J. BERKELEY.

"Goodbye Pa." I said to myself and took a long swig.

Chapter 4

Anonymous Author

Disclaim to Fame

Of the many myths and stories born of this eventful period, it is this tale, I feel, that has twisted the most. Countless retelling and infinite, innocent additions have subverted the stories of these compelling lives and the perpetual curse that entwined them.

As a passionate enthusiast of the subject and legacy in question, I endeavour to tell the tale authentically here, through compiled research, archived records and journals interconnected through my own creative vision.

With regret, I must remain anonymous throughout this body of work. Such is the price of the trust and respect I have earned in order to be in such a position to present the truth.

Ben Hoby

Town of "Basin"

Deep West

What I thought was night seemed to last forever. Haunted by memories and thoughts of my family, I dreamt of my Pa shooing me away with his hand like vermin on the ranch. Eventually my mind grew tired of torturing itself, and I took in my actual surroundings. I realised it was not night at all; we had obviously ridden through the night as there were bright shards of sunlight spearing through the wooden slats of the stable outside the wagon.

Bright specks floated in the air, and I could hear muffled voices outside.

Quietly, I climbed out of the wagon and went to the door. I peeked outside; the sun hurt my eyes. The town was bustling with activity beyond two arguing men; one kept pointing angrily towards our stable and occasionally spat on the floor by his feet. I tried to listen, but couldn't make out why they were arguing. Then the angry man shoved the other aside and came stomping towards me. At first, I froze, then a wave of something primal came over me. I grabbed a pitchfork from the wall and stood defiantly as the door flung open, almost blinding me as the light rushed in. The angry man, spittle dripping from his long moustache, was at first startled, then angry.

"WHERE'S YOUR PA BOY?" he shouted, looking around the inside of the stable as he squeezed a meaty fist.

"HE'S NOT MY PA!" I screamed back; a rage from deep inside burst out at the mention of my Pa. The man hunched slightly, his voice quieter as he snarled.

"I don't give a damn who he is, WHERE IS HE?!" the man's taunting coupled with the whirlwind my life had suddenly become broke something inside me; I lashed out with the pitchfork as the man jumped back, the tine catching him in the shoulder. A thin red squirt flew across the stable as he roared with pain.

"You little swine!" He screamed as he slapped his hand to the wound, pure rage in his eyes. I stood my ground as he pulled the door closed behind him and rolled up his sleeves, his shirt now soaking up blood. I braced myself for his knotted fists, strangely unfazed by the fury aimed at me.

Callus

Got caught in the daytime and picked up a partner
Stopped off in Basin to wait out the day

Now, usually if I get woken up in the daytime, which don't happen that often, it's because the shit's seriously burst the bag! Sleep ain't like it used to be; nice fluffy dreams, then you wake up eight hours later grinning at

the day to come. No, since the curse, sleep's a necessary twelve hours o'
black stillness where my body does all kinds of painful and grotesque stuff,
eventually releasin' me into the night with a hunger that groans and rips its
way through my stomach and into my veins. After over a hundred years of
this nightly torment, I've become as used to the yearning as anybody could
and can usually handle the urges until I'm in a fit and sensible position to
deal with it.

On that day, though; already days behind schedule and rudely awoken,
in daylight, to face a damn thug; a bleeding one at that, in the middle of a
threat to the boy. I burst from the old wardrobe with my head ringing. I
wouldn't say that the sight of blood turned me into a monster, but my need,
especially if woken up early, is akin to a man crawling through the desert
finding a bulging fruit tree. The oath I'd taken the day before had marked a
turning point in my long life, and the nobility I felt protecting the boy was
bigger than anything I'd felt in years.

Despite feeling like shit, I leapt out the wardrobe, bore the thug to the
ground and sunk my fangs into his unshaven neck. The first mouthful killed
the hunger, I remembered myself; I turned to the boy, now terrified, as I
leaned over my prey.

"RIDE!" I pointed north through the stable door, unaware I spat bloody
spittle on my hand. "Ride until dusk, then wait for me. I'll come to you!"
The boy was nodding like a wild horse by then; I looked him in the eye,
tried to sound gentler. "Take the wagon! If you'll wait for me, I will come."
He'd hitched the horses, opened the stable doors and disappeared with the
wagon before I'd finished my feed.

I was in the shit. Blood drunk and staggering, I dragged the sorry bastard
to the back of the stable and sat beside him. I knew people would come
lookin'. I was in no state to turn them away as I'd over fed; I knew as soon
as I'd let go. The situation had made me ravenous, and I never did know
when to stop when my own blood was up. So I barred the door as best I
could and went and sat with moustache man in the shadows to nap it off.

Luckily, I got a couple hours in before they started hacking at the door.
Beams of sunlight bursting through the gaps.

"Shit!" I felt more sober, but it was still daytime and, like I say; sleep to me sure is a precious thing. I stood and unhooked my hatchet. It felt good in my hand; a link to the man I used to be.

CRACK! The bar gave way and everything was quiet for a second. I spun my hatchet to use the dull end; I'd made a promise to myself to be a different person. Walking to the door slowly, I tried my best to ignore the hot beams as they passed over me. The first face came through the door, Thunk! He went down; probably never even saw me in the gloom.

"Shoot!" a voice called from outside, then the shots came. They didn't have an arsenal, but one of 'em caught me a couple times. As bullets tore holes for more sunbeams, one bit me in the side, another glanced off my scalp and hurt like hell! I roared as pain went through me; didn't even know which hurt worst but I was real angry! I kicked the door open and leapt onto the nearest gun man, turns out there was only two of 'em but the nearest got thrown into the other, there was a loud crack but it was just an arm or leg I think, I hurt too much to care. One fella remained; trembling as he stared at me. In the distance, I could see more shapes cautiously moving towards me, and a few more quickly moving away.

"Horse!" I shouted as I walked towards him. He jabbered something and reached for a six gun at his hip. Before he'd cocked it, I was on him, hatchet to his throat.

"You a fucking idiot?" I asked politely. "Get me a horse and send me on my way, then I'll not have to chop you into pieces; sound good to you?"

"Yes, yes sir, no problem with me... sir." I let him up; he backed away slowly, arms raised high and pointed round the front of the stable to a swishing tail. "Take her, I don't want n-no trouble." He stammered and tried to smile, but the bulging, terrified eyes were all wrong.

"That's more like it!" I grinned, despite the pain and the sun sizzling my wounds. "A man with a br-."

Another bullet *popped* into my left shoulder! I roared and spun; as I came back round, I hurled my hatchet with everything I got at a patch of gun smoke behind the horse guy. A gurgle and a splat of bright blood rewarded me as I saw him slump to the ground; it was a legendary throw. I remember how it felt to this day!

Despite my weary state and the holes I was collecting in myself, I smirked at my aim; went to remove my sticky hatchet and made for the horse. A couple shots hit the wall beside me, but I just wanted to get out of there and back on the trail, see if the boy had waited; think I was hoping he had, but knew it was a tall order. I got hold of the horse and gripped firmly to steady it; the gunshots weren't helping. I'm not great with panicked horses, but brute strength sometimes seems to reassure them.

I climbed on and she bolted. Any direction was a good start, so I let her have her way; she galloped straight out o' town like she knew. Then she threw me what seemed like a hundred yards over the boundary fence onto the hard dirt.

"Christ aches!" I hollered my frustration as I sat up and straightened my head. When I'd recovered and got to my feet, the damn horse had vanished.

I was roughly north of the little town and as far as I could tell, there was no pursuit yet. My body felt like it had been on fire for an hour; I pulled my hood up and limped onto the road, headed further out o' town, fast as I could manage. Before long, I looked up to find three crows circling. I hung my head. "Damn crows." I muttered to myself as I stopped to rest and check my wounds.

"Need to take better care o' myself," I said as I limped along. Saying it aloud somehow made my growing list of goals easier to remember.

Chapter 5

Excerpt from *The Basin gazette:*
1ˢᵗ Thorsday, 3ʳᵈ, 829 AF

"He hit this town like a beast from a storybook." One upstanding citizen told
the Gazette the following morning; according to witnesses, the crazed tribesman
laid waste to Main Street before holding up in Mr Berriforth's stables, where he
took part in a gruesome and sadistic tribe ritual. Luckily for Basin, local hero
and gunslinger, Tom Gibbet scared off the native before his magical cursing took
any effect. *"Biggest man I ever saw!"* Tom told me on that sombre morning. *"He'd
killed Vern and Skeech before I got there, but he soon went runnin' when I had
sights on him. If it weren't for my shooter jammin' justice would've been served."*
The red-skinned murderer took flight on a stolen horse while the good citizens
of Basin mourned and buried their dead. Although the Basin Gazette cannot
condone the idea of vigilante justice, it seems something needs to be done to stop
these tribal savages from trying to take back their land.

Ben Hoby
Outskirts of "Basin"
Deep west

Oddly reminiscent of the first time we met, I saw the crows first.

I'd ridden the wagon's horses to near exhaustion to escape the town and the flailing horror of my mind as it ranted to me. The town was far below when I stopped, but my thoughts were not to be outrun. Surely the same fate as the mustachioed villain in the barn had befallen my Pa, but if so, why had Cal dragged me along with him? A sudden and vastly alarming thought nearly stopped my heart. What if I'm just a snack? What if I was just Cal's equivalent of trail rations? I panicked; I climbed down from the wagon and paced the small plateau I'd stopped on, my mind reeling. Luckily, after some nail biting and nervous stomping that unsettled the horses, reason kicked in. Why would Cal have been so angry at the man threatening me, and why the story about Pa? Having seen the strength and speed Cal possessed, he didn't need to lie to me. Perhaps it was all true and my Pa had suffered from the blood being sucked from his veins in that brutal manner I'd seen with my own eyes. I shuddered at the thought, but could not shake the bizarre loyalty and fascination I felt for Cal. Eventually, I settled on a deal within myself to ease the growing conflict in my thoughts. Cal had said he would come for me; he'd looked me straight in the eye and said he would come. The town was full of people; he could have any of them if he wanted. Also, he could leave in several directions and leave the town behind; never giving a second thought to the boy he was saving for a snack. So, I decided that if Cal did indeed come to where I was waiting by dusk, I would trust in him and forget my fears of him feeding on me like he surely had my Pa. If he didn't arrive by the next morning, I would find my own way back to the ranch and discover what had happened to Pa.

I looked up confidently as soon as I had decided and casually glanced south; in the sky was a clustering flock of familiar black specs. They seemed to drive a crooked figure towards me.

Soon, Cal had arrived at the wagon and seemed to be in a terrible state. Hooded once again against the sun's rays and stumbling around a wounded leg. Without thinking, I ran out to him and helped him back to the wagon. He'd bled, but it had dried on his clothes; he didn't say a word, and neither did I.

As the surrounding crows settled on the wagon and nearby rocks, I helped him onto the back of the wagon and instinctively opened the doors to Pa's wardrobe. He pulled back his hood and revealed a painful line of missing hair and sun-baked gore on one side of his head; I winced at the sight of it. Cal did his best to smile at my concern, but was clearly in a lot of pain and had gone through a lot to get to me.

"It's you and me now, boy." He grunted. "Time for our new life." He stared into my eyes. "Leave the old life behind now." He was nodding as he settled on his back in the wardrobe. "We have a job to get done, then we can do what we like," he continued, "be whoever we want; we just have to find Rev. Osset and look after each other; sound fair?" I nodded as I took his massive, outstretched hand and squeezed as hard as I could. His voice was becoming distant. "We just have to end the past and find ourselves." He said solemnly. I knew what he meant. He gave me a minute to let it sink in and closed his eyes. "What's your name, boy?"

"Crow." I said proudly. "Call me Crow." I closed the wardrobe doors and lay beside the box containing my new partner. The sun would go down soon, and I'd need to keep watch.

Callus
Boy saw me feed
Back on the trail to Osset

Crow! Soon as he'd said it, my dead heart sank; I hated those damn birds. Sure, occasionally they'd come in handy for a bit of effect on the hunt, got the adrenalin flowing, but who wanted to be hounded by filthy, flying rats?

My existence don't have many restraints, 'cept daylight. The sun burns, it weighs on me like I'm underwater, I'm suddenly dead weight, and the damn birds! It's like they can smell me; if I'm out and about in the day, which preferably is rare, they'll find me with their twitchy black eyes and continuous damn cawing. One always becomes more and before I know it, I'm hounded by a damn flock of the critters; makes it hard to blend into the shadows. Imagine, over a hundred years of being sniffed out and tormented by crows, you make a pact with a man, his life for yours and his Child. Hell, you swallow down your own needs to ease the kid's transition and teach him a thing or two. Any name! He can pick any name for his brand new, damn near immortal life with a legend such as me.

"Crow." He said; all wide eyed and excited.

Damn birds!

He closed the doors on the wardrobe, and I let out a sigh of relief as the dark enveloped me. I knew I'd be good as new when I woke up, just had to make sure I had control of the hunger.

Chapter 6

Excerpt from "lost hopes"

**a collection of letters sent to the front line of Western civil wars that
never arrived**

Dearest papa.

*Moma told me I should write you on account of all the pestering I've been doing.
Apparently, with you away fighting, her chores are such that she hasn't the time
to 'indulge my fantasies.'*

*I keep telling her that what I have seen is not a fantasy, but she keeps shooing
me away and so I thought that if I don't tell anyone I will burst.*

*I have taken to collecting shells by the bay, don't worry I don't go anywhere
near the seafront, in fact I stay on the clifftop, but the waves can be so fierce that
often they smash shells into the cliff and pieces fly up and over into the nets I've
built to collect them.*

*One night I'd stayed later than I should and when I returned home, Moma was
furious with me for staying out past dark. The nets had been full from the storm
the day before, and the pieces they'd collected were incredible. You should see how
many spirals I got, and intact too!*

*As I was saying, when the sun went down I realised I would be in trouble so I
packed up my things and stowed my new treasures in the box that you made me,
you know the one that I used to use for my wood carving? Well, I use it for sea
treasures now and it's already getting full.*

*From on top of the cliff wall you can see right down past the bay and as I was
about to leave, I saw that there was a procession of horses and carts heading out
towards the sea! I thought about how angry Moma would be, but I couldn't help*

myself, so I stayed a while to watch what happened.

They set up a camp, I could see the fire but couldn't make out who they were or what they were doing, and it was getting so late so I went off home to face Mama but you won't believe what I saw the next night!

Crow Hoby
Outskirts of Basin
Deep West

Before the sun sank, I knew that pursuit from the town was more than likely and made ready to ride. I had no idea of the geography of the lands we found ourselves in and so decided to just create distance between us and the town we had offended. I climbed into the driver's seat and set off at a steady pace so as not to wake Cal prematurely. I was fairly comfortable with the reins; Pa had often asked me to drive into town to fetch feed or supplies while he worked through his chores. I shook my head; that was my old life now; I squeezed the leather straps in my hands and fought a pressure behind my eyes.

Eventually the sun dipped and smouldered against the horizon; with the darkness came the strange vision I had experienced on our flight from the ranch. Though I could still make out the shadows, they were thinner somehow; I could pick out details amongst the blackness, but could not quite understand why. When the last slice of sunlight vanished, I pulled up the wagon on the side of the road and spent a while just looking across the landscape, picking out creatures I'd never seen before, skittering from hidden warrens or stalking their nonchalant prey. The night was alive with activity; it was like it invited me to a secret place that nobody else knew about. My hearing, too, seemed enhanced; I made out the calls of a myriad of creatures surrounding me, *bleating* and *screeching* to their kin and *buzzing* around my face, hoping to find food or, at the very least, a lamp to surround.

On the outskirts of my attention there was a loud *creak* and before I could recognise it, a heavy hand startled me as it clasped my shoulder.

"Good evening... Crow." Cal said as he nodded his approval at our surroundings. "I was hoping you'd move us away. Good job!" I grinned at him, pleased with his appraisal. "You tired?" I shook my head. "Right then, shall we get going? My turn to drive, I reckon." I moved aside as he climbed up and passed me his hip flask. I drank.

"Where are we going?" I ventured as I caught sight of Cal's previously wounded scalp; the hair had grown back and was already an inch long, but it was now pure white against the jet black of the rest.

"Reckon we should get away from civilisation for a bit, get into the wilds, see if we can't teach you a thing or two, what d'you reckon?" I nodded excitedly, eager to charge off towards our new life together. We set off into the long night.

I guess three or four hours went by before my mind's excitement dwindled and reality nibbled at my thoughts. After all, the man I was sitting with, making comfortable conversation, was also the man who had potentially killed my Pa. The image of the man in the stable kept appearing in my mind's eye. His shocked face paled so quickly.

Despite the bumpy ride, I eventually fell asleep, my dreary thoughts entwined with the bitterness I felt at the treatment of my Pa and echoed through my dreams as I no doubt jerked and muttered under my blanket.

It was a long, hard summer before I forgave him. Night in, night out, I did as I was told and pushed myself through his lessons with an icy determination, spurred by the resentment and grief in my heart. Only when I slept did I allow myself to be a boy again, taken from the arms of his Pa. The image of Cal sucking at the angry man's neck, his mouth twitching as his eyes bulged, fixed in my mind every single night for that long summer in the wilds. The same question haunted me; was that how Pa looked in the end?

We slept mostly during the day; at night he taught me about the night sight he had "blessed" me with, how to tune my eyes to the shades of blue-grey and realise what I was looking at. Sometimes I let my guard down and obviously thrived on the thrill of the new skills I was learning. I didn't let Cal see my excitement, though I sometimes think he could tell, otherwise why would he have persevered through my dark, ungrateful moods? He taught me the crafts of the woodland, hunting and surviving, and living as one with the wildlife and fauna, how to use a hatchet as both tool and weapon.

Cal mostly ignored my frosty attitude towards him, but on some occasions, when I really let loose, he would snap at me; his face snarled and his eyes barely contained his rage. The first few times I had quaked in my worn boots, my recurring nightmare image leaping into my mind and my heart hammering against my breast; I pictured his sharp fangs in my throat. Each time, though, he managed his anger, and I found myself stood tall before his monstrous fury, evidently looking braver than I felt.

By the time the nights grew cold, I had learned many ways to survive in the wild, and a few other things besides. With nobody else around, I thrived on Cal's approval and slowly I eased into our relationship. Many times I would catch him looking into nowhere, lost in thought; I realised it was probably just as strange for him to have me along as it was for me to be with him.

On his recommendation, we staggered the nights so we would have time to ourselves, me in the day and him at night. Even when we were together, he would often disappear for long periods and come back full of energy and back slapping pride for me. I loved those parental moments but still occasionally guessed at where he had been and the answers I conjured were not always agreeable.

We had a good little camp going with our backs to the foot of a ravine, the cart all covered in leaves and vines Cal had me tie together. I was showing great promise in hunting and could easily feed myself; with enough to spare for what little Cal ate. One evening, as the sun dipped behind our corner of the great forest, I came into camp baring a couple of rabbits ready for gutting. Cal was already up. This surprised me; I thought I'd have time to prepare some food before he rose.

"We need to talk." Cal stood chewing a finger; his brow furrowed with apparent worry. His usually throaty voice was serious, but I tried to ignore it and act casual.

"Okay, what's up?" I replied as I lay the first rabbit down and started the well-practiced routine.

"Leave that." he gestured at my work. He seemed agitated. His hands flexed and closed nervously. I stood slowly as he sat on one section of log we'd cut for chairs. Silence grew between us and the anticipation mounted; just as I was about to speak some babble to break it, Cal stood up suddenly.

"Are we partners, Crow?" The question took me by surprise; I feared something terrible had happened.

"Of course." I replied jovially. I remember being pleased that my voice didn't break as I kept up the cheery facade. Cal paced up and down as he continued, whereas I took a seat on the log opposite the one he'd vacated.

"This place is good." He was nodding at our surroundings approvingly as he paced. By this point, I had become nervous; Cal wasn't acting like himself. "Yes." He continued, "It's been a very good spot. I feel I've got to know you and I think we make a good team." He looked at me questioningly, only I didn't know what the question was; I looked around before answering hesitantly.

"You want to leave?" I questioned quietly.

"No, it's not that." He shook his head. "Well, yes it is, but, argh!" He put his hands on his head in frustration, took a huge breath, and then let it out slowly. I had no idea what he was trying to get out, but he was making me very anxious. Even the way he talked was different; since I'd met him when he talked, he'd barely moved his lips. I'd got used to it, but at that point he seemed wild, somehow untethered; I could see the points of his elongated fangs as they caught in the moonlight. As he spoke, his voice grew louder.

"You know what I am, Crow, what I do, what I need to do! God damn, I don't normally have to explain myself to anyone! It's so damn hard with you 'cus were partners and… I saw your face." His shoulders slumped like a massive weight had slipped off him as he ranted. I still didn't know what he was referring to, so I kept quiet. Obviously relieved, he lowered himself back onto the log across from me and spoke in a softer voice.

"I saw your face when I fed back in town." We looked at each other for what seemed like hours. My mind was spinning at his anguish and I suddenly felt guilty for all the thoughts I had harboured during our time together. He'd seen the sheer terror on my face as I'd watched him take down my aggressor back in Basin, the pale shock I'd felt as he dropped to the floor and the horrifying realisation as I'd pieced together the events of the night we left the ranch.

"It's what I need to do to survive, crow." I think I already knew, but as Pa used to say, I'd kept my head in the sand. Strangely, the realisation didn't seem as bad as the fear of it. Now I knew the man who was confessing. "I get hungry. Been slipping out, catching beasts or jumping the odd traveller, but keeping it from you is nigh on impossible. We need to at least pass through civilisation, and I need to bury the hatchet with you." I wasn't ready to speak just yet. I opened my mouth to try, but he continued.

"I've got a mission, an important one, more important than anything, and I've been here with you instead of my mission. 'Spose the thing is whether you wanna join me?" He looked at me straight. I barely heard the question as my mind painted the picture, slotting the events of the last few weeks together into some kind of understanding.

"Do you kill just anyone?" I said, trying to keep accusation out of my tone, but I felt I had to explore this strange 'curse' as he called it. "Like them." I pointed to the limp rabbit carcasses on the camp floor. He sighed again before he spoke.

"They don't have to die." His shoulders slumped again. "But yeah, was a time I went for anyone and everyone! I wanted to get back at the world for what it had done to me. I got a story too, Crow. It goes back a long, long time. Before I met him." He tossed me his engraved bottle; I caught it easily and looked at the familiar lettering.

"Wilf." Cal looked into the sky and briefly smiled. "Since my world went black, I've known three people I could call friend. Without Wilf, I'd still be angry, still be killin' wherever I could. I'd still be an 'abomination.'" He said the word like it was never his to use.

"I got things I need to do for Wilf, Crow. Things aint pretty but need doin'. Question is," He paused, "you comin' or not?" I looked at the man before me in a completely different light. He had remorse, he had history, and he had a wealth of feelings that had burst out of him that night. The silence came again, but this time it was comfortable. We both sat chewing over what had he'd shared; I had never felt so much like an adult. I felt trusted, and the huge, powerful man sat in front of me wanted to be partners.

"No more secrets?" I asked as I looked into his dark eyes. He shook his head.

"We're partners, we're partners." He said and offered me his hand. I grasped it with a passion I had never felt before.

We talked into the night now that the barrier between us had fallen. I asked him about his long life and he regaled me with stories of his travels, adventures, and also dark deeds. When we spoke of the time before his 'curse,' as he called it, he asked that we not speak of such things yet, they were painful memories he would like to hang onto himself for a while, I agreed although I was still mighty curious. I too held back the stories of my youth, a period that seemed to end that fateful night.

After hours no better for counting, I tired beyond belief; though I had already wrapped myself in my blankets, I felt it necessary to climb in the cart to sleep. Cal stood and stretched with a satisfied smile. "Till tomorrow then, partner." I smiled and nodded as I pulled down the cart's curtain. Then a thought came unbidden to my mind.

"Cal?" I asked through the fabric

"Yup,"

"Who were your other friends? The other two?"

"You are, you fool!" He chuckled, and I heard him walk away.

"The other?" He stopped. There was a pause as I lay down next to his box and closed my heavy eyes.

"Your Pa... now get some sleep." Another time I would have jumped up at his mention, but I barely heard as I fell into a deep, deep sleep.

Chapter 7

Excerpt from "lost hopes"

a collection of letters sent to the front line of Western civil wars that never arrived

I promise I didn't go too close to the sea- I know you and Mama always say that they can reach further than you expect, but I had to get closer and see what was happening. I'd climbed down into the woods, but then I couldn't see anything, so I had to climb a tall tree.

Papa, they were children! Lots of children and adults all tied together and the men in black were mean to them, pushing them around and shouting. I panicked, and I knew I shouldn't have climbed down from the cliffs, but it was too late!

I climbed down as quietly as I could, but I was quite far away and I didn't think they could hear me, but Papa, I was so scared! I just wanted you to come and take me home.

That wasn't even the most exciting bit! As I climbed down from the tree, I saw a light out to sea, actually in the sea! I've tried to tell Mama so many times, but she never listens. Papa, there was a boat coming across the sea! It wasn't like the river boats; it was much bigger and had spikes everywhere and little lights pointing into the bay.

I think it was coming for all the children.

I ran as fast and as quietly as I could so I could tell Mama, but when I got home, she was just angry again and made me promise not to go back there and not to make up stories. I did promise, but I'm not making it up, Papa. It was real! I know you will believe me and I know that when you come home, you'll come with me to see where it all happened and you will know what to do.

Please make it soon, Papa, we all miss you and I need you to come with me to investigate this mystery. It's more important than your fighting, so please explain to the captain that you must come home.

Ivy x

Anonymous Author
The past that follows

The small homestead was a scene of wind-blown desolation. Loosened, clattering gates and creaking paddocks long since abandoned surrounded the central building. Weeds lay claim to the stonework as questing desert shoots climbed the old walls, reaching for the light. To the back of the place, a couple of crows cawed to each other over a dried-out carcass, baked beyond stench and devoid of carrion meat.

Jake shielded his eyes as the low sun splintered off a broken window. He squinted and reached for his canteen before dismounting. He spat before he swallowed, washed the sand and grit off his teeth, and tethered his horse next to a dried-out trough. His hand still at his brow, he peered the way he'd come, but saw nothing; he scratched his grizzled chin and opened the front gate. Time to get to work.

With the ever-shifting sand, there was nothing he could track from here. With careful, measured steps, he moved into the abandoned house as the others breached the horizon.

There were four of them, riding the corners of a two-horse cart.

"Boss!" Broderick shouted. The sound ventured ahead on the hot wind. "He found a place." The second in command glanced at the covered cart for a reply, but none came. The posse made their way towards the old ranch. They'd ridden long and hard through the relentless sun. As they approached, they quickened their pace in anticipation of shelter, food, and water.

"Aint no water here!" Jake, the outrider, was shouting as he emerged from the front door, "Aint nobody either." The other riders were tying the horses as he approached, canteen to his lips.

"Then where'd you fill up?" Dev replied, nodding accusation towards the sloshing canteen. His long mustache curled back with his lip. Jake finished a long draught and smacked his lips over zealously. Jake stared at his colleague for a moment before replying, "Go check 'you don't believe me." He lifted the near-empty canteen, "I just aint greedy." He said with a smile as Dev stomped past towards the house. "Stay out of the barn, haven't checked it yet." He called after him; Dev answered with a middle finger.

Broderick climbed down from his driver seat with a groan and a stretch. He cast a glance at the back of the cart but saw no sign of his boss. He followed the others towards the front door when it was suddenly flung open.

"This is fuckin' bullshit!" Dev stormed from the house and shouldered past a smiling Jake.

"Told you."

"Fuck you!" He replied. Philips, the nearest to the wagon, took off his spectacles and raised his hands to calm him.

"Out the way, Philips."

"Just calm down, Dev." Broderick was older than the rest of them and usually talked the most sense; he intervened and put his hands on Dev's shoulders. "You take this shitty mood to him again and I aint responsible, you understand?" Dev shoved him aside and marched towards the back of the cart. The older man called after him, "Boss didn't say last chance for nothing, Dev!"

"Aint even any fuckin' water!" he muttered to himself as he reached the back of the wagon; Broderick swallowed hard. There was a creak of shifting weight as the cart lurched slightly, then suddenly a thick arm appeared from the rear opening and grabbed Dev around the scruff of the neck. In a display of illogical strength, Dev was instantly dragged through the opening like a rag-doll. Once inside, he let out a long and gurgling moan, and the sound of his thrashing limbs made the five onlookers wince and twitch. The brutal clamour seemed to continue far longer than necessary as the posse looked on uncomfortably. Dev's body never came back out.

As Broderick anxiously rubbed his brow, Jake, the posse's outrider, spat. He replaced his hat and headed for the stable in search of tracks. Jones, a towering, unwashed brute and Bean, a half-blood tribesman, followed. Philips stood mesmerized; he slowly replaced his bowler hat, his eyes transfixed on the now silent cart, and a hungry rictus cracking his dry lips.

Chapter 8

To: Lord Grivnen, Cthonic Order of the Reach

My Lord, it is my great honour to inform you we have arrived at the requested destination and have prepared operations. It is fortunate that we have arrived as the allies have suffered heavy casualties and local forces are close to routing. Though we are a small force, I am confident that we can now hold the line until suitable armaments arrive.

I feel I must warn you, however, that this is an uncivilised and lawless land and we should take every precaution to deliver the armaments safely and with adequate security.

From: Commander Rostrom, Cthonic Order of the Reach,
Rear camp four,
Northern Efrin,
Zandal Province

Callus
Showed Crow a thing or two
He's joining me on the hunt for Osset

We'd left the forest days behind; we were travelling across endless, barren plains with nothin' but distant hoodoos masking the horizon. Although it'd been my idea to move on, I was getting bored and not to mention hungry. I think I'd been spoiled. It was the first time I'd not thought about Osset for a long time. In the back of my head, a voice kept telling me I'd let the trail go cold. I was getting' good at ignoring that voice.

Crow'd been driving through the day and I knew somethin' was up soon as I awoke and opened my box. He was waitin' for me. I have to hand it to him; he didn't wake me early even though he was bursting to tell me what he'd found; it wasn't excitement exactly, but worried eagerness.

"There was all this noise, BOOM BOOM BOOM, and men shouting!" he blurted out soon as I emerged.

"Whoa, slow down, partner." I stopped him with my hands in the air; he was beckoning me out of the wagon as he spoke.

"There's something you need to see." I caught the scent then. My stomach churned something fierce, and my blood sped up. He took me to the edge of the camp he'd made whilst I was out. I heard soft and fast panting as we approached a pale wretch of a man dressed in a black uniform. Crow had laid him out on the ground. He'd been bleeding, still was, but he was on his way out. His eyes were yellow and twitching as they stared up into the night sky.

My instincts were a force to hold in check; I'd not fed for days, and even then it'd been some critter I'd snared. I barely held off as Crow surprised the shit out of me. He nodded encouragingly at the man and said,

"He's not going to make it. We've talked, but he made little sense, thought you might..." he hesitated. "Need him by now."

Don't get me wrong, I didn't hesitate, but it shocked me how the boy had come to terms with things. I crouched over the pale stranger and took my fill. His pulse was weak. My lips were numb when I came up sated and I think his wounds had got infected; there was an ugly zing to his blood.

Crow looked a little pale himself when I'd finished, but was eager to press on with his story. He led me out of the camp as he told me what had happened. My body was coming back to life again after a long time without blood. I passed him my bottle and gave him a proud nod; he threw back a quick swig.

"I had to pull up the wagon; I could hear so much noise over that hill." He gestured to a rise in the landscape. "There was an almighty BOOM BOOM, like ten shotguns firing one after another, and men shouting and fighting and well, wait 'til you see." We eventually reached the top of the rise to look down on a small battlefield. There were corpses strewn all over the place. That's when I realised Crow must have dragged the fella over the hill to bring him to me; looking back, it was a strange moment to be overcome with pride.

As we approached the scene, Crow continued.

"I waited for it all to die down and watched as some men took a wagon over that way." He gestured with one hand and pointed to a body with the other. "Look at the state of him." He was right. There was hardly anything left of the ragged red man lying in front of us.

"What in hell happened to him?" I asked as I moved to the next body to find a similar mess o' gore. Crow was taking it well, didn't imagine he'd seen a man all torn up back then, but he didn't seem too fussed. He passed me back my bottle; I hesitated before putting it in my pocket.

"They had a weapon." His excitement interrupted my thoughts; his eyes were gleaming in the moonlight. "I think, and according to the man who survived," he frowned for an instant before carrying on. "These men had a wagon with a special weapon. It must've been the sound I heard. The weapon was to stop bandits from stealing whatever was on the wagon. It didn't work. They took off with it, and the wagon."

I checked some of the other bodies; mostly torn apart by whatever the weapon was.

"I've been around a long time, Crow. There's not much that can excite me, but this is something I've never seen! Let's get after it." By the look on Crow's face, we were both more than eager to get near that thing and find out what was going on. Once again, I'd let myself get carried away by our new friendship. It had been so long since I had anyone beside me. Deep down I knew I was turning away from my salvation, my redemption and my chance for a new life, but neither of us really took the time to think about what we were heading into, considering we were amongst a field full of corpses.

The wagon left deep and obvious tracks.

"Must be heavy." I muttered almost to myself as we followed the two lines that gouged away into the night.

"It's the treasure!" Crow said excitedly. He skipped about behind me as I scanned the horizon; I had to stop and put my hands on his shoulders to stop his dancing.

"Don't you lose focus, now." I said, looking into his gleeful eyes. "These men are killers. We ought to be quiet and careful here," he nodded. "You do as I say when we find 'em, OK?" Crow stilled his jigging and nodded back at me. "Sorry partner. I'll be careful." He cleared his throat and looked away, a little embarrassed. We pressed on; I took my hatchet from my belt. Must get Crow a weapon, I thought to myself, although it was a bit too late.

We needn't rely on our night sight to locate their camp. They still had a dwindling fire, and the odd, gruff voice carried on the night's breeze. We both lay prone and crawled up to a rise to peer over; I got my first sight of the wagon they'd stolen and the strange, and massive, weapon on the back. The covered wagon had a great chimney stickin' out the top and what looked like a cannon stickin' out the back; I'd never seen anythin' like it.

They'd hitched their horses near the strange cart and, as I saw them, a man strolled past. Obviously on patrol, a rifle rested on his shoulder. Across the camp there were tents scattered about, a couple more guards sat round the fire and a naked fella tied to a pole shiverin'. Looked like he'd taken a beating. His head was floppin' about as he sat there on the ground, hands behind his back, the fight gone out of him.

"Reckon you could hitch a couple horses to that wagon real quiet?" I whispered to Crow. His head turned instantly to the fella patrolling. "I'll take care of him." I said, "You just worry about the horses and be real quiet, you get chance climb on that wagon and wait for me, OK?" He nodded but I could smell the fear on him. "Hey." I looked him in the eye and smiled. "It's just an animal in a snare; you get to it while it's not panicked and see to it, understand?" I watched as his mind went back to the woods and the lessons he'd learned through summer; he nodded at me and I slipped away. Inside, I felt a fear for him that threatened to make me turn back.

Chapter 9

Crow Hoby
Bandit Camp
Western Scrub land

Cal silently slipped out of sight and left me with my fear and the hard lump in my throat. "It's just an animal in a snare." I muttered to myself like a mantra as I crept away, keeping low and moving like a snake through grass. The knowledge was there in my mind. I could almost hear Cal's voice as he talked me through every aspect of the hunt. This time it was for real though, and the prey had guns!

As I approached on the outskirts, way beyond the dying firelight, the men's voices got loud. This was good; I needed something to mask the jingling tack once I'd got to the horses. With held breath, I stalked towards them with my head low, placing each foot carefully and lifting it only slightly to maintain balance. I'd crept to within spitting distance of the first of the horses before I let out my breath slowly, then suddenly a powerful hand gripped my shoulder. I gasped as I spun around and raised my hand instinctively thanks to Cal's grappling lessons.

Cal's massive hand slapped over my mouth and nose as his face silently loomed before mine. I relaxed and he let go. I felt like an idiot, but there was no disappointment on his face.

"D'you hear that?" I thought I heard one guard say, though I couldn't be sure if it was fear playing tricks. Cal carefully and quietly passed me a rifle and beckoned me back to my task. Then he slipped from view once again.

My partner's proximity bolstered my courage, and I closed the distance to the horses and stroked and softly reassured them. Before long, I was stealthily unhitching two animals and walking them towards the nearby wagon. Each inevitable sound made me wince as I drew closer.

I arrived at my destination and began tacking the horses to the wagon as I tried to keep them calm with quiet, soothing tones; they were understandably becoming more excitable with each second. With the first completed, I glanced up to check my surroundings. Then from the back of the wagon came a deep, wet *thud* and a low grunt.

"Best hurry it up, Crow." Cal hissed. His urgent voice made me jump, and I got to work with quicker but louder movements. I heard another thud and a muttered curse. My heart beat fiercely as I tied off the last of the tack and ran to the back opening of the wagon.

"Shit!" a nearby voice startled me and a loud gunshot followed it. I threw myself into the wagon and was immediately hit with the foetid but familiar stench of manure as I braced myself for the chaos that was surely coming. All around the camp, voices hollered and cursed. There were a couple more gunshots that sounded disconcertingly close. I looked around the inside of the wagon for anything of use as I cocked the rifle Cal had given me. Then suddenly, the weight of a naked man crushed me as Cal hurled him through the opening. We struggled together for a moment, then separated and regarded each other in shocked confusion. His beaten face looked grim; one eye swollen shut, and his tightly gagged mouth was bleeding from the sides. I noticed his mottled ribcage was black and yellow as he lifted his tethered hands aloft, a pleading look in his one visible eye. I reached into my pocket for a blade when the wagon suddenly lurched and we collided once again in a painful yet comedic fashion.

"Yeeeaah!" Cal had obviously reached the driver's seat and was giving the horses hell. The wagon bumped and jostled like a mule as I tried to cut the prisoner's hands free, careful not to add to his wounds. As soon as I cut through the thick rope, he reached up and tugged his gag free, working his cracked and bloody mouth with obvious relief.

"Thanks! Let's get this bastard firing." He was nodding to the huge cannon-like machine poking out of the wagon. Apart from the colossal barrel, the thing looked more like a stove than a cannon from this angle; it had three large iron pots with gaping mouth-like slots and a series of long metal levers sticking out in all directions. The man scurried around the back of the wagon, rummaging through wooden boxes I'd not noticed earlier as I gawped at the machine.

"Crow! Rifle!" Cal's voice jarred me from my fascination as I realised the sound of guns discharging behind us and the angry shouts of their owners.

I popped my head and rifle up simultaneously and immediately saw several pursuers galloping towards us. We were obviously moving at a much slower speed because of the weight we were carrying. I took aim at the nearest rider and flinched as he fired; a cloud of grey smoke obscured my target briefly, but as it cleared, I pulled my trigger. It never occurred to me I was intending to kill a man for the first time, over the years since I have heard so many talk of their first kill and the resounding effect it had on their psyche. For me, it was a matter of survival. My mind and body had gone through so much change over the recent months I had ceased to question it. I put a bullet somewhere in that man's torso and he flew from his horse and never shot at me again. His friends, however, were not subdued by his demise in the slightest.

I'd taken down three of them when I noticed the naked man was loading a fat belt made of shotgun shells into his machine, which was now smoking, and stank. He fanned one of the metal pots with one hand while he fed the shells into another slot with the other.

"Out the way!" He shouted with a crazed look in his eye. He pulled on a couple of levers and cackled like a madman.

Callus

Neck deep in shit

First time I'd felt alive in a long time

I was givin' them horses all I could, but we were getting' nowhere on account of the weight we were pullin.' It was like we were riding through oil. I could hear the snapping sound of their guns firing; a few shots whizzed past my head but my concern for Crow. I kept turnin' back but couldn't see a thing 'round the strange wagon's cover.

"Crow! Rifle!" I shouted against the wind. It was his only hope of dodgin' them bullets, to put them gunmen down. He'd told me he was an excellent shot, said he'd practiced a lot with his Pa back home; just hoped he'd been truthful. To be honest, my blood was up; with fear for Crow, and the damn excitement of it all. I could feel the adrenaline, if that's what it was, pushin' my body on; I was more alive than I had been for a long, long time.

"Yeeah!" I kept screaming at them bolting horses as they sped through the night; my voice sounded high pitched and manic even to my own ears.

I grinned as I heard Crow's first shot; couldn't tell if he'd hit or not, but I had faith in the boy. I craned my neck to see past the wagon, but still couldn't see a damn thing. Then an idea came to me. I glanced round quickly; couldn't see any nearby danger, long as the horses kept their route. I tied the reins under my seat and had another look around. All clear; I leapt onto the wagon's roof, grinning like a wild child as it dipped with my weight but held. As they crept up our flanks, I could see the attackers tryin' to get to me while driving. Crow seemed to do well; I could see a few bodies in the distance, rolling amongst clouds of dust and more riders.

Approaching fever pitch, pumped up with the thrill of escape, mixed up with the danger I'd not felt for so long. I looked down as I balanced and saw one rider just as he saw me; he had to look twice in the dark. I saw him reach for his gun, but at that moment, we were both distracted by a long and demented cackle from inside the wagon. Then the weapon fired up.

I've heard shotguns a plenty, many aimed at me, even, but the sound that night as I clung onto that roof pushed the wind right out of my lungs. It was like a hundred shotguns, one after another, echoing through a tunnel. My head felt like I'd laid it next to a train track as the metal beast screamed past. Me and my would-be shooter both looked back to see the devastation; his hand still fumbling with his holster. The riders behind were flying from their horses in violent bloody clouds as it struck again and again, both before and during their flight through the air. That crazy cannon pushed my wild mood up a notch, and I leapt across the gap between the wagon and that sorry fella. I didn't even realise I had my hatchet out, but I'd soon buried it in his head; I kicked him from his horse and snatched the reins as he fell. The irritated horse squealed and slowed down in protest as I swapped with its owner, taking us further behind and closer to another rider. This poor bastard was more concerned with avoiding the booming death machine than watching out for me as I leapt to his saddle; all it took was my boot, and he was rolling through the dust into the distance. I looked back to see the rest of the riders were veering away; the cannon had got too many of 'em for comfort and they were fleeing.

I spurred my new horse on to get back to my driver's seat and glanced ahead; they weren't retreating! Ahead, the open land dropped away to nothing as the track we were on suddenly curved to the right along a cliff's edge; the horses pulling the wagon were charging on in panic on account of the booming cannon.

Chapter 10

Excerpt from "Savage Seas, Fauna or Fear."
  By Vadchek Spirious

According to Cthonic law, the study of sea creatures without an official licence is tantamount to heresy. Despite efforts far beyond any logical reason, I have, unfortunately, been denied such licence at every opportunity and am forced to embark on my heretical journey into the depths to study the beings that surround us.

The validity of my writings is often questioned and this, in part, I feel is a matter of fear of the unknown and the mystique garnered by the Cthonic Council. This taboo subject is one of the many reasons that I have craved this knowledge, this forbidden and oh so delicious knowledge.

The second motivation for my critics is the credibility of my research. How, they ask, am I able to study these creatures beyond the occasional washed-up corpse or glimpse from afar?

As I have made my decision to remain in the shadows and hidden from the many eyes of the council, I feel it my duty to explain my methods and whence they came from. My former duties as a Magnite, and my talents in scientific application have gifted me knowledge of certain aspects of how the council succeed in crossing the sea aboard the Aileron Dwarf.

It is with these principles in mind that I can delve into the sea. With meticulous safety checks and rigorous testing, I am able to not only discourage the creatures from coming near me in my submersible but also potentially scare them away should they venture too close.

Crow Hoby

A high speed gun fight

Approaching a cliff edge without control

"Crow!" a cold, fleshy smack accompanied his shout, "Crow!" another smack and a white flash forced my eyes open. My body came to life in a slow flare of pain, an involuntary groan escaping my burning lips.

"You hurt?" Cal's question seemed sarcastic as I focused on his vacant face; it took a moment to blink away the blur. He slapped my shoulder and thrust his familiar flask into my hand before he stood and fled from my sight. Even my hands hurt as I unscrewed the top and threw back a mouthful; instant relief coursed through me as I took in the scene.

The wagon was on its side. Great chunks of wood had torn through the canvas like broken ribs, exposing the bright orange flames as they clawed their way from the interior. Cal cautiously approached, silhouetted as the flames took hold of the wagon's frame and spewed thick smoke into the night air.

Suddenly my memory kicked in and my head snapped around to see where we were; the vast expanse of cliff drop was still to our left, we'd avoided plummeting over! I was sprawled amongst the shattered seating from the wagon, entangled in the remaining tack as Cal had ridden in close and hacked the fleeing horses free. Detangling as I stood, my mind filled the blanks in my memory caused by the trauma of the high-speed disaster. I'd seen Cal come riding into view, swinging his hatchet and leaping from horse to horse like a deranged and sinister rodeo performer. Pure panic had caused me to tear through the wagon's canvas to get to the empty driver's seat as the steaming contraption behind me boomed and echoed through the night. Finally emerging, I froze as the vista opened up before me; the horses sped blindly towards the edge, and the massive weapon hissed into silence as if it sensed our approaching doom. I yanked on the reins with all my weight as I leaned out over the edge, dangerously close to the speeding ground beneath me as the wagon tilted. The bolting horses finally got the picture and switched direction in a heartbeat; the entire wagon lurched towards the cliff's edge and toppled. The beams beneath my seat splintered and cracked as the weight in the back rocked the bulk of the wagon over onto its side. That was when Cal had arrived. As always, at the moment of pure despair, he hacked through the tack in one furious swing and the inertia was too much to take.

My sense of smell was the last thing to right itself. The stench of burning, acrid dung assaulted me and was all-encompassing. The billowing smoke was thick with it. I retched, but nothing came. I spat and took in the scene before me again, my vision sharpening, my night sight compensating for the glaring inferno. That's when I saw the body. He'd crawled in desperation away from the fire, smoke rose from his seared skin; he'd made it some ten yards and given up. I ran over, shouting to alert Cal, who stood transfixed as the flames demolished the wagon.

I knelt by the prisoner. His burned skin smeared in black filth; his entire body shook as he mumbled incoherently. I touched a clot of the black stuff and it seemed to sizzle beneath my finger.

"Shit!" his shout startled me.

"I'm sorry! What shall I do?" I realised how pathetic I sounded straight away; he laughed, a demented and maniacal sound. I looked to Cal for inspiration, but he still gazed into the fire. Frustrated, I turned my attention back to the poor wretch before me.

"I'm gonna clean you up, OK?" His laughter dried up, and he looked at me, his eyes twitching.

"Sh… shit." He whispered, as if pleading.

"I know. It's bad now, but I'll take care of you." I began wiping away the filthy smears, and he hissed in pain.

"It's shit!" he sounded angry now. No surprise. He'd had a rough night! "We c… call it a shit cannon!" He raised a shuddering hand to point at the bonfire behind me. His eyes bulged as the pieces clicked into place in my shaken head. The smell, the fire. The weapon burned shit for fuel! I reflexively drew back my hand. Shit completely covered his burns!

"This is not good."

As if he'd waited for me to figure it out, his head flopped as I spoke the words and he lost consciousness. His night had just got rougher.

Callus

Could've been worse.

I hate fire.

Them flames took me back soon as I rode up. I climbed off that horse and saw to Crow, but my mind never left that fire. When you've lived as long as me, memories get blurred, but not that one. It was me they'd come for; I knew it as soon as I saw that smoking treeline. I'd ran as fast as I could, till my legs burned fierce, but the fire'd smashed them stained windows before I got there. That house of God burned by one of God's own.

Might be that moment was the first on my new path. I could hear the whoops and cheers of Osset's do-gooder posse as they rode away, but I knew Wilf was still in that Church. I pounded on them thick burning doors, ignoring my scorched fists. There was a time when vengeance would have been my first and only thought, but Osset's posse floated off into the night; I knew Wilf was still in there.

It was too late, I already knew. I knelt there that entire night as them flames purged me. Too late I realised Wilf would have gone down to my cellar to escape the fire, but a blaze that big took everything. All I could do was wait out the night on my knees, every second stretched out, every memory burned into my soul. Wilf would have said it was a cleansing, but there weren't nothin' clean 'bout that night. In my mind I could hear His voice preachin' as he did, 'bout the ghosts of my victims, 'bout reversing the curse and the long hard road to redemption. If there was a hell, that night was my homecoming.

There weren't much sun in the morning, I didn't care anyhow. The fire'd gone, left a few bricks that smoked like stoves. I jumped down where the stairs used to be, into the cellar. Wilf had given me this sanctuary, a kindness I didn't deserve for a price. Until that night, I couldn't pay.

I found his bones and his hip flask. I buried him with my old life in that Churchyard and kept his flask, case I ever forgot Reverend Wilfred J Berkeley and the burning need inside me to murder his killer.

Crow Hoby
Entangled in the wreckage of a Shit Cannon.
Middle of nowhere.

Cal eventually shook himself from his fiery reverie but remained withdrawn and quiet; I suppose there wasn't much to say until he swung the prisoner over his shoulder and looked at me.

"Run!" Then he was off, not at a sprinting pace, but I still had to push to catch up to him; my legs were still a little befuddled, but at least I wasn't carrying a fully grown naked man!

I'd wiped most of the excess dung from him, but it still ingrained many of his burns; I knew that meant trouble. I'd seen what infected wounds could do to cattle without clean water and extra care, but Cal did not seem interested in having that conversation. It was the fire that had spooked him, not the threat of pursuit.

We jogged in silence for a long time, longer than I thought I was capable of. I reached for my pocket as I ran and felt the bump of Cal's hip flask; for a terrible moment, I thought I'd left it in my jacket pocket, way back, crumpled and covered in excrement of an unknown origin. I think I always knew what the flask contained, but whenever my mind skirted over the subject, I shut it down and locked it away along with the image of my Pa that I'd created as my farewell lament.

We'd run through the night; a grey streak was bleeding over the horizon, highlighting details of terrain on the higher ground. Cal stopped; he was tiring but as he looked at me he appeared focused again. The run had shaken off whatever had passed over from the fire.

"He needs a bed." He said as he twitched his head to one side; the prisoner had not so much as stirred, even when Cal had stopped to switch shoulders.

"What about you?" I looked out at that ominous grey as it brightened before our eyes. The loss of Cal's box went unspoken, but a fear was creeping up on me never the less.

"Think there's a cattle town out here somewhere; we got another hour or so." He hefted the prisoner and turned.

"What then?" I asked, obvious worry squeezing my voice. He turned back and grinned at me before he set off.

"You'll have to bury me."

Somehow, the pace increased. My legs burned and my lungs felt like they were getting smaller with every stride. I couldn't tell if Cal had been joking, but his grin was not one of a worried man. Such was the exhaustion that was ravaging my body. I could not bring the assessment of it properly to mind, and so I just kept running.

Each small rise offered a view of the landscape ahead, a barren place scattered only with malnourished trees and randomly scattered rocks. Despair whispered over my shoulder.

We relayed between strange metal occurrences, like twisted stumps that rose from the ground, usually in groups of four. Cal seemed to use them as landmarks. I was too tired to care; the idea of finding this town he'd spoken of was getting more and more futile as the sepia sky prepared for the sun's imminent arrival.

I set my eyes on a ruined structure that maybe once housed one of the obsolete structures, clearly our current destination, and this was surely our last. My dry lips hung open as I staggered towards it. Even Cal had slowed by then. The sun would have been upon us if not for a tall, weathered wall just ahead, our final shadowy shield in Cal's hour of need.

Cal unceremoniously dumped his human burden as he reached the shaded corner. He stretched his back, and we both dropped to the ground, entirely exhausted.

"Flask." He gestured at me with his fingers; It amazed me he could still speak. I tossed it to him, but he dropped it. Then, kneeling with his back to me, he seemed to make a fuss of picking it up; his arms moved as though he were tying a knot. Then the flask landed in my lap.

"Fraid the work's not done yet, friend." He nodded at the flask, then dug into the earth with both hands. Once again, I pushed all thoughts of the thick red liquid's origins away and swigged it down without mercy. The clarity it proffered made me suddenly more aware of my surroundings; the air was cool with a welcome breeze and on it rode a sound I had not noticed before. I sat up and strained to hear as vigour writhed through my spent muscles.

Music.

Music and voices carried on the wind. I looked at Cal hopefully; he had scooped a sizable hole from the earth. He looked up and rolled his eyes.

"Just beyond the ridge." He said whilst grinning at my wonder, "I told you!"

I returned the smile, my despair carried away towards the distant voices.

"Now get digging!"

It's no surprise that there's something very unsettling about burying your only friend in the ground while he continues to talk to you nonchalantly. He assured me it had been a standard routine before he'd acquired my Pa's wardrobe, but the force of will it took to scoop earth around his upper body was phenomenal.

"Just keep going," he said when only his head poked out of the ground. "I'll come find you tonight when you got somewhere to stay."

"I don't understand." I was really struggling with this idea. "How will you breathe?"

"I won't." He answered as a curtain of golden light broke from our sanctuary and edged across the ground towards his face. The sun had breached, and it was probably the only thing that could have actually forced me to do it. He spoke again, a little faster, a little more anxiously.

"I don't sleep like you do..." He frowned and spat out a lump of loose earth. Unable to shrug his buried shoulders, he raised his eyebrows and spoke.

"I die."

Chapter 11

Excerpt from 'Holy Scriptures of the Western Creeds'

... and YES, it is true that our landcestors lived in harmony. And YES, it is true that they took strength from the strong creeds and gave knowledge to the weak of mind. But is it not also true that this way of life led our people on the path to the communion? Is it not true that the joining of creeds gives rise to those of mixed blood, those of low character and those of little faith? I stand before you now, filled to the brim with faith and blood of pure breeding, and I say this.

"We do not sin by using the strong arm of another creed! Nor do we sin by using the crafts of those creeds beneath us! It is our duty as pure creeds to work alongside these lesser creeds, to learn from them, to watch them and to make use of their strengths. But I also say this. We allow these creeds into our towns! We allow these creeds into our pockets, our saloons, and our minds even, but I tell you this, people. We do NOT allow these creeds into our beds! We do NOT mix our precious blood with theirs, and we do NOT call them brother!"

Reverend Osset

Crow Hoby
Outskirts of Hatton.
Western desert

I'd thought of leaving him several times. I clambered across the dry earth with his pale limbs flopping over my shoulders and tripping my legs. Luckily,

Cal had thought to provide his massive coat so the anonymous man was partially wrapped, and the more tender areas of his flesh covered. The sun had risen in full. It brought with it a mild headache, not pain exactly, but more of an incessant buzz in the back of my mind.

It surprised me how much ground I'd covered despite the dead weight that was sprawled over me, but eventually my strength gave way. He flopped to the earth without protest; I wondered if he had actually died. Inside me, frustration argued with guilt; I did not even know this man, yet could I really just leave him to die? This unidentified, near naked man had tapped every drop of my strength and was lying before me, silent, stinking and ungrateful. I paced around him, my head in my hands and visions of my Pa reminding me I could make a difference in this world urging me on. I almost failed to realise how close I had got to the town I so desperately sought. Roofs of roughly shod buildings and sounds of civilisation poked over the desert terrain as the place woke for the day. Hustle and bustle drifted across to me as I struggled with the idea of what to do next, all the while trying to juggle the vexatious memory of burying Cal.

Eventually I stopped my shamble and stared down at the broken man; like an echo from a life now lost. I heard my Pa reach into my mind and grab hold of my hesitance. There was no way he'd leave this man where he lay. Not only that, but Cal was also relying on me to get him to safety; a formidable will washed over me. I spat like Pa would have done in the same situation and bent to continue my work. I straightened his body and pulled out the folded length of Cal's coat from under him. With his skin protected, I pulled him across the rough ground. His weight seemed immense as I dragged him, but my spine had protested at the idea of trying to pick him up again. I grunted and groaned as he slid, inch by inch, towards the town and potential sanctuary.

It was only my single-mindedness and perhaps a little desert madness that gave me the strength to carry on; my legs shuddered, and my knuckles bled as I gripped and lost the coat's collar repeatedly and heaved with all the might that remained inside me.

"Youneedhelpboy?" A deep, foreign voice surprised me, the mangled question breaking my desperate focus. I lost my grip and my backside hit the floor unceremoniously. Shielding my eyes, I looked up towards the strange voice's source and I fear my mouth fell open.

He was a large man; his face was mostly beard and shadow caused by a peaked helmet from under which flowed his long, braided hair. He wore few clothes, just a leather tabard which hosted hundreds of woven metal links. I stared up incredulously as he waited for a reply. It was not only his bizarre appearance that caught my tongue and almost convinced me I had fallen into some exhaustion-born fever dream, but the realisation that beneath the rider sat a six-foot tall, muscular goat.

"Hello." I must have sounded like a simpleton, but my sense of reality was wrestling with the fatigue that threatened to put me to sleep. The man laughed heartily, a booming laugh that seemed not to mock; he shouted something over his shoulder and quickly swung down from his mount.

"Do you need help, boy?" He spoke slowly, as if trying to communicate with an old man with old ears; his smile never left his shaded eyes. Still dumbstruck, I looked back towards the giant goat. Behind it, more of the strangers were riding up the track towards us; more goats pulled a heavy cart.

"It's called a goath." He said, nodding and scratching behind the ear of the grateful animal. "They always cause a fuss in town." He said fondly. Then he looked at the body beside me as if noticing him for the first time; his smile dropped and changed to an expression of concern. He shouted something back to his arriving companions and reached over to put a hand on the unconscious man's neck.

"He'sstillbreathing!" his words were fast, but I caught most of the meaning through his thick accent. "He'sinabadway, yougotanysalts?" Another bearded man dismounted and came to his aid; they fussed with him until I heard a faint murmur. Then, as if my body had realised it was in capable hands, it switched off and I passed out.

I awoke in a bed with crisp white sheets. I was in a dormitory; two of my benefactors sat at a table in one corner playing some kind of game at a small table, and the man I'd dragged across the desert was in a bed next to mine. He was even paler than before.

"Ah, yourawake!" one of them stood from his game and approached with a warm and familiar smile.

"You'reahero, I'vebeentold?" I tried to understand the question, but his accent left me confused. "You're a hero, I've been told?" he repeated slower, with only a hint of patronisation.

"That's better." I smiled. "You speak faster than I'm used to." I said, trying not to slow down myself. He nodded eagerly and gestured at his friend. "This is Vulf; my name is Elger." He seemed genuinely excited to know my name in return.

"Crow." I said and held out my hand to shake his. He strode over to my bed and, quick as lightning, he slapped my outstretched hand; I tried not to let the sting show on my face.

"Nice to meet you, Crow."

"And you." I said, "thank you for bringing me." I looked around the room in confusion. "To safety?"

"It is not a problem, friend. It sounds like you deserve the help after what you did for Jarad." The bearded man nodded towards the man in the other bed.

"You know him?" I asked. It was strange to assign a name to the man.

"Only today. He woke up when we gave him some salts. You've just missed him." I looked over at the pale face of a man near death; waxiness had developed on his brow and his chest rose and fell with fast, shallow breaths. As I watched, Vulf, the other man, an even larger fellow than Elger, stood and took something from the table. He hunched as he approached as if he carried a great weight; his empty hand almost seemed to touch the floor.

"Hewrotethis. Said you were to have it." He handed me a sheet of folded parchment. On one side was a hastily scrawled map. Before I opened it, Elger Spoke in an excitable tone.

"We are Vikens, from the mountains. Where are you from?" Vulf rolled his eyes and strode from the room; he had to turn slightly to fit through the door frame.

"I don't even know where I am now." I replied, sounding like a lost little boy. Wincing inside, I quickly added. "Gunmen chased us through the night." Elger nodded and gestured to the window. It was getting dark outside. "Hatton; we come to trade before we go home." A silence fell as I wondered what these strange people had to trade.

"Look." Elger said. Reaching into a fold in his tabard, he handed me a thin slip of parchment. "Can you read it?" the eagerness was radiating from him, he suddenly seemed just a boy, even to me. I looked at the slip; beneath an unfathomable drawing, I read it aloud *"NO PROSPECTS? TIRED OF THIS ENDLESS BARREN LAND? SEEK A NEW LIFE OF PLENTY; CTHONICA AWAITS YOU. SET SAIL WITH THE AILERON DWARF: AN ARC TO THE NEW WORLD!"*

The words seemed to mean nothing to Elger, nor to me. I looked at the drawing again, but it made little sense; it seemed to depict some kind of river boat crossing the sea. I gave the parchment back to Elger with a sceptical smile; everyone knew there was no way to cross the sea. Elger stared in awe at the little slip before folding it carefully and offering it back to me with a nod and a smile.

Callus
Six feet under.
Time to find Crow.

It'd been a long time since I'd had to dig myself out the ground. 'Fact, it'd been a long time since I'd seen a decent sized town. Soon as I saw the lights, my hunger rose, along with a bunch of memories of the feasts I'd had in years gone by. I pushed 'em to one side. Had to find Crow first, make sure he was OK, then I'd take care of my thirst.

The town was bigger than I expected, not just some knocked up cattle town that'd probably burn to the ground before it prospered. It had some decent buildings and, by day, seemed to have been doing some good business. The sign on the gate read: *HATTON, WHERE PROSPECTS PROSPER.* As I arrived though, it was dark, and 'Hatton' really came to life.

As in most towns, with night came music, muffled inside inns and whorehouses, enjoyed by drunks and brawlers, bums and tinkers. Gunshots and the sound of smashed glass came from every direction and eventually forced the revellers into the street to jostle and threaten and get in my way. I could sense Crow was pretty close and at ease so I figured he could have done with a bit of freedom to explore by himself, might have been the hunger talkin', but I let him have his time and went to go treat myself. Joining the shadows, I disappeared into an alley, following the sounds of drunken vagabonds.

I admit I went wild, got greedy. My head got straight as the guy threw up over my shoulder. I was holding him in the air by his collar while I drained his drunken friend. I looked him in his terrified eyes whilst licking liquor-tainted blood from my lips.

"He'll be OK," I assured him, but his eyes were getting bigger, his breath like a train. "He aint dead!" I promised, thinking back to the talk I'd had with Crow about my feeding. That's what did it. Didn't think Crow'd approve of me taking up old habits and gettin' greedy. I shook my head and let go of the feller who just laid at my feet lookin' up, pleading with them eyes. "Go'n, get gone!" I shouted and the lucky son of a bitch scrambled to his feet and ran; didn't seem too drunk no more.

I wiped the chunks from my shoulder, didn't care too much, but supposed I'd stink if I left it; that's when I went to get us some supplies; Crow needed a hatchet!

Crow Hoby

Hatton

In the company of Vikens

I talked through the evening with Elgar and found him fascinating. Likewise, when the other Vikens invited him downstairs for ale, he refused and instead stayed with me to swap stories. I'd got dressed and was wearing Cal's long, now practically ragged coat to guard against the drafts in the creaky wooden beamed room. They were traders in ore from the mountains and spent most of their time mining down in the ground, and only teams who had been selected had permission to come into town to trade. Elgar seemed to take great pride in his place in the group; I got the feeling that he'd only made the trip once before. This accounted for his excitement and the questions he was asking me.

I had not so much as mentioned Cal; I don't know why but my stories were all of my old life. I suppose it would be hard to swallow the fact that I was waiting for my friend who I'd buried the night before, several months after he'd murdered my father.

During one tale concerning my Mother's illness, Elgar suddenly lifted a finger, and I stopped. He slowly turned his head towards Jarad in his bed; my gaze followed as the room became insalubriously silent. Elgar slowly stood from his creaking chair and went to place the back of his hand over Jarad's mouth. He shook his head and looked up at me.

"Is he dead?" I whispered. I found it hard to muster grief for the man as we'd hardly spoken, but the quiet room and the fact that he could have slipped away unnoticed whilst we chatted somehow left a peculiar sensation up my spine and above my ears. Elgar nodded solemnly. We stared at him for a long while, each lost in his own thoughts. I wrapped and buttoned Cal's coat.

"What do we do now?" I breathed; the sensation I was feeling was making my heart beat faster. I suddenly yearned to be with Cal. It felt like my blood was lacking his company. Elgar unfastened the armour he wore; he'd told me they called it 'mail.' He looked at me solemnly and placed it on his bed.

"I've never done the rite myself, but I should do it. He was under my protection." I saw a brow-twitch of guilt as he spoke and walked over to the weapon propped in the room's corner. Vikens use a strange pick as a weapon, modified from the tools they use underground; They connect a long wooden haft to a metal bladed spike similar to a scythe but much shorter. He lifted the pick and turned to me with earnest eyes.

Without warning, the door to the room smashed into the sombre scene as it burst open to reveal Cal in motion. Before I understood his arrival, he hurled his hatchet through the room with such force and speed that it seemed to disappear. The weapon only became visible again as it buried itself into Elgar's neck just above the collarbone, the handle angled up to part his beard. There was a loud wet crunch followed by the sound of Elgar's limp body hitting the boards midst the red that cascaded from his hideous wound.

Chapter 12

Anonymous Author

Trouble's Wake.

The humble town of Basin has the illusion of protection from its surrounding hills. Built at the bottom of a vast recess in the dry land, it had one road through and out the other side. Strangers rarely visited Basin. It was often easier to miss the area altogether, skirt the great dip and head for the horizon. Once on that spiralling road, though, travellers slid down like a spider towards a plug hole with no choice but to make a stop. If you travelled by day, the inhabitants could not miss your arrival; there had been other visitors recently. The people of Basin had viewed visitors with increased disdain since then.

Jones had drawn the short straw again.

"You're the newest member." Philips had said, he sat on a table with his feet weighting the seats of two separate chairs.

"Gotta earn your place." he lifted a golden bottle to his lips. Jones licked his own cracked lips without thinking; he knew he could best Philips easily if it came to a brawl, but he didn't trust the way he'd fight. He squeezed his massive fist, and a knuckle gave away a quiet click.

Looking around the bar, only Broderick looked sympathetic. The rest continued their loud and incorrigible conversation.

"That's why we're here and not over there." Jake, the outrider, was saying to the rest of the gang. Bean was shaking his head; a section of his long black hair dragged through a pool of spilled ale.

"What?" Jake seemed angered by the tribesmen's dismissal. "What you shakin' your head for? You don't believe me?" Bean just grinned and took a long swig from his bottle; Jake shook his own head and copied the motion. Jones saw Philips tip the rim of his bowler hat with a wide grin across his face before he joined in.

"Bean doesn't believe there is an 'over there' do you Bean?" he jumped down from his table seat and patted one of the tribesman's massive shoulders as he walked past.

"Over where?" Jones interjected and silenced the conversation. Philips stopped and turned to enjoy the prospect's embarrassment. Nobody answered. They just looked at him as if he were stupid. The silence held until Philips snorted and started laughing and shaking his head.

"Crave can sure pick his prospects." He said as he wiped laughter's tears from his eye and continued to the bar; Jones suddenly stood up; his chair screeched along the floor.

"What does that mean?" he said, clenching solid fists, "I'll…"

"Alright, alright" Broderick stood up and Jones stopped before his threat went too far. Jones knew better than to go against Broderick. He was thick with Crave. He spat on the floor and marched out of the common room, giving one silent patron a sudden start as he feigned to punch with a growl.

Crave's cart was horseless and tied for the night by the stable hand. The boss insisted one of his own men clean out the inside whenever they stayed in town, or so Philips had told Jones on the road. Jones did not know what needed cleaning, but figured it couldn't take long. Then he'd be back inside with a beer or two, taking his frustrations out on the locals. He got to work untying the many cords at the back. Inside the inn, raised and angry voices gave him a smile. Maybe someone else was having a pop at Philips.

Finally untied, he opened the slit and threw back the canvas to reveal an inner net in the stable's gloom. He climbed up and swept the net aside with his thickly muscled arm. Unlike any netting he'd felt before, it stretched and tore with his motion, the fine strands clinging to the hair on his hands and forearms. Frustrated with the sticky sensation, he swung his arms around erratically; the movement causing strands to settle across his face.

Agitated, he grabbed handfuls of the stuff in anger, but the weird substance seemed almost to dissolve in his grip. At nearly seven feet tall, Jones stooped as he flailed around the cart, swinging his arms like a man on fire, then he tripped on a covered mound on the floor and rolled into the corner, cursing as he went.

Muffled gunshots rang through the stable from inside the inn then, followed by mocking laughter and a solitary *smash!* The trouble had started without him. It was inevitable really, thought Jones, a gang of Outlaws like them, holed up in a quiet town with everyone shitting themselves since they arrived. Jones kicked at the mound that had tripped him. It rolled down the wagon and out into the stable. Angered and keen to join his posse, he started scooping at the weird stuff now, scraping the cart walls till it gathered in sticky balls on his hands. As he cleared the wagon, air circulated. It released a stale stench that permeated the dark trailer. Jones repeatedly spat; the substance tickled his lips and was infuriating him. Eventually, he could take no more; he jumped from the back of the wagon and flicked the cloying balls from his hands and sleeves.

Inside the bar, it seemed the ruckus was in full swing. Furniture *crashed* and *snapped*, always followed by Philips' cackling laughter. There were no more gunshots, which suggested the fray was strictly fisticuffs. Jones grinned; that was his favourite.

With the excitement, he almost forgot the mysterious mound on the floor; the light was brighter outside the cart and he could see it was maybe five feet long and rolled into a bundle. He looked closer; someone had tightly wound it in the same substance that already covered him from head to foot.

Crouching to get a closer look, he saw it was cobweb; the stuff was spider webs! Jones ripped off his shirt and rubbed at his head and face manically, spitting as he danced around the straw covered stable.

He was eventually as clean as he was going to get; he put one foot on the curious webbed bundle and with a disgusted face; he rolled it over.

Jones threw up in the corner, his empty stomach yielded little but ale but he continued as Dev's mangled and desiccated face stared up through the webbing towards the stable roof.

Chapter 13

Letter to the local Sheriff's office
Dated: 12th Weresday, 7th, 829 AF

Dear Sheriff,

I feel it my duty as a concerned citizen of this region to implore you to take action against the villainous slavers that are in operation in the area that you call your jurisdiction.

Only yesterday I received word from a cousin out in the wilds about how he and his kin were forced to flee their farm on account of the swine that had already come for their neighbour. These foreigners have come from beyond the mountains and they're stepping on our land like it's their own. Now I'm not in favour of our Viken neighbours but even those heathens are running scarred and keeping their heads down and we know those brutes like to swing their picks if they get a chance.

My husband, rest his soul, had a cousin out East who escaped from the very same slavers. When he came back, his own Mother didn't recognise him. They'd painted one of his arms in pitch. Said it was like leather. Poor fella lived in fear till he died nursing a black arm and a wicked thirst for strong ale.

As I write I am making plans to visit town and speak to you person to person, we need to do something, Sheriff, else they'll keep coming closer and closer to town and taking those they need and dragging them off to the Lord only knows where!

Irene Galdursgate,

Concerned citizen

Callus
Thinking with my hatchet.
In the eye of the storm.

Seems I only ever think about life before the curse when I've done somethin' stupid. Think I knew before I let go of the hatchet, but some weird twist in my guts stopped my brain. I was so concerned that I'd left Crow in danger and I'd felt his heart was pounding.

As we ran down that busy street, barging and dodging drunks and doorsteps, my mind went way back to the forest as I fled to escape from my tribe. They'd held her back as she tried to run with me. They wouldn't hurt her, but my own tainted blood was worth nothin' to them. Arrows stuck into trees as I passed and wild hunt calls came from everywhere. Always knew what we were risking, but the elders could never have kept us from each other, or so I thought.

A weird horn echoed behind us, followed by furious calls for revenge; back on the busy Hatton Street, I picked up the pace, Crow kept up, I guessed he was enjoying the chase, didn't really have time to ask.

"This way!" I pulled his arm down a side alley and his legs went from under him; he scrambled his way up again as I pulled him up and into two men.

"Watch wh...!" Crow's shoulder sent the first man flying as we dashed past and away from more angry shouting. I think I heard Crow laugh, but someone hurled a distractingly enormous man out of a saloon and into my path; I had no time to dodge, so I tripped and rolled over him and into the dirt, cursing as I went. With Crow now ahead, I got up and ran after. At the end of the alley was a ramped cellar door. There was nowhere else to run and for a second I thought he'd stop, but up he ran and leaped off the top to disappear down the other side. I followed him up; I could sense his pounding heart as he landed far below in the shadowed stable yard. I landed next to him and had to grab his shoulders before he ran again.

"In here." I put my finger to my lips as I led him down the side of the stable to the side door I'd been through earlier. He followed in silence into the darkened shop I'd stashed our supplies in. Out in the street above, another angry horn called across the town.

Crow Hoby
Dorm of a Hatton saloon
Before my friends became my enemies

I stared in all-encompassing horror at Elgar's still body, my mouth agape; my head was spinning as my pulse quickened. In that heartbeat, it appeared it was my body that had decided between my two guardians. I'd relished Elgar's company and had felt a bond between us as we'd talked, but as Cal scooped me up in his arms, the relief that surged through my blood left no mistake where my place was; I gripped his shoulders and braced as he ran us headlong towards the glass window. Booming footsteps echoed behind us and in the back of my mind I recall a deep, sorrowful and angry roar follow us as we crashed through the window and plummeted towards the street far below.

Crow landed effortlessly amongst the shocked denizens of Hatton's nightlife. Shards of glass splintered and burst onto the hard packed street as people fled. He put me down and we ran.

The initial despair at Elgar's sudden death had gone; all that mattered was our escape together. We ran with speed and agility that seemed supernatural. If not for the crowded streets, we would have been long gone by the time the first horn called across the town. It was an eerie and bitter sound, like it reached for us and there was nowhere we could go to avoid it.

Eventually Cal stopped me in a distant, shadowed alley; he put his finger to his lips and led me through a doorway. Silently and without protest, I followed, surprised I was barely out of breath after our escape.

He quietly barred the door behind us and turned to me with gleaming eyes and an ecstatic grin. We shared a moment of pure euphoria before another horn sounded not so far away.

"I stashed us some gear." Cal said as he lifted a bundle onto a table between us. Not only had he led us to this place, but to my surprise, he'd already been here to stash supplies. He saw my expression in the gloom and smiled warmly.

"Been here already, figured we'd need some supplies." He fumbled amongst the items. "And you need a weapon." He handed me a hatchet; it was my own, not Cal's I'd borrowed for practice, but my own weapon. Elated, I inspected it thoroughly as he talked me through the other things he'd stashed. Amongst them were two new greatcoats, one for each of us. I quickly put mine on and admired the stitched-in hide at the shoulders and hems, a sturdy coat that my Pa would have approved of, but most pleasing were the similarities with Cal's. His was a lighter garment and had the addition of a hood, but together we looked like a team, two equals.

Like children, we went about strapping our new packs and belts on in an excitement that almost drowned out the ever approaching Vikens outside. I told Cal about the Vikens and what I'd learned from Elgar, almost forgetting that my new friend now lay in a pool of his own blood.

I realised it was a hunting shop that we were in and found some jerked meat to chew on as we prepared to leave with a new sense of capability.

"There's a wagon out back. Just need to hook up a couple horses." Cal was saying as he moved towards a door, then suddenly he stopped. There was a loud metallic clunk, and an unfamiliar voice followed the barrel of a shotgun around the corner into the room.

"Yup, there's MY wagon out back and that's where it's stayin', boy!"

Callus

Gearing up

Finally, back on the trail

It's unusual I let someone close enough to point a shotgun at me. No doubt I'd survive the blast, but it'd leave one hell of a mess of my face when I woke the next night. He was old and nervous, kept twitching his nose like he could smell somethin' bad. I quickly decided I could take him first.

"Stop!" Crow's hands were up. "We can sort this out with no one getting hurt." He was talking to me; the old timer held his breath.

"We'll pay for what we've taken." He looked at me. His face was a question.

I knew he was right; this fella hadn't done us any wrong, was my fault he'd caught us.

"You aint got the gold for all this!" he waved the barrel at me and Crow. He was nervous, but he wasn't backing down, had to give him credit; I could have his throat out before that bony finger pulled.

"Okay." I said, didn't raise my hands, not my style, but I showed him one palm as I reached for my pouch with the other. He didn't like it. His eyes started blinking like there was sand in 'em. The barrel lifted an inch.

Didn't want to risk it; I lunged across the room and spun away from him, pulling the barrel with me; his trigger finger gave a loud click as I yanked the gun from his hands and tossed it across the room.

Now his hands were up, his breath coming fast and furious, and a pretty nasty smell filled the room. Crow was looking at me strange; couldn't decide if he was trustin' me or not. I reached into my new coat pocket and pulled my pouch. That damn horn sounded again outside, sounded very close.

"Aint got time to mess around, old man. What's it gonna take for this and that wagon of yours?" I pointed at the gear me and Crow were already wearing and untied the pouch. He looked at Crow, thought it was a trap, like I was just gonna gut him where he stood. Might have done a few years back. I started tossing coins into a patch of moonlight next to his cash register; I saw his eyes bulge, not too scared to turn down my gold.

"Them's pre-war coins." He licked his lips, his nerves chased off. I threw a couple more.

"You happy old man?" he looked at me and then back at the small pile.

"One more for the horses?" he was smiling now, so was Crow. I leaned forward and put a coin in his hand, then grabbed it and squeezed.

"One more for the horses." I agreed and put another on the counter. "And another, so no one knows we were here." He nodded frantically; I patted him on the shoulder with a firm hand as he scooped up his coins.

The old fella watched us without a word as we tacked up his wagon and climbed aboard in the backyard. Just as we were ready to leave, there was a booming knock on his door, back in the shop. A voice with an unusual lilt shouted.

"Openup!"

"Let's see if too much gold can keep a man's mouth shut." I said to Crow, think he knew I wasn't pleased, but he said nothing, fact he looked quite pleased with himself.

Chapter 14

To: **Commander Rostrom, Cthonic Order of the Reach,**
   Rear camp four,
   Near "Sanctuary" School for the lost, civilian educational facility,
   Northern Efrin,
   Zandal Province
   Dated: 2nd Redsday, 5th, 126 PC

It is with great regret I must inform you that the weapon, that which I am charged to deliver will not arrive. I docked on these shores via The Aileron Dwarf, 4th Maanday, 830 AF, and made haste to the front. However, native bandits immediately overrun our division and commandeered the weapon. I was, as the only survivor, tortured and held captive until liberated by the two men who hold this missive; it is thanks to them I can write this letter before my demise and inform you that the weapon was destroyed and therefore will not be available to the enemy.

I humbly ask as my dying request that the two men in receipt of this message earn the respect they deserve and not be considered responsible for the fate of the weapon and our mission to engage with your forces.

Yours Faithfully
Jarad Tinian
Cthonic Officer of the Reach

Callus
Heading West
A fork in the road

We passed through the next couple towns, only stopping to ask about the place in the letter and get our bearings. Crow needed to deliver it at this 'Sanctuary' place, said he'd come so far he might as well go all the way. As we rode, I realised it could fit with my plan. Bit of time on our own would probably do us both some good. I'd gotten so close to Crow it was showing, I was making mistakes I'd never make on my own, and the need to catch up with Reverend Osset was a continuous weight on my mind, I'd lost so much time getting to know Crow that I felt I was letting Wilf down and stretching my redemption beyond the horizon.

He didn't like it, but we agreed. He'd go deliver his letter, maybe learn a thing or two at the School and I'd go finish my business and come back to meet up at 'Sanctuary.'

"If we're partners, least one of us needs some education." I'd said. He nodded, but still had a scowl on his face. He knew I was right. Hell, I'd struggled to read Jarad's letter back then.

We had a couple good nights talkin' round the fire, and I showed him some more things with his hatchet. He was getting good; I was sure he'd be okay on his own for a spell.

We rode as far as we could together before our paths had to split. When the time came, there was no scowling; he knew I'd be back soon and with one less demon on my back.

I'd taken the wagon and one horse, I'd need somewhere to sleep in the day, and we were far closer to 'Sanctuary' than we were to Osset's place when we'd split.

As I rode, I wondered why I'd rarely come this way before. The need to get hold of the good Reverend had always been there, but I'd never actually searched for his place. Crow would probably say that I was more of a beast back then, cared less for people and my redemption, but that boy had sure put a change in me. I felt somethin' akin to loss at parting ways, but the need for revenge and to clear my debts just kept getting' heavier and heavier.

I'd never seen Osset's Abbey, but Wilf used to say 'bout how grand it was, how close to God Osset must be to have such a place to worship; I spat at the thought. Close to God or not, I'd tear it down right in front of him.

Crow Hoby
Heading West again
In search of Sanctuary

Another day closer to 'Sanctuary' and I realised that the land was drying up. For a while I had followed a small stream, but it had dwindled and just a small trickle remained. I encouraged my horse to take a drink and painstakingly filled a canteen. For a moment, I thought about emptying the bottle Cal had given me and refilling it with water, but thought better of it. I took a swig while it was on my mind and sat as it coursed through me, making me feel more alive.

I took out the strange letter that Jarad had written in those impending hours. Little of it made sense to me, but something tickled my mind. I reread it, trying to understand the brief message, when a spark of insight suddenly came to me. I quickly took out the paper poster that Elgar had shown me back in Hatton.

"Aileron Dwarf." I spoke the strange words out aloud, matching them to both papers in my hand. Jarad had come to this land on the Aileron Dwarf. My mind raced. A boat that crossed the sea! It had to be true; the two papers were from entirely different sources.

"He came from across the sea!" My horse looked up at my exclamation and dipped his head again, nonplussed. I knew little of the big cities in this land or the wonderful things forged with metal and fire, but one thing I knew was that men had never crossed the sea, not until then, it seemed. I suddenly felt part of something huge, something secret, and I was on my way to meet with Jarad's superior, who could surely shed light on this phenomenon. Packing up my things with increased vigour, I mounted my horse and set off.

As the land dipped and swirled around gigantic sandy hoodoos, I could see for miles. The landscape seemed devoid of green flora or the signs of inhabitancy, but somewhere out there was a path to a new world.

Callus
On my way to Church
Making good time

I'd almost got back into my old lonesome routine by the time I got there. Rising, I pulled back the wagon's curtain; I'd ridden for a time in daylight but didn't take any notice around me, just kept my head down and rode to make good time. If Crow'd been with me, it might have been easier, I thought to myself.

Small hamlets had spread over the land like a rash since I was last there; I rode through twitching curtains and disdain, stayin' clear of Wilf's ruins; didn't think I'd approve of what they'd done to the place. I had no love for these people; they were Osset's people.

Another night's ride and the lights of his Abbey came into view; I hid the wagon in a nearby copse and got my head down before sunup. It'd been a rough night; I had no injuries to heal but as I stopped breathing, dreams of before the curse haunted me.

"You must go now." Her voice trembled as she spoke, but she looked away, chin up. She would not look at me again. I stood and her first tear pattered onto the bark floor of the tent.

"I will only go to protect you. I leave my heart behind."

"They have already taken your heart, my love, where they send you, I cannot follow." Before I turned, I saw her hand go to her belly.

I turned and stopped before I lifted the flap, the golden sunlight eager to flood in.

"This world will pay for their curses."

"I know." She whispered through the rush of tears as I left.

Knock knock!

"Anyone in there?" It must have been dusk 'cause I woke up strong. The hurt left over from my dreams filled me with hate; I tore down the wagon's curtain to reveal two shocked Abbey guards.

"I am here." I dropped from the wagon and moved towards them. They stepped back, spears still held upright.

"W-what are you doing here?" the first asked. He finally had the sense to point his weapon. "This is God's property." The second now lowered his spear and rolled his shoulder. These two had never seen trouble in all their days, was obvious in their pompously clean velvet uniforms, their pale faces sitting on spotless ruffs.

"Osset!" I snapped. "Where's Osset?" I grabbed the first's spearhead and moved it from my face as the other advanced.

"Father Osset is in the new world. He isn't here." They shook their heads together, fat, freshly shaven cheeks wobbling.

"You must go now; this is God's property." The first repeated. I was not in the mood for this; I took his spear from him and snapped the shaft two handed over his partner's head. He dropped unconscious with his own spear still in hand. I grabbed the other's face in both hands, his cheeks bunched up like a baby's.

"Where is he?" I said through gritted teeth, his face crumpled in terror.

"He's across the sea!" he sobbed. "See for yourself." He dropped to his knees to moan when I let go.

"I will." I turned towards the Abbey feeling invincible but for a coiled snake of worry that I'd let my prey get beyond my reach.

Chapter 15

Excerpt from 'Holy Scriptures of the Western Creeds:

It is not for my vanity that I have gathered you, my congregation, my children, my flock. It is not to comfort me as I step into the unknown, carrying, not mine, but our precious cargo to unknown lands. But to allay the fears and concerns of some of those amongst you.

God's earthly ears have become alerted to concerns around our involvement with those from across the seas.

Fear, it seems, has been nibbling at the toes of the weaker amongst our brethren. These whispers, though bordering on heresy, have worried me, my children. My worries, so great, have they become that they have almost put an end to my journey before it has begun. It was not until I had spoken with God that your safety in my absence was reassured. He has given me the faith to take my pilgrimage despite adversity. The faith to trust in those amongst this flock that would stand strong in the face of heresy and stand strong in the shadow of my absence.

This family's actions questioned. Though it pains me to reveal, there are those amongst us that say we should not meddle in the politics of these lands.

Now I ask two questions of you, my children.

What is politics if not the management of power?

And who, if not God, may wield power as he sees fit in the world he alone created?

I can tell by your silence that the truth has settled across the flock and the sun has risen to share its gifts.

My last word, before I take God's wisdom across to our brothers and sisters in the new world, shall be this.

It is God who has connected our nations.

It is God who has shone his light on the people across the sea and enabled them to travel to our land.

It is God who has encouraged their participation in our battles and the clasping of our hands.

And it is God who has invited me to cross the sea after the years of purgatory caused by the Communion.

I WILL NOT REFUSE GOD'S INVITATION!

Callus

Locked up and Hurtin'

Losin' hope

Bloody idiot! I woke up as I slipped off the stone bench in my cell. Reckon I'd tried to move my face outta the sun and fell. My head felt like it'd been used to pull a wagon and not just 'cause I'd woken up in the day; also with the beating. Memories of my night came back slow and sure.

I'd marched into Osset's abbey, leaving groaning men in my wake. As far as I knew, I'd not killed anyone, and I'd not even had my hatchet out. They were a soft bunch, kept saying the same thing.

"Reverend Osset is across the sea, spreading the word." It made no sense to me, and I was getting angrier as I searched through the old place. Then the cramps came. From nowhere my guts twisted and my chest pounded, I roared in frustration as I doubled up in pain, sudden concern for Crow flashing in my mind.

"This is a place of God." An unfamiliar voice with a weird accent echoed across the hall I was in. I stood up as the pain slacked off.

"Where's Osset!" I shouted, my voice boomed around that grand chamber, and more robed men in white hurried away from the scene.

"Reverend Osset is not here, and you have outstayed your welcome." This one was calm as he walked down the strip of red carpet towards me; he was a funny lookin' fella, not a creed I'd seen before. He had long black hair braided up like a woman's, and silky, flapping robes. As he got close, I noticed his eyes, squinted and snakelike, never saw anything like it 'till then; he was the first one didn't look threatened by me.

He stood in front of me, surrounded by pews and made like he was about to dance, just as another gut wrench got me down on one knee; the world went white and then black immediately.

Everywhere was iron bars and painful sunbeams. Felt like there was no escape from the light 'cept in the corner where the hay was sodden and stinkin' at least they'd left my boots on.

From the shadows I looked around, more pompous guards with pointy spears and further across the dank corridor, another prisoner. She paced and dragged something across her own bars. The loud clattering was nothin' compared to the sunlight, headache and all-round bruising I was already suffering from.

"Stop that!" A guard got off his ass and tried to look threatening. She carried on a little faster. "I won't tell you again." He poked through the bars with the haft of his spear, but she moved away all easy and sniggered. He tried again, then again; she started laughing now; she was playing with him like a rattler as he got redder and clumsier. The other guard stood up.

"Leave her, brother; she'll drive you to distraction." He put his hand on the flustered one's shoulder, but he didn't stop trying to jab through the bars. It was amusing to watch. There were a few more tries, and then suddenly she pivoted on her heels and yanked the spear clean from his hands. He fell back on his ass and let out a yelp. She spat at him and threw the spear to the back of her cell. Sounded like it hit others piled back there where it landed; she'd been busy.

I laughed, and the embarrassed fella came shaking his finger at me and ranting. I stayed in my corner, noticed his bunch of keys, and kept my head down. If I was going to make a move, it'd be after dark when I at least had some strength.

Later, the guards changed, and my fellow prisoner collected another spear. I'd never come across a more fiery woman. Unfortunately, they eventually got wise and started lobbing buckets of water at her as the sun went down. She kept her spears but her desperate shivering through the night did nothin' for my mood.

Not only had I fucked things up in the Abbey and got myself locked up. I'd spent too much time with Crow, too much time playin' the happy father and pretending to be normal. Osset was mine, and with his death, my revenge and redemption would have been earned. I'd lost sight of my prey and it had bolted. Despair was my new partner, and it was pushing me back down a familiar hole.

Crow Hoby
Nearing Sanctuary
Sandy plains

According to my map, I was right on top of 'Sanctuary' but from the high ground, I saw no evidence of the place in Jarad's letter. I'd stayed high to elevate my position to get a better look at my surroundings, but I began to think that the pathways and undercliffs below concealed another landscape. I tied my horse and began tentatively approaching the edges of the gigantic rocky platform I found myself on, looking for signs of habitation. I did not know the wildlife of the place and I was around forty feet above ground level. Occasionally, I had to stop my search and override the panic that threatened me; especially at the distant and victorious yowl of what had to be a large cat in the vicinity.

Just as my hope was ebbing, I noticed something across a broad vista between clifftops; it was fleeting but something glinted unnaturally amongst the flora. I studied the area but saw nothing, then I climbed a few feet up a nearby tree and watched with intense concentration, to no avail. I sighed and untangled my limbs from the curled tree to disembark when something else caught my eye... smoke.

It was distant and thin, but there was definitely smoke rising from a natural chimney down below me, in the adjacent rock face. I was right. The entrance to 'sanctuary' must be far below.

Reluctantly, I had to let my horse find his own way to freedom. I untied him and made my way, climbing and scrambling wildly to the thoroughfare below.

Captain Lazarus Badstock

A God damned pilgrimage o' woe from start to finish! Soon as I get into the meat of it, I get foggy. Now I'm one smart fella when I ain't all foggy but on account of my age, and all the killin' I done, I have these times when things get too rough for my little ol' brain. I been caught wonderin' and cavortin' from bar to barley. Anyway, by the time I get halfway to this sanctuary place I gets tired. Real tired. Got myself spun round a few times 'fore I stayed put, then I found myself a spot under a cracked old tree.

When I came round I wasn't under no tree, got my leg stuck fast in a creek with my ass in the air. Finally got my bearings from the sky and set to get back on the road.

Took me two days to get back to that tree!

I finally get to the place, and it takes two hours to climb up. Lookin' down on the front doors is always a suitable spot. I set myself up and put a couple nets up to hide my camp. Interestin' place; the front doors look like the maw of the great hoodoo God behind it. At night, the eye-windows glimmer with fiery oversight.

I'd been sat a few days with nothin' happenin'. My mind wanders. I don't get somethin' to chew on; I get all kinds o' crazy.

Sometimes them kids came outside and played, not all of 'em but most and that's the times I remember 'fore Crow showed up. Watchin' them jumpin' and bumpin' was a joy, pure and simple. It kept my mind busy enough to hold off the fog while I sat and waited. Through my scope, I could see their faces clear as day; don't need no words to know what's goin' and I watched 'em. In a couple days I got to knowin' who played with who and which teachers they liked. Couldn't read the teachers. They had their big white hoods up, just caught the odd laugh or dressin' down.

I got too carried away watchin' them kiddies, forgot to keep my eye on things. It's essential that you keep an eye all around your defensive position at all times. First, I got to know about my mark was when he fell out of a tree up on the next plateau. I'd just lit up a smoke to prepare for a bit of shuteye when I heard the thump. Damn him, he'd gotten right up my ass 'for I even spotted him. Anyway, I was watchin' him then; he was stumblin' round lookin' for somethin' and fallin' off this and that. I got my scope and had a good look; he was younger lookin' than I was expectin', good thick hair, not too short. Thought he'd spotted my lens then, so I put it away.

As harsh as it was for me to get up on that damn hoodoo it was twice as bad for Crow to get down, course I didn't know it was Crow then, I was just laughin' up there, quietly as I could o' course. He finally found his sorry ass at them enormous doors and they gathered him up and swept him inside.

I couldn't rightly remember what was gonna happen next, but I could tell by how he moved young Crow had absolutely no idea of the black clouded shit-storm that was coming for him. I loaded up my shotguns and took a few rounds out the rifle to reload from scratch; she preferred it that way.

Chapter 16

Anonymous Author

Keeping the troops in line

Accustomed as he was to the glances at his size, walking with Bean made Jones feel like ten men. People fell over themselves to be out of their path. Broderick had given his familiar twitch of the head, which meant "With me!" He'd come out of Crave's room like he always did, looking slightly relieved. Jones hadn't even met Crave yet, but the way everyone spoke about him like he was so bad ass made Jones' elevation to the posse seem better and better. The only thing lacking so far was a decent job; Jones thought this was about to change as they entered the thriving Bank in Hatton.

The place was alive with commerce. Tellers scurried this way and that with scraps of paper and furrowed brows. Customers competed for status as the ever-continuing competition in self-importance raged. Apprentices torn over which customers required the most bowing and scraping. Only an experienced teller could give them the all-knowing nod in-between their own customers. It was money induced pandemonium.

The floorboards creaked as Broderick, Bean, and Jones entered. The guard's eyes bulged and he quickly, yet casually, stood ready for trouble, hand on his pistol butt.

As one finely dressed customer made to move around Jones, he gave her a little growl; she squeaked and hurried out onto the street. Jones grinned and turned to Bean for approval, but suddenly got cuffed across the head by Broderick.

"What the hell is wrong with you, boy?" Broderick was significantly shorter and older than Jones but intimidated by his prospect's size or youth he was not.

.

"I was just..." Broderick hit him again; Jones' unruly hair flopped comically.

"Well, don't!" Embarrassed and angry, Broderick continued in a venomous whisper. "You wanna stick with us? You stay in line, understand? We're here to do business, that business aint scarin' off the fine customers of this establishment, you hearin' me boy?" he gestured pointedly at the skittish guard.

Jones looked at Bean again, there was no expression of support there, Bean just waited, hands on his belt, nonchalant. Jones sulked like a child as they moved into the bank, and Broderick got to his business.

When they emerged from the bank, Broderick was carrying a weighty cash bag and put himself between his two hulking sidekicks. He lit a cigarette and shook his head disapprovingly at Jones. Before he stepped off the decking and into the street, he looked up again.

"Think it's time you met Crave."

Thanks to a considerable amount of coin, the landlady of the "Belle of the Ball," where they'd been staying, had offered them a place to conduct their meeting. Broderick had given the boys a couple of hours to relax beforehand and had explicitly said,

"No trouble... we got business."

It was a large wooden paneled room with a huge gaming table in the centre. This sat on a large, once colourful carpet. Broderick was smoking up the place by the time they all filed in and took a seat. There was an order to where they sat. Jones obviously didn't know this and bounced about like a pinball until he found his spot furthest from a seat left empty for Crave.

They sat in silence for a time, a big contrast to their usual banter and social abrasiveness. Their only entertainment was to watch as Broderick's thick smoke curled and traversed the beaming sunlight shards, vanishing as it moved to the shadowed rear of the room. Jones tapped anxiously on the table with increasing speed until Philips slammed his hand on top to silence it. Jones opened his mouth to complain, but stopped as the door at the back of the room opened.

Crave stepped in, drowned in shadow. As he meandered around the room, that shadow seemed to cling to him. He put his battered Stetson on his chair back and rounded the table, his back always to the wall. He wasn't a big man, but the power that exuded as he circled was oppressive. Still in shadow, he tugged thoughtfully on his thick black beard, where it poked out from beneath his kerchief. He moved fluidly from gang member to gang member. As he passed each, he placed a hairy hand just between neck and shoulder, a subtle caress as his long middle finger brushed above the major artery found beneath. Not a word spoken.

Jones stared in horrific wonder as their leader moved around them. As Crave came close to one light beam, he saw a thin thread lift on the slight breeze in the room, another attached to Bean's hair to fall out of sight. Jones' mind wandered back to his discovery when he'd cleaned out Crave's wagon back in Basin. Their leader stopped behind Jones and his bony yet darkly hairy hands slowly slid over Jones' shoulders and onto his chest, his thumbs resting on his collar bones.

"I've had word from my brother." Jones jumped slightly as Crave addressed the room. His voice was deep and resonant, coarse from the blackened bones of an inner fire.

"He thinks he knows where our prey's headed." he sniffed, unconvinced. "Heard it before. Now me." He paused for effect and casually untied his kerchief. "I KNOW where he's headed, and I intend to be goin' after him!" Craves hand gripped slightly along with the stifled anger in his words but then relaxed again and slid from Jones' shoulders as he moved away, tucking his kerchief into a pocket.

"Question is," he said as he arrived at his own chair. Bathed again in shade, he slid out his chair and slowly removed his greatcoat to hang on the back. As he squatted as if to sit, he suddenly slammed both hands on to the table and propelled himself over and on to the table across the room to where Jones sat terrified. He pinned him back into his chair with hands on his shoulders. Now in the light, his great black beard parted to reveal the sticky black mandibles that came out from his jaw and opened, threateningly to close on Jones' face.

"Who's coming with me?"

Chapter 17

Excerpt from Archives of Heresy, Vol. 4

Dearest Anneka,

I know you hold my recent opinions in disregard, but I urge you with all that I have and all the years that we have been neighbours, to at least hear me out.

Father Osset is a great man. Of this I have no doubt, he has been our shepherd and saviour throughout these hard years, and I know he has the ear of God. He has, however, made a decision with grave consequences, and I fear he is mistaken.

Anneka, he has made this deal with the foreigners and we know nothing of their heathen ways. The only thing we can be sure of is that they have power! Power to cross the seas, power to send weapons and soldiers into a war that is not theirs. What will be their price for such aid?

When father Osset reaches their shores, what will they want in return? I fear the leave he has already granted them to come and go as they please, though appreciated, is hardly fair compensation for helping us to win our war!

Please, consider my thoughts and offer your loyalty with care. I fear that Father Osset has opened the gates that will lead to our downfall.

Garren, your friend and neighbour

Callus

It gets worse before it gets better

Fire in the gloom

While locked away in them cells, we'd get visits from that guy, the one got me locked up, a sick piece o' work. He'd come down tellin' us what he'd do when he got the go ahead back from Osset. He gloated 'bout how easily he'd taken me and Silk. She was the one in the other cell; I didn't know her name 'till we got out.

He goaded the both of us.

"You are welcome to try your skills again." He'd say, smirkin' "You need only ask," In his weird, gently hissing speech. I was getting angrier with each visit, but was smart enough not to show it. Silk spear charged him through the bars on damn near every visit, screaming like a banshee. He stepped aside easily and knocked away her spears with that damn smirk on his face. One time, he grabbed her spear while she still held on and thrust her end into her guts. She crumpled, and my rage came on proper. I stood up. The sun was down, but I'd starved for days, my strength gone. Just stupid fury had me facing him. He smiled and came to my cell, swinging the keys like a dead mouse by the tail.

"You don't look so strong, dark one." He said, still grinning while his weird snake-eyes stared right into me.

"You need some exercise?" I saw Silk stand in the background and I made a fool's decision. I stepped back, stretched my neck, and nodded at the lock.

"Get it done." I said as my stomach rumbled, already knowing he'd beat me.

When the gate opened, he threw a flap of his robes over one hip and waved me over. I wasn't used to being the underdog. I threw myself at him, but his foot smashed into my eye, then a fist in the guts, and I stumbled back, coughing. Damn, but he was fast. I went in again, but he swung out the way and I ran on past over towards Silk's cell. He laughed, and it urged me to try again. I swung for him, but he kept playing with me. I was way too slow and getting more exhausted with each pass. He started dancing around like a damn fawn, always out of reach of Silk, who tried to grab him more than once. I could hear her yowl like a cat when she missed.

"Perhaps you need to rest, old man?" he mocked and held the key up again, not even sweating. I looked up, my hands on my knees, then went for him again, hitting the floor when he took my legs out from under me, then kicked me square in the jaw. I think it broke.

He was looking a little confused as to why I wasn't unconscious. The pain across my whole body was like I'd been under a stampede. But when you die every night, you learn to get ready for what might come when you wake up. I couldn't talk, my jaw hung funny, and I was drooling. The bastard relaxed. I stepped forward, and he turned his body and stepped back into his fancy stance. He was over near Silk, but way out of reach. I was determined to hurt him before I crept back into my cell like a damn whipped dog.

I moved in as I saw Silk reach out and from her sleeve a red cloth shot out like it was alive. It wrapped itself around his leading arm and then up past his neck. The thing never left Silk's hand, but pulled tight around him. He lost his balance for a split second; I saw it in his eyes. I leapt at him and grabbed his head between my hands. He was damn near looking backwards after I twisted his head around, snapping his neck. I threw his dead body at the wall and it crunched again. Then I watched as the red cloth quickly slid back up Silk's sleeve; I saw it move under her clothes and wrap around her body, just like a child would run to its Mother after a fight. One corner just poked out at her neck as it stopped moving.

"That's my Mother." She nodded downwards and then looked at me. "You going to let me out?"

Crow Hoby
Sanctuary, school for the lost.
Sandy Plains.

The first of the Sisters of Shearn to greet me was Sister Kirin. She pulled me in through the massive doors and grinned from ear to ear, her hands clapped together quick and softly like a sparrow's wings.

"Welcome, I am sister Kirin and we are very pleased to meet you." As she spoke, she glanced behind, highlighting the crowd of faces, all eager to fill the small, shady chamber we were in and investigate the stranger. I was then subject to many gleeful introductions and questions as they somehow moved me into the place proper, seemingly without moving my feet. Eventually, the handful of Sisters, recognisable by their pure white robes, clapped loudly and ushered the crowd of kids and adults of all ages back to where they came from.

Sister Merryn sat me down and put her hand on my shoulder. To this day, I find I can never remember the words she spoke to me, but I remember the massive sense of relief and security I felt when she'd finished. I was weeping and completely exhausted. Sister Merryn hugged me tightly, and I remember no more.

I awoke to a gentle prod in my side, and then I met Mouse. She was the sweetest person I have ever met. Although she poked me, she gave me the most innocent and warm smile and then beckoned me to the door. I quickly got dressed, not really stopping to think who'd undressed me or where I was. I was eager to follow little Mouse and share in her excitement.

She skipped around the subterranean metropolis of Sanctuary like she knew every little corner like the back of her hand. When I slowed she'd grab my arm then, as we built up momentum, she'd let go, lift the hem of her grey dress and skip ahead. She spoke very little, even to the other kids and adults she introduced me to; she seemed to communicate with a series of squeaks that were perfectly followable.

The school itself was vast, and amazingly, carved out of the rock it sat within. Huge high chambers and pillars gave way to the smaller cave like tunnels and corridors. In the higher sections, obviously above ground level, there were very few windows. We occasionally passed white-robed adults who were about the business of keeping the place's many candles refreshed or reignited. Almost everyone we passed had a warm smile for Mouse and an introduction for me, the names forgotten instantly as Mouse tugged on my sleeve and led me to the next area. My legs tired as we climbed one spiralled stone staircase that seemed to go on forever. When we finally reached the landing at the top, we passed a couple of sisters, and Mouse beckoned me to a small hole in the rock wall. A beam of bright sunlight shone through, causing a rare illuminated patch on the opposite wall. Mouse's smile vanished, and she put her finger to her lips before stretching to her tiptoes to peer outside. After a short time, she waved me over, and I curiously leaned into the light.

Immediately blinded by the sunlight, I shouted as I thought my eye would explode with the pain. It was fleeting, but when I could eventually open it, an unfamiliar pain bloomed in my stomach and I bent double. I heard Mouse squeak behind me, followed by her frantic footsteps as she ran down the cold stone steps to fetch help.

After what seemed like an eternity, I got a handle on the pain and stood up straight. I heard louder, but no less frantic footsteps rising towards me. The light from the window seemed so much duller than before; I tentatively peered out without the pain of the previous attempt. The hole overlooked the clifftops across from the main doors; I realised it was similar, if not the exact place I had been clambering around the previous day trying to find Sanctuary. Suddenly my eye caught by a quick glint of light to the left.

Nothing. I idly scanned the landscape for my horse in case it had returned to where I had set it free. Then I saw the flash again. My gaze fell on the source. This time, it did not disappear. In fact, it seemed to shine right into my eye and I ducked away. I jumped as Sister Bevre gently put her beefy arms on my shoulders and guided me back to my room without a word.

Chapter 18

Intercepted Vendorrin missive

As promised, we have located the school which you have identified as a rich source of human commodity. I presume I need not reiterate my concerns over the quality of the assets after the previous target yielded so poorly. Our supplies, heavily depleted since forced to firehide most of the aforementioned yield, are depleted to unacceptable levels.

It is during these raids that I weigh the cost of firehide materials against the quality of the commodity that is produced after processing. I am sure you can understand my concerns as my party makes our living from this process and no amount of back slapping and ass kissing from foreign ambassadors can wash the vile taste of a poor deal from my mouth.

Having expressed my thoughts, it also seems that I am bound to form some kind of frail alliance with you and your sea crossing brethren, despite whether I deem it prudent. To that end, I merely suggest that you arrive at the designated coast in due time to receive the assets that I have collected. I am eager to be done with this charade of partnership and I do not wish to draw my blade in anger over a late collection.

I hope you judge the quality of my work and the sincerity of my threat on merit.

Vaurus

CHAPTER 18

Callus

On the run from Church

Out of the stew pot...

My knees were shaking like a damn dying dog's.

Despite having just fought my way out of a prison cell guarded by many fellas with big spears. Starving, beaten and exhausted, I'd been steady as a rock till I got to the boat.

"Don't be a fool!" Silk was shouting; I could hardly hear her as I gripped the last sturdy post before the plank reached across the river towards her stretched out hand.

Appears, I am terrified of water!

Realising I'd never really seen a river since cursed, I was discovering new challenges every day. I clenched my teeth and leapt across rather than risk the thin plank. Silk grabbed my hand, and I saw her Mother coil round her wrist in readiness, but then flit as I finally got on board. Back then, all the weird stuff I'd seen had been about me. That was until I'd met Silk's Mother. She'd gasped a brief explanation as we ran, claiming the red cloth was somehow blessed with her soul after Osset had killed her, which explained our shared eagerness for vengeance but left too many new questions in my head to even begin to ask.

She insisted they'd not follow us on the boat. I was OK with it but couldn't shake the fear of the moving water under my feet; it hummed through my boots. My head was swimming. I reached for Silk and my hand started shaking. My need to die was getting urgent.

"I need to be alone!" I shouted through my clamped teeth.

"You are a strange man." That's all she said, but she turned away as if to give me some privacy as I looked for somewhere dark to lie down. I found a hatch to a large box containing the anchor. I heaved it open and with the last of my strength dragged the anchor to one side and fell in beside it, I reached for the hatch, but Silk's hand grabbed it and closed the lid for me, she didn't understand my desperation but then, why would she.

I reckon I was louder than usual as I went. The agony o' death was akin to the worst I've ever felt.

Strangely Silk, nor the Captain never said a word about my daily anchor box retreat; each evening, after I slept, I'd wake up to a cup of juice and Silk's arm as I climbed out of the box. She always shook her head, but showed no unkindness. The captain kept to his own business. His skin was near black and his voice was a low bellow.

Back in the Church's guts, Silk'd led me to her old clothes and effects. She threw mine at me while her Mother covered her modesty and she dressed in her hide and leather armour; links of metal fastened it, and it seemed to look right with her sword and long boots.

We fought off more than a few guards. Usually Silk was there first with her sword; she was ferocious! I just wanted out of there so I could find a dark hole to hide in, but she wanted payback.

She was as strange as she said that I was, a raging fire one minute, then a concerned companion the next. As we travelled, we shared each other's company more each night. We didn't always talk, but the silence got more comfortable as we rolled down the river. I thought I hated Osset but Silk carried it like the anchor I slept with each day, got the feeling nothing would stop her from getting to him, which made her a suitable partner. Just couldn't shake the need to fetch Crow, too.

"I can't wait for you to fetch your boy. I'm sorry!" She stood up and paced around the deck, chewing her thumbnail. "I need Osset, you don't understand!" she sat down again, then stood up and wagged her finger at me, "If I miss him again because of you!"

"Just calm down... sit." I waved her down as if she were cattle, but it seemed to work. Least she stopped arguing with herself, anyhow. "I'll come with you. Damn it, I'll come as far as it takes, but we need Crow." She flashed me a look could've killed a snake. "The three of us, that's how we'll get him. No good getting ourselves banged up in another jail." She looked down at her boot, thinkin'. "I saw you cuttin' down Osset's men and you're good, real good, but you're like me, y' get yourself all worked up and there aint nobody can stop you! Crow can keep us both in check. He's a good kid."

"How long?" she was swingin' my way.

"Not long. We get to town then we go fetch him, few days at the most."

She closed her eyes. Even her Mother was gettin' riled; I could see her under Silk's armour, curling round a shoulder again and again, all worked up.

"Listen, you have my word. I'll see this through to the end, whatever it takes, but… but I need Crow." I insisted as I scratched my head. Somethin' felt strange hackin' on about Crow like I needed him so much, but somehow I felt it in my guts. I needed him back to feel right again.

She nodded. Her Mother squeezed round her waist. Then Silk suddenly looked up at me, shakin' that pointy finger; her eyes blazed, then she sighed out and nodded in agreement, looking back at her boot. I relaxed; I needed Osset as much as she did, but I needed Crow, too.

We had a deal, or that was how I saw it anyhow.

I'd like to say I got used to the boat, but I didn't.

Night after night, we slid down that winding river while my guts churned and my feet buzzed. Silk was right, though. Nobody seemed to follow us.

Whenever we got the chance to stop, I got on dry land and went to find something to feed on and help with my guts. Silk never said a word about it. Even one night when I came back limping, I'd drank from a beast that damn nearly kicked my leg out from my ass. She just frowned as I jumped the gang plank and crawled into my anchor box.

Chapter 19

Crow Hoby

A place to call home

Sanctuary, School for the lost

Time passed with ease in Sanctuary. My studies often kept me from venturing outside, which suited me, but would occasionally earn me a kindly telling off from a sister. I relished the dark gloom of the place, whereas other students often stared hopefully out of the crude window holes, coveting the intense light that they gave way to.

I had all but forgotten the reason I had come out into the desert in the first place as I fed my hunger for learning and toyed with the idea of friendships with similarly aged students.

My stomach cramps remained, though, and seemed to come at random. I think it baffled the sisters, as they would constantly inspect, poke, and berate me for what little I ate. They would whisper amongst themselves after each medical examination. It seemed I was becoming quite the exotic mystery.

Despite my enjoyment of my surroundings, my satisfaction with my studies and the pleasant company, I increasingly missed Cal; occasionally I would decide to leave, but would each time be dissuaded by a sensible sister.

Most nights, I would wake in a state of intense anxiety. I'd say drenched in sweat, but my body was going through strange changes since splitting from Cal and sweat was not something I suffered from. I didn't feel cold despite the obvious chill in the air out there in the desert, but I felt numb, the tips of my fingers and toes often losing their sensitivity. On particularly dreadful nights I drank from Cal's bottle, more out of a craving of closeness than any physical need, or so I told myself.

One night, as I paced the empty tunnels to clear my mind, the smell of burning on the slight breeze that traversed the ancient catacombs alarmed me. I attempted to follow the smell, fearing a fire inside, but wandered in fruitless circles as the sun crept up outside.

I got dressed; the day had begun, so I knew I'd not find any more sleep, not as Sanctuary came to life. Descending the stone steps towards the dining hall, I decided I'd help with the breakfast chores. The increase in students and sisters milling around on the stairs frustrated me. I grumbled under my breath as I squeezed between huddles of bodies, ignoring the protests behind me. I all but lifted sister Betrice to move her from my path.

"I beg your pardon, young man!" she turned on me, putting her bony but strong hand on my shoulder. "Your urgency for breakfast does not give you—"

Suddenly a thunderous boom echoed through the whole of Sanctuary, rock dust fell from the ceilings and an inquisitive silence spread throughout the residents.

Boom! Only a handful moved towards the source of the omnipotent sound. The rest, still paralyzed by the all-encompassing vibration as it shook the walls. I moved towards the staircase that led to the front doors, another level down, and I would reach the dining room.

Boom! This time, a splintering crack accompanied the noise, and a series of terrified cries came from the floor below. I took the steps three at a time, my heart pounding in my chest. I turned the corner and saw the front doors explode into splinters of wood below me.

The surrounding screams intensified as several black clad arms pushed through the ruined doors from the outside, tearing chunks of damaged wood and hurling them aside to gain entry.

Callus
On the water
Against my best judgment

Still don't know why or how but my eyes opened early. Usually heard Silk's puffing and panting as she swung that sword around, but that night I woke up to boots stomping around me. I tried to listen 'for I got out my box, couldn't see any light coming in but it still felt early, like I had a couple hours left to sleep.

"Woah, woah! He's all yours!" it was the captain. Nobody else had a rumble like his. He sounded a bit panicked. "You don't have to…" he went quiet then, something was wrong.

Something heavy hit my box and the voices of the sailors got louder, then they all started shouting and screaming. I pushed on the lid, but there was a weight on it. Something was very wrong.

As the boots quickly stomped all around me, I squeezed my knees up to get my feet on the lid above. It must have been late 'cause I felt strong, just couldn't get my legs right to heave. Then I heard Silk.

Sounded like she'd torn the cabin door off its hinges! Then she roared. I heard her sword swinging and the pure fury in her voice. It gave me a kick in the ass, and I shoved the lid open and threw myself out onto the deck. First thing I saw was the captain's dead face staring at the sky as he rolled off my anchor box, an arrow in his neck that was smoking. Everywhere was smoking! Flames were catching up the side of the cabin and the deck was filling up with burning arrows.

Fire always put me back in Wilf's place. The agony I'd caused by taking his help, the searing pain in my burning fists as I pounded on them Church doors… Osset.

The sailors were jumping in the river to escape the flames. Silk was yelling at them as they fled; she had blood all over her, likely not hers. A burning arrow sunk into my chest, then another snagged at my hair and clattered on the deck. I pulled the arrow out; the flames tried to catch up my sleeve, but I flung it into the river.

The Captain'd tied the boat to the riverbank, although the rope itself was smoking. Just beyond, lined across the bank, were maybe twenty of 'em. Hooded and masked, all in red. Two of 'em on each end were still picking arrows out the ground, lighting and sending 'em over. The rest chanted some weird Church drone whilst waving their burning torches around.

With my blood up, I hardly thought about that burning rope and how it could leave me stranded on the water. I started running towards the gangplank, a sick feelin' in my guts that it had gone overboard. Silk was already leaping across to the bank ahead of me.

Chapter 20

Excerpt from "New Roots: The Viken's Descent."

Matwan's Mother said nothing as he left. As was Viken tradition she simply reached up and touched his hand as he rode by, He saw the slight glint of a tear on her cheek, but her face was passive and calm, she would not want to summon ill fortune to his journey and risk his eventual return.

He had spent almost a year convincing the elders to let him go. It was only because of the recent disappearance of Vulf and his crew that they had finally relented. Matwan had proved his worth, but his helm had only recently bonded. He feared they presumed he could not defend himself in the harsh world below the mountains. They were unaware of the fierce and dedicated training he had undergone since his brother's disappearance last year.

He swung his pick one handed as he rode down into the valley, his other hand controlling the goath as it picked its way down between, and over, the rocks along the pathway. His teacher, Antallen, would not have approved; he'd taught him to always have both hands on the goath's reins whilst descending.

Though Matwan's purpose ran deep into his soul, he also found an excitement at the chance to see more of the world than the mountains he had, until then, never left.

His first task was to investigate in the town called Hatton. Vulf's crew were on a well-established trade run with a merchant there. Matwan's people had no reason to suspect the merchant, as he'd traded with them for years, but since Vulf had never returned, Matwan could not stop the suspicion from forming in his mind.

Matwan's brother, Bearlen, had disappeared under entirely different circumstances. Raided whilst foraging, or so the scouts had reported. They had fought bravely; the mountains strewn with the corpses of their enemies, yet there was no sign of the survivors. Many feared they became prisoners, but this theory fell on deaf ears. What use would Vikens be beyond the mountains?

The mystery and the need to avenge his brother had burned within Matwan for so long that he often feared that there would be no horizon to his quest.

Crow Hoby
Peace under threat
Sanctuary, School for the lost

As the main doors gave way, a tide of black cloaked men burst into Sanctuary, each of them grabbing the nearest person within their reach and tightly embracing them against their kicks and screams. The sounds of terror were deafening. Attempting to resist the wave of fleeing bodies as it pulled me deeper into the School; I had to defend these helpless people. I forced my way into the kitchen against the flow and grabbed the biggest blade I could find; I hefted it and in my mind I saw it chopping through bone with enough strength behind it. A couple of others had the same idea, two sisters I didn't know, and a lad of a similar age to myself. They were scrambling to arm themselves with anything they could find when the inner door was flung open.

His hood had fallen in the chaos, revealing a black leather-like substance that partially covered his pale bald head. Even though he moved in a frantic and threatening manner, his face remained calm, nonchalant. His eyes seemed to stare elsewhere as he ran towards me, arms outstretched.

Something within me stirred into life. It was almost as if the cramps I had been experiencing deep in my stomach had turned tail and were now on my side. Energy and strength pulsed through my entire body as he neared in what seemed like slow motion. To the side of me, I could feel the pulsing life throbbing through the lad as he readied a large fork and saucepan lid. Determined, but horrified.

The fear that had infused me when I'd first seen our attackers had completely gone. My mind found a focus on putting them down. I stepped in, towards the assailant, and swung my knife down into the side of his neck. The blade bit deep through his collarbone and into his chest to produce a sluice of dark blood. My other hand pushed his arm away and although I could feel strength there, I was far stronger. He fell to his knees, but continued his attempts to grasp me around the waist. I hacked sideways into the remaining neck flesh and the head lolled to the opposite side as the body dropped.

The lad vomited behind me and I stormed back out towards the main doors with more savagery in mind. I cut another down as he came for me. Again, he did not stop until I'd chopped my knife into his skull. I recall a distant cracking sound that seemed to echo around the walls, but I was intent on the black-robed enemies I stalked. I came across another who was dragging a young girl towards the entrance; the fight had gone out of her and as I approached; she stopped thrashing; her face was a mess of tears and damp hair. I almost took his arm off in one swing and the girl bolted while the hooded face barely registered my presence. His working arm reached for me and I grabbed it. Suddenly, another black form barrelled into me, and the three of us rolled onto the floor. Three arms reached towards my neck as I squirmed around what I feared was a lifeless child's body beneath me.

The loud crack I'd barely heard before rang louder and one of my would-be stranglers suddenly looked up to the ceiling, then collapsed. I stood and as I rose; I thrust my knife up under the jaw of my original prey. He instantly stopped moving as the blade ascended from under his chin into his brain.

The room was suddenly quiet and empty. Blood splatters and torn clothing adorned the vestibule. There were no live residents and no signs of the attackers remaining. My shoulders sagged, and I had to fight a mild wave of nausea.

The silence shattered then by what I could instantly recognise as a shotgun followed by an insane cackle, a reload, then another shot.

"No!" I shouted aloud and ran towards the sound, fearing the carnage a gun would wreak on these innocent kids.

As I turned the corner, I almost ran into a large man, covered in red plates of leather that were edged with pure white bone. He spun at my arrival, and I saw his sneering, ghostly face. The only colour was in the thin blue veins that crept towards his features and his pale blue lips that opened to bare his teeth. He dropped the body he'd been examining and pulled out a long sword that rasped as it came free of its scabbard. I noticed another of his kind to one side who barely noticed me; he continued his work amongst the dead.

The wretch before me took a stance and whirled his blade confidently; I noticed four red cuts down his neck that bled a thin trickle, and my stomach rumbled.

He stepped forward and readied his sword, then span violently as a shotgun blast tore into him. Now, with his back to me, he took another blast. His ruined remains dropped at my feet, his dark blood speckling my face.

The shotgun wielder cackled again, "Yeeehaw!" a tatty, bearded rustler type stood in front of me; he poked the rim of his hat up with one of his two sawn down shotguns and gave me a wink. The second bone wearer stood and was reaching for his sword; the hunger took me.

I leapt onto him before his blade left its scabbard, too quick for his free hand. I bit into his neck; clamped on hard and sucked until I felt life and energy leave him to fill me. For a fleeting instant I saw a picture of my Pa in the hands of Cal but brushed it aside with the exultant feeling as it filled my body with newfound strength and a strange sensation of many voices fighting to be heard as I consumed them.

"Time to go, Mr Crow!"

The guy was maybe in his sixties, reloading two sawn down shotguns, surrounded by the bodies of some children, some weird, pale fanatics and who knew what in hell those bone wearers were, and his smile was huge and infectious.

"How do you know my..."

"Ahhh c'mon now, I aint the strangest thing in this room and we aint got time, let's go!" he threw me one shotgun, I caught it clumsily and followed.

Strangely, I felt comfortable in his presence, a feeling that, until that moment, I'd only had with Cal.

Stopping briefly before following, my mind found the faces of those I'd met and befriended in Sanctuary, probably dead, but I would join them if I stayed. I took a step, then remembered Mouse. I stopped, my head in turmoil. The stranger looked over his shoulder and made a clicking sound like you'd make to encourage a horse.

"S'bout to get busier round here and you and me got bigger problems."

Chapter 21

Excerpt from "New Roots: The Viken's Descent."

Fortune indeed favoured the bold as Matwan arrived in the town of Hatton. The busy market town was no stranger to trouble, but the trail of carnage left by a group of Outlaws stood out like fresh tracks to the young Viken. The natives to the town were mostly pleasant, trading between our two homesteads had stood strong for a few years and our differences were, if not understood, then respected.

He discovered the Outlaws had already left the town and, despite his desire to investigate further in Hatton; he raced after them, with only his intuition to suggest a connection to his vanishing brothers.

Progress was slow. Matwan's goath, like all goaths, was a creature of strength and dexterity at the sacrifice of speed. Fortunately, Matwan's prey had little fear of being followed, and the tracks they left were like a call to glory.

Again, the Outlaws' effect on the locals was obvious as he arrived in small towns and villages in their wake. One town called Oaken denied the Viken entry; he lost precious time as he rode around the town's walls to continue his pursuit. The detour took him up onto the cliffs and hills that reached towards the distant sea and as he first looked upon the wonder of the dark water and watched it swallow the horizon, Matwan was glad of the inhospitality he had encountered.

Callus

Osset's people fought back

I would follow the trail of blood

Silk tore into 'em like a wild cat. They'd expected us to go down with the

99

boat; barely raised their spears before she landed.

I ran to the rail and saw the water down below; it stopped me in my tracks! I damn near fell on my ass. I could see the hooded swine turning back now. Silk was on her own. They'd swarm her. I ran further up the boat, alongside a small jetty; it was closer, but that damn water seemed to get in my head whenever I saw it. I heard her fighting and screaming at them, but she wouldn't have a chance once they all turned.

"Cal!" she screamed my name; she knew she was on her own, but my feet wouldn't let me over that damn gap. The fighting stopped. They'd surrounded her. I looked up. She'd piled a few bodies, but they circled with their spears; eyeing and nodding each other to go first.

There was a snapping sound. The rope holding the boat whipped up and smacked me in the face; the boat was loose! I can't explain the cowardly terror that came over me. There was only one way off that boat.

I made a noise like a trapped deer and flung myself onto the jetty, which knocked the wind out of me. I rolled over onto dry land and got my ass together.

Roaring as I ran in. hatchet swingin', I hit the circle they'd made. I felt a couple spears sink in but kept swinging. Bits of them flew this way and that. Untrained; they were used to the simple life. Silk's anger kept coming and more bodies dropped till one fella, the last one, ran.

My hatchet took him down at 20 yards.

I looked at Silk over my shoulder with a smile. But she'd gone!

There was a splash as she disappeared into the river, heading towards the now burning boat. I watched in horror. I never wanted to see another boat in my days and she was chasing one down!

I thought she was done for, and I needed blood.

I found one fella dragging his sorry ass away as quietly as he could; I drank 'till I heard another splash from the river. Silk climbed out, dripping.

"Catch it!" she was shouting. "You were supposed to catch it!" she was angry at me now. She stalked up to something on the jetty. It was a book she'd hurled from the boat while I fed. My bad. I joined her as she was checking the pages.

"It's OK." She sighed with a smile, first time I'd seen one on her.

"What in hell is it?" I asked, still couldn't believe she'd swam onto a burning boat to get it.

"My journal" is all she said. Then she started stripping one of the dead fellas and drying herself on his robes. I stood for a while. Got all thoughtful about me and Crow and what was next.

We had a job to do and a posse to do it with, but I had nothing in this world I'd jump into a river for. I looked over at Silk as her Mother wrapped around her head, drying her red hair and the usually angry woman smiled.

"Christ aches, I best get me one of them journals."

Crow Hoby
Lost and following
Deep west

Thankfully, we walked in silence for what seemed a long time. I needed the time. There was a notion in me I'd become something wicked, something wrong.

As we weaved through the undergrowth, keeping from the path, I replayed the last couple of hours through my mind. I somehow felt that I should feel more remorse over the lives I had ended, but although I willed it so, it did not come.

I had fed.

"Name's Laz." The stranger said over his shoulder as though we'd just met; we'd been walking in silence for an hour at least.

"Gotta lotta other names, but I'll give you that one."

I looked up from my feet to his back. He had a long-barrelled rifle over his shoulder that he'd almost seemed to nod an introduction towards when we'd first left Sanctuary. We'd passed many bodies outside the main doors, mostly robed, but I saw at least one of the bone wearing masters In their red armour; each of them had a hole in or around their head and an expanding pool of red.

"Who the hell are you?" I said to his back as if I'd just realised what was going on around me. He stopped and roared with laughter as he turned around, slapping his thighs.

"I'm sorry, boy, you must be like a rat in a box. Shit." He was still chuckling as he reached up and pulled a pair of thin goggles down from the brim of his hat. There were still at least three pairs still fastened up there. He stepped close and eyed me, close enough to see there was only one lens in his goggles. Scratching at his thick beard, he looked around and put his hand on my shoulder.

"Tell you what, boy, when we put some distance in, we can hole up and get acquainted proper like, but we best keep movin' now, y'understand? He grinned at me, nodding. His face was filthy. He wore a long, ragged coat and had pouches and skin bags hanging all over the place, not to mention several guns. He turned and led the way, muttering something about a smoke.

Strangely, I followed.

Callus
Back on the road
Heading towards Crow

Every night of that damn journey, I wrote in that journal. Then, an hour later, I'd tear it out and throw it onto the road. We'd walked all the way to the nearest town and eventually found a wagon heading out our way, place called Port. Apparently, it was a straight road from there to Sanctuary. Seems Port was a trading town on the coast where we could settle a little before heading to get Crow. Our friends in white had left us a few coins for our services, so we'd paid for passage. Fella didn't ask questions, but I think Silk slept with one eye open every night. I played I was sick, kept my head down.

Every night when she climbed in her bunk I got my journal out, bought it in the station before we left, leather bound, real nice. I'd write about what we'd seen, what we talked about. About Crow, and how I missed him. It felt good to write it down, like it mattered somehow, but damn, it was as boring a book as I'd ever read!

I ain't proud but one night I slipped Silk's journal out of her bag for a look. I watched her like a damn hawk as I did it. She'd've killed me if she caught me. Just as I grabbed the book, her Mother wrapped further around Silk's sleeping body, but didn't wake her.

I only read a few pages, right in the middle, figured we all had a past that should stay in the past.

The way she wrote made me wanna read more, but I'd got what I came for and slipped it back in her bag. Neither Silk nor her Mother moved.

I tried writing like Silk, told the story like I was explaining to someone, not just ramblin'. Soon I enjoyed writing in there, pulled out my book once in a while and scribbled stuff down. I picked one up for Crow in town when we got there. I'd heard some funny rumours about Port, but it was on our way to Crow and Osset and nothin' would stop me from that.

Crow Hoby
Sitting with a stranger
Woodland, heading East

"Now, here it is, Mr Crow." Laz said, then licked his rolling paper.

"Just Crow." I said sulkily as I swept the leaves away from my spot and sat down.

"Well, looky here, boy's got a voice." He reached over with a bit of tree bark and set it to burn on the fire.

"Don't be that way, I'm only messing with ya. Fact is, you've had plenty to be thinkin' on and that's alright by me." He sucked on the large cigarette he'd rolled, and a plume of dark smoke drifted into the canopy of leaves above.

"Another fact is me and you gotta make an accord." The stench from his smoke hit my nose. It was revolting! He seemed to get pleasure from it as he drew one long drag after another and blew out the acrid clouds.

"Now mostly when I'm talkin' I'll be comin' over all wise and the like, and you should listen to what it is I'm sayin'. Fact is, I believe that you and me we gotta go on a journey together." I looked up, suddenly missing Cal.

103

"You're headed somewhere, kid, and I gotta help you get there and help you when you find out why. Problem is, I aint always gonna be wise. I have these times when I don't know what I'm doing." He shook his head in disappointment at himself. "I act all crazy and don't speak or nothin'." He threw up his hands and looked me right in the eye.

"That's when you gotta keep me with ya! Ya'understand?"

"I need to find Cal!" I interrupted, suddenly panicking that we could travel away from him. Laz continued as if I'd not spoken.

"I won't be no good to ya while I'm like that, but you gotta keep me taggin' along." He was frantically nodding for me to agree, his eyes wide.

"You'll need me where you're going boy, you gotta see through them bad times and think of the endgame, Ya'understand?"

"OK." I realistically had no choice, but I felt that somehow, I should to go with the unusual man. He grinned and had another draw of his smoke.

"What in hell are you smoking?" I said. The mood had suddenly relaxed around us. He gave me a sideways grin, exposing a large hole in his stained teeth. He bowed forward and slid off his hat. Beneath his hair was a tangle of unkempt salt and pepper, with handfuls cut short and shaved. With his other hand, he patted the pouch by his side that I'd presumed contained tobacco.

"Don't you worry none 'bout your friend," he said as he took another drag.

"He's gonna be waitin' for us down the road, you two aint finished yet."

Chapter 22

Excerpt from "New Roots: The Viken's Descent."

This unknown land, the likes of which Matwan had never imagined, stretched for mile after mile in all directions. The unbroken horizon circled him with only the occasional interruption. The coastal paths that he traversed placed him along the spine between two worlds, the never ending flat lands to one side, and the dark, brooding and uninhabitable sea to the other.

Matwan at first felt uncomfortable in the open expanses. He was used to the mountains and the confinement of the mines, the verticality of the rocky land as it reaches towards Vallen, beyond the sky. The sea also filled the young Viken with foreboding, for despite its alluring vista and the sheer size of its dark surface as it stretched beyond natural vision, it teemed with life of an alien and hostile nature. When studied as Matwan had, for a lengthy period as he rode beside it, it gave brief and surprising glimpses of the fauna that dwelled within. A striking tentacle or a fleeing prey would occasionally burst from the surface briefly before vanishing back beneath. Matwan was grateful for his elevated position along the cliff top, both for the chance to observe these phenomena and for the position of safety it offered.

The further he ventured from the mountains, the more naïve and vulnerable he felt as the new world around him unfolded. Though he bore his trepidations with honour, he was glad to be approaching his destination. The coastal city of Port would be full of strange and dangerous people, but the enclosed and clustered dwellings would offer temporary yet familiar relief on his long journey.

Captain Lazarus Badstock

Boy, didn't trust me anymore 'n I trust myself, but he came along. Once I 'splained the nature of our future together, his pot of options was gone. He wasn't one for questions, so I enlightened him while we went 'bout our business puttin' a few miles behind us. First night he was all sneers and fat lips, but he soon got to talkin' on account o' my way with people.

"Why did they come for us?" he says while we're puttin' out snares one night. S'pose I knew he'd ask but didn't give it a thought till then.

"They's slavers, boy. Know what that is?" he looked confused but was noddin' his head. "They wanted to take them boys 'n girls and get em' workin'." He looked down at the ground, a real angry look on his face, thought he was about to pop.

"Ya know, why build a damn when you' got a whole mess o' beavers in ya back yard." I looked at him, but he was still fightin' inside. "That's what my old Da used to say anyhow." I finished up with the snares and gave him a nudge to walk on back to camp. He didn't say another word till we got settled for the night and I'd got a smoke goin'.

"Shouldn't we be heading back?" his eyes were wide, like he was ready for a fight. "Shouldn't we have stayed to fight back? If... if Cal," he was workin' himself up proper, ballin' his fists and standin' and sittin' again. "If Cal was here, we'd have..."

"Too many, boy!" I 'cided to stop him; make him think. "You saw them fellas with the bones, right? I aint no expert, but I've been thinkin' them swords looked awful pointy!"

"But we killed them! You were laughing! We could have handled them, surely?" he stood up again, lookin' hungry.

"Too many, boy!" I said again. Now I don't enjoy havin' to repeat myself. It gets stuck in my gullet so I stood up too; that made him think. The two of us stood like a couple idiots in the woods, eyeing each other for a while. Then he slumped back down.

"How do you know so much, anyway? And where the hell did you come from?" I laughed then. I liked the boy, didn't take him a week t' get over himself like most folks.

"You got some fire boy, you and me we gonna do OK." I threw him the tin kettle and a waterskin. "You boil us up some tea and I'll tell you where I come from as best I can." He got to work, and I lit my smoke.

"Then you gonna need some blood."

Callus

Outskirts of Port

Reluctant negotiations

For the first time in a while, my guts felt calm, like a storm had passed and the rain was slowing down some. Silk sat on her bunk, tending to her sword when I woke. Her Mother held out a candle from her waist to work by. It flickered as the wagon rumbled on.

"Should be in Port by morning." She said with a small smile.

"Then it's a straight road to Sanctuary?" I asked, and her smile vanished. She sighed, and it got my dander up.

"I aint goin' nowhere without…"

"I know, I know." She waved her whetstone to shush me and shook her head. "I just want him so badly!" She'd been cooped up like a chicken in this wagon thinkin' all day. She needed some air. I thumped on the wall a few times, and the wagon stopped.

I could see the town on the horizon and the sea beyond. We'd been following a river which ran beside us and was getting wider with every mile, but I'd made Silk cover the windows to block the sun so neither of us could see outside 'til we got out.

Somehow, I could feel that I'd see Crow again soon, and right then that was all that mattered.

Silk was swinging her sword while her Mother stayed under her armour.

"How long do you think it'll take to find Crow?" she asked between gulps of air.

"I know where he is. Just gotta go get him. He's studying over in the place I told you about."

"If he found it?" she said, and I looked over at her with a frown.

"Course he found it!" I snapped. "It's you and me that's been stupid, getting' ourselves in all kinds o' trouble! Crow's had his head in his books." I felt proud and couldn't wait to see him. It surprised me how much the fire had cooled inside me at the thought of finding Osset; it was a good job Silk had enough fire for the three of us.

Crow Hoby
Forever following
The ruins of war

"Wait a minute, this is the camp!" Laz looked up at me, baffled. We'd stumbled into an abandoned army camp. There'd been a slaughter by the look of it. My mind jumped back to the camp where me and Cal had stolen the strange cannon in the night. Scattered mounds with softly billowing uniforms lay at regular intervals, the scent of old death.

"The Shit Cannon!" I pulled out the letter I still had in my pocket and read it aloud.

"Boy, I don't got a clue what you're barkin' about, but we gotta keep movin'." Laz dropped an abandoned rifle he'd been inspecting after he'd emptied the ammunition into one of his many pouches.

"I should have delivered this letter." I waved it at him. "To captain…" I checked the letter again.

"Rostrom! Captain Rostrom at rear camp four!" Laz approached and put his hand on my shoulder.

"He aint here, boy." He said in a gentle tone, "Likely it was the same slavers that hit your place." The realisation that I could not deliver the letter and complete my task dawned on me. There was nowhere for the letter to go and my journey had only just started. I felt tiny and overwhelmed by the world around me. I slumped to the floor and stared into nowhere while the camp litter swirled around me. Now that my excitement had dissipated, I noticed the scent of blood past its best. There were dark stains everywhere. It had been carnage! My stomach growled as I looked through a tent flap and saw a bedroll drenched in red. I took out the letter again and held it in the wind for a second or so before I let it fly.

"Sorry Jarad." I said into the breeze.

"This used to be me." Laz was right in the middle of the camp, his arms raised. Trekkin' round the land, goin' where I was told; killin' who I was told to kill." I looked up from my reverie, and last night's conversation all made sense.

We'd talked into the night about Laz's previous life, how he'd been a slave to his masters, and how he'd been the best of the best at what he did. He'd said that he had another, different calling now, and it involved mending the world. I didn't really know what he was saying the night before; it was late, and my eyes were begging me to lie down for the night.

"Now I'm trekkin' the land with you, and these sorry meat bags, they's from the war." He gestured to the East. "See, they set up camp and they shoot each other." He made a gun shape of each hand and proceeded to 'fire' from left to right, then right to left. He repeated the motion as he spoke. "Now they'll shoot each other 'till there's no-one left, and when there's no-one left, they find someone else to shoot, you understand?" I looked at the nearest corpse and nodded solemnly. "These soldier boys is close. Hell, I can smell their powder and their shitty britches." He took a breath, then gave his head a shake. "So let's go mend this world 'fore everyone in it gets killed!"

Captain Lazarus Badstock

We'd settled in, snares'd got us a critter on the fire and the kettle had finished whining. Crow set to brewing up some tea while I smoked.

"I see's it as a big old bucket." I said between tokes. "Ever'body gotta be good at somethin' and that's a drip in that big old bucket." Boy was listenin'. I had a way with stories. "Some folks' good with growing trees, some's good at learnin' them little kiddies, sellin' goods; you know my meaning." I had another pull, thinkin' my pouch was getting' awful empty. I'd have to fill it up.

"Me, I was the best damn shooter in the army! They wanted anyone gone, they'd pack me up with a bag o' bullets and I'd get it done, no questions. Now, I wasn't too sharp up close, but give me a rifle. I could take the seed from an apple and leave it swingin'."

"So, there I was fillin' up my bucket. Bang... drip. Bang... drip, one poor fella at a time." Boy was real keen now; sat, arms folded, watchin' me like a hawk.

"So, turns out the last fella was my captain.

I was walkin' into this town where the enemy was hidin', see I'd taken out the guards on the gate so that our men could charge on in there." I sometimes find it real hard to tell that story, so I take my time, have a few pulls and realise my smoke's nearly gone. I get to makin' another while the boy watches on.

"Anyway, I hear this screamin' and it aint no soldier; sounds like a lady in there havin' some trouble. So I set up my rifle to have a look see." Sometimes my head gets real scratchy, I ought to get a blade to it and fill up my pouch, I thought, then the boy's face reminded me, I was in the middle of my story.

"So I have a look and I see my men and they's pushin' round this lady and she's cryin' and hollerin' but they keep pushin' her round see." I stopped smokin' and looked Crow in his eyes. I see he's not likin' my story now, just like I ain't.

"Now you gotta understand that in them days my bucket was real full... real full! I'd been shootin' for th'army for years and years, even back then. It was my talent, so my Da used to say. He packed me off with a rifle when I was just a boy, younger than you are now, even!"

"So I'm watchin' my friends, the folks who I live and eat with ever' day and they're pushin' that lady and she's cryin' and there aint nobody stoppin' em. Now I'm too far away to shout even so I can't stop em'. Then Cap'n Bolo comes swaggerin' up and I think he's gonna go mule shit on them soldiers, so I relax a little. But he didn't. He unbuckled his pants while them friends o' mine held that lady down." I'd finished rollin' my next smoke, so I lit it on the fire and pulled real hard. Crow wasn't sayin' a word. He never did when I was talkin'. I loved him for that.

"I took 'em all out, one by one. Bang... drip. Bang... drip. Bang... drip.

Bang… drip!" now Crow's mouth was open, he was thinkin' hard. I finished that smoke in silence. We both needed it.

"When my bucket was overflowin', I got another callin', another bucket to fill. Now, I don't know who's handin' out these buckets, but I know they been speakin' to me. Ya see, I know things, things I didn't know before and I can do things; don't ask me how, but I know what I know and I know I got a different job now."

"That's why you came for me?" he was quieter than a mouse when he finally got to talkin'.

"Yup! Me and you, we gotta job to do, I've been told. I had to get myself to that school so that I could take you off one path and on t'another." I looked at him then, thought he was ready t'hear.

"Mr Crow, we gotta haul our asses across the sea and I aint sure yet, but I think we gotta kill a guy, a real, real bad guy!"

Chapter 23

Anonymous Author

A gateway to a new world

"God damn, would you look at that!" Philips was riding up front with Jake as they left the main drag and approached the coastal district of Port. Neither of them paid any attention to the bustling town around them or the market banter of the traders and hawkers. Their eyes locked ahead.

The posse had ridden hard down from Hatton, Crave had insisted. He'd pushed his men further than most would dare. Tired, thirsty and getting at each other's throats, but he'd pushed, anyway. The sight that greeted them was almost enough to make them forget their sore behinds and cracked lips. Philips and Jake rode, transfixed. They were a click ahead of the others so they could arrange some accommodation, but they were so in awe of what was slowly emerging from the sea mist, they stopped riding and just stared. Without shifting his gaze, Philips broke the silence.

"Bean owes me big time!" Jake rubbed his sandy eyes as if to make sure what he was seeing was real. He kicked his heels and clicked his horse onwards.

"Yup."

The two of them approached the seafront where the walls were, the cheapest places were up there, people wouldn't pay much on the front just in case those walls weren't strong enough to keep them safe. They'd built the town itself around the massive defences in the early days. It was said that Port was the first town on the coast, the Mayor back then was one brave settler and it had eventually paid off. Port was now a vast town full of thriving businesses, both legal and illegal, and every coin that changed hands in the place was reliant on those twenty-foot walls and the forest of sharp stakes that adorned them.

As they got closer, the perimeter seemed to rise, and they had to crane their necks to see. Up near the front there were others staring in awe, people everywhere in the street stretching their necks, oblivious to the surrounding traffic. Jake's keen eyes also caught watchers clustered up on the rooftops like seabirds on a cliff top; he looked for the tallest inn he could find and led them toward the stables out back.

"Ride back and meet the boys. I'll get us a place up there." He pointed up to a top window above an inn and trotted away. Philips was about to reply with some foul retort about Jake's authority, but thought better of it. He just wanted to see more and claim his gold from Bean.

By the time they had paid their way and muscled their way into the dorm with the best view, the Aileron Dwarf had fully emerged from the fog and was docking against a gigantic pier that bravely reached out into the foreboding water. The posse all stood in a half circle behind Crave and looked on in silence. Bean's hands were on his head; the usually unshakable tribesman was having trouble comprehending what they could all plainly see, the first passenger ship ever to successfully cross the sea.

The Aileron Dwarf was a gargantuan metal beast; it rose above the height of some of the nearby buildings and bristled with huge metal spikes and cylinders that crackled with some kind of energy. Its vast tail, like that of a creature that it shared the sea with, stretched along behind it and floated on the surface. From their distance, the tail itself seemed as broad as a train and covered in glass and iron panels. An enormous wedge that jutted out like the chin of an ancient and sinister God fronted the main body. On one side, its spikes were dripping with blood and black chunks of a monster that had obviously confronted the huge metallic impostor. The ship's 'head' displayed many strange cylinders that seemed to share the bright energy as it travelled from one to another like barely controlled lightning. Great plumes of black smoke gathered and then dissipated from an unseen system of belching pipes, just out of view.

As they watched from their vantage point, they saw people, like black and white insects, alighting and joining the waiting crowds inside the walls. The sea breeze carried a faint music and an occasional roar of celebration before the crowds parted and eventually merged back into the town, leaving the giant iron behemoth sitting in the water; small, glinting round windows mimicking the sinister eyes of an insomniac predator.

The following morning, Broderick ripped open the curtains and flooded their dormitory with light.

"Wake up, you useless bunch o' mules!" he wrestled open the window, allowing the gull's chatter to filter in along with the distant and ominous crackle that drifted up from the Aileron Dwarf.

Only squirming shapes and grunts followed.

"Wake up!" Broderick kicked Jones's bed, and he sat up immediately, quickly scanning the room with swollen and bleary eyes.

"Crave's in his room." Broderick reassured him as the others climbed from their bunks, mostly holding sore heads.

"OK boys, you deserved last night's party, but it's time to get work."

"What's next, boss?" Jones had shaped up since his encounter with Crave back in Hatton. He wasn't the sharpest blade in their arsenal, but he was becoming more willing and a little more able.

"We got one week!" Craves right hand gathered and checked his revolvers as he talked. "We gotta be ready. Crave's got the scent and we don't want to let him down now, do we?" He one-eyed Jones, who nodded frantically despite the obvious headache he was suffering. Bean thrust open another window, and Jake joined him as he stared out at the monster in the bay. Broderick slapped his hand on Bean's massive shoulder.

"You're gonna love it, Bean." He winked at Jake. "Soon as we find our man we're going for a ride on that beast!" just as Bean's face contorted in obvious dismay the dormitory door slowly creaked open to reveal Crave. Jones stood up quick, almost as though he was about to salute. Philips shook his head and laughed at the prospect's eagerness.

"Mornin' boss." Said Philips with a smile. "How's that head?" Crave stepped into the room, partially leaving the shadows behind him.

"You boys are animals." Crave rasped, his voice even more rough than usual, but he grinned before he pulled his bandana up to his nose, covering his mandibles. Everyone grinned at that. Even Jones relaxed a little.

"Gonna be a busy week, boys, but…" Crave gave a long and audible sniff, "I can smell him." He turned to leave the room, then stopped.

"Philips."

"Yes, boss." Philips stood up straight.

"Get me someone t' eat, would ya?" He closed the door as Philips grinned ear to ear.

Chapter 24

Excerpt from "New Roots: The Viken's Descent."

Relief settled over Matwan as he approached the town gates. He could see the enclosed streets beyond, illuminated by row after row of windows and personal oil lamps. Even at the late hour of his arrival, the town was busy and loud with commerce. He climbed down from his weary goath and walked it towards the gate as the guards approached him with drawn cudgels.

The coastal town of Port met Matwan with instant hostility and arrogance. He argued with the guards, but they gave no quarter and when he saw fit to lift his pick, more guards swarmed him. The clattering of an alarm bell ringing from within the boundary gate.

Without offering a chance to appeal, they incarcerated Matwan in a dark cell with a man of later years and frail bones. Harsh treatment had dulled his mind and so conversation was difficult, but Matwan eventually discovered the man was of Viken origin.

The man spoke of his captors in red, who had taken him and his brothers from the mountains and tried to feed him to their iron monster of the sea; his resistance had left him starved and beaten and left to die in his cell.

Matwan had found a clue towards understanding his brother's torment, but the knowledge he had gained crushed his heart. Deep inside the young Viken, his quest still smouldered, and would eventually become a roaring fire of revenge.

Callus
Finally got my feet up to wait
No rest for the wicked

"You're in a good mood!" Silk said as she looked in the mirror. She dabbed at a wound on her face. She'd been into town and got herself into trouble again.

"I'll be seeing Crow again soon; can't explain why I know, or why it's so damn good to know." She shook her head at my grin.

"Things rough in town?" I asked, but she just carried on cleaning her face. We'd arrived in the daytime, so it should've been me in a foul mood. She'd damn near carried me into our room and dumped me in a bed. When I got out, I saw she'd covered all the windows.

"You people just don't know how to treat each other!" she blurted out, then started taking off her sword and shaking her head.

"These aint my people."

"I mean East of the spine!" she snapped. The spine was a mountain range, apparently where she'd come from. I thought it best to keep quiet. She seemed furious. She carried on banging around our shabby room for a while, then she seemed to calm down a bit and looked at me with an evil lookin' smile.

"You hungry?" she said, as my guts started growling.

Crow Hoby
More flat lands
At the edge of the world

It felt as though me and Laz had walked for thousands of miles. I started out missing my horse, but eventually I craved a wagon and a seat; the sun was beating down and seemed to drain me of all energy. I longed to be in the shade while somebody else took the reins.

I didn't always understand what he was saying, but Laz kept some kind of conversation going to occupy our minds as we trudged along. He had a saying for everything and always had a story to tell, "in his back pocket" he would say. His body was tough and wiry, and he never complained, but occasionally he'd force us to stop so he could collect his thoughts. He repeatedly warned me he would have "foggy patches" as though I didn't believe him. I wasn't exactly sure what he meant, but I was sure I'd find out, eventually.

"There it is, boy! The edge o' the world." He was pointing out over the flatlands to the horizon. Then I saw it, the ocean. I'd never seen it before, but my Da used to tell tales about how it stretched on forever towards the unknown.

"Not meant for men." He would say, "only the monsters that would gobble you up as soon as they saw you." I could only see a dark smear on the horizon, but it conjured those tales I'd heard in a life I'd left behind. Those distant memories quickly retreated when we heard a gunshot echo off the sky and around the valley we were approaching.

"Rifle, two point two." Laz reported instantly with an agreeable smirk. He looked around, finally taking his eyes off the distant sea.

"There!" he said, pointing to a rise in the land. A faint hint of smoke was drifting up in a continuous line before it merged with the sky. He put his hand on my shoulder suddenly and closed his eyes as if he were listening.

"Yup." He said nodding.

"This way!" He abruptly changed direction and jogged off; though my tired legs protested, I followed.

Just as we reached the lip of the rise, there was a cluster of gunshots and a series of whoops and yells down below. Laz lay down before he approached the lip and crawled. I copied him, looking out over the lower plain; there was a train down in the valley, panicked steam billowing from the engine. Scattered around it, easily keeping pace, were riders shooting their guns into the air. From the distance, I could just make out two of them riding up close with a mind to board.

"Time we got ourselves a ride." Laz readied his rifle and peered down the sights.

"From here?" I was incredulous. "You'll hit no one from back here."

"Quiet boy." The train was slowing as it gradually arced around us. "You get yourself down there; make yourself real comfortable like, jus' don't be lettin' that train pull off without me."

I slid down the bank as I mumbled. Had little faith that Laz could hit the riders from this distance. I thought maybe this was one of his foggy patches, but I didn't want to offend him, so I started down towards the train at a reluctant jog; it was all I could manage.

Callus

Memories of the coast

Making friends with the natives

Silk was still in a mood. She stomped alongside me, not sayin; a word; we'd taken the path down the side of the wall down towards the front.

It wasn't the ship that shocked me, but the size of the damn thing. It was as tall as a building and covered in spikes, real mean lookin' piece 'o' work. It was mostly black against the last bit 'o' sun as it went down behind the sea. Hell, even Silk stopped as she saw it. I walked into her and she grunted.

"This way." She snapped as she carried on stompin'. I laughed.

"Where we headed, Silk?" I said to her behind, "Someone's got your flag flyin'." She just kept on stompin' down the path. I followed, shakin' my head. Then to my side there was a loud slap on th'other side of the wall, then the sound of the water as it splashed up. My head wandered back to the last time I'd been in Port, a long time ago, before the curse, a time I thought I'd forgotten.

She was always fearless. She pulled me by my hand, down to the seafront, surrounded by tall walls. Folks were crowdin' round, but she weaved through, worry in her eyes. It was the estuary pipe, where the water comes into town, 'fore it gets boiled up. We almost got to the front before a big fella held us back. Five or six men were jabbin' at something in the channel. People were fightin' to get a look, but still seemed weary. I tried to pull her back, didn't like her being surrounded. The people in town didn't always welcome our kind on a typical day, even less so in a mob. Then I saw it. A huge black tentacle flicked up from the channel like lightning. It hit one fella, who then flew into the wall with a crack. The crowd suddenly stopped jostling. Then it came up again and wrapped another fella, pulled him down into the channel. Everyone fled. It was like a stampede. Already trapped, I had to let her hand go just to stop her arm from breaking. Even now, in another lifetime, I still think about the relief when I found her later, bruised but not really hurtin', still sittin' near the break in the wall and starin' out to the sea. They had eventually boarded the hole up when the creature realised it wasn't gettin' into town and fled.

"You!" Silk's shout snapped me out of it. We'd wandered onto a planked street close to the front and she was pointing at a scruffy-looking boy as he sat on a beam that crossed the road and made a bridge above. He didn't seem affected by Silk's rage, but when she got close and pulled her sword out, he quickly stood up and blew a whistle. Silk turned to me with a wicked grin and rolled her shoulder as hard lookin' men and women with clubs seemed to appear all around us.

Crow
Hitching a ride
Laz is full of surprises

My exhausted jog into the valley was a surreal experience. My crudely calculated route to the train's nearest door, which included its present speed and course, took me into the path of the bandit furthest from the slow-moving vehicle. He was still sat on his horse and barely noticed me as I approached. The moment his eyes met mine, a hole appeared In his forehead as a crack echoed round the valley. He dropped to the floor before me, leaking red. With barely a hesitation, I straddled him and fed. He tasted wrong, but I suddenly felt more energised. Somehow, I knew the taste of his blood was that of a creature that was no longer living, but still it fed my soul. I quickly wiped my face and picked up the pace towards the train with renewed enthusiasm. Having seen their friend come off his horse, two more of the men turned their mounts towards me and charged. They were at a distance from each other and so they aimed to convene with me in the middle. One of them raised a revolver. Another crack rang out, and another dropped from his horse. His partner looked confused for a moment before another gunshot suggested he join him in a dead heap on the valley floor. The repeating echo seemed to distract the men from the train and encourage them to run me down. I kept running, a strange euphoria seemed to carry me to the slowing train; I could hear a screech of brakes mingling with the pounding of hooves.

He struck each rider that came within 30 feet of me or raised his weapon, from his horse, never to stand again; it was like my guardian angel flicking them from their mounts. The horses continued in their general direction and had all left the valley by the time I reached the train doors and looked around.

"Come on now! You hurt, boy?" a big man with a thick leather apron was saying as he straightened his cap and reached for my hands. I could see Laz making his way down from his position with all his belongings and, to my surprise, there was no one else left upright; he'd taken them all out In the time it had taken for the train to stop.

The big man heaved me on to the carriage and was wiping at the blood around my neck.

"It's OK." I said as I moved his hands away protectively. "It's not mine. We need to wait for my... friend." I pointed out towards Laz. I still felt like I was in a dream.

Eventually a panting Laz climbed aboard the train and the driver and a well-dressed man both thanked us, and shook both our hands, though he eyed my blood-stained clothes with dismay.

They offered us an empty carriage, out of the sun, all to ourselves, and a slightly nervous woman brought us some tea and bread.

"Should've used magic." Laz said before he stuffed a slice of buttered bread into his mouth. I looked at him quizzically, and he rolled his eyes.

"My ass wouldn't be so whacked if I'd used magic!" he spoke with frustration, as if I was being dim.

"Magic?" I countered with a smile and a raised eyebrow. Laz shook his head and scowled.

"You seen what you seen and you don't think there's any magic?" he was incredulous and was slowly getting covered in the butter and crumbs he spat out as he talked.

"Well, yes, but… not actual magic!" I wasn't sure what he was getting at, but it was not making him happy, so I looked out the window as the train picked up speed.

He couldn't let the conversation go.

"You need to be listening to some things, Mr Crow!" he sat up looking serious. "I hate the fact, but I think I'm headed for some downtime and you got to take care 'o' me, okay?" I nodded once again.

"Now listen up." He shuffled up to the edge of his seat and put his hands on his knees.

"You got this dual mortality thing going on. You got some 'o' him, he got some 'o' you, okay?"

"Okay?" I didn't mean for it to sound like I was answering a question with a question, but I wasn't quite on the same track as Laz. I can't imagine anyone ever was.

"Now, the more you're like him, the more you'll be him, understand?" A picture of Cal flashed into my mind and I understood vaguely what he was talking about. I wasn't sure if he was warning me or congratulating me. Laz looked like he was about to say more when he suddenly yawned and blinked rapidly. He stretched his arms above his head.

"I'm done for." He mumbled, then slumped back into the back of his seat with his eyes shut and whispered,

"There's only room for one." He licked his lips once, then slipped into a deep sleep, just like that.

I shook my head at the cryptic old man and turned back to the window. Everything seemed to be clicking back into place and we were approaching Cal at speed, plus I'd never been on a train before.

I had a snooze myself in the comfort of our carriage and woke as a woman of middle years opened our door with a smile. I smiled back and stretched; it was dark outside, and the train had stopped. A hissing sound accompanied the bustle of the passengers as they climbed onto the platform and went about their business.

"We've arrived in Port, gentlemen." She said in a soft, Motherly voice, "do you need a minute?"

Suddenly, I knew Laz was standing up behind me. He wore an unusual expression and he spat on the floor.

"Well, Missy! Why don't you go givin' me one good reason I can't leave this sorry establishment?" The woman and I looked at each other, equally confused.

"Now, go on, get!" he thrust his pointing thumb down the train and was looking between me and the dismayed woman. His face was strange and quite scary.

"You OK, Laz?" I asked hesitantly. He turned on me and put one bulging eye and his chin in my direction.

"And who in hell are you and how d'you know my name?

Chapter 25

Excerpt from "New Roots: The Viken's Descent."

Matwan endured what must have seemed like an age in his cell. He exercised often, attempting to keep his body strong despite the meagre food offered, but eventually, his mind strained.

Without warning, one day, they dragged him into the light and paraded our brother through Port in chains with those who had suffered similar fates. Through the deterioration of their physical fitness, many fell and were then violently encouraged to stand and continue or helped by their fellow prisoners before the aggressors noticed.

Before his eyes could open fully to the light, Matwan plunged into darkness once again as the procession boarded the hold of the Aileron Dwarf. Here, they would live and work together under the watchful eyes of their cruel masters.

Matwan's inner fire still burned brightly deep inside him, though his mind was dulling by the day; with the last ebb of his will, he set his thoughts to his new surroundings and how he'd escape them.

Callus
Hornet's nest
Old habits die hard

There were six of them, more lurkin' in the alleys behind, but six for the first test of our resolve. They were smarter than they looked, but when I saw one had a blade; I took my hatchet out. Fight was more serious than I'd thought. Turns out the kid Silk had dealt with a few hours before was just a lure for the hard ones, him and his posse had given her the runaround.

They came at us all together. Silk just seemed to spin round and two of them were down. I grabbed mine by the throat and squeezed before he had time to smack me with his club; he dropped it.

The masses that had been gathering outside surged forward like a damn wave; I threw the terrified fella I had hold of into the oncoming bodies. Silk was like lightning, spinning and dodging through attack after attack whilst cutting them down and sending them out of the fight, but eventually they closed in and she had nowhere to spin. Likewise, my ass was getting pinned down whilst I smashed away with hatchet and fists.

A combination of the blood splashin' at me and the fact that I was getting trapped and panicked turned me into a beast. I started flinging bodies around and fighting against the hunger to just choose one and satisfy my thirst.

They tired before us and after what seemed like a damn age they fell back, but my blood was up; I followed. Causing pain and death wherever I turned, I gave in to the insistent nagging of my curse, and took my fill from a large fella who still looked shocked to be beaten. I flung a kid into the wooden wall of the street; he was younger than Crow; he cracked and laid still. I took no notice of Silk and how she fared as I raged, chopping and biting as more critters came from the surrounding streets.

Eventually, they stopped coming. One was in front of me while I held a young girl in my left hand. I'd carried her for a while and I can't say why. Fella in front went still and glanced around at the bloody carnage round me. He looked like a hard man, scarred and weathered. I turned and looked at the girl, lifting her up to eye level; the man just turned and ran. The hunger burned, and suddenly an amazing feeling came over me as I looked at the girl's squirming neck. I thought it was an instinct to feed again, but as I moved in to latch on, everything stopped.

"Cal!"

Crow's voice. I turned round whilst still holding the girl. He was there, stood holding a small sawn shotgun aimed at a fella that attacked us. Can't explain the relief that went through me. I put the girl down slowly and marched up to him.

We embraced like reuniting brothers after a long and bloody war. The massive rage inside me was suddenly gone. The thug that Crow had threatened just turned and ran, one of a few survivors that fled, no doubt counting their blessings.

"You Crow?" Silk didn't deal with affection. Until then, I didn't think that I did. He nodded at her, and she flashed a tiny smile. Then it was gone.

"Osset." She said, slightly out of breath and speckled in red, nodded at me and turned to go.

"Wait!" Crow still had one hand on my shoulder. He understood from that one word what we needed to do next. "I have another friend who needs to come with us." Silk threw up her arms impatiently.

"He's…" He thought for a second, "Capable." Crow smiled at me, and I accepted this new fella right away. Another one to add to this strange family.

"Where is he, Crow?"

"He's tied up in a room I can't pay for and he's angry."

Crow Hoby

The town of Port

The edge of the world no longer

The only way I got Laz in a room was because, for most of our trip across town, he was chasing me. The man had become a nightmare. His mood would switch in a heartbeat, trying to kill me for my attempt at stealing his goat one minute, then an emotional outpouring the next because of his apparent lack of fatherly skills with his hundreds of children.

His usual confident and adept persona vanished, and it left behind a violent and confused old man who rarely knew where he was or what he was doing. I had to remind myself often of Laz's sincere face when he'd asked me to "take care" of him during his "foggy patches." I finally got him trapped in a room in an inn where he became subdued and blatantly scared. I waited with him in silence while he gathered the ends of his thoughts, wondering how long these periods would last and whether I could cope with them.

I had decided on a plan of action should things get out of hand again when Laz stood suddenly with anger wiped across his face. He came at me, so I reversed the shotgun on my belt and grabbed the barrel. In a flash, I'd hit him on the temple without too much force, and he flopped to the ground. I gently lowered him onto his bed and tied him with a rope I'd found on his person, amongst many, many other items that I could not fathom their use.

I'd told the landLord that my father was sleeping upstairs and that he would pay him when he woke up. The landLord did not look impressed; I looked down at my still bloodstained front with a nervous look on my face.

"He is a violent man." I said and looked at the thick shouldered man with all the pleading I could manage. The tactic just popped into my head. His expression instantly changed. His brow knotted, and he gestured me away and onto the street.

I felt confident. I had a sensation running through me that events were about to collide for the better and that I would be with Cal again soon. I set off to explore the town while Laz slept off his dark period and I felt an almost imperceptible pull down towards the seafront and the magnificent and enormous black shadow that sat beyond the walls and crackled with light and power.

The walls prevented me from getting to the station where the beast was waiting. Two very serious-looking guards eyed me sternly, and one hefted a strange club that buzzed with a life of its own and a thin, blue crackle of energy. Their uniforms were like nothing I'd seen before, mostly jet black with small and random patches of white with long white straps across their chests. Each wore a triangular hat and a long black leather-like skirt that covered the origin of the cable that connected to their sinister weapons. I would later discover that these were the infamous 'Mariahs', the hard line of the law that ruled across the sea.

It was a strange pounding rumble that stopped me from attempting conversation with the guards. The curiosity was about to burst out of me, but the sound and its origins distracted me. It seemed to echo all around and as I watched, people, mostly men, appeared from doorways and alleys and run as fast as they could back towards town, the wooden flooring bouncing as they went. With my curiosity diverted, I followed the commotion as more and more people joined the stampede into town like rats fleeing a flood. As I followed, One boy landed from a low rooftop beside me and jostled into my shoulder.

"Look alive!" he said over his shoulder, "Grimmer's blown 'is whistle, there's some beating goin' on." Then the hurried crowd swallowed him as they weaved through the wooden maze towards the source of action.

I continued to follow, and when I rounded one corner, the smell of blood stuck me. My stomach growled as I took in the sight before me. It was like a nest of snakes, all striking for the same two critters, only the critters were chopping the snakes down one after another. The woman was like a dancer with a sword; she moved so fast that the thugs couldn't land a blow; only sheer numbers were slowing her down. Splattered with blood, she growled like she was enjoying herself. I could barely see the other defender; the bodies were on top of him, punching and kicking down into the morass. A handful of the crowd held back, obviously unsure who was actually winning the fight. Though I had no place in this strange and violent clash, I felt rooted to the spot. My stomach groaned at me to feed as the blood flew freely around the street. I held off the urge and watched in awe as the man beneath the biggest cluster of bodies roared and flung the bodies from atop him. Like straw dolls they flew away from him and many then lay still, as the violence continued he grabbed a girl who had been pathetically swinging a wooden club into his side as he fought, he merely held her as he moved from victim to victim until he became visible through the thinning crowd.

Cal.

The joy I felt was a strange juxtaposition to the vile carnage that was unfolding before me. The bodies and the screams suddenly did not matter, only the seemingly slow motion vision of Cal as he tore through his enemies.

As I took a step towards him, a man to my left reached into his tunic and produced a long and jagged blade, intending to join the wilting efforts of his friends. With one quick motion, I levelled my shotgun at his face and took my eyes from Cal to lock with his. I heard his blade clatter onto the floor and we both glanced across to the fight. Only the strangely attired swordswoman, Cal, and one other man stood upright.

There was a weird and sudden stillness to the scene. As I watched, Cal took his eyes from his last foe standing and lifted the thrashing girl, bringing her neck towards his mouth. Something felt wrong, like it was important to wake from the dream I was in. My stomach yearned for me to grab the guy I was aiming at and feed. I could anticipate the feeling of the pulsing vitality running through me, but somehow I knew it was not the time to indulge myself, other things had to remain important, not just for me but for Cal and his redemption, I must hold back his inevitable fate.

"Cal!"

Chapter 26

Excerpt from "New Roots: The Viken's Descent."

They forced Matwan to work in the beast's belly. A darkness lit only by the blazing fires of its many engines. Driven to their knees, they fuelled and stoked till their fingers bled and their eyes wept. Their only salvation was the food they fed them to keep them strong enough to please their masters. The heat and isolation broke many of their minds. Matwan tried in vain to rally others to escape, but such was their fear they left him alone to plot his ascension from the metal cell to which he was confined.

Eventually, through pure and resolute determination, he escaped the confines of the lower levels of the ship to discover the Aileron Dwarf had left Port and there was nowhere for him to flee.

Callus
New friends reunited
I wouldn't trust me either

Crow had told me about the attack at Sanctuary and how this Laz fella'd saved him. I was honestly grateful and looking forward to meeting the man, but when we locked eyes, somethin' weird happened.

We'd walked back through town to our place to wash. We looked pretty bad. Nobody came anywhere near us all the way back. We hurried. Was only a matter of time before the law got wind of what we'd done.

Good as it was to see Crow he was harpin' on 'bout Laz and what he'd said and what he'd done and how he'd gone foggy, which I didn't really understand but Crow seemed to hold this fella pretty high up, so I went along.

The town was coming alive with bells and torches. They were lookin' for us. When we finally got to Crow's place, it seemed there was a posse waitin' to knock the door in and give Laz a beating. Just in time we showed up and Crow said that he'd brought us to make sure his pa got what he deserved. I wasn't sure what was going on, but Crow seemed to have it all stitched up and ready to go. He'd got real clever since I'd last seen him.

Not sure exactly what I was expecting, but it wasn't what I got. Trussed up good, Crow'd tied him to a chair, which he'd smashed the legs off. He was laying there on the floor, covered in bits of wood and straw from holes in the walls, his belongings scattered all over the place. He looked up as Crow arrived with the warmest of smiles, despite his ass bein' on the ground.

"Now there you are." He said with a big old grin. His hat had fallen during his escape attempt, and his head looked like a blind tribesman had scalped him. Big wisps left long dangled in front of his grinning face. Then he saw me.

We locked eyes for a long time, too long, but he lost me in them crazy eyes. I couldn't seem to look away 'till he'd let me. Can't say why, but after that he was one of us. He'd rescued Crow and wasn't about to let nothing bad happen to him whilst he was around. Me, on the other hand; there was somethin' he wasn't sure of 'bout me, could see it plain as day as he stared through me. Maybe he could see my past, dunno, but I let him have his doubts. Had a few myself.

"I aint complainin', but if I don't get free 'o' this chair soon, I'm goin' stink worse than a shit house in a sandstorm."

Anonymous Author
A glint in the haystack
The door to Crave's room opened slowly, and a flood of daylight arced across the simple furniture, sending a slight but visible breeze through the residual webbing that coated the place.

"You expectin' a letter, boss?" Broderick moved into the dark room, slowly but confidently. He brushed the seat of a wooden chair and sat as he tossed an unopened letter onto the table. Crave sat opposite, his hands on the same table, his legs widely placed and crouched, ready to pounce at any moment though he was currently still. Broderick knew he was awake. He'd heard his breath whistle quietly through his mustache, but his eyes remained closed as he replied without the slightest movement other than his dry lips.

"This better be good, Brod, I aint in a great mood."

"Jones brought it to me, said some guys from the ship came looking for you, don't feel right to me." He reached into his waistcoat pocket and brought out a smoke. Before he lit it, he lifted a boot and placed it on the table with an audible clink as his spur made contact.

"Read it." Was all Crave said; he remained deathly still, only his tongue flicked out to wet his lips. Broderick shook his head slightly as he reached over and opened the letter. He placed a second parchment to one side as he read the letter in silence while he smoked.

Broderick sat up, quickly dropping his boot from the table and straightening his back.

"Says it's from your brother."

Craves eyes flicked open.

Captain Lazarus Badstock

Now I don't consider myself a normal kinda guy, but this here group we got goin' was some kinda messed up snake pit and that's for sure. The woman, Silk, she didn't talk too much, just kept on scowlin' at me, but she felt alright, inside like. Somethin' was hungry inside her and she was hell bent on feedin' it. I knew, like I did sometimes, that she'd be rollin' a big old dice when the time was right.

Callus, or Cal as Crow called him, now he was one big stinkin' mystery, even to me. Crow loved that Tribesman all the way over the moon, but there was somethin' I couldn't shake, somethin' I couldn't decide yet. Ya see me and Crow was on this path, I could see it and I'd been try'na tell him 'bout it. This path was one big beast of a path and at the end we'd put the world right again, only problem was there was this big old fella blockin' the path, a real dark son of a bitch and he'd need to be taken care of. By taken care of, I mean he needed killin'. Now I ain't scared of killin' long as I know it's right. The problem was no matter how hard I thought 'bout things, how deep I got when I listened to the world, I couldn't tell if Callus was our brother or the son of a bitch we was meant to kill.

Now, I'm a polite kinda guy so I kept on smilin' and bein' all friendly like, seemed like a good guy so far as I could see, so I made friends 'til I got the message and then we'd have to see how things played out.

Crow had come back for me; I knew he had to at one point, but I never know what's gonna go down when I get foggy. Wakin' up tied to a chair, covered in my own piss, ain't the worst way I'd woken up, that's for sure. The boy seemed nervous at first, not sure if he'd had to knock me around, I can be a big old pain in the ass when I'm not myself but I don't remember a damn thing so it's all as easy to forgive as forget.

Apparently where we were stayin' there was a lynch party after my blood, so we had to get out of there real quick like, was probably my fault but I didn't think to ask at the time. Out on the street, I could hear all kinds of clatterin' and hollerin'. Torches were everywhere and I could hear militia boys knockin' doors in and shoutin' at folks. As we rushed through the dark town, Crow turned on me.

"What are you smiling at?" he said, his brow all crushed up and serious. I put my hand on his shoulder and laughed.

"Hell, boy. You can sure kick up a shit storm in a hurry! I've been told I'm a trouble causer more 'n once, but you is another level. Boy couldn't help himself; a big old grin came out of nowhere.

"Quiet!" Silk sure made every word out of her mouth count. She followed Callus when he took the lead, draggin' us from alley to alley. 'Ventually we all huddled in a big old shadow, could hear the sea crashin' against the walls all 'round us, we'd got ourselves stuck down near the seafront, I couldn't see how that'd help 'till Callus explained.

"Where do we go now?" Crow was soundin' nervous, but Callus put an arm 'round him and held him real close like he was his daddy. He pointed up into the darkness towards the seafront. I couldn't see shit with my old eyes.

"We gotta get inside." The tribesman said, still pointing at nothin', I peered into the dark just as a cloud moved off the moon and lit the massive beast just sat there in the water, bigger'n two houses and buzzin' with tiny blue lines, my mouth fell open, but no words came out.

Anonymous Author
Trepidation

Crave slammed his flat hand onto the table.

"Get Jones in here!" Accustomed to Crave's temper, Broderick didn't flinch, despite his boss's mandibles, as they seemed to reach for him with dilatory hunger. Broderick slowly stood with his palms up.

"I'm just sayin' it doesn't seem right, that's all." Crave shot him a menacing glance and stood.

"I'll go get him. We can check this out. You're right to get Jones." Broderick backed towards the door and spoke like he was calming an angry child.

"I just think it stinks a little, why would Sidian send us all round the country looking for this guy but before we actually get a hold of him, he just turns tail and says, 'Come on guys, just jump on the boat!' something's out of place, Crave, surely you can see that?" Crave sat heavily with a sigh, his mandibles drooped a little.

"I'm tired, Brod." His voice was a rusty whisper. "I can't travel like the rest of you; I want him so bad, want him to pay, but" His hairy hands gripped the sides of the table and it shook with his controlled anger.

"Sidian's got a place for us! The new world! Maybe we can come back when we've lived a little. I'm so damn sick of endless deserts and mocking horizons." Broderick, sensing the change in mood, slowly closed the door and returned to his seat.

"You deserve it. We all do! I just want to be sure, OK?" Crave nodded gravely. He knew his chief was right.

"Sidian is not a man to change his mind." Crave admitted, at this Broderick nodded slowly, understanding.

"And what was the condition? can you remember his exact words?" Broderick's question brought a wistful smile to Crave's face as he remembered.

"He looked me in the eye; he was as close as you are now. He said, *'Brother you will only be welcome in my new world when you bring me that bastard's head'* and that was the last I saw of him. That was a long, long time ago."

"Boss, boss!" Jake's booming footsteps accompanied his shouts as he took the steps two at a time. Crave seemed to snap out of his memory and gave his head a tiny shake. Broderick stood up again, ready to receive the scout. He gestured around his face with a finger and a nod at his boss. Crave pulled his filthy kerchief over his mandibles, and his expression became hard again.

Jake knocked loudly on the door, and Broderick swung it open. The outrider was out of breath, but clearly excited.

"I've found him!"

Broderick shared a look with Crave, and Jake continued.

"He's on the boat."

Chapter 27

Crow Hoby
Heading for a coffin
Then into the abyss

"Never underestimate the greed of a mortal man." Cal had said as he knocked on the door to the undertakers. On a typical night I'd worry about the noise, but all around us, other doors were being pounded on. Militia men shouted up to furious residents in candlelit windows.

When the disgruntled undertaker finally answered, he was brandishing a rifle of the like I'd never seen before. Its barrel was like a trumpet and he seemed barely able to lift the thing. As Cal had promised, the gold he had on his person was enough to buy our way past his crude defences and get us a coffin each to hide in for the rest of the night.

The coins Cal had produced seemed to have a mesmerising effect on the old man; this was not the first time I'd seen it and before we climbed into our hides, I questioned him.

"What are those coins you've got?" He took one out nonchalantly and tossed it to me. It just looked like common money to me.

"They're from the wars, when the good folk tried to wipe out the tribesmen. Worth a fortune now." Cal's eyes lost focus for a second as he obviously fended off a dark memory. Laz sighed loudly and interjected.

"Blood money always is, friend." He winked at me happily and pulled his coffin lid closed.

"Where did you get them from?" I asked as I climbed in my own coffin, stood at an angle that felt strange but not completely uncomfortable. Cal looked at his feet.

"I earned them." He said no more, then pulled his creaking lid shut.

The undertaker had been most accommodating once he'd seen Cal's gold, he'd promised us he could secure passage on the Aileron Dwarf, but we'd have to wait until morning, none of us liked the idea of sleeping in coffins except Cal as it was his preferred end to any night, and Laz who appeared to be enjoying the best day of his life.

Luckily the undertaker's place avoided search that night and, by the morning, we were all where we intended to be but with various degrees of ill humour. The plan was to leave our weapons with Cal, then wait for the returning undertaker who would guide our motley procession on to the gigantic death trap that would then set off across the sea. What could go wrong?

"Load me up." Said Cal with a smile. I could sense his good humour was annoying Silk as she stood with her hands on her hips. It was the first time I'd seen her Mother as she unfurled from Silk's waist and wrapped around her sword's hilt. She unsheathed the blade and held it out towards Silk's hand; Silk rolled her eyes and shook her head almost imperceptibly before she took the sword and placed it in Cal's coffin. Laz produced various gun parts and bladed items from his travel bags and stacked them at Cal's feet, and I threw in my shotgun and hatchet, feeling somewhat naked.

Remarkably, the undertaker was true to his word, mainly I suspect, because of the war coin he received on completion of each stage of the plan.

Before we knew it, we were walking in a sombre procession towards the gigantic ship with Cal's coffin riding in a miniature cart that me and Laz pushed along. We followed the undertaker's melancholy stroll. People were everywhere, marvelling at the Aileron Dwarf and all its deadly splendour. Even the crows seemed to enjoy our charade, as one by one, they alighted on the surrounding walls and armaments and watched intently for any slip ups. There was a slight hush as we trundled along the dock, and people showed their collective respect for our dead. It almost made me laugh out loud. Our 'dead' was the only one not having an unpleasant morning. The sun seemed to blaze down on us despite the cool temperature. I wanted to shield my eyes, but the coffin cart required both hands.

As we got close to the ship's doorway and away from the bulk of the crowd, I noticed a handful of disgruntled crows trying to settle on the massive ship's various overhangs, amongst the spikes, and barely contained lightning emissions. A gang of black-clad coffin lifters approached to relieve us of our coffin, and Silk spoke up under her breath.

"I feel like we're getting herded into a trap. I blame Cal." She hissed. Laz grinned at her and replied happily.

"There aint no doubt 'bout it, Missy. An expert hunter always knows when he's bein' hunted."

Once we were inside that ship, the world became a different place.

Chapter 28

The Pilgrimage

A desperate marsupial scream rang through the hollows as some hapless creature plummeted down to the depths to be smashed on the stone table. The sound was not uncommon. The table was not only a marker for how far the hollows reached into the earth, but also served as a primary source of food.

Magan shuddered and attempted to sit up. Rudely torn from his pollen addled machinations and weighted by the limbs of his two bedfellows, he growled out his frustration and flung an arm and leg over onto one of many woad-smattered furs.

"She comes." He grunted.

He quickly washed his body, wiping away the twins' woad as memories of the night's passions made him grin. Lela had been slow and delicious, every curve of her body fitting into the shape of his whilst Gudr had been forceful, his stone hands clamped onto Magan's with a troll's grip.

He lit a torch, and the flame growled as he passed through the hollows with purpose; the passing light showed glimpses of the myriad tunnels and alcoves that wormed deep into the earth and rock of the hollows. Occasionally, areas sealed off by the ever-shifting earth itself blocked his way. Dust and dirt flickered in the torchlight as it dripped from above.

"Wake!" he shouted into the rough-hewn chamber where the elders slept, and before they could arise, the cavern was brimming with fur-wearing torch bearers who held sharp stakes and murderous glares. They did not attack or even touch him, but such was their body language that all knew that they would if told to do so.

"She comes." He said again as the elders moved through the crowded guards surrounding him, occasionally and gently lowering a thrall's weapon.

"My vision, it is time." Each of the five elders clearly understood his meaning as they stopped their advance as one, but did not speak a word. The druids were a very expressive people and communicated with few words, favouring gestures and facial subtleties over constant noise. Eventually, the elders displaced the belligerent guards surrounding Magan. Liriss, the youngest of the elders, reached out a patronising hand to place it on Magan's, but he snatched it away and grunted. Liriss jumped slightly and showed confusion.

"It is time!" he insisted. He glanced around the chamber and raised his hands to question who would join him.

After some time, filled with grunting and indecisive gestures, Magan finally gathered a sizeable group of followers before readdressing the elders, who had by now covered their nakedness with furs and adornments. The communication continued towards dawn with occasional, almost violent outbursts as Magan wrestled to gain influence or looked to his followers for support. There were obvious objections coming from most elders and their advisers, but eventually Magan's influence caused a rift within the druids. One faction would stay in the hollows and reap the lifestyle they had strived to create and the other would follow Magan as he began his odyssey to find a woman of two souls who would right the world and lead the druids to their rightful place by her side.

Soon they emerged into a pale dawn and made their way through the dew-soaked foliage, away from the Hollows. They had little time to prepare, but each of them wore all the furs they could gather in the time Magan had permitted.

Above ground, the air was cool and damp, rivulets of melted frost wound their way through the vegetation as they ascended the hills. The towering, skyward horizon was a foreboding sight, especially as it was their destination; the climb was no small feat.

The pilgrimage walked without communication for the first few hours, thoughts of the lives they'd left behind commandeering their minds away from the journey ahead. Each of them had chosen, and they were steadfast in their approach towards their vows; Magan knew he would not need to waste his time convincing them to aid in the prophecy's fulfilment. They had followed him, and so they would continue to. Some of the older druids had been alive when the people had originally settled in the hollows, and now they were facing this hardship to continue the tribe's growth in the only way they knew how.

The climb from the hollows itself had been fraught; They had given two lives to the table during the ascent of the deep crevasse. The remaining druids would consume their flesh in return for their good will and their acceptance of Magan's calling. The exodus had significantly thinned the druid's population, but all knew that it was nature's way to decimate before life could once again flourish.

A further four lives were lost to the cold as they traversed the mountainous ridge that bordered the woodland, these brothers and sisters would not go to the table and Magan felt sorrow at this, death should always feed life and so the druids dragged their fallen with them as they descended beyond the mountains. When the land turned from white to green, they left the bodies to feed the life of the new and alien forest. Magan felt certain that this offering would bode well as they entered the unfamiliar territory.

The air became warmer, and many removed furs to stow them as they walked. Eventually, as the forest thinned, flatter lands arrived on the distant horizon and a warmth of spirit spread throughout the procession. As one, the druids stood to rest and point out their destination and the distance they had come. The woodland they were in felt very different to their own lands. The colours and shapes were strange and Magan insisted they only eat meat until they could understand the vegetation. There were no objections.

It was the hunting party ahead that first encountered familiar fauna. The troll had signalled its annoyance at their arrival by crushing three of them with its massive arm. Its roar echoed through the trees, back to Magan and the rest of the druids, who quickly advanced to learn the fate of the hunters. Many of them reached for their stakes with aggressive instinct, but Magan raised his arms.

"Whooooah." He called out to his people loudly but softly. His kin looked to him but showed conflict at first. Then a crunching of tree trunks warned them of the approaching troll, and suddenly all the druids turned to Magan with stricken faces.

"His land." He said, receiving a few hesitant nods. "We wait." He touched his hands briefly to the front of his head and then slowly crossed his legs and sat as the devastating sounds grew louder. The troll, an animate, huge and angry rock formation charged towards them. The rest of the druids followed their leader and sat as the monster emerged and stopped. His massive hands made fists onto the ground as he surveyed the scattered druids. He moved around them slowly as he growled out his claim to the area. His shorter, but no less powerful, legs following where he planted his fists, his head nodding upwards at each druid as he approached, as if he challenged them to stand. The troll was around twice the height of the tallest of the druids and made of stone. There was no temptation to take up the challenge, but the urge to flee warred inside all of them.

Magan knew he could easily lose everyone to the troll, but most of them had encountered their kind before and understood that to defer to the beast's authority and claim to his territory would be the correct way to show respect until it left them alone. His concern was, how long would that take? They'd all heard tales back at the hollows of hunters sitting out a troll's rage. By the time they had earned the right to stand and leave, many had near starved or insects who also claimed the land had ravaged their bodies.

Day turned to night and then day again as the druids sat in their meditative states, many of them shivered uncontrollably but the conflict was not about stillness, more a battle for dominance and whilst the druids remained submissive the troll would find satisfaction and eventually leave or sleep. The monster continued its patrol, and with each planting of his fists, a shudder rumbled through the ground. The vibration was almost imperceptible, but never the less, made it challenging for the druids to lose themselves in their trances.

After a further few hours, there was a sudden and loud crack as the troll stuck his own chest with its mighty fist. Tiny chips of stone shrapnel flew into the air. The beast then grunted in satisfaction and finally, after almost two full days, it settled down amongst the druids and relaxed, the rocks of its limbs clacking together as it piled itself on the gentle hillside and slept in complete silence and utter stillness.

Daroch, friend and brother, placed his hand on Magan's shoulder to rouse him from his dreams and offered a hand. With his aid, Magan stood and nodded his thanks. Daroch gestured with his arm across the sky, and Magan understood his worries regarding the time they had lost. The prophecy which Magan followed was not specific, yet he feared the druid's path would not cross with that of the woman with two souls if they did not hasten towards the conjunction.

Hungry but triumphant, the druids continued their journey into the new world.

Chapter 29

Excerpt from "New Roots: The Viken's Descent."

Matwan's resolve had broken. He made a desperate break from his back-breaking chores in the steaming hot chamber and fled his captors to climb above deck. Sadly, the notion of escape died as he emerged, and the salted winds battered his face and beckoned tears to his scorched cheeks. Though the Mariah gave loud pursuit with their crackling and unnatural weapons, he stopped and took in the sight of the dark sea that surrounded him. To the horizon in all directions, he gazed, his mind unable to understand the expanse of lurching water all around him. In the back of his mind, despite his dark reverie, he heard the metallic, pounding boots of the Mariah as they suddenly retreated. He grabbed the metal rail to steady himself as a feeling of utter doom, greater even than the feelings he had harboured during his time below decks, overcame him.

"Spiger!"

The call repeated around him as the strange word rang from the alien tubes that entangled the entire ship, both inside and out. Matwan's body froze as a gigantic shadow swept across him before wrapping him in an iron grip and tearing him from the gantry. The enormous tentacle released him to fall to a small, wet platform far below. Utterly maddened, Matwan stood, unable to comprehend his predicament as an enormous eye slowly rose from beneath the surface of the roiling water. He held out a shaking hand as if to ward against this evil when suddenly the soft island beneath his feet plummeted down into the dark doom, sucking him with it into the crushing depths of the sea.

Callus

Awake from death

To find a new level of hell

When Crow lifted the lid from my coffin, his damn face was smiling like a kid with a new toy.

"We're at sea!" I almost filled my damn britches.

The floor moved just like on a riverboat, but not so bad; it was the idea that made me prickly, couldn't help it, no solid land. I shuddered and climbed out into our room. There was a crackling yellow light up on the low ceiling. It flashed each time Silk paced past it.

"He's trouble." She said as a greeting. I could see her Mother scurrying about under her armour, just as tense as Silk was.

"Who's trouble?" I asked as I stretched. It'd been good to be in a coffin, always was, but the feeling of being on water just didn't sit right.

"Laz, he's out there chatting with everyone, I don't like it." Crow sat down and started writing in his journal. That gave me a smile. I closed the coffin lid, leaving our stash of weapons in the dark.

"Let's go get him." I sighed, and she grabbed the door to heave it open. Crow looked up.

"I'll catch up. See you in the bar."

It was like no bar I'd seen before. Everything was shiny black with yellow, buzzing lights everywhere. The ceiling was low, just like in our room, but the floor was lower in places with ramps to get down there to sit at the tables. People chatted all around, sat at the bar, stood 'round metal pillars and around what looked like gamblin' tables. Silk stomped past me and down a ramp to one o' the tables. I followed and saw Laz surrounded by people. He was swingin' his arms up and 'round chatting up everyone. They were laughin' and jokin' like they'd known him a lifetime. It was a gambling table, but everyone was more interested in Laz's tales, so the chips and cards were just sat there gatherin' dust.

"Howdy partners!" he seemed louder than usual. "Come sit down with us, less you wanna go grab me a drink 'fore you get all cosy like?" I sat down. Silk just stood with her eyes bearing down on the old man. I tried to think if I'd ever seen her relax.

"I'm just tellin' some o' my old stories." He picked a drink; he obviously had a few waiting in front of him.

"Meet this fine fella." He put his arm round a man's shoulders. He looked like a fat rancher but was head to toe in white; he took the cigar out of his mouth with one hand, tipped back his wide-brimmed hat, and reached for my hand with the other.

"Dolomon." He spoke strangely, but his smile seemed real. I shook his hand. He pushed over a drink and nodded. I eyed the rest of the folk 'round the table and a few vanished, don't think I had the same charm as Laz. Silk finally sat down. No sign of her Mother.

"Don't let me stop you." I said as I threw back the drink; Dolomon put up his hands.

"I can barely take any more, friend, give someone else a chance, yes?" he winked at me and I couldn't help liking the man. He leaned over and whispered.

"So, what brings you to our new world, friend?"

"Looking for a man." He smiled and slammed his hand down on the table; I saw a quick flash of Silk's Mother disappearing like a rat into a hay bail.

"Ha ha! I like your honesty, friend. Looking for something we all are, eh?"

Crow Hoby
Inside a metal serpent
Crossing the sea!

Inside, the ship was like another fascinating world. Everywhere were dark corridors of a black metal which twisted and shaped around the structural innards of the boat itself. The surfaces were rarely completely flat, which gave a strangely organic and withered feel to the walls and floors despite the iron like solidity and the cold, hard feel of its many panels. Glass spheres, set into the walls every few feet along any walking space and, as far as I could see, within each room. The yellow light they gave out flickered and swelled in an incomprehensible rhythm and seemed to buzz angrily at each passing.

The communal areas were alive with conversation and a collective excitement. This new world dressed its people in black or pure white and nothing in between. This made it obvious who had boarded in Port and those who were native to the new land that we were heading to. Those in white had a lofty air about them, like the ladies and gentlemen I'd always imagined were aplenty in our bigger cities and towns full of industry and business.

On every corner, and often moving through the ship, were the guards I'd first seen at the dock when I'd set eyes on the Aileron Dwarf. These also were in black, but many sported white, mis-shaped patches on their uniforms. Their entire outfit, from the tricorn hats to the high boots they wore, appeared to be made from an unusually marked leather which comprised tightly woven strands rather than stitched panels that were common back home. The guards, or 'Mariahs,' were a stern breed and barely said a word. They watched and judged in twos, occasionally hefting their batons, which were connected to their belts beneath a black skirt.

On that first day, I'd just watched in awe, exploring everywhere that I was able and soaking in the unusual and alien décor and people. Prohibited from many of the areas, I presumed these parts were the inner workings of the ship; I asked a Mariah but a surly snarl was his only answer.

In some corridors, I noticed wide tubes that ran along the ceilings. These tubes, made of the same metal as the walls, were thinner and some sections had a series of holes. At one point, I saw a small, black-clad figure squeezing through with practiced movements. I imagined soot covered engineers moving about unseen as they fed the massive engine that powered the ship like a gigantic train.

As night fell, or at least it seemed to fall; there was no natural light for reference. I woke Cal and felt a weight return to my shoulders. A responsibility I'd not felt whilst exploring the ship on that first day, returned; It was time to continue our mission in an entirely new world, a world full of threat and alien technology where danger could lurk at every corner.

I joined Cal, Silk and Laz at their table, Dolomon, who I'd met earlier was leaning over his ample belly, talking in serious tones to Cal. Laz was looking worse for wear, several empty glasses sat before him and Silk shook her head and rolled her eyes at me as I noticed them.

"It's not just the twitchers that you have to watch, no no, they're the easy ones," Dolomon's eyes included me as I sat down.

"What's a twitcher?" I asked. I found his accent compelling; his conversation seemed like an easy way of gathering information about the people who would soon surround us.

"You see their beady eyes, yes? It is a drug. They use too much, their eyes cannot move." He lifted his beefy hands incredulously, as if to say 'why?'. He leaned back in his chair, then quickly moved forward again, clearly a little agitated.

"Believe me, I have enough money, but I also have the brains." He tapped his temple with two thick fingers.

"Twitchers, pshht!" he threw up his hands again. "I'm sorry, friends, this Black gets me angry, is what we call the drug, yes?" he stood from the table, for the first time in a good while, I guessed. He centred himself and then leaned in to speak to the four of us earnestly in a hushed voice.

"You watch the twitchers; they will do anything for black." He paused, lending drama to his warning, and continued. "But you watch the rest too, yes? They are not so easy to read, my friends!" he tapped the table twice and left towards another table, one with gambling in full swing.

"Do you trust him?" Silk spoke up.

"What's to trust?" said Cal in response, "he's just warnin' us, we aint getting in bed just yet."

Laz finished his last drink in a quick jerk and opened his eyes wide, as if to help him stay awake.

"I aint on top form right now, but there's always been two things I could do better'n anyone." He held up a wavering, solitary finger. "Killin' at range." He dropped his finger, "and figurin' a liar. Now that there fella in white, he aint no liar; sure as I aint no priest."

We sat in silence for a while, and I watched Dolomon with casual interest as he joined another table. Cal finished his drink and looked towards the bar, obviously considering buying a replacement. To my surprise, it was Silk who broke the silence.

"What are you drinking?" she asked Cal with a touch of disdain.

"Damned if I know." He lifted his glass and gave it a sniff. "Some kind 'o liquor; I aint too fussy if it takes the edge off. Do we know how long this ride takes?" He looked at me with the slightest hint of fear in his eyes.

"I think we're going to be here a while, I'm afraid" I sympathised, but still found it strange to see him so disturbed by the water. The man was fearless otherwise. He put down his empty glass and stood.

"You in?" he looked at me and Silk. Laz was in a daze, mumbling to himself happily. We both nodded enthusiastically.

Before he approached the bar, he leaned in, his deep voice only just cut through as he whispered.

"Watch the big tribesman. Somethin' aint right." His head motioned slightly across the busy room. Then he left us for the bar.

I don't know how I'd not seen him before; the man was massive, and sitting alone holding his drink. His skin was slightly darker than Cal's, but his hair and features undoubtedly marked him from the tribes. I casually observed him as his gaze followed Cal to the bar, then returned to his drink. Silk's hand went to her side, but she remembered she'd stashed her sword in Cal's coffin; she put her elbows on the table and I saw her Mother coil slowly around her left wrist.

Cal returned with three drinks and pushed them over.

"Relax." He said, a little forcefully. I realised we sat rigidly and forced a slump. As I reached for my drink, a commotion snagged my attention towards the table that Dolomon had joined. Raised voices caused two gamers to throw in their tokens and stalk away angrily; I was suddenly feeling full of energy and not entirely comfortable about it. I threw back my drink and liquid fire engulfed the inside of my skull. Coughing desperately, I tried to suck in air to cool my throat. Cal and Silk were smiling at me whilst I clamped my hand to my neck and coughed the last few flames from my gullet.

"Slow down, aint no rush!" Cal's good humour was obvious as he looked from me to Silk, who also smiled. This was a rare sight; had I not been so stricken; I would have appreciated the moment of bonding at my expense. She reached over and touched my shoulder with surprising tenderness.

"First time?" I nodded as I coughed a couple more times and couldn't help but join them in their mirth.

For a moment genuine warmth passed between us, and despite my scorched throat, it felt good. Then, as if he'd woken from the dead, Laz lifted his head; his face was lucid and deadly serious.

"Stay calm now."

He said, and I looked at Cal, whose brow knotted suddenly in confusion. To our right, amongst several other patrons, Dolomon roared in frustration and stood up abruptly, lifting the edge of his table with him. Drinks and betting chips flew across the room, and pandemonium ensued.

Callus
In a box in the sea
Actin' natural

Now I'd seen gamblers lose their cool before, but Dolomon turned himself into an animal. Couple 'o the other fellas were reachin' for blades and hollerin' at him but he just reached down and pulled two 'o the most polished, shinin' six guns I'd ever seen and levelled 'em across the wreckage 'o that table.

I reached for my hatchet 'fore I realised where it was, and then I clocked Laz. His eyes were burnin' into me like he was sayin' 'do not move!' The action behind him was only getting' wilder as we sat, not movin'. Dolomon was threatenin' to put a hole in the other fella's head through his gritted teeth when the Mariahs showed up. I glanced over at our tribesmen friend an' he was just starin' straight at me, not even flinchin' at all the commotion. Every pound of me wanted to get up and start swingin'. My blood was up an' ready to go, but Laz kept on clockin' me with them mad eyes. I felt trapped between the two of 'em. I looked up as the Mariahs got to Dolomon, who was still growlin' at the fella across. 'took me by surprise when one of them

150

black jacks suddenly started buzzin' with blue light, like lightening sparkin' out of the thing, the Mariah swung it at Dolomon from behind and the big white fella dropped like a hog, his six guns hit the floor just after he did. That took the tribesman's eyes off me, just for a second 'fore he was starin' again.

That crazy bar was silent as the Mariah's dragged poor old Dolomon out 'o the place; wasn't sure if he was dead or alive. We all just stared while the room got put back together by bar keeps. I almost jumped when one arrived at our table. She seemed real nervous, like a damn bird, her head jumpin' about as she grabbed our empties.

"Sorry for the commotion, travellers. Is all OK, yes?" She spoke like Dolomon but couldn't keep her damn head still; she filled her tray and left us. Laz closed his eyes and started chucklin' to himself again. Silk was watchin' the woman. Then she looked at me like I should know something. She nodded as the woman retreated. Silk and Crow both spoke at the same time.

"Twitcher."

Chapter 30

Anonymous Author

Spitting distance

"Speak, Bean! I know it aint your strongest talent but tell me, what does he look like? Who is he with? Damn it, we've waited too long for you to clam up now!" Crave was pacing the small room and squeezing his hands into fists; Broderick and Jake were both straddling chairs with equal enthusiasm.

"He looks like... a tribesman." Bean's head dropped slightly, a sign of the shame he felt occasionally since leaving his tribe to pursue more individual gains. Crave smacked a gloved hand to his own forehead in exasperation.

"Speak to him, Brod! Jake, with me!" Crave stormed from the room and hammered on the solid metal door across the dim hallway. Philips answered and recognised that Crave was in no mood for his charm.

"What do you need, boss?"

"With me." The three of them marched off down the black and twisting corridor towards the bar, Jake and Philips exchanging looks of excitement as they followed.

Broderick placed his chair closer to Bean and lit a cigar.

"You know how he gets, Bean. What's wrong with you? Last thing we need is one of his moods on this damn journey to hell." Bean looked up with a genuine apology written on his face.

"Don't know what else to say. They had a couple of drinks and then left." Bean had not been himself since they'd boarded the ship. He'd insisted that people should not be in or even on the sea. It was not their place, yet here they were. Miles from the coast, in a metal box floating amongst a myriad of unknown horrors.

"It's them Mariahs we need to worry about." The huge tribesman's shoulders lifted and Broderick saw a flash of excitement in his usually solemn eyes. "That fella went down fast, Brod. One hit and he was out. We got to watch them, Mariahs."

"OK, I get that Bean, and we will, but tell me about Callus. Hell, we've been hunting the man for months! What do we need to know?"

There was no sign of Callus in the bar, at least not from the meagre description Bean had given them. They sat down at one of a few remaining free tables, and Crave sent Jake to fetch drinks. The leader was a fearsome character but had never been comfortable amongst crowds. His hands were continually adjusting his kerchief around the bottom half of his face and the horrific mutation that it concealed. He took in the surrounding scene. Gaming tables and sunken booths were everywhere, with people hurrying around, spilling drinks and shouting to be heard. The crew that ran the bar were, to a man, dressed in black, fitted uniforms with the occasional overseer in stark white. The patrons were a mix of new worlders, who were also in white or black but with less formal clothing and the mismatched travellers from back home in mis-matched riding gear and merchant attire.

Crave continued to squeeze his fists, and beneath his kerchief, his mandibles moved in small anxious circles. When Jake returned with drinks, Crave looked at Philips almost pleadingly.

"Find out where he is." Philips practically jumped out of his seat.

"Got it, boss." He tipped his bowler hat and disappeared into the crowd to blend in and ask questions.

"Relax, boss, it's getting late. He'll turn up in the morning." Trying to inspire confidence, Jake pushed over a drink to Crave and rested his boot on Philip's vacant chair. Crave grimaced and held a breath while his hairy fists clenched, a knuckle popped, and he looked Jake in the eye.

"He won't be out in the morning, he'll be sleeping all day, have you forgot who we're hunting, you fool?" through gritted teeth and his filthy kerchief Jake only just made out his boss's words, he put his foot back down on the floor and threw back his drink.

"What do you want me to do? I'm all yours, boss, but he aint here!"

"Watch your tone, Jake! I'm in no mood for it." Crave threw back his own drink and added, "and I'm hungry."

Philips soon got word of a man calling himself 'Captain Lazarus' who'd associated with a tall, half-blood Tribesman, a youngster and a woman. Philips grinned, more through satisfaction that he'd bested Bean than a job well done. He'd been able to find out the direction they'd headed in, but wandered a series of twisting corridors that all looked identical. Against his better judgment, he decided to report back to Crave, but as he approached another identical nexus, he noticed a small face observing him through a mesh-like slot in the pipework against the ceiling.

"Hello." He said as he approached to stand directly beneath the face. An obviously female child's voice answered him.

"Hello." Philips could see her shift uncomfortably. What little he could see of her face smeared in black soot.

"What 'you doing up there?" Philips moved slightly closer. An idea was brewing. This little girl had probably observed a lot from her little hide hole.

"We're not allowed to speak with travellers." Her head twitched from left to right, looking up and down her pipework for her superiors. Philips noticed her eyes didn't move, only her entire head, like a little bird poking its head out of its nest.

"It's OK to talk to me, especially if you like presents." The Outlaw's voice was gradually softening, his usually sinister grin merging into a cheerful face that anyone would trust. The girl looked confused at the word 'presents.'

"Is there anything you'd like me to get for you? Then maybe you could help me?" The girl's face split into a hungry grin of her own, her eyes wide.

"Erf!"

Crow Hoby
Finding my sea legs
Approaching the new world

Cal was pale and very agitated. We'd spent a couple of nights, mostly in our room but occasionally in the bar, chatting to fellow travellers and citizens of Cthonica, the city we were heading towards. Strangely, I was enjoying the lack of natural light and somehow felt at ease knowing that we'd escaped the blazing sun of our homeland, and with little else to do but remain cautious it was easy to forget the pressure of any predestined fortune that may await us. Though I'd gradually woken later each day, I'd spend my time continuing my exploration of the ship in solitude. Silk had made several comments about watching my back since we'd seen the mysterious tribesman watching us. I'd later seen him around the ship, sometimes with others, but I'd stayed out of sight. As everyone on board seemed to be armed, we'd taken to wearing our weapons and had, so far, not aroused any unwanted suspicions.

"I hate to say it, but I need to feed." Cal's sudden announcement stopped all movement in the room; the idea made my stomach rumble despite the ample meal I'd eaten about an hour before. Silk looked up sharply but said nothing. Laz scratched at his beard and mused.

"There aint no critters 'round here to be keeping that thirst 'o yours in check." Laz somehow had a way of knowing things he shouldn't know. I repeatedly felt that there may actually be some truth to what he'd told me about his calling. Silk stood from her bed and started pacing once again. Then she turned to Cal when an idea struck.

"There's got to be some live animals on board for them to cook. Would that keep you going until we get off the boat?" Cal seemed interested, if a little ashamed. He thought for a moment. Laz squinted his rheumy eyes as if concentrating, then sighed.

"Black is comin' y'all, season's changin'." As was often the case, Laz's interjection went ignored.

"Worth a try." Cal pulled open the door and turned back to us. "You best stay here an' I'll see what I can find."

155

Suddenly, two enormous hands appeared from behind Cal and an immense man in worn travel clothes pulled him violently through the door. I saw a gun appear, levelled at Cal. Without thinking, I leapt forward to find the first person I could with my hatchet held high.

Anonymous Author

Premature instigation

Philips pulled his hand away as she snatched the Erf eagerly and disappeared into the pipework.

"Thank you, my little spy." He called after her, but she had instantly scuttled away to enjoy the fruits of her labour. It had taken no time at all to discover a source of the drug they all seemed to use. They sold black at the bar in tiny black lumps and after some research, it became apparent that 'Erf' was Black in its most primitive form. Throughout the ship, he saw passengers chewing on the stuff in apparent delight.

Satisfied with the information, Philips turned back to Bean and Jones and pointed with both hands back up the corridor and back to their room.

"Let's see now!" Jones' massive frame blocked the corridor. His face was a picture of mischief. "We've been hunting this guy forever; let's just go look." Philips was shaking his head, but it was obvious he was in favour of the reckless idea. It was too tempting after all this time on the road, all this time building to the moment they caught him. Bean just shrugged. He would join them, whatever they decided. It was difficult to get a reaction out of him at the best of times.

"OK, but keep your mouth shut and do exactly what I say." Philips put his hand on his holstered six gun and moved up the corridor, the other two followed, trying their best to keep quiet despite the rattling of boots and the jingling of bullets.

"This is it." Jones whispered almost as loud as he usually spoke, and Philips shook his head with his finger to his mouth. Jones put his hand on the solid door wistfully. There was nothing to see, just another huge, solid door along a hall of other doors, but the excitement was palpable; Jones could not stop switching from one foot to the other. Bean looked unimpressed; he even tied his knife back in its scabbard. They stood there for a few moments in silence and Philips realised nothing was going to happen; he holstered his gun and pointed with his thumb back down towards the bar. Just as Jones's face fell with disappointment, there was a loud thump from the door, and slowly it glided open.

Bean stepped back out of sight, Philips pulled his gun and Jones just stood there, vacantly. The door opened, spilling a little more stuttering light onto the corridor, and a deep, rasping voice said,

"You best stay here an' I'll see what I can find."

On hearing Callus's voice, Jones relinquished all control of his senses. He stepped into the doorway, partly shadowed by the door itself but directly in sight of the occupiers. Their prey stood there with his back to them; it had to be him; he had hair like Bean, the long straight mark of the tribesmen but for one dull white stripe.

Philips was incredulous as Jones suddenly reached around Cal and heaved him out of the room and amongst them.

Callus
The trap finally closed
And I wasn't ready

Bein' honest, it was quite the thrill bein' pulled out 'o' that room. 'Round normal people, I've always got the drop, but that big guy had me by surprise.

Soon as I got my feet down, I twisted in his arms. He was strong, but not enough. That sudden attack and my hunger weren't any good for that fella. I went straight for his throat and clamped my arms 'round his body. It shocked him when I bit him, hardly tried to stop me, then he went down and I clung on, feeding like a damn rat.

By the time I climbed off him, Crow was pinning the other fella down, his

157

gun had scattered, sliding through the blood that came off a big old hatchet chop in the side of his head; the fella was still strugglin' like a wild cat though. Silk was in the corridor too, pointing her sword at the tribesman we'd seen watchin' us a couple of days back. He was still, no hands, no weapons, just lookin' at us, like he was expecting a beatin'.

Was one 'o' them times when the world stays still, just for a moment, then all hell breaks loose.

Seemed like a hundred Mariahs came thundering down the corridor, some from in front, some from behind. I turned to face the closest as everything lit up blue and I guessed they powered up their black jacks. I tensed up my guts and knew I'd be able to take the blue lightning if one got through to me; I dodged the first swing and turned to avoid another.

My entire body went harder than a damn rock, every damn muscle wanted to pop, and everything went black.

Chapter 31

Dearest brother, Crave,

As you have inevitably realised, word has reached us of your incompetence, despite being across the sea and many, many leagues from your embarrassment.

Aligning with the wisdom of ages and the old mantra, "if you want something doing, do it yourself." We have planned to put a stop to this potential breach in our rise to power. Sadly for you, one of us has failed in the essential task of conveying the importance of stopping this wretched man from arriving in our new world.

As a result, this has forced us to ensure that neither of you arrive in Cthonica. It may come as a surprise to hear, but Cthonica is not the mecca that you have been expecting. This city is a jewel left in the grave of another world. Its power grows every day and ascends us towards the sky with every glorious discovery. It is not a place for the remnants of your old world. There is nothing for you here, brother, and sadly, your time has passed.

Sidian

Grand Maal of the Reach

Cthonica

Anonymous Author

Ripples of betrayal

Crave reread the crumpled letter in his hand for the third time. Jake and Broderick had both read and given it back to Crave, who'd screwed it up and hurled it away both times. The stark room they'd been thrown into was more like a chamber of the weird metal that comprised the entire ship. Completely free of any furniture or decoration, the floor curved slightly, which even made sitting down uncomfortable.

Crave had a right to be in a sombre mood. Even before the letter arrived in their cell, their capture had incensed him. Shortly after Bean, Philips and Jones were due back, Mariahs had invaded their rooms. Crave had fired a couple of shots into the throng, but they'd quickly rendered them all unconscious with their Bolt Rods.

They'd no contact for hours before they threw the letter through a small hatch on one wall, the letter that had caused Crave such inner pain from the almighty betrayal he'd endured.

They sat in silence while he seethed and digested the words before him. They'd hunted their prey for almost a year, never getting close, or if they ever did, he was long gone by their arrival. Every lead was a gamble and their winnings had been meagre. Suddenly, the reason for their tenacity snatched away, their purpose entirely obsolete. He still hated Callus, but currently, Sidian was his favoured target for his hate. Craves mind could barely take the hurt, his own brother! His memories flittered around his past, picking up pieces of conversation and scenario and violently hurling them against the details of Sidian's deception and treachery.

Hours later, though it still surrounded them, the air of misery was clearing. The three of them had eventually talked through the situation. Though Crave had always kept his plans close to his chest, they all knew that Sidian was Craves brother who'd left to, apparently, secure them a place in a new world, a place of riches and power. Their one condition was that they had to kill Callus before Sidian permitted them to follow him.

Sidian had sent previous letters to random towns across the land, letters full of encouraging words and promises of a new life when their quest was complete. Within these letters, he'd seemed humble and eagerly awaited his closest brother. He talked of the new city and how they would all find glory when they finally arrived.

CHAPTER 31

Callus

Yet another cell

Got to be doin' something wrong

It was one strange, dreamy sleep.

As I was so unaccustomed to dreams, it had me hooked all the way, convinced I was back in the tribe with her for real.

"What has he done to you?" her voice was like cool water on burning lips. I stumbled into her tent, shakin' all over and hungry, hungrier than I'd ever been.

"I don't even know! They had me bound for days, some kind of rite." I lay down, and she wrapped her arms 'round me. I could feel her worry through her skin, and something else, something pulsing that I craved.

"What happens now? Are we banished?" she was the daughter of Cazique. She knew it would only be me he would banish. I knew she would come with me if I asked, but what would she have to leave behind?

We talked into the night and entwined our bodies, our lovemaking was intense and ended with teary eyes. The hunger I had only got stronger each time her skin came close to mine, but somehow, I kept my new thirst at bay as I knew this could be our last night together.

Eventually, the shouts outside her tent announced that my presence had been discovered.

"Cal!" Crow's concern woke me from my memories, but her face still lingered in my mind.

"My first damn dream in years and…" I'd completely forgotten where I was and what had happened. I opened my eyes to find we were all in a cell and my head hurt. Silk was pacing. There was no surprise there. The rest slumped around, lookin' like they'd been awake for days. Strangely, the fella, Dolomon, was with us. He seemed comfortable, like this wasn't his first time in a cell. Laz did not seem his usual grinning self. He was anxiously searching through his bags, counting his belongings. Crow was just relieved I was awake; he sat next to me, idly tapping on the floor.

"Guess we're in trouble."

"Guess so." My voice needed to wake up, too. I stood up and joined Silk

161

as she walked, tried to get my head back together.

"Is OK, friends, relax!" Dolomon also stood up; I noticed he still had his guns on his belt. "They will let us out soon. Is too much trouble to keep us down here forever, yes?" it was Silk who replied, to everyone's surprise.

"You speak like you've been down here before?"

"Yes, each trip I end up here, I cannot help myself!" he laughed and seemed to put everyone at ease a little. The fella certainly had charm. Even Silk had a smile and sat herself down before Laz's panicked voice interrupted.

"Y'all listen up good, you need to be payin' me attention, not sittin' round gigglin' like it's tea party time, y'understand?" he was getting frantic as he started stuffin' his things back in his pockets with a wild look in his eyes.

"OK, I need anything you got, anything that don't work no more, y'understand?" we looked at each other, all confused."

"God damn it! We're heading down, deep down into the water, and I can't help you fools unless you dig deep!" For the first time, I looked at the stuff he was countin' through on the floor. Empty bullet shells, bits of metal and stone, seemed like junk, but I'd not seen him this serious before. I checked my pockets, if only to put his mind at rest.

Crow Hoby
The walls closing in
Less likely to reach the far coast

Laz grabbed me by the shoulders and shook. His eyes were pleading behind a pair of goggles with one lens missing. Part of me wondered if he was falling into one of his 'fogs.'

"It's like the bucket, ya get me? Just like me! I need the things aint got no use no more!" I recalled our conversation back on our journey before we'd all met up. He'd spoken about his calling and how he'd got a new job to do once he'd filled his 'bucket.' I looked at a pile of things he had gathered on the floor and realised what he was after. I nodded and went through my pockets.

"OK, he needs anything that has no use anymore." I said to the room, everyone started panicking apart from Dolomon, Laz's hysteria was spreading and unnerving everyone.

Eventually, we'd all submitted a couple of random items to Laz, and he seemed satisfied as he stuffed them into his pockets, counting and muttering to himself as he did so. Cal and Silk seemed completely befuddled by the idea but went along with it anyway. Just as Laz's mood seemed to change, and a smile appeared on his face, Dolomon approached and handed him a single bullet casing, and Laz's eyes lit up.

"Yes, this is good, just look at it!" he showed the casing to everyone and finally seemed happy with his haul. We exchanged confused looks and sat back down to await our fate just as the door to our cell squealed and slid open.

The Mariahs marched us out of our cell in near silence, the only sound, the crackle of their Bolt Rods and our footfalls as we made our way towards the back of the ship. It seemed like the corridors were getting narrower the further back we got. Even the ceiling closed in. It may have been my imagination, but I couldn't help the feeling that the floor was less stable, like the entire corridor was floating on the sea's surface, a small panic rushed across my skin at the thought of being so close to the water, then more Mariahs joined us, along with the fella I'd chopped and the huge tribesman.

His face was a mess of bandages that left only the left-hand side of his face exposed, his one eye fixed me as soon as he arrived, cold, driven murder filled that eye and although his hands were bound, it was an intimidating stare not easily ignored.

Chapter 32

Anonymous Author

Inevitability

It was like a mountain of blistering lava plunging into arctic seas.

Crave, Broderick and Jake sat talking amiably to help pass the time when the doors opened.

Callus was the first in the room followed by his motley crew and a bandage strewn Philips being led by his own three Mariahs. He looked a mess but had obviously put up a decent fight.

The standoff was complete when the small army of Mariahs left the chamber, slamming the doors behind them, leaving the prisoners and their conflict behind. Crave got to his feet, locking eyes with Callus. The half-blood tribesman they had hunted for months looked tired and mean, but there was no aggression in him. Crave, however, was bubbling with pure and barely contained rage.

Jake and Broderick shared a look and hesitantly stepped forward as Philips shuffled over to join them. Bean just stood where he was, looking stoic; Broderick was the first to break the silence.

"Now, think about this first boss." He put a tentative hand on Craves shoulder and seemed relieved that his leader allowed it to stay there. "Now the table has turned, and killing this fella is as likely to please your brother as not." Crave said nothing. His eyes burned into Callus' just as Philips stared down at the boy stood next to Callus.

Crave squeezed his fists tighter and tighter before replying through clenched teeth.

"I know your talking sense, Brod. You always do, but this fella's got crimes to answer for if Sidian's involved or not."

Callus's brow knotted slightly before he joined the conversation in a tense and lowered tone. The imminent conflict between the two leaders had a choking effect on the whole chamber. All eyes watched as their audience collectively swallowed one by one.

"Aint we all got crimes, friend?" Callus' measured voice started the proceedings, his hands rising like he was moving in on a venomous snake. Crave answered in a slow and steady whisper, his rage still palpable but obviously at war with his reason.

"I aint your friend, devil."

Silence.

Nobody moved. One side of the room was a slowly erupting volcano, the other side had greater numbers but knew nothing of the root of the tension or the best course of action. Crow became locked in the battle of wills with Philips, a simpler situation. He'd damn near chopped his face in half and the fella was, after revenge, pretty straightforward.

Crow's mind raced. Somebody had to defuse the situation before it popped, and it was getting close. Just as he snapped off his gaze from his own enemy, Philips' bandages shifted and a smile crept over the visible side of his face. He opened his mouth for the first time.

"They killed the prospect, boss." The fire was lit.

The room burst into an explosion of violence.

Callus
Out the stew pot
Into the inferno

I had no damn idea what the fella's beef was, but as soon as his man spoke up, he was on me faster 'n a rattlesnake and he was strong. We wrestled while the whole damn room went into commotion. He kept tryin' for my throat and spittin' out curses, 'was all I could do to keep him from chokin' me. A couple gun shots went off amongst all the hollerin' and I could hear calls for us to stop rollin' round, but the little man would not let go of me.

Eventually, I got a boot in and thrust him away long enough to get to my feet. His boys grabbed hold of the fella and Crow put his hands on me. Comin' to my senses, I realised everyone was now lookin' up. There was an almighty noise like a damn train crash and steam hissin' up above us. The floor was shudderin' and a sick feeling started at my feet and got to spreadin' all the way up my body.

"Don't any 'o' you fools be sayin' I didn't warn ya, now!" Laz's voice was gettin' on for bein' a shriek, despite the violent standoff all around us he gets down on his knees and starts emptying' his pockets, right in the middle of that round room.

Nobody moved. Even the fella that attacked me was lookin' up as the ceilin' started slidin' away. A pale, grey sky was suddenly above us, not the strange black metal we'd gotten used to in the ship. We were outside and every one of us was chokin' on panic.

Crow Hoby
Finding my feet
In the depths of chaos

I looked around at the stricken faces, now suddenly bathed in a gloomy but natural light. On both sides, pure fear replaced the contention as all eyes looked up to the widening sky above. Even their leader who'd attacked Cal was clinging tightly to his men and staring up, knowing that if they were outside, it was more than likely that they would soon be in the sea. Only Laz remained focused. As before, he was on his knees muttering to himself in fast and inaudible sentences and rooting through his pockets, occasionally holding up an item to study before giving it a squeeze and putting it back on the floor.

Suddenly, the whole chamber seemed to drop for a split second and the light outside swept in from below, revealing the dark sea below us. We dropped a few feet and hit the surface with a muted splash. The black casing of our chamber retreated above us to complete our abandonment.

We birthed in a glass bubble from the chamber in the ship and the Aileron Dwarf slowly but progressively moved away from us. Like a none-viable egg, they had dropped us into the most inhospitable place on the planet without means of defence or survival; we were doomed.

To see so many hardened characters in such utter terror was disconcerting. Even Silk's Mother was out of her sleeve and caressing Silk's face like she was saying her last goodbyes. Pretty much everyone else was curled into a ball in silence or gibbering to whatever Gods they believed in.

Laz continued his muttering, and I saw no need for me to curl up and weep.

"What can I do to help?" he didn't look up but replied in a stern yet desperate tone.

"Get me more items!" suddenly imbued with a sense of purpose and an attitude of do or die, I began kicking the curled-up Outlaws around me.

"We need to get him more items! Check your pockets, there's no point in giving in now. Get to it!"

"What do you need?" at least a couple of them had broken free from their terror. The surrounding water completely immobilised Cal and the gang's leader. I have to admit I was struggling to keep down the rising fear myself.

"Anything you got that doesn't work no more, come on! Broken stuff, bullet casings, stale bread!" they got to searching, and it seemed to keep their minds off the sloshing, blue doom all around us.

There's only so much searching you can do in a glass bubble. Once all pockets and pouches had yielded, I actually took time to look around, beyond the bubble and across the vast sea.

The unending vista was quite surreal. In all directions, there was only the black-blue water as it roiled and occasionally formed the odd wave pattern. The bubble itself didn't roll over. They'd obviously made it in such a way; quite the marvel of Cthonic technology.

In the distance, against the dipping light of the fading sun, silhouetted against the horizon, I could see sinister shapes venturing out of the water as they preyed or played. I stumbled to the outer edge of the bubble to get a better look when a huge, dark shape rose from the surface just beyond and wrapped itself around our vessel from top to bottom. Huge suckers the size of a man's face splayed as they attached themselves to the glass all around me.

I feared I could not take any more despair. Then, violently, it pulled us under.

Captain Lazarus Badstock

Now if I'd had time just to take a minute, I'd have been proud as a big old pig pie when that there tentacle grabbed us. See, I talk and I talk, but there ain't nobody listenin', fools be runnin' round like chickens without no head, even when I done told them what they need to be doin'.

I'd seen that big old tentacle afore. Kept tryin' to tell them folks, but they's all too flustered with fightin' and commotion to listen to old Badstock. One thing I know is that when I see somethin', I mean really see somethin' that stuff is goin' happen. Might be the next day, or the next year, but it's damn well goin' to happen.

So that there huge Octusk is draggin' us down to a watery hell and everyone's gone quiet, 'bout time 'you ask me! So we're getting' deeper and deeper and there aint no light no more, just the damn black pressure all around us, getting' heavier and heavier. We got Dolomon's bullet holes lettin' in that black sea, drip by drip, and we got that high pitch creek as them holes start slowly spreadin' across that glass. I can't see the lines in the dark, but I can feel em'. They were inchin' across the surface like a damn spider's web, getting' louder and louder.

I reckon I'd just about finished pullin' the power out 'o' everythin' I'd got, but it wasn't enough. Now, I'd gotten some pretty powerful stuff in my collection and a few bits passed over from the other folks, but I could feel the gap 'tween how much we needed and how much we got. All 'round me I can hear the breathin' getting' faster and faster and some fella's whimpering like he's a scared kiddie, but I aint got time for distraction so I focus. Focus on the gap we got, not enough purpose left in them items, they're all gathered up in my arms and I can feel it all swellin' inside me, all that purpose, all that unspent power.

Then all the other folks is gone, it's just me and the bubble and the Octusk. Man, he was keen to crack us open and fill his belly; he was mighty curious too, never come across no bubble before, just floatin' there, abandoned.

Seemed like I'd sat there a while too long when I 'ventually figured it. It was me that had to cough up the rest, aint nobody else gonna give any more for the pot. I dug deep, tryin' to stop my thoughts from distracting me. Many thoughts comin' thick and fast. Memories, good times, bad times, even my poor ol' Ma comes poppin' up with a story to tell me, but I keep on pushin' them thoughts aside, these folks relyin' on me and they got one big job ahead, least I can do is give em' a hand along.

The bubble stopped. Think we reached that big old mouth. I felt the beast's glee when he opened up wide. It was do or die time for me, maybe do and die, I didn't rightly know.

I mustered everythin' I got, then, like a damn barn door, I opened up the rest. I had more in me than I'd realised.

Suddenly there was so much white!

Crow Hoby
Valuable lessons
Unexpected truth

I was on the verge of giving in to the fear as the crushing black swallowed us. Only Laz's muttering and the occasional moan in the dark broke the silence, which strangely felt deafening. It seemed right to make amends with my maker. Then an urgent sense of loss came over me. I scrabbled in the dark until I found Cal's trembling hand and a relief calmed my panic as it squeezed back earnestly.

Laz's voice rose and fell until it seemed to reach fever pitch, and the bubble suddenly stopped. The motion would have put us all on the floor were we not already huddled like children in that spherical glass coffin.

Then there was white. I couldn't tell if my eyes were open or not, there was just white. Laz stopped his tirade, and it suddenly seemed that the pressure all around us was receding. There was a sense of relief that permeated the white. There was more air to breathe, then motion, fast motion.

The massive bubble suddenly burst from the sea, and daylight rushed us. We left the water and flew into the air. Individually, we were all lifted from the floor for a moment of surreal stasis before the glass bubble, now textured with sharp and sinister cracks, fell back to land on the sea's foamy surface with a loud slap.

I imagine the jolting of our dramatic release was akin to a train crash, but the relief amongst us was overwhelming. As the bubble settled, people were on their feet, laughing and clapping each other's shoulders. Cal and Crave were still deep in their trauma, both had heads to their knees and neither joined in the celebration.

I turned to Laz with an incredulous smile. He looked terrible. His face was a clammy white mask of sudden ageing. His hands were shaking, and he reached for me.

"Get me my journal boy, quick as you can, now, I aint got long." His voice was a whisper, but his hands gripped me firmly and sincerely.

"Aint got long for what?" I replied, but he shook his head.

"Them monsters surround us, my friend. I can keep em' at bay 'till we get to land, but I'm using everythin' I got, y' understand?" He looked me right in the eye, the way he did when he had a serious point to make.

"I need to write what I just learned before I aint got the strength to do it. Help me, Crow!"

I retrieved his journal and settled the old man with my greatcoat as a blanket. As he wrote, he continued to mutter quietly under his breath. We'd escaped the belly of a beast and somehow, I knew we were now floating in the right direction, though whatever the old man had done had taken a heavy toll.

Chapter 33

Excerpt from 'Shadow of the Reach.'
Author unknown

Reverend Tiberius Osset continued to sit in his moulded, Skelatin chair and stare at the black, Skelatin wall as it curved out of sight and twisted deeper into the innards of the tower of the Reach. He knew full well that he was the victim of The Grand Maal of the Reach's power trap. Kept waiting until the point of despair in order to highlight his meagre status when he eventually stood before the Grand Maal in person.

He let out a long and frustrated sigh, already weary of Cthonic politics, and this was only his first year in the city. He repeated his own words in his head like a mantra, 'accept the sins of the minor in order to convert the major'. He once again evaluated the decision to come and see the Grand Maal in person. Was it foolishness or boldness that brought him to the tower so early in his campaign of conversion? He took a moment to close his eyes and consult God.

Yes, he opened his eyes and smiled, assured that he was indeed the voice of God, and his crusader in this strange land and therefore, his decision had been the right one.

Anonymous Author
Brave new world

The fractured bubble miraculously maintained its upright position along with the glass's shattered integrity; it bobbed along, propelled by some invisible force. Whether Lazarus Badstock had encouraged the bubble's

171

motion as he'd suggested or it was the sea's current that brought them into a tributary remains a subject of debate to this day but arrive at land they eventually did.

It was a strange, swamp ridden region. Alien black mud formed the banks of land and seemed to choke any native vegetation, supporting only the weight of tall, ragged birds the like of which none of the motley party had seen before.

As they drifted further inland, stunted black trees appeared through the low and thick mist, their limbs barren and cracked. The land itself gradually became firmer as they floated on, new species of wildlife became evident, burrower's refuse piles, claw and footprints of various sizes and they could see the twisted trail of serpents on the swamp-like banks.

The black, oily matter permeated the entire area. It collected in nooks and coves like sap from a bulging tree back home; it seemed to taint everything like a thick ink that eventually dried into stone. As the sombre group floated onwards, a handful of them watched with mesmerized fascination and chatted in hushed tones, whereas Callus, Crave, Philips and Lazarus kept their own company and fought their own demons.

Crow observed all that he could of the unknown land as it slowly surrounded them and rolled on with the bubble's motion. It was a bleak place but so diverse and removed from anything he knew, he couldn't help but smile as gradually the area revealed itself to him. It was quiet but for Lazarus' whispered incantations and the occasional belching that bubbled up from beneath the water's surface, releasing foetid gas as it burst.

Eventually the bubble came to a stop as it beached onto the black land, an open area dotted with large black rocks and the rotting remains of a once tall forest. Crow realised that Lazarus's quiet voice had ceased. He turned to check on his weakened friend to find he had simply gone.

Crow Hoby
Arriving in a new world
Nothing is the same

"What the?!" I jumped to my feet and the entire bubble rocked slightly. "Where?" I looked around in complete confusion and panic. Laz was just... gone.

My exclamation seemed to wake everyone from their reverie and all around me people got to their feet with confusion on their faces and fear in their eyes. Even Cal and Crave stood to investigate, though they each found it hard to look away from the other.

I moved his blanket sceptically with my foot. There was no trace of the man that had laid muttering beneath it. I was incredulous, as I looked around the faces before me, all were equally dismayed except that of the one called Philips. His eyes still burned into me with pure hate. Cal also noticed this and positioned himself between us as he addressed the group. His confidence and bearing seemed to return the instant we hit firm land.

"Look, I don't know what kinda black hell we've gotten ourselves into, but if we wanna get out of it, we're gonna have to level with each other." He looked at Crave and then Philips, his eyebrows asking a silent question. Silence answered him.

"What in the damn world have I done to you, fella?" he asked of Crave, who slowly stood. Philips joined him and they both raised to full height. Philips wasn't a big man, but he was half a foot taller than Crave. He didn't carry the same power that his leader did; Crave was pure menace. I noticed that Silk's Mother quietly slid Silk's sword an inch out of its scabbard and the stoic woman's hand wrapped around it. Crave's other men stayed on the floor, almost a gesture of neutrality. Their boss's voice was slightly softer than the last time he'd spoken, the fire less furious; we'd all had ample time for reflection.

"See, for a long time, when things got hard in my world, I had you." He pointed a long finger at Cal while pushing Philips gently back down to a sitting position. "Now I don't know up from down right now, but I recognise you." He pointed again; he was angry but conflicted. "I've blamed everything

173

on you for so long. I'm not sure I know how to stop."

"But I don't know you, friend." Cal's ordeal had softened his edges, but there was iron in the way he stood. "I've done a lot 'o things I aint proud of but I aint the same person I was. Hell, by the looks of it, you aint no angel!" That actually brought a disconcerting smile to Craves eyes. His mouth covered, as always, by his kerchief.

"And maybe there-in lies the problem, friend." The sarcasm as he emphasised the word 'friend' almost broke Cal. I could see his inner battle playing out. I thought he might just attack, but some hidden strength held him back. He snarled, revealing a long fang. In response, Crave reached up to untie his kerchief and revealed the horror beneath. Hidden amongst his thick, black beard were two mandibles. Once released, they moved with insect-like speed and seemed to reach out to us all. Even Bean sucked in a shocked breath at the sight of his boss's mutation.

"My black deeds are all on you." He spat, then continued to speak as the black mandibles stretched and enjoyed their freedom; we all stared in stunned silence.

"See, not only did you murder the only woman that ever cared for me," there was a very slight waver in his voice. Crave was clearly not a man accustomed to sharing his inner feelings. "But you also abandoned me, your own son."

Callus
Left the world behind
But the past keeps huntin'

I'll be damned if Crave's revelation didn't hit me harder than a train. I knew straight away. Damn it, I knew as soon as he said the words. My head was spinnin' already tryin' to figure who his Mother could be and what I'd done to her when he hit me with the line.

"But you also abandoned me, your own son."

As soon as the damn words were outside his mouth, I knew it was true. This man before me was my son, my son from another life.

We stared at each other for a while longer. Somethin' made him relax a little; the truth had a way of doing that to you when it finally escaped.

"Why in hellfire would I kill your Mother?" My voice stumbled too, the pain reachin' all the way from the past to that stinkin' black swamp. "The heart of my heart, the light in my life. I went away and dealt with this damn curse for an age to protect her from the justice her father spat out." I was livid suddenly. From nowhere, my memories of before were sittin' right on top of me, weighing me down. I ranted and raved, got on the high horse; hell, I don't even know half the things that I said, but I knew for certain that when I'd left she was alive, more alive than most.

Any chance he got and Crave came back at me, pointing his finger, his mandibles workin' overtime. He ranted back and worked out his demons one word at a time.

Somehow, the fight was different now. The threat gone, only the heart takin' the wounds. We talked for a time, everyone else starin' or mumblin' to each other as we thrashed it out.

I told him of our last days, the curse that her father had put on me with his shamans. The damn oppression I lived with as a half blood and my forbidden days with Cazique's daughter, Crave's Mother.

Eventually, we wound down. Lots 'o thinkin' time for us both as we unleashed the past piece by piece. Became obvious that Cazique and the tribe had lied to him his whole life. His Mother had more than likely died giving life to her baby, that or some other sinister intervention from her father. There was a sadness at the thought of it, but this was a life I'd left behind so long ago. The tribe told Crave that I'd raped and killed his Mother. As a child, he believed what he was told, as any child does. He'd spent his life looking for vengeance against me and here I was, turnin' that life upside down.

And he was my son.

We were sittin' all puffed out. Seemed like people were up and plottin' all around us, figurin' how to get out of the beached bubble. Crave stood scowlin', but the fire in him had died. I felt like I'd been under a horse a couple 'o times. He shook his head to clear his mind and looked at me.

"You should know." I looked up at him. I felt like I knew too much already, but he pressed on.

"I've got brothers and sisters." He winked enthusiastically.

Chapter 34

Excerpt from 'Shadow of the Reach.'

Author unknown

"Grand Maal, Sidian will see you now!" Osset jumped. The oration came from a Mariah of later years. His uniform was patched with more white than black; a visual statement of the loyalty, respect and authority he had garnered over those years.

The Reverend followed the Mariah through the twisting black corridors of the tower of the reach, seemingly ever deeper into the metaphorical snake's lair. He was eventually seated in a black chamber which was empty other than an oversized desk and two chairs which seemed to be cut from white stone. The indiscernible rear of the room disappeared into shadow. Osset smirked, knowing that this would be how the Grand Maal would make his dramatic entrance.

The Grand Maal of the Reach, his sibilant voice entered the room before he did.

"Osset, you finally make good on your promised visit." Before he'd finished the loaded remark Sidian, Grand Maal of the Reach, materialised from the darkened void of the chamber. Osset suppressed his annoyance and stood to greet him as the Grand Maal shifted from shadow to the unnatural light that hummed from a recess in the ceiling. His appearance alone, once lit, was enough to instil a deep intimidation. Osset had seen the man before, but always shrouded in robes and a deep hood. Currently, he dressed more fitting for a Lord in his own home, though no less dramatic.

His dark, creased skin was adorned with white tattooed symbols and line work, which entirely covered the left side of his face. Only his deep eye socket remained unblemished; the light from above picked out a shine from his eye within. His

177

attire complemented the Mariah's uniforms, ornate white bands rimmed the tunic from collar to skirt, accentuating his office. He gestured with a gloved left hand for Osset to sit and he did so, noticing that the Grand Maal's right hand was ungloved. Sidian then seated himself with a small smile, which could have been mistaken for a disdainful snarl in alternative lighting.

Crow Hoby
The only way ahead
Into the unknown

We eventually hacked our way out of the cracked bubble and spilled on to the black bank like the contents of a giant, alien egg. I tried to swallow the fact that Laz had just disappeared, but my eyes kept searching the group instinctively, as though I'd just misplaced the unique old man. Cal and Crave's discourse seemed to have died down somewhat. Both looked utterly shaken by recent events, but we were all lost on foreign land and action needed to be taken.

As we moved further in-land, the ground became firmer, and no longer tried to claim the boots from our feet.

Gigantic rock faces walled off the horizons all around us. Despite the enormous scale of the mountains, they were many miles away, and it was possible to put distance between us and the tributary that we'd arrived by. We checked weapons and kept them to hand as we gathered our wits and pressed on, each of us overwhelmed by the journey we'd undertaken but driven towards its conclusion.

After deciding to find civilisation, we traversed narrow cuts through and around huge white boulders, never able to see very far ahead as we wound into the unknown land. The black mud-like substance could still be seen bubbling from the odd hole, but it had a much less oppressive reign the further inland we ventured. Trees became prevalent; they were leafless but somehow were surviving without the cloying blackness choking their roots. We could see green ahead, a relief to most in this new place that vegetation was not all struggling for survival.

Eventually, we emerged above a vast clearing. The relief to be out in the open was palpable. Suddenly Jake, Crave's outrider, was barring me with his arm; Cal did the same.

"Everyone, quiet!" the Outlaw put his flat hand to his brow, I think out of habit as there was very little sunlight, the sky seeped in grey, just like everything else. I could just about make out two figures over to one side of the open area. They were too far away to hear conversation, but a strange metallic ringing echoed rhythmically around the depression, a din not unlike a hammer strike.

"We should investigate first." Jake looked at Cal and then over to Crave, who was the only one who had not ventured from the tunnel-like pathway back into the rocks.

"I aint heading out there without a reason." He grumbled, both hands planted firmly on either side of the thin tunnel, obviously comfortable where he was.

Cal and Jake crouched and slid off towards the mysterious figures, leaving the rest of us to sit and get a rest. I noticed that Silk had appeared next to me the instant Cal had left; she blocked the hate-filled line of sight between me and Philips. I'd tried to ignore his stares, but my instincts told me that eventually something would give, and it would be explosive. As I crouched to sit, the massive frame of Bean pushed past me with some urgency. He trotted off toward Jake and Cal, his fellow Tribesman.

Callus
Blowin' off steam
And making new friends

We arrived pretty quiet; well, neither of them noticed us, anyway. Jake was good. He took his time and made his moves carefully, confident. Bean was a tribesman through and through, could tell by how he moved, watchin' him left me wonderin' why he'd left his people.

When we got close enough, we could see was one 'o' them guards with the blue lightning sticks and a young boy. He was goading the lad as he

179

hammered topping' strange into the ground. Now and then the lad got a smack from a short, tasselled weapon that looked like a horsewhip, only more painful. We crept closer. The light in the bleached clearing was good, the grey sky somehow kept the sun from bothering me, felt good not to have to hide from it.

"Faster, boy! I wouldn't want to be you if the nodes weren't in place in time."

"I… trying, master." The lad was out of breath and in a panic, tryin' to knock that thing in the ground, reminded me of Crow 'fore he'd cut his teeth. The Mariah took another strange device from a large sack and walked away, placing it exactly where he wanted it whilst shakin' his head.

We got to maybe twenty feet away, all hidin' behind boulders and listenin' when I got to thinkin'. All round my head was the Mariahs and how they'd tossed us all into the sea without a care. I remembered the pure panic as the roof slid away to let the sky in and the drop! Then there was Crave, my son. Had to shake my head a little at that thought. Point is I'd spent a lot of years wonderin' and throwing my power around, takin' what I wanted and usin' folks. I'd learned that it was not the right way, hell I'd been happier than ever since I'd met Crow and started this damn adventure. It got into my head so that I was thinkin' 'bout all the people in our way, the Mariahs, the jailers, the Church, everyone stopping' us from doin' our work, getting' to Osset!

Before I knew it, I was walkin' at that Mariah and heftin' my hatchet. His back was to me as he ranted at the lad.

"Get a move on, boy! When that horn blows…"

"HEY!" I called out and stopped him in his tracks. He turned on me, maybe fifteen feet away.

"That aint the way to talk to people, especially not a boy!" I carried on walking.

"What the hell are you?" said the Mariah as he unhooked his lightening stick, a sick smile on his face as he thought about putting me in my place.

The boy just stared at me, as confused as his master. He carried on hammering, but the heart had gone out of it. The swine was walking towards me now. He had no fear, could tell he'd had nobody to fear for a long time. He threw his whip on the floor, not even concerned that the boy would take it up.

"What are you and who are you to stop the work of the hive?" he said with his nose in the air. I'd thought it through as I walked; it just felt right to go with my guts.

In a blur, the fella was dropping to his knees, my hatchet handle sticking up out the top of his head, pinning his pointy hat to his skull even as his body slumped forward to lie in the dirt. His hat flipped over. I carried on walking to collect my hatchet when the boy shouted.

"NO, no, no!" he was even more panicked than he'd been before. He looked around for the fourth device that was not hammered yet. "How will I get back?" his hands went to his head as he approached the weird, staked box. Confused, I joined him as he held the spike onto the ground and tried to bring the strange hammer to bear. I took it from him. Drove the thing into the ground just as I'd seen the boy do it only in one swing. Then I held my hand out to him. Up close, he had red lines all over his back, thick crusts where old lines had not healed yet. He looked up at me, his eyes unmoving, fixed straight ahead inside a terrified face.

"I'll take you where you need to go." I smiled and meant it, too. Beckoning him closer with my hand, I realised I was going through some serious changes.

Just then a loud horn call came echoing out of the surrounding trees and the boy's eyes bulged! He ignored my hand and bolted for the boulders where we'd been hidin'.

"HIDE, HIDE, HIDE!" is all that he said.

Crow Hoby
Beset by enemies
Hostile territory

Cal reached the strangers in the clearing, and something inside me suggested I should be near him. I set off running. Silk, though surprised, followed me without question.

As we got close, we heard a horn calling from the thin forest ahead. Cal was waving at us to get down as he slipped behind a boulder. As I crouched, I noticed a stark movement from one tree; it juddered to one side, branches and small leaves cascading to the floor, then an awesome sound answered the call of the horn. It was a roar like nothing I'd heard before, almost deafening; the hairs on my arms and neck stood on end. Another tree violently lurched as I turned my back on the scene to dive behind a boulder. Silk was close by, but didn't seem as terrified as I was. The sound from the forest developed into a loud crunching noise, pounding into the ground and vibrating the earth all around us as it got inevitably closer to our position. Silk's confidence inspired me, and I lifted my head slightly above the rock that shielded me, the sight taking my breath away.

Four men, stripped to the waist, were running for their lives towards me. Each of them was bound by a long metal bar that encircled their necks. They ran well together, in perfect rhythm despite the heavy contraption. Suddenly, their motivation for such desperate haste burst from the trees and came bounding after them. I can only describe the monster that chased them as an animated pile of gigantic rocks, with arms, squat legs and a furious face. It ran in a strange gallop as it planted its long arms before swinging its body forward. Despite the sheer size of the thing, it was approaching at an alarming pace. I heard Silk's sword leave its scabbard beside me and saw Cal stand from his hidden position. The two of them were fearless.

The four men suddenly skidded to a halt just in front of us, one of them crouched by a strange device while the others lined up behind him, panting and panicked. The gigantic monster approached at speed and lifted its mighty arms above us all; its reach must have been over twenty feet. The front man of the four smashed his hand down onto the device before him and the clearing suddenly felt energised, a loud, crackling buzz emanated from the device, of which I could now see three others, surrounding the beast who dropped to the ground in an instant. The floor shook and Silk yelped as her sword flew from her hands and stuck sideways to the beast's face with a clatter.

Entirely immobilised by unseen energy, they'd lured the rock behemoth into a trap. Without stopping to celebrate, the four men were straight back into action. They filed past a large sack on the ground and each of them took an item except the first, who then guided them to climb onto the monster's back. The five of us were now out of hiding and approaching like bewildered children at the scene before us. A small boy wandered out from behind Cal, his skin striped with thin red wounds. He watched with casual interest.

The second man hacked at the rock that formed the beast's neck, chips of stone flying into the air as he swung some kind of pick again and again. A rumbling groan filled the area, the only protest the victim could manage. It was uncomfortable to watch such a powerful being held helpless. Eventually, the picking stopped, and the four men moved in perfect synchronisation. They had obviously done this before.

The third man hefted a large metal tank and seemed to inject it into the exposed neck. I could hear a series of clicks and cracks as the rocks comprising the monster's body eased, and the weight settled into position as the rumble stopped and the thing's life drained away; Silk's sword detached and clattered to the ground. The last man then approached to insert a tube into the hole his colleague had dug and pulled on a lever, sucking up black, viscous liquid.

Their job complete, the four men turned and jumped to the ground beside the now inert pile of rocks. It had taken them minutes to reduce the ferocious beast to nothing more than an addition to the boulder-strewn landscape. I briefly scanned the clearing, wondering if all the boulders had once been massive predators. The men slumped to the ground exhausted and, for the first time, looked up at us as we approached, silenced by the spectacle we'd witnessed.

The front man scratched at his heavily stubbled chin.

"Youlotbestgo." He looked back towards the forest, "They'llcometotakeus back." The fourth man answered with one word, more discernible than his friend.

"Bastards!"

They spoke like Vikens.

Chapter 35

Excerpt from 'Shadow of the Reach.'
Author unknown.

Osset began.

"I trust you are well, Grand Maal?"

Sidian fixed the Reverend with a stare that lingered just long enough for the faint-hearted to become anxious. The Grand Maal then seemed to consider his response.

"We are prospering. Thank you for asking, and how, I should ask, are you finding your temporary new home?" The word 'temporary' not lost on Osset but once again he suppressed his aggravation.

"I am glad, and hope that your prosperity continues, Grand Maal." Osset bowed his head before continuing.

"I would like to take this opportunity to thank you and the Cthonic council for the home you have provided for me. It is very much appreciated and will surely aid my work in your great city." Osset smiled. They were clearly engaged in a game of minor victories and annoyances. He knew well that Sidian would have voted against housing the immigrant from across the sea and that he would happily aid in bringing about the end of Osset's campaign if he could do so without losing favour from the council. The Grand Maal of the Reach was obviously engaged in a campaign of his own to garner power over the city. Osset's ideas of religious conversion could only get in the way, but they both needed allies.

"The council did indeed offer you succour while you pass through our city, but I feel it my duty to inform you that not all council members voted in your favour, Reverend Osset." Now the term 'Reverend' comes into play, thought Osset. Now

185

he will create an enemy for me to hide his own animosity.

"*Within the council, there are those with their own... religious aspirations.*" *Sidian's feigned smile was becoming difficult to endure. "I am a man of science and magic, of betterment and evolution. If your God would like to assist in my machinations, I would not oppose his influence." This time Sidian's smile was genuine, a feral and hungry grin. He had set his traps.*

"*Though I appreciate your acceptance, Grand Maal, I feel first I must encourage Grand Fraul, Rachnis of my good intentions towards this city and its people." They both sat back a fraction once he'd released her name from its cage. "Despite your obvious loyalty and unquestionable diplomacy, I feel she would be the most unlikely to sympathise with my plight." Sidian simply nodded.*

"*We hope you can convince her of your good intentions, Reverend.*"

Crow Hoby
Crossroads
The pull of fate

Despite their insistence that we go into hiding as quickly as possible, the four Vikens were very amiable. At galloping speed, they explained they were slaves from a mine close to where we stood. The Mariahs would come to check if they had survived the hunt and take them back in the unlikely event that they had. Despite the physical size and strength of these men, not to mention their effectiveness at killing monsters, they seemed fearful of their masters; it was disconcerting.

We eventually complied with the Vikens and made our way back to the group before their masters returned, eager to spy on them from our vantage point.

I explained what had happened with great enthusiasm. When I'd finished my summary, Jake spoke up.

"There seemed to be two pathways out of that clearing, one back into the rocks to the North and one East which, I'll bet, skirts 'round the outside, past this mine."

"We go North." Silk astonished everyone by speaking up, loud and assertive. She nodded, "The boat was heading North."

It made complete sense, only I couldn't help thinking about the mine the Vikens had told us about. Something made me itch to see it, to get a glimpse of the people of this land. We all looked at each other, but before anyone said a word, the sound of nearby hooves drifted up from the clearing.

We hunched lower as we observed. There were five of them, four mounted Mariahs, one of which was pulling a black wagon. The fifth caught my eye immediately; dressed differently than the others. He was wearing the same attire that I'd seen back across the sea, working their way through Sanctuary, killing indiscriminately; my stomach rumbled, and the memory almost caused me to vomit.

I couldn't put the pieces together in my head. It was like I was reading a book and skipping sporadic chapters. I still watched as my mind reeled. They loaded the Vikens into the wagon and turned their peculiar mounts. I looked closer at one, something familiar.

"They're riding goaths." I exclaimed. Cal looked at me, slightly confused, but said nothing.

"Giant goats that the Vikens ride, incredible." Just then, as I watched them ride away, I realised they hadn't taken the boy. He was nowhere to be seen. I scanned the clearing, checking each boulder for signs of him, when something very strange occurred.

Crouching amidst the rest of our party as we watched the slavers depart easterly, I felt a sudden jab in my ribs. I quickly turned, expecting to see the boy I was looking for.

Sat cross-legged, right next to me was the grinning face of Laz; I couldn't speak. A ripple of shock went through the entire group as they noticed him and stared silently. Only Crave broke the silence as he spat on the ground. Laz rolled his eyes and chuckled before he nodded toward the retreating Mariahs.

"You wanna get yourself after them, do you all good to see what they got goin' on down there." He whistled as if to emphasise the importance of his suggestion. "Need all the help ya' can get, boys and girls." He smiled as he looked around the assembled misfits; he seemed proud, fatherly almost.

187

"Oh, I'll be around when I can be, don't you worry none."

Everyone stared in silence. Then, without warning or explanation, he vanished. The only evidence was a faint smell of burning hair on the breeze.

Callus
Crossroads
Crossed loyalties

Damn it, things were gettin' too strange, even for me! That crazy old fool just poppin' up and then he's gone again. I put my hands over my eyes, rubbed my face all over.

"I want to see the mine." Crow decided. He had a glazed look, think we all did, but he went with Lazarus' words. I had my doubts about the old man's wisdom when he was actually here, but damn it, if it wasn't him that got us out the monster's jaws, and out 'o' the sea, I don't know what it was.

"I'm in." I said. Jake said the same. Then Bean nodded solemnly and put his hand across his chest, a tribal gesture that meant respect. Philips laughed and shook his head at the big tribesmen. Nobody else spoke up.

Just like that, we split. Didn't sit right that Silk was with them but there wasn't a thing I could do to slow her down on her way to Osset. Damn, she had it worse than I did.

Me and Crave locked eyes for a moment before they set off. Neither of us idiots knew what to say, but Crow came to the rescue.

"We're all heading to the city, this Cthonica, so we can just meet up there?" Everyone was nodding and hesitating. Only Philips and Silk had already set off. For the first time since we'd broke out of that bubble, Dolomon spoke up. His white suit splattered with muck and his confidence had taken a beatin', just like the rest of us.

"When you get to Cthonica, you ask for me, yes? My place is big and believe me, I have the room for my new friends, yes?" I smiled at the man. His own people had left him to die in the sea. He'd been quiet, mullin' over that since we set off. He looked to the East and continued.

"You be careful, friends. This world is growing, yes. It is a greedy place.

In Cthonica, you are on top or far, far below."

Bean, Jake and Crow took turns to pat me on the shoulder and we made our way back down to that big old pile 'o' rocks that just tried to kill us.

We found the boy wanderin' like he was lost. We said we'd take him home, and he started jumpin' around all excited. The five of us found them goat tracks, and we got movin'. They were easy to track; three of us could track a damn bird if we had to. That thought got me lookin' at the sky. No damn birds and no damn sun. Things weren't all bad, but I didn't enjoy splittin' with Silk. I had to go with Crow. I owed him that much, but I was lookin' forward to getting it done and getting' back on the trail to Osset.

The Pilgrimage

Daroch was still holding the boy's head as it drooped. The remaining water he'd taken trickled from his slack lips. His eyes remained open.

Magan approached as Daroch lowered the body and closed the eyes. They remained still. Both of them knew the decisions that had to be made, no need for unnecessary words. They had lost many druids to the elements of this new world; they were unaccustomed to the dangers and discomforts of living above ground. They had travelled for miles in a race against time to arrive at a prophesied place and time, the conjunction. They would meet the one with two souls and begin to right the world. The dwindling pilgrimage had followed Magan with little question, despite there being no proof of what he'd seen in his visions. Each time they lost a brother or sister, Magan feared that the revolt would come and they would take his place at the head of the Hearth, the pilgrimage would end and all the death and suffering would have been for nothing.

Daroch stood and placed his hand on Magan's shoulder, knowing his leader's woe. There were so few of them now and the air was getting colder by the day. Their thick furs kept them warm in the daytime, but the nights were becoming longer. Soon the sunlight would vanish for what seemed an age as the night cycle began. They had already lost many to the cold and more to the treachery of the land and the beings that called it home. Magan knew Daroch would stand with him to the end but feared the two of them would not be enough to continue their work after the conjunction. This journey was only the start; the testing ground before the pilgrimage began in earnest.

As they stood in silence and shared the troubles of leadership, more druids arrived, like shadows, to take away the boy's body. His last task would be to feed his people, to add strength to their diminished numbers so they could continue. This was their way.

Fast falling footsteps put an end to Magan's reverie; he opened his eyes and turned towards a quickly approaching scout. What more could they endure?

Gulni was out of breath. His frame was skin and bone. He reached for Magan's face with bony fingers and wide eyes while he laboured to fill his lungs with air. Magan waited with a questioning tilt of his head. He feared he could take no more news of the perils ahead. Daroch took his hand to lend him strength.

"City." Gulni managed a single word; such was his urgency. He continued to draw breath with withered lungs. Finally, he regained some of his composure and looked into Magan's eyes with barely contained glee.

"We are in sight of the city, my brother! We are at the crossed roads!" Magan's eyes bulged, and an uncertain smile blossomed across his face.

"Truly?" Gulni nodded frantically, and Daroch squeezed Magan's hand. The scout continued.

"It is as you said each night around the fire, brother. The black towers, the spirals and the smoke of industry!" Magan swung his arms around Gulni and squeezed his malnourished frame. Daroch lifted his arms to the sky and bellowed across the camp.

"Brothers and sisters, we have arrived at the crossed roads! We need only wait for the one with two souls to deliver us. We have made it to our calling!" A series of weak but triumphant calls spread around the camp, building in volume and euphoria. Magan also lifted his arms towards the sky.

"We may yet spare this world!"

Chapter 36

Excerpt from "The Cthonic Orders."
Chapter 9: Skelatin Society.
Anonymous

To use the term 'mine' to describe a Cthonic facility under the rule of Grand Fraul Rachnis during the mid to late Cthonic era is akin to describing an ocean as a mere body of water. The facilities were indeed mines and produced vast amounts of the raw product which, through labour and industry, eventually became Skelatin, arguably the physical and metaphorical building blocks of the whole of Cthonic society. However, the mines, or 'Hives' as they were known, went far beyond the mere production of materials.

Each Hive comprised an outer settlement of indentured workers who, through continual exposure to the raw materials deep within the earth were, to a man, physically dependent on the consumption of Erf, a primitive form of Black, the popular substance used by the nobility of this era of Cthonic evolution. Because of this widespread addiction, the workers were compliant and easy to control; the Mariahs stationed at each Hive who watched over security and production were considered ruthless but were often; it is recorded, seen rewarding certain behaviours with extra Erf or, to the contrary, using violence and misery to punish those who tarried or spoke out against their oppressors.

Not only were the workers treated as the property of the Cthonic Hive, but also their offspring. Grand Fraul Rachnis was famed for her breeding program, which she conducted for many years without the consent of the wider Cthonic Council. During fertile periods, female workers were taken to cells and inseminated by *their Cthonic betters; the children born of this perverse system removed from their Mothers and schooled to become the next generation of compliant workers.*

Morality aside, the Hives produced tonnes upon tonnes of material, which was 'seasoned' at the Hive itself before being shipped back to Cthonica during the summer. The seasoning involved the harvesting and scientific application of the stomach acid of various breeds of native Troll. This process, as one can imagine, was not exactly risk free. Grand Fraul Rachnis relied on the Order of the Reach, under the leadership of Grand Maal Sidian, to provide capable workers particularly for this area within the Hive. These workers often came from distant lands and had to be controlled both psychologically and physically in order to gain the correct results and avoid hindering the production process.

The Hives were incredibly productive and successful facilities; however, their oppressive practices had huge and irreversible effects on the workers. Most remained fearful of human contact, social norms and interaction entirely broke down, whereas a few amongst the masses could resist the psychological effects and plotted towards rebellion and eventual uprising.

Crow Hoby
Sneaking into a mysterious lair
Cthonic Mine

Our quick, curious visit to the mine had not gone according to plan.

The boy's name, we discovered, was Nich. As we approached the mine itself, he became more and more anxious. He practically crawled through desperation not to be seen by the Mariahs who patrolled the gate. His fear was so great that at one point, as we were dragging ourselves through a hole in the outer fencing, he soiled himself at the sound of approaching footsteps.

We got inside, into a dilapidated shanty town. The makeshift huts seemed to be positioned at random and often left little room between dwellings. Nich took us to his family home, and we entered unseen. He visibly relaxed once inside and went straight to a covered hole in the ground, producing a small sack which he emptied onto a low table. Unsure what he was doing, me, Cal, Jake and Bean watched in silence. Bean was practically on his knees in the low-ceilinged hut. The skinny boy set up a small burner with a dish and began using a flint to ignite it.

"What's next, little man?" Jake was clearly impatient; he kept putting his face to the ramshackle door to peer through one of its many holes. The boy seemed not to hear him. He got his burner lit and placed a tiny lump of something on the dish, then covered the whole thing with a black funnel. We shared glances, wondering what he was doing while he looked through the funnel into the dish and waited a few moments. At apparently the perfect moment Nich removed his eye and sucked on the funnel's spout, he seemed to get a good chest full and blew out a vapour like smoke. The boy then slumped to the floor with relief and euphoria lazily scrawled across his face. He gestured, invited us to use the strange devise next before he closed his eyes and lay on his back.

Bean stalked over to the prostrate boy and gave his cheek a hearty slap, but he seemed unresponsive. Jake shook his head, and we all sat dejectedly in a rough circle, unsure what to do next. We'd seen a small amount of the place as we entered, the outskirts seemed to be completely different to the ominous black buildings in the inner circle, that seemed like the place we needed to see but we didn't know how safe it was or how to get there. Bean rolled a cigarette and offered one to Jake, who shrugged his shoulders and accepted. My stomach rumbled, and I looked up into Cal's eyes. A mix of hunger and worry danced in his gaze as he raised his eyebrows.

Callus
Followin' Crow
For better or worse
Id seen folk use all kindsa stuff to get high, kinda understood Nich's

craving better'n any of us, but I didn't 'preciate his timing. My mind started wanderin' over to the guards outside. Maybe I could get a feed while the boy slept it off? Nothin' else to do, just didn't want to bring the whole damn army down on us. I thought 'bout it while we were quiet, then got to my feet. Jake and Bean were talkin' real quiet. Crow was lost in his own head. I went to the door and before I could grab the handle it opened from the other side and in walks an old man, wizened and unfed, he looks up at me and drops his bag, and his jaw.

Now, I have control these days but I have to tell ya, while I grabbed the fella and put my hand over his mouth, my eyes never left his soot covered throat, I could almost taste him already. Instead, I span him round and kept my big ol' hand clamped on his mouth. Everyone jumped to their feet, Bean hit his head on a beam and swore.

He had little struggle in him. He was all bone and old age. I took my hand away slowly.

"Nich! You are, idiot!" He barked. I clamped my hand back in place to shut him up, though I agreed with the old timer. Crow walked forward, his hands up like he was surrenderin'.

"We're not here to hurt you." He said like he was calmin' a horse. "Let my friend take his hand away and let's talk?" the fella gave a quick nod, and I let go. He surprised me and didn't move a muscle. I figured we probably scared him to death, filling his home with men twice his size.

The old man stretched his bare foot across and gave the boy a quick boot, then said, quieter than last time,

"Idiot boy!"

Crow pointed to the floor and sat down. The fella followed, and I nodded at Jake and Bean to do the same, relieved I'd not had to hurt the man so far, despite my rumbling guts.

Crow Hoby
Making friends with slaves
Cthonic mine

When Nich awoke from his stupor, we had already made rudimentary introductions to what turned out to be his father, Burl. Nich explained the situation and although the man was fearful of the concept of harbouring us, he agreed to help until we moved on. As we talked, more individuals arrived home to be greeted by Nich and his convincing explanation; the hut became quite cramped.

Each of the ragged inhabitants made use of the burner though in a gentler fashion, they stayed awake and able to talk in hushed tones as they told us about the mine and how it worked before having to return to whatever oppressive workload the Mariah's had planned for them.

They agreed to harbour us and, when able, help us escape, the risk for our casual investigation seemed suddenly too high. The ragged family was clearly malnourished, and it was touching to hear that they would share their food and what little hospitality they had.

That night I barely slept as my mind could do nothing but ponder their oppression and wonder what, if anything, I could do to help them.

Chapter 37

Excerpt from "Roots of Rebellion."
By Marius Maxslimov.

Arton Bravlav was a member of great standing in the early years of rebellion in Cthonica. He was born in the region and experienced a time before the name Cthonica was implemented. He was a childhood friend of the Dolomon's and so, as they grew in number, he rallied to their cause, thinking nothing of the danger he was embracing as the steel eyed Mariahs steadily multiplied across the city.

He was extremely passionate about the cause and stood against the tyranny of the Cthonic Council wherever the Dolomons would allow it. The organisation was esoteric and hidden in plain sight. Any undertakings were strictly secretive, and victories never claimed or celebrated.

It is in these early years when one of his children, Grauta Bravlav, became embroiled in the dangerous game of rebellion and circumstance forced Arton to pledge his life to the cause in return for the rescue of his youngest child from the hands of the Mariahs. The operation was bigger than anything the small group had ever attempted, but they achieved the rescue with seemingly little impact on them as a group. It was not until several months later that the wrath of Cthonic retaliation arrived and the rebellion was torn apart. Helder Dolomon, the founder and driving force of their alliance, suffered punitive execution.

What remained of the group went back underground and each day Arton thanked Helder for the life of his daughter and pledged to one day pay it back. The lifeless statue of Helder Dolomon always stared back with marble eyed indifference, but Arton was a man of integrity and would hold true to his word.

The city of Cthonica grew at a phenomenal rate and soon the Mariahs were an ever-present army of oppression that squeezed the city of every drop of freedom for all except those in the nobility that prospered and rose through investment into the industrial boom.

The rebellion also grew. With a rise in power, it stands to reason that there would be a rise in those that would oppose it. With Helder gone, it was down to his brother, Fredre, to lead them. Fredre was a cautious and humourless man, but his drive to fight the powers that would crush the citizens was no less furious than that of his deceased brother.

It was Fredre that finally asked Arton to repay his debt from so long ago, to sacrifice his life for their cause.

His children were older now and fighters in the rebellion themselves and so Arton agreed to perform his final assignment so that his children may have a better life than the one he must sacrifice.

Anonymous Author
Hesitancy

"I'm telling you; this is madness!" Jake's voice was hushed but angry and frustrated. The four of them huddled in a corner, the only space available without venturing outside. "We need to get out of here, now!" Jake was adamant whilst Bean just silently nodded his agreement. Crow had his own thoughts on the matter.

"We need their eyes out there!" he pleaded. "We can trust them. They have no love for these Mariahs." He paused. "As soon as the way is clear, we can slip out."

Bean continued to nod his head whereas Jake's shook in disagreement.

"Look, no disrespect meant, Crow, but it was your idea to come to this horrible pit in the first place. Let's quit now that we know we're ahead and get out of here." He looked pleadingly at Callus, urging him to see sense. The dark tribesman scratched at his chin and looked at each of them. He then flexed his shoulders.

"I go with Crow."

Jake put his hand to his forehead but stilled his tongue. Bean kept nodding;

he looked from face to face, trying to hide his inner conflict.

Just as we reached the stalemate, the door swung open to admit Nich. Concern contorted his youthful face; he chewed the end of his finger as he sat in the corner and reached for his sack of Erf.

"What is it?" Crow and Jake asked in unison. They all watched the boy expectantly as he prepared the instruments of his favoured oblivion.

"They know you're here. They want people to come forward if they know anything." The worry on his face was slowly increasing as he thought it through. His fingers worked absently as he assembled the funnel and burner, his head bobbing as if in conversation with himself.

"When can we leave?" Jake's voice left no room for argument. Callus stood slowly and addressed the group.

"I aint any good to any of ya if I don't feed soon." He cast a quick, self-conscious glance at Nich as he spoke; the boy only had eyes for his devise. "Let me go see what's going on out there. Do what I gotta do." He lifted the hood on his greatcoat and, before anyone could argue, he slipped out into the gloom of the perpetual dusk outside.

"Nich!" Crow exclaimed a second time, trying to get the boy's full attention. "What would they do with us?" the black smeared boy looked up for the first time from the burner, his face a drooping mask of worry. He stared with wide eyes at Crow for some time in silence; then a slight tremble played across his bottom lip.

"They're cutting Erf rations."

Callus
Steppin' out for a bite
What the hell were we doin' there?
Damn, it felt good to leave that hut!

I figured it was getting late, was hard to tell in this land; seemed like dusk all the time. I kept low and weaved through the huts and shelters, looking for Mariahs. The thirst was damn near crippling me and the workers had trouble enough already without being preyed upon by the likes of me.

The area was full of ragged people rushing to and from their shacks to the central entrance that led to a huge black building surrounded by metal fences. They seemed not to notice me; they were like ants moving about, barely lookin' where they were goin'. I tried to move along with the flow until I saw the first Mariah. I stayed behind the corner of a hut and watched as he loudly encouraged people past him with a shove; he was alone but surrounded by the workers on their way past.

It seemed to take forever, but the crowd got thinner, and it seemed like they'd all made it to their work. I swore as he straightened his tricorn hat, sniffed and set off in the opposite direction. I was about to call his attention my way when there was a racket back from where I'd come from, followed by a desperate scream. He heard it too; he pulled his weapon from its holster and reached round to his back. A sudden memory hit me of the pain that those damn things caused, and I made a move before he switched the thing on.

He didn't see me coming, but a few stragglin' workers did and fled. He noticed them run and looked up as I got to him. Just as the Bolt Rod came to blue life, I grabbed him by the arm and neck and pulled him to the ground; he tried to swing the thing at me, but I had his arm locked as I went for his throat; his panicked shout ended in a gurgle when I sucked hard until he passed out. I would have kept going, I was so ravenous, but his limp hand let go of the Bolt Rod and it sparked as it hit the floor. I jumped back, the sudden fear breakin' my concentration.

Then I heard gunshots.

It came from where I'd left Crow. I ran back through the alleys and gaps between the huts; I was fast; always at my best after a feed.

I got close and could see through a narrow pathway that Mariahs were all around the shack, their rods blazing blue light. There was another gunshot, further out towards the outer fence, but I couldn't tell who it was. It wasn't a shotgun, which meant that maybe Crow was still in the shack. I moved closer. There was a scream from inside and hostile voices.

My blood was up. I ran at two Mariahs as they stood with their backs to me, their attention on the shack. Heedless of their Bolt Rods, I reached out to grab them both by the neck and swung their heads towards each other in front of me. There was a crunch, and they both went down. I kept moving, but most of them had heard and looked up at me as I got near; I charged at one with my hatchet now in hand; he was on his own, took a swing at me, but I ducked under and swung my own weapon up and into his jaw. They were shouting and crowding towards me, still no sign of Crow, thought maybe my distraction might have given him a chance to get away. Another one took an angry swing. As I stepped aside, I tripped on a body on the floor that I'd not seen in my rush to get to Crow; I rolled over it and stood as another rod came at me. I took a chunk out of the fella's arm and twisted to face two more closin' in on me. As I moved, I'd glanced at the body on the floor; I let out a roar as I saw the face; Jake stared at my feet through dead eyes. A huge black burn across his neck had almost taken his head off.

I tried to stay focused but was gettin' surrounded. Another swing and another red spray as I'd chopped at his arm. I wasn't sure that my hatchet would stop the sparking weapon if I'd parried it. I spun at a furious shout behind me and prepared to duck the blue flash when another Mariah found an opening and dropped me to my knees; the pain sent everything black, but I remained upright for a second before another bolt of lightning finished me.

Chapter 38

Anonymous Author

Best laid plans

Every bit of Bean's body hurt like hell.

To give his accomplices as much chance as possible to escape his own painful fate, he remained silent. Through each beating, each vengeful interrogation, and each time they dragged him, bleeding and broken, from one dark room to the next, he never said a word. He'd passed out frequently and each time he awoke, he was more confused and the world was more brutal and hopeless. They'd dragged him incrementally deeper into the facility until they roughly shoved his damaged and exhausted body into a small metallic black room. The only feature, other than the pale, flickering light, were two other bodies already slumped within feet of the excrement they'd amassed in the shadowed corner.

The huge tribesman had no energy to move. He remained where the four Mariahs had hefted him until a dark and twisted sleep took him.

Crow Hoby

The start of my descent

Beneath the Cthonic mine

Indiscernible hours or days passed. The darkness was all-consuming;

even Cal's eyes would have struggled in the crawling tunnels. The weight of rock and earth that surrounded us seemed to squeeze the very air from our lungs. Enslaved, along with so many others that were forced to drag their scabbed and skinny frames through the tunnels to reach the digging sites.

As I inched my way along, continually spitting out the crunchy dirt that was kicked up ahead by my fellow slave, I remembered our betrayal.

Astoundingly, it was not the fear of repercussions that had made them cave in; it was the threat made to cut them off from their precious Erf. I have pondered the situation many times and each time I war within myself. Am I not just as dependent on human blood? What lengths, what betrayals would I be capable of should I be unable to obtain it?

I worked tirelessly under the eyes of the Mariahs, surrounded by waist-stripped slaves who swung their picks in mute fixation to avoid attention and the wrath of the electrically charged weapons that our guards carried. After hours of the same repetition of dig, carry, move, return, they ushered us back into the crawling tunnels and eventually back to the caves to eat. A thin gruel which I secretly poured away each time. The increasing hunger I hosted was not for leaves and vegetables dipped in hot water, it was for the confined and pressurised blood that pumped around the poor wretches that shared my fate.

In the dark caves, I had learned there was ample opportunity to make people disappear. Nobody would look or find any evidence in the pitch black. Only a predator could appreciate such conditions.

In my conflicted mind, I had already designed my feeding pattern, though at first I believed I would fend off the hunger with a shield of morality. The daily silence and hard labour left plenty of time for my mind to converge my resistant feelings towards those of a ravenous survivor. Parts of my soul vanished in those unlit caves, never to return.

After each time I sated myself was a period of inner conflict, with nobody to share my thoughts, my mind rambled until it hardened against its own judgment. I looked for people to blame, sometimes offering my pain to the slaves I fed upon and sometimes I remembered the family who had taken us in and offered us safety but plotted against us when we turned our backs.

Anonymous Author

Reunited in misery

When Bean finally awoke after a timeless void in his existence, only one eye would open naturally. He could feel the bulge of swelling covering his face and indeed much of his body. His jaw felt to be on fire and his teeth no longer met where they had before; he closed his eye again and embraced the void.

Eventually, enough energy returned for the tribesman to prop himself up, though he slipped in his own sticky blood on the cold floor. Everything was pain, but as his eye slowly opened, he found a measure of relief to see Callus at the other end of the room.

They were both naked, as was the third inhabitant who sat with raised knees. Bean could not tell if he was awake, though he knew from the outlines of his face that he was not Jake or Crow. Crawling painfully towards Callus, the metal floor felt almost frozen to the touch. He slowly stood instead and limped across to find his fellow tribesman staring straight up, wearing death's face. He dropped to his knees and put his hands on Callus' chest, a sting building in his one open eye, the tear unable to find passage through the swollen flesh around the socket.

Suddenly Callus' hands snatched Bean's and his head lifted, his eyes burning with hate and fury. Bean and the stranger both gave a mumbled cry of alarm while the presumed dead tribesman lifted himself painfully to a sitting position.

"Where's Crow?"

The two tribesmen conversed in hushed but urgent tones, each of them baring their misfortune with stoic resilience.

Back at the shack Bean had seen the Mariahs incapacitate Crow with their Bolt Rods and carry him off towards the entrance to the central facility. The huge tribesman had escaped the immediate area but found trouble as he'd attempted to follow the detachment who'd taken him. Callus, though of a considerably dark and justified mood, closed his eyes as if to thank his maker for his ward's survival.

Crow

Into the abyss

Never to return

I thought I was blood drunk, a term Cal used to describe the intoxication he'd felt when he'd failed to limit himself and sucked a victim beyond mere sustenance.

I hid the body in a deep recess in the rock, without light and a willingness to crawl through the low tunnels. It would never be discovered. My eyesight was becoming more and more effective in the dark with each day I spent underground. Navigating the cramped tunnels was becoming easier so long as I could feed.

I made my way back towards the sleeping cave, my mind pensive. My victim had not attempted to scream or even call out. He seemed almost grateful for the relief as I'd took hold of him and dragged him further into shadow.

As I approached a cross-roads of a sort, I noticed a faint light flare and fade to my right, in the opposite direction to which I was crawling. Accompanying the strange light was a sharp and familiar smell; I took the tunnel and soon could crouch as I made my way towards the acrid scent, the upper ceiling rising as I moved deeper. I rounded the corner to find Laz, sat contentedly smoking one of his bizarre cigarettes in a shallow alcove in the rock. He smiled at my arrival; a genuine smile such as one you would give to a lost, and eventually found loved one.

"Now looky at you, damn it boy, you' been fixin' yourself good!" There was no judgment in his voice, but I immediately dropped my head as a convulsion of guilt swept through me. I couldn't speak, which made him laugh heartily. He reached out and patted my shoulder; I half expected his hand to pass straight through me, but it was as solid as it always had been.

"Don't you be worryin' 'bout what you gotta do to survive now. You got a job to do, aint gonna get it done down here with an empty belly!" His good cheer was like a cool wind on a baking hot day; I sat beside him and lifted my head.

"What happened to you, Laz?" my voice was quiet. It cracked as I formed the question. I realised I'd not spoken for such a long time.

"Don't be concernin' 'bout me neither. I'm where I need to be, and you need to keep strong. Aint gonna lie, I've had some doubts 'bout the company you keep, but now I can see we're all just where we need to be." He took in the cramped cave and his face twitched slightly as he sniffed. "Place aint ideal, but we gotta work with what we got."

"I don't understand. This is hell and it's swallowed me whole! You don't know what I've become!" I tried to stand but realised there wasn't enough room, had there been I would have been anxiously pacing. Laz just smiled, crushed his cigarette into the rock face, and put his finger to his lips. His voice dropped to a lower tone, and he looked me straight in the eye.

"Now listen good 'cus I aint gonna be here long. I need you to hear what I say, OK?" I nodded before he continued, suddenly feeling like a boy again, not the ravenous beast I'd become.

"Now, I thought your Cal might be the heart of the darkness we were headin' towards, was makin' me twitch some, but now I know, like I told you, I just know stuff! Thing is, I now know he aint. 'Fact, I know a whole lot more, but aint got time for that right now. Hell, didn't even have time for my smoke!" he looked at the extinguished stub wistfully. "Now, you just sit tight and be doin' what you're doin' and be ready to strike, ya understand?" as always Laz was cryptic, it took a while for any of his words to settle in my head, I just stared at him, and he took that as a nod. "Cal is comin' for ya. You just gotta be strong when he gets here!" he shuffled closer to me. "Thing is, Crow, you'll be him eventually and you aint the darkness, 'spite what you think right now you are the one, the one that will mend this world."

I was about to bombard him with questions and resistant statements when I realised he'd gone. I crouched, looking into an empty crater in the rock wall, and shook my head.

I made my way back to the silent community I was now a part of, unsure if I'd actually seen and heard anything in reality. What I felt and accepted was that the guilt was subsiding, and Cal was on his way to get me away from this place. Laz had said to keep strong, and so I would. I would need strength to exact my revenge on the twisted masters that had imprisoned and abused me, along with so many other dwindling souls.

Chapter 39

Excerpt from "Roots of Rebellion."
  By Marius Maxslimov

Despite his talents, skills honed throughout years of rebellious activities, covert assignments and the passion and drive of one so utterly wedded to the cause of a free Cthonica, Arton failed to end the reign of Hive Lord Nestor. I theorize that had the Lord been situated anywhere but deep inside an active Cthonic mine, Arton's resources would have facilitated the assassination with relative ease. As it was, the celebrated activist and assassin spent every shred of influence and ability just to gain entry to the facility. Once inside, he had nothing with which to supplement his craft. Rumours suggest Arton's eventual attack caused the scars that striped the Hive Lord's neck, and the fact that Nestor's voice had never sounded the same since the two met suggests validity. A further misfortune struck the rebellion as Nestor's formidable reputation had only grown from his survival and his broken voice only garnered further fear in his prey since that pivotal day.

Scattered records and former slave testimonies lead us to believe that an assassin gained entry during Hive Lord Nestor's tenure and was quickly and brutally subdued. This information can only concern Arton Bravlav and so sure are the writers of this history that they assume this to be so and offer no apology or disclaimer.

As an example of Cthonic resilience and dominance, Arton was kept alive as reference for any further rebellious ambitions, it is said that each time he would appear before other slaves his physical condition had markedly worsened and that by the time of his eventual death Mariahs were under strict instructions not to use Bolt Rods to subdue him lest his heart stop, and their woeful example become

207

obsolete.

Anonymous Author

Redemption

The shivering form of bean tentatively rose and limped his usual circuit around the black room, each footstep sending a cold ghost of feeling through his numb feet. The large tribesman could not think whilst sat still, an opposing trait to Callus who seemed to have been statue-still for hours, if not days. Pensively chewing on his finger, Callus occasionally looked at their silent neighbour and then at Bean as if they were his only assets in a grand plan. Eventually his head would slump, and a visible shudder went through him as he fought with himself and his rising hunger in the black cell that was slowly consuming their minds.

"Redemption" Bean spoke the word aloud and Callus looked up questioningly. Bean continued almost enthusiastically, like he'd solved a puzzle "Only you can do this, Cal. I've got nothing left; only pain and shame."

"What you sayin'?" Callus croaked with a hint of exasperation. They'd stopped whispering long since, as their fellow prisoner never spoke, they suspected his native language was not the same as theirs. He sat huddled in shadow with the occasional sniff or scratch but said nothing and offered nothing to their musings.

"You need to be strong; I know what you are, what you can do, dammit, I've followed Crave all these years!" the big man was becoming passionate, coming to terms with a long-buried conflict. He staggered over to where Callus sat and flicked his long hair over his shoulder with a wince. "You need strength and I need forgiveness," Callus creased his brow,

"Forgiveness for what?"

"For turning my back on my tribe, my people. I am a tribesman. I bring them shame, a stone I have carried for too long. I cannot carry it from this room. I am done. It's time to pay my price." His head hung, the hair sliding back around to cover his face. Callus stared at the man before him in silence for what seemed like an age. He finally opened his mouth to speak when interrupted.

"You two sorry shits don't need redemption. You need me, yes?" the silent prisoner stood, his bones crackling as he rose. He held out his hand. "My name is Arton. You may have heard of me?"

Callus
A light in the tunnel
But a hefty price

Just like that, the fella was in the room! I stood and took his hand, tried not to notice his pulse through my fingers. I was getting' so hungry, worried I'd lose control if I moved, but it felt right to stand and meet him. Bean was done for, he still crouched there lookin' sorry for himself, I wanted to tell him it was a tribe that had cursed me and Crave, that they were not worth the hurt he was feelin' but this Arton fella had offered some kind o' deal, it was worth hearin' him out.

"OK, you two must listen to me, now," he pulled back his hand and looked at it for a second, didn't like what he saw and put it behind his back. He talked like Dolomon, figured he came from Cthonica too, but there was no meat on him like our chunky friend. He was skin and bone and most of that was black and bloody, fella had been through hell before being dumped in that room.

"There is just one way to make it past the Bolt Rods. You need two, yes? One takes the hit and the other well, he gets the best job," he grinned at that, his eyes shinin' with somethin' real mean. "The rods, they take time to charge, yes? This is when you strike!" he clapped his hands together for effect, but it sounded like a damn kid's clap, fella was wastin' away. At this Bean looked up, was suddenly getting' interested. Arton went on, his long, tangled beard twitching as he spoke.

"Sacrifice! That's the only way, yes? Only two will escape, yes?"

"Ill do it." Bean stood up; suddenly keen to get involved, but Arton shook his head.

"No my friend, I have earned this," he slapped his chest with both hands,

"I will not survive the bolt, it is my time to go and it is your time to get out of here, yes?" he stepped up close to me, I could smell the rot on his breath, "You make them pay with blood, yes?" he gritted his teeth and said it again but slower, "You make them pay with blood, yes?" his eyes got big and he stared right into me, fella had madness sittin' right there just behind them eyes.

"He doesn't have the strength." Bean said solemnly as he shook his head. He looked at me and I knew what he was thinkin'.

"Only one of us leaves this room," he nodded slowly while pointin' at me, "And he makes them pay."

Crow Hoby
Still falling
At least I'm moving

If I were to be truly honest with myself, I would say that I went beyond my basic needs. I fed beyond survival and into the realms of luxury. Each slave that I ushered into those natural catacombs gifted me with strength and vigour beyond anything I'd ever experienced. I remained, to outside perception, a malnourished and mentally broken slave, but my soul seemed to burst with excess energy. The notion that Laz had planted in me to feed and ready myself for Crave had garnered a sense of purpose and somehow released me from my ever-increasing guilt.

I'd performed my tasks satisfactorily, and the Mariahs did not need to notice me. To them, I was just another wretch scraping an existence under their watchful and predatory gaze. Inside I was waiting, waiting for Cal to release me so I could finally unleash the building rage on my masters and put this hell into the past.

Had I not thrived on the hunt and the blood that it provided, I feel I would have eventually lost hope. As one day merged into another and the monotony of the crawling caves battered against my aspirations like a petrifying drip to my soul, I found excitement where I could, and lost the remains of my human youth.

Then, as I returned to affect the pretence of eating food after my morning's labour, my world shifted once again.

I stood as soon as the ceiling of the feeding cave allowed and stretched my back with a satisfying click. I felt strangely alive considering the amount of black rock I'd shifted, a feeling that seemed to intensify. It started in my guts, a vaguely familiar thrill that built as it moved through my body, a euphoria that was hard to suppress.

I went to the pot to pour myself some of today's thin slop under the ever-watchful eyes of the Mariahs; two on the door and one monitoring those with empty bowls, ready to send them back through the crawling caves.

I found my usual spot, on the outer edge, in shadow. It was the only place I could dispose of my food without drawing attention. Just as I stooped to sit, I felt a warm hand envelope my shoulder and a faint smell of burning hair invaded my nostrils.

"It's time." Laz hid in the dark recess, but his voice was unmistakable.

"You need to get yourself two friends and get to that there door right now." He sounded uncharacteristically serious. His hand gave me a strong shove, and I staggered back into the dim light. My mind spun. It caught me in an instant of indecision as a muted clatter came from the main door into the cave, its two guards suddenly looking at each other.

I grabbed two slaves by their upper arms and dragged them both to a standing position, noticing their wasted muscles and their inability to resist. Everyone focused on the door as the two guards stepped back and it swung open.

My inner excitement reached a crescendo, and somehow I knew exactly what I needed to do. I launched the two unfortunate slaves towards the door.

Time seemed to slow as Cal stepped through; one Mariah fired up his Bolt Rod. Cal fluidly grabbed the oncoming slave I'd shoved and spun dance-like to position the poor wretch between himself and the Mariah who swung his Bolt Rod into the wrong target.

Cal then reached over to the other Mariah and grabbed his weapon hand as the rod came alive with blue power. He thrust the guard's arm and rod

211

across and into his fellow Mariah; his strangled grunt echoed that of the slave as they both dropped to the floor immobile.

I looked on with a mix of shock and relief to see Cal again as the third Mariah barged past me to join the fray. I instinctively kicked at his back leg. The surprising strength completely spun his body as he careered onto the floor. I glanced up to see Cal dash the remaining Mariah's head into the framework of the doorway he still stood in. Slaves scattered as the tangled Mariah beneath me tried to get to his feet. His efforts died as my weight pinned him back to the floor and I sunk my teeth into the back of his neck.

I looked up at Cal, the spoils of my kill dripping down my chin. His eyes showed relief at being reunited, but shame and regret also lurked on his face.

He entered the cave and took in the cowering slaves all around, then he threw a sack bag to me, my belongings inside.

"We gotta get out o' here and quick!" I quickly dressed and strapped on my hatchet, and the Shotgun Laz had given me.

"You need to feed?" I asked as Cal gestured for me to hurry; he winced at the question and shook his head quickly.

"Any of you lot want your freedom, you better keep up!" He addressed the whole cave. A few rose, but many appeared broken beyond any ideas of a new life. Cal clasped his hand on to my shoulder and gave me a small smile before he looked around the cave and spoke up again.

"We're gonna need some of you!"

Chapter 40

Excerpt from "The Cthonic Orders."
   Chapter 9: Skelatin Society.
   Anonymous

During the initial onset of winter, the Cthonic Mine facility began its yearly stockpile of supplies to prepare for lockdown during the deepest of the frozen period. This short and swiftly changeable season meant many Mariahs were seconded to logistical duties to prepare for the closure of roads both to and from Cthonica itself. The period nicknamed 'the gloom' by many Mariahs and facility staff forced into unfamiliar operations and then cut off from the outside world until the snows thawed.

Without the constant shipping to the city, the facilities used this period to concentrate on manufacturing and processing raw forms of black to then later fashion into Skelatin. It was a dangerous and tense time throughout 'the gloom' as the volatility of troll product and raw black could spell disaster if treated without extreme caution.

It was also a time of reflection and low morale for those stationed at said facilities, as there was no line of communication to Cthonica until the ice gave way to the passes and roads that connected the nation. Sadly, historians agree this period led to an increase in the barbaric treatment of workers, as many Mariahs, and indeed senior leaders, found distraction in mistreating them and, with no real accountability in place, many workers suffered and died providing amusement for their masters.

Crow Hoby

The taste of freedom

Soured by shame

There was an element of guilt as the last of the escaped slaves dropped lifelessly into the snow. We both knew we had no way of keeping them alive, considering the cold. Cold that strangely kept at bay from me and Cal as we moved further into the dark wilderness of the new land. On our escape Cal had been savage, physically hurling the slaves into Mariahs to shield us from the glowing Bolt Rods, I try not to think back too often but I feel he encouraged escape just so he could use them as bait for our own freedom.

Escape we did, and as we emerged from that evil place, the world outside had completely changed. Thick snow covered the land and thick dripping claws of ice reached down from the surrounding trees. Cal eventually told me of his meeting with Arton Bravlav and all that he had passed to him, of his rebellion back in Cthonica and, importantly, how to get there.

The deeper we moved into the forest, the darker it became. It tested even our ability to see without light in the dense frozen forest. This was a time and place where humans did not stray, and we had to venture through to the other side in order to survive. Our goal was to find Cthonica and our companions. Laz's vision for me was to help the people of this place, and their rebellion seemed like the best place to start.

Our pursuers fell away as we buried ourselves deeper into the inhospitable valleys and hills, they presumed that the forest itself would finish their work for them but they were unaware of the physical changes that Cal and I now shared and the desires we had forged to right the wrongs of these people and their tyrannical society.

"Aint proud of what we did back there." Cal said after he called for a rest, it felt strange not to have a fire to focus on, but everything was frozen or wet for as far as the eye could see. We both looked at our boots.

"Me neither." There was a silence then; it stretched out while the creatures of the woods created their own music amidst the soft droppings of snow from branches above. In that quiet moment amongst the chaos of the last few weeks I mused I had failed, failed myself and failed my Ma. When she had died, nothing but my promises seemed to matter and I had vowed to hold back the forces of nature that ravage us unjustly. Now it seemed I was on the opposing team.

I eventually broke the silence, pushing away the shame and regret before it swallowed me whole.

"I saw Laz in there. Strange as that seems."

"Aint nothin' strange to me now, Crow." He looked up and I could just about make out a smile in the dark.

"He told me you were coming. I knew he was right."

"We got Bean to thank for us getting' away, ya know? I was done for. Bean and that guy Arton, they laid down their lives for us." Another silence as we came to terms with that.

"Then we best make it worthwhile." I said, trying my best to muster some enthusiasm while I sat there dripping wet in the dark. He looked up at me and nodded.

"Made a promise. Said I'd make them pay with blood. You in?"

"Where we go, we go together."

Callus
Knee deep in trouble
Usual story

Snow ain't somethin' I was familiar with. Yeah, I'd seen it before, back during the war I'd even marched in it, but this was something different. There were places you'd disappear if you walked in; it was so deep in parts we had to use branches to check the depth before we moved through.

When you're fightin' through the snow and concentratin' on where you're walkin', you get to thinkin' a lot.

At first I kept beatin' myself for how Crow had turned out, kept seein' him on top o' that Mariah with his blood sloppin' everywhere and thinkin' I'd let him down. Thing is, we were in it together and Crow was becomin' a man and not just any man, a man that was sharin' my curse. This curse had caused me some real pain over the years, but it had also saved my ass over and over again. Reckon the same could be said for Crow. We shared a purpose now, 'fact we shared more than one, and it just so happened all our roads were leadin' to Cthonica. We just had to get through so much damn snow to get there.

"What the hell was that?!" Crow was just in front when he stopped. There was a low rumble and the sound of lots of landing snow.

"Just keep still. Let's wait and see." I whispered, tryin' to keep us both calm. As we stood there, knee deep in snow at the foot of a ridge, the hill we were climbin' started to crumble and slide. Great boulders of snow started rollin' towards us and the rumble came again.

"In the trees!" Crow urged me as he moved as fast as the deep white would let him. I followed but watched the crumblin' hill. From above a large stone face emerged, followed by two arms.

"Troll!" we both pinned ourselves to thick trees and hope'd he'd not seen us.

"Arton said these woods were full of em' and they're not always asleep!" I kept my voice quiet and kept dead still.

"Why are you telling me this now?" Crow hissed back; he was not seeing the funny side.

"Aint no getting' away from it, Crow. We gotta cross this land, like it or not." He was about to spit somethin' back at me, but the beast was comin' close. We hugged them trees tight and kept our mouths shut.

From behind the tree, I couldn't see its approach, but the deep crunching of snow was getting' closer. Crow was itchin' to run, but I held up a hand, knew there was no runnin' in that snow. Then, as we stayed still and listened for signs that it'd spotted us, an almighty howl echoed through the woods, unmistakably a wolf's howl, and it was close. The crunching movement stopped.

Silence.

Before I could look, there was a massive crash that almost uprooted my tree, great damn chunks of ice rained onto me, and a loud whine filled my ears as I staggered forwards. There was blood, too. I could smell it right away, not human; the troll let out a loud roar that seemed to bounce off the sky, fella was enraged.

Crow Hoby
Knee deep in new experiences
Few of them pleasurable

I could not tear my eyes away from the troll as it clambered its way free of its snowy bed. At this distance, it seemed huge. Every movement sent a vibration through the snow and earth; I wanted desperately to run, but I looked over at Cal and he gestured to stay where we were.

I looked back and my eye caught a large black shape moving towards the beast, who was now completely free of the snow. Another on the opposite side melted through the trees. The shapes moved quickly. My mind told me they were four-legged animals, but my fear said they were too big.

Then the closest let out a howl that tore through the ice-choked forest surrounding us and more dark shadows converged on the stone monster. As I watched, transfixed, one shape made contact and suddenly came hurtling towards our position to smash into the tree Cal was hiding behind. There was an explosion of snow, ice, and blood as the creature impacted and then fell, sinking into the white forest floor. It was a wolf; it was near the size of a horse but a wolf nevertheless, now motionless and leaking steaming red into the blanket of white around us. Somehow, the realisation that it was a familiar animal eased my panic a little, but I was still keen to leave this battle behind.

Luckily, Cal was coming to the same conclusion, and we made our way from the fight as quickly as we could. All around us more shadowed wolves were joining the pack, the snapping, growling savagery echoed down from the hilltop as we fled.

We moved painstakingly away, relieved to discover there was no pursuit. The wolves were obviously using their numbers, attempting to take down the troll, attention fixed on their own survival. We trudged on in relative silence until we could no longer hear the echoes of the clash behind us.

The landscape was hard going, even without the deep snowdrifts and treacherous gulleys. Hills rose on either side of us. Every turn led us into a valley or a steep climb. On more than one occasion, one of us suddenly and alarmingly disappeared as we slid out of sight, eventually coming to a stop and climbing back to catch up.

Without sunlight, it was impossible to discern how long we trekked. It felt like days had gone by with painfully slow progress. My body hurt, not from the cold, strangely, but from the exertion. Every step was a challenge and an ominous feeling began throbbing within me. It started in my stomach, but soon my whole body felt like it was drying up and attempting to twist inside out. I tried to ignore it, but something was wrong.

"Cal... I" I remember speaking, but then I was on the floor. My body convulsed, panic surged inside me and increased the twisting, slow agony that was inflaming my insides.

Instantly Cal was there, knelt by my side. He looked grey, his brow creased. There was a small amount of relief to know that he was with me, and he'd know what to do. I stared up at the dark sky while he fussed with something out of sight.

"Knew this would come, eventually." He said as he worked. He was mumbling as if he spoke to himself rather than to me.

"Curse has gone far enough, tried to hold it off, but we gotta go through it, my friend." The pain kept intensifying as I tried to concentrate on the stars above. They blurred and shifted as I stared and Cal continued, as if distant.

"Not gonna lie. This will feel weird, and it's gonna hurt." I was losing sensation in my limbs. They were finally becoming cold, but my stomach seemed to relax a little.

"I'll be right here with you, Crow, you listenin'? I'll be right with you and when you come back, we'll get back to it, ya hear?" Suddenly, I couldn't see the stars anymore. Cal was covering my face. There was a threat of more panic, but I couldn't move my body to jump up, so I tried to embrace the feeling. I was covered and cold, sinking deeper into nothingness. My guts stopped twisting but something altogether darker and inescapable was approaching me, something that I couldn't outrun and made physical pain seem infantile.

"You just gotta lay down and die first."

Chapter 41

For the ultimate attention of The Grand Fraul of the Hive,
By the hand of Fraul Nemiah,
The Tower of the Hive
The Enclave of Orders
City of Cthonica

My exultant Mistress, Grand Fraul, Rachnis,

I write this letter with an update from the Cthonic mine that you have graciously left in my capable hands. Production levels of processed raw product are strong and see us easily meeting suggested targets before the Gloom descends and closes our supply routes through deep winter.

I have, however, a frustrating report to deliver regarding an attempt on my life. Unfortunately, a rebel from our great city has made his way to us and, through inside information and buried contacts, secured entry into this facility and prepared to assassinate me.

You will, I'm sure, be aware of Arton Bravlav, the notorious elder of the group, through his insurgent exploits over the last few years. You will be pleased to hear that we have thwarted this attempt and now have him. We are holding him as an example of the strength of the Hive and are using his insalubrious visage to inspire fear in those who would act against us. Now broken by our Mariahs, he has become somewhat infirm; no longer posing threat to our great nation. Equally, my agents are hard at work discovering the identities of those who granted his passage into the facility. We shall afford an equal level of tolerance to those who would plot against us from within and this will ensure this kind of situation shall not reoccur.

In other news, our new program of future security is also producing promising results. Training has begun in many cases, and thanks to our long-standing control measures, we have had very minimal resistance from worker's families.

I remain your loyal servant and continue to understand the sensitive nature of the esoteric and pioneering work you commission at our facility. I only hope to one day present our successes to you personally.

Yours faithfully,

Nestor Gradisan

Hive Lord,

Cthonic mining station Beta.

Anonymous Author

Machinations

Reverend Osset lifted his robes in disgust as he stepped from his carriage into the thick mud that seemed omnipresent in the slum-like outer district of Cthonica. Taking the offered hand of Joeson, his newly appointed priest for the region, the religious ambassador waved his other hand to his driver to stand him down, though the Reverend did not intend to stay long in this impoverished district.

They clearly threw the outer areas of Cthonica together with what materials the early builders could gather. This was in stark contrast to the inner city where curved black lines dominated the cityscape and spiralled towers reached towards the smog choked sky. Skelatin was expensive if you were not in the right circles of Cthonic society and so rare sections and repurposed panels stood out triumphantly in the shacks and shelters of the slums. As a gift, Sidian, Grand Maal of the Reach, had commissioned the entryway to Osset's new Church in sculptured Skelatin. The symmetrical black metal formed perfectly, creating a welcoming, if slightly overzealous, doorway into the sanctuary beyond.

Osset was resentful of the positioning of his first Church in Cthonica, but he also recognised the strategy of converting those with nothing initially as a foundation for a larger and eventually formidable religious community. As in all decisions, he'd asked God for the path to be presented to him and here it was, laid out before him, surrounded by mud and naivety. The Reverend entered the Church with barely a word to his priest. His immediate concerns were more related to his stained robes than the progress Joeson had made in feeding the poor within.

Inside, the Church was lit by small lamps that tainted the crude walls with an orange and oddly misty glow. The Reverend made his way to a rear room after a brief exchange with Joeson. The priest was passionate about God's work but focused only on his small yet gathering flock; a visionary such as Osset had eyes that always scanned the horizon and the matters beyond the short term.

"Reverend Osset." Vishtuum stood as the Reverend arrived, his once broad shoulders stooping further as he affected a small yet respectful bow. Osset smiled in return. His eyes flicked to the shadows behind, alert to more potential visitors.

"Grand Maal, Vishtuum." Had I known my visitor was so esteemed, I would have brought refreshments and surely arranged for a more… comfortable meeting place."

"There is no need, Reverend. I am not a man to be bought by pleasantries and refreshments." The Grand Maal's tone was serious and to the point, almost having the effect of dismissing Osset's smile, but not quite. The large man looked tired; he was clearly a man who enjoyed good health in his younger life, but the signs of weariness were all too obvious in his later years.

"I am told that you have garnered a personal relationship with our Grand Maal of the Reach." though not a question, the Grand Maal waited for an answer as he sat and gestured for the Reverend to join him. The insult induced a small cough as Osset held back his retort. They were in his Church after all.

"Merely a show of respect to my host, such as I would show to any of the Grand Maals and Frauls, I can assure you, Grand Maal."

"Yet you have failed to visit me." There was a silence then. It stretched across the small room. Neither occupant wished to fill it, yet it grew into an unseen defiance that served nobody until the Reverend changed the subject.

"How do you like my Church? It is young but the start of something special, I think." Osset's smile crept back into place, his mask of deference returned. His visitor leaned closer and attempted to summon the baring of a younger man.

"I am the Grand Maal of the might, Reverend Osset. Though we have allowed your work and have offered you welcome to this city, it would serve you well to understand where its power lies." The old man stared into Osset's eyes, a further attempt to intimidate the smaller man. With his statement made, the Grand Maal of the Might simply stood and stalked from the room. As he made his way back through the Church two previously unseen Mariahs slipped from the shadows and joined him as he left the building. Osset frowned and clenched his fists in disdainful anger.

"Oh, I know where the power lies, my friend," He gave a snort of derision, "and clearly you do not."

Fraul Nemiah passed through a myriad of Mariah guarded doorways without interruption as she progressed further into the Tower of the Hive. Like a spiral drilling deep into the ground, the curved corridors steadily wound past doorways and hallways as she approached the intentionally darkened quarters of Grand Fraul Rachnis. The Grand Fraul of the Reach preferred her quarters to be beneath ground level as opposed to many other Grand Maals and Frauls that chose the heights of their towers to oversee the various aspects of governing the city and its endeavours. Somehow, Cthonic society seemed to value the spectacle of its building and the heights of the towers. Often referred to as 'close to the sky', these dramatic heights had helped, over the years, to garner the idea that the Grand order had power close to those that were once called Gods in older civilisations. Grand Fraul, Rachnis went entirely against the grain and buried herself deep in the foundations of this new world that they had devised. Although a relative newcomer to the Grand Order, the foreigner made her home in the depths of the city, amongst its roots.

The air became cool and the lamps more irregular in their placement the deeper she went. Unphazed, she continued until the last lamp disappeared, pulling over her black hood to fend off the chill. She took hold of the thick cord that would lead her into Rachnis' quarters proper. She was used to the dark maze that led to the private chamber, but the pitch black tunnels could be treacherous without the wall mounted guide.

Eventually she pushed open the heavy door, releasing warm air and the orange light from the roaring fire of her mistress's private sanctum.

Draped on her shadowy bed, Rachnis grinned as Nemiah entered, a genuine grin. Typically, it was only in Nemiah's presence that she ceased to be a predatory creature.

"Oh, what tonic it is to see you, Nemiah. Please warm yourself." She gestured to the fire with a long, willowy arm. "I've been above all day. I grow weary of the men and their phallic contests." Nemiah smiled a knowing smile and briefly closed her eyes.

"They drain you so, Grand Fraul Rachnis. You are right to retire when you have the chance."

"Oh, they have their uses." They shared another smile; this one had a more playful edge. "but you are right. I must retire to my lair to rejuvenate when I am able. Do you bring any news?" Nemiah took a letter from her pocket and approached the bed.

"A letter from station B, a report, I would imagine before the passes close for deep winter." Rachnis' hand reached from the shadow, revealing the dark veins that wandered her pale skin. She almost snatched the letter with her eager hand and opened it.

"News from our project too, I would hope." She read the letter with interest and nonchalantly threw a question at Nemiah as she stepped to the fire.

"Vishtuum?" Nemiah smiled.

"The Grand Maal continues to behave as if you pull his strings. He went to visit Osset in the slums. He did not go alone, but he made his first move in the, how do you put it so eloquently... phallic contest?"

Chapter 42

Excerpt from 'Concerning Wraiths.'
By Rhona Hubbard.

What is a wraith? Not a question that is often, if ever, asked in Cthonic society. Indeed, so wrapped up in layer upon layer of fear and awe is the subject that it is a source of fear itself and one that is guarded by the Order. This position of defence could hint at their involvement in the phenomenon or, more likely, that the all-powerful and infallible Order have no answers to questions regarding wraiths and therefore see the exploration of the subject as an affront on their reign and their superiority. Indeed, it is considered subversive to not only explore the subject, but to even ask the question.

It is for this reason that I write within the protective embrace of a pseudonym, such a sad and demoralising state of affairs, but one that must be accepted if one wishes to pursue, or even share, wisdom in this glorious age of industry and evolution.

To the minds of many, wraiths are linked directly to faith and some kind of belief structure. This theory, however, crumbles time and time again with events entirely dislocated from religious groups or spiritual movements.

It is my opinion, albeit an unpopular one, that wraiths are an appendage of our own creation as a society. They are a by-product of a species grown too large for its environment, a side effect of our illusory rise towards Godhood.

To me their random, yet powerful effects upon the world during recorded encounters speak of a desperation to set things right. The powerful abilities and phenomena that they apparently wield comprise the area that causes the most academic challenge and, I feel, is the source of the common opinion that a deity of some kind grants this power.

An opinion I hope to dispel in the pages of this book...

Crow Hoby

Hopeful

Beyond the grave

I cannot say that I have experienced death, despite dying for the first time in those frozen woods, surrounded by dense vertical trunks and mounds of snow-laden undergrowth. There was no experience; there was nothing. I ceased to exist for a period while my body rectified the effects of time and my misadventures. My mind, thankfully anchored to my body, was also absent during this time, though the memory of the exquisite agony I went through immediately before my... passing remained a way to regather my thoughts and bring me back physically to that frozen forest.

Hours later, it occurred to me that had I not been fumbling towards the sound of Laz's voice as I awoke, I might have struggled to find my way in one piece, with memories intact.

This experience was akin to waking from a deep sleep. His rhythmic and nonsensical monologue was already in full swing before I realised what I was listening to. Once again, I later worried whether I'd missed crucial information as I clawed my way back to reality and understanding of his voice in the dark.

"... Like I'm always sayin' it's like that damn bucket, drip drippin' till there's no more room for water. Time to get a new bucket, but don't you go throwin' that one out. Everything still has its uses, even when you've moved on. You just gotta tune in is all. You got a new bucket just like everything else has." He didn't seem to care if I was listening, but I tried to centre myself in the blackness that I suddenly realised was deep snow. He'd buried me in snow! A panic threatened as I realised it was a struggle to move. My mind told me that the soft snow had frozen solid, it might encase me in ice forever more. I couldn't actually feel a speeding heartbeat, but I imagined that if I could, it would thump against my eardrums as it squeezed up my neck and into my brain, steadily increasing in strength and tempo. Then, before my imagination could completely turn on me, I felt a burrowing finger wrap around my wrist, then more fingers and an iron grip.

Cal pulled me from my frosty grave and into the pale blue night. I spat icy residue and wiped my eyes clean as I sat and affected to breathe deeply despite the newfound inability.

He looked terrible. Despite the temperature, the surroundings and the entirely polar opposite scenario I found myself in, I was reminded of the first time I'd seen him, the fear, the wonder and the surrounding crows as he's dragged himself across the desert and into my world.

"Let's move." With his ebbing strength he pulled me deeper into the woods as I silently recounted the last few hours, well those in which I was still alive.

We trudged a slow pace even though the terrain was angling slightly downhill. I occasionally shivered, a strange sensation that flittered across my skin, but it was more habitual memory than an actual physiological reaction; I could not feel the cold, though I could tell it was biting. Cal's gait was no longer the comical high kneed march. His legs slurred for want of a better word, forcing their way through the snow, leaving great gouges. I walked with an instinctive arm propped behind him, barely touching but urging him on while my mind reeled, searching for a solution to the inescapable predicament we were in.

Then, out of nowhere, came an edge. We were both of us focused on the immediate snow and when it suddenly stopped, we fell; only a few feet, but we landed in a crumpled heap. There was no explanation, no sense of heat or signs of a physical clearing, just an abrupt end to the snow, it created a three-foot wall behind us like a white barrier that we'd fallen from to arrive in this blessedly dry area.

We detangled and a modicum of mirth returned, a relief passed between us without a word as we stood. We were on the edge of a small, dilapidated hamlet. There were no signs of current life, but certainly people had lived there once. A few shacks with tattered roofs and a central clearing surrounded by a low wall. There was not a single snowflake within that vaguely circular perimeter.

Callus
Crow's first death
Bitter sweet

I was getting' alarmed.

I was hungry. No point in denying it, but more than that, I'd missed a night. Damn near no way to tell in them parts, but I know I'd watched over Crow when he'd gone, a full night he'd lasted before I pulled him out, it was his first time and damn I was angry 'bout having to keep him movin' after that.

I kept goin' for his sake, but I was driftin' bad. Had to get him some place safe before I could go. Could've cried when that snow parted like an oasis, only there was no water, just a beat-up little town, folks long gone.

We started kickin' doors in to find a place. Crow was near carryin' me by then. My head was wanderin' somethin' fierce. I felt the need to spill my guts about Bean and Bravlav.

"Rebellion!" I called out, suddenly sat up straight.

"Alright, just give me a minute." Crow had to keep leavin' me slumped while he scoped the place, then on to the next shack if it was no good.

"I can still see the sky in there, no good, just hang on, Cal!" I could hear his concern but just had to tell him where I'd been, what had happened in that damn cell.

"It's Dolomon's lot, Crow, damn it, it's Dolomon!"

"What is?" he was humouring me as he dragged my ass across the village.

"Bravlav! One of Dolomon's boys, he came for the hive Lord, but they caught him."

"Hive Lord?" Don't think he was all that interested, just tryin' to keep me talkin' while he went about findin' somewhere.

"Gradisan! Caught him and messed him up proper." I was furious at the man I'd never met, but my strength was like a child's.

"This is the one, Cal!" He'd found a place. I closed my eyes in pure relief while he banged and scraped about, a screech of a rusty hinge and he was liftin' me again.

"Here we go, Cal, time to rest." I could see him floppin' my arms around like they weren't mine; I tried to look him in the eyes but they were swirlin.'

"I took Bean, Crow, it's what he wanted! They both went down so I could get out!" He was closing the door on me then with a smile, I had to spit it out before it was too late.

"So I could get you! We gotta make 'em bleed Crow, you and me, we gotta make 'em bleed!"

Sweet blackness.

Crow Hoby
Blessed respite
Amongst the ruins

I closed the door on the shabby wardrobe I'd pushed over, yet another reminder of the early days of our relationship. Sitting on top of it for a time; I could hear his voice dwindling beneath me like that of a tired child as its brain dumps the rest of the day's thoughts before sleep finally wins the battle.

We had been on quite a journey. Physically, and emotionally, I was now an entirely new person. In fact, as I sat there fondling my now pointed canines with my tongue, the thought came to me; was I even a person anymore? The youth in me would have been filled with anxiety about that very question, but I just sat there; I'd seen enough and indeed done enough in my new world to render existential concerns irrelevant. I was who I was. Life was in front of me, and it took all I had just to keep up with it.

I sat there in the dark beneath a slate bare roof and felt oddly at one, complete.

I stretched my back and stood. My only immediate task was to feed. My stomach rumbled as the idea crossed my mind. I wondered how long it'd been since Cal had fed.

As I approached the remains of the wooden door to the outside, I caught a familiar smell of burning hair. I smiled fondly as I pushed the door open and was shocked as it revealed a huge inferno in the centre of the village.

The pyre was maybe twenty feet high and burned with a fierce intensity that seemed unnatural in its restrained tower of flame. It hurt my eyes to behold. I lifted my arm to shield the glow as the sound of the roaring fire intensified and buffeted my ears. Then deep within my head came a woman's voice, hindered by outraged fury and somehow a disbelief in my gall to set foot in that place.

"You return on your knees to right your wrongs. I will relish watching you try!"

Chapter 43

Crow Hoby
My journey continues
New levels of hell

At first my mind simply watched like a passenger as surreal events unfolded, then as my body was physically flung around the central clearing like a marionette, I felt as though perhaps I was indeed conscious and that something was very wrong. I had no control over my body or my reality.

My arms pinched at my sides as I flew around in the grip of a seemingly enormous and invisible child. The voice I had originally heard ranted incoherently inside my head; she was angry but gleeful as she paraded my body around the small village. The physicality of my predicament kept asserting itself in my mind; I could feel the air rush against my face as I swung around and see the breeze my motion caused as it brushed the remaining flora of the dead village. From my occasional vantage point, I glanced at the encircling snow wall that it held at bay. Suddenly, it felt more sinister than it had when we'd arrived. I was entirely immobile, and the terror was becoming overwhelming. The living nightmare I was suddenly part of made no rational sense. I kept trying to close my eyes to steady the world around me, but each time I would receive a little shake that would strain my neck, my feet wobbling like the head of a deceased chicken ready to be plucked.

Then, without warning, I slammed into the ground, my legs buckled under me and I cried out in pain. My anguish only seemed to cause more mirth for the entity that was toying with me. The voice inside my head seemed to shift from deep within me to right by my ear, though there was still no visual sign of its owner. She spoke like an elderly woman. The child suddenly vanished; this voice had a rich wealth of experience of this world and the suffering it could harbor.

"Before the burning, the agony and the screaming, before you brought your God, there was the sickness. Do you remember?"

I felt a sense of release then as I lay crumpled in the central oval of the bizarre hamlet; She was no longer watching me. I took a ragged breath and looked around the abandoned place. It was in better condition than it had been on our arrival.

Before I knew how, I realised she'd dropped me on grass peppered with small white blooms; the air was fresh and smelled remarkably pleasant.

My mind still spun; I had no way of understanding the experience I was being forced through. All around me, the quaint thatched homes were bulging with wooden adornments and splashes of bright colour. Planters scattered around and filled with greenery and bright bulbs of fruit and berries.

As I settled in my current surroundings, I felt an uneasy tightness in my wrists and neck. My skin became warm and then hot. As I scrambled around in a mild panic, the floor beneath my backside bulged and lifted, rolling me off as a small hump pushed its way through the earth. The tightness crept around my body, my arm pits flaring hotter and hotter as my panic increased and the lumps multiplied across the oval. My hands felt fat. As I looked at them, dark blue veins thickened and reached towards my fingers from the cuffs of my coat. Like rivers finding their way through mountainous flesh, the veins spread through my body, some visible, some beneath my skin and surrounding my organs. The surrounding bulges formed into prone forms of villagers. Some reached out as they moaned in pain. A girl beside me reached for me in desperation, her face covered by a cascade of lank sweat soaked hair; she tried to speak but her throat sounded thick and bulging; there was barely enough room for air to escape her distended neck.

I tried to scramble away but soon collided with another poor wretch behind me. All I could see were the bodies of villagers squirming in pain and suffering. Men, women and children surrounded me and each one begged for me to help them as I lay there bloating myself. Vomit threatened, but had no way of leaving my stomach. My eyes watered and my nose ran. Then time stood still entirely.

She came from the opposite end of the oval, dressed in rags and walking with a limp. The wizened old woman reached out to brush the outstretched hands of the villagers as she passed, her other hand held a nobbled, and equally ancient cane. As she touched them, the villagers climbed to their feet and followed behind her at an agonizingly slow pace. I dragged myself back to the far edge and sat on the low wall as she slowly gathered her flock and shuffled towards me.

My swellings vanished in an instant, my airways were open and the strains on my circulation eased immediately; the surrounding village was back to its dilapidated state. Only the pain in my legs remained from my crude collision with the ground. Nothing broken, but I would not be running any time soon.

The old woman was getting closer. Her gathering crowd also seemed to be free of their earlier symptoms. Stoic disdain displaced their moans and desperation, judgment and cold malice urging their approach. Each of them stared directly towards me, their pale faces focused only on me; their collective hate made me feel breathless.

The crone lifted her head as she stopped her advance; she was maybe fifteen feet away. The crowd fanned out to block my view of the clearing and then stopped.

Her eyes were pale and deep within wrinkled hollows; her eyebrows grown unruly, twitched as they untangled from a lock of thin white hair.

Her voice, not as powerful as when it had been ringing in my head, still sent a shudder through my entire body as she spoke.

"You brought this plague to us. This sickness that raged through our hearth taking children, parents, brothers and lovers without question." She spoke as though the accusation pained her, but she had already made a judgment. Though terror stuck my tongue to the roof of my mouth, I tried, with a warbling voice, to plead my case.

"It wasn't me; I've never been here before!" I sounded like a babbling child. She simply raised her hand to silence me, then pointed over my shoulder.

"She brought the plague, your mistress." I spun around to find a robed woman stood behind me. She had the baring of a powerful leader; she reached up to remove her hood as she looked upon the crowd with a smirk of satisfaction. Her face, when revealed, was so pale it appeared blue and dark veins reached out from behind her ears and the collar of her robes. Her eyes were both predatory and infallible. As I looked at her, the old woman behind continued to speak. Her voice was in my ear again and I started and spun around.

"But it was you who brought your God and the fire that finished her task."

Before me stood a mighty wooden pyre. It was over twenty feet high, a tower of broken planks and branches, smashed furniture and the trappings of village life. As my eyes climbed up the monstrosity, my mouth fell open as my gaze alighted on Cal, tied and thrashing at the top.

"Cal!" I screamed out in dismay. There was no sign of the old woman or the former residents of the village. I tried to move towards the tower of wood but found my legs to be steadfast. I could not move at all and the panic increased.

It momentarily blinded me as a torch was lit, and a sickening feeling threatened to consume me. The torch was in my hand.

I tried with all my might to stop myself, but my legs walked towards the pyre, the torch burning brightly aloft. There was a feeling that the old woman watched me, although there was no sign, only a solemn inevitability, as she controlled my diabolical actions. I pushed and pushed against my own muscles, but could find no purchase to resist.

As I arrived at the pyre, there was a familiar cracking sound that echoed around the village. The familiarity tickled the periphery of my mind, but I could not focus during my present predicament. The crack sounded again. This time, my burning torch splintered and flew from my hands. My movement stopped. I saw the shattered torch's flame disperse into the floor but as the relief caused me to look up; I saw there was instantly another in my hand!

There was another crack. This time I was unfortunate enough to see it shatter the stave and remove the ring finger of my left hand in an instant. Pain flooded through me, but I had no control of my body to brace against its effect; I roared my frustration privately in my head, the searing agony merging with the helplessness of the situation.

"Stop it, you damn crone!" it was Laz's voice. I suddenly realised that the cracks came from his rifle.

"There is nothing but vengeance left in my heart. Stay out of this, wraith." The woman retorted, also inside my head; I could feel Laz somehow pushing against her inside me, but she was so incredibly powerful. I continued my motion towards the pyre, the flaming torch held high whilst the stump of my missing finger sent throbs of pure torture through me.

"They're strangers here, woman, they's huntin' another man of God, they want him as bad as you do!" A chuckle of doubt, but I felt a hesitation.

"Go on stranger; tell me their tale while they burn." I was reaching out, the flames tangling into the wood, smoke gathering, when my mind's eye burst into flashes of memory. It was our journey. From meeting Cal to this very moment, images fired into my brain at such speeds I could not perceive them. I only knew they pertained to us.

There was a sudden and omnipotent pressure across the entire scene, like I was violently shoved onto the ground by an unseen weight, and the world went black. The last thing I remember from that horrendous event was her voice. It was gleeful again, but unapologetic as it whispered directly into my mind.

"Bring me Osset."

Chapter 44

Excerpt from "Tribes of the West."
Book 2 of "The Wise or the Woeful." series
By Snaaris the Seeker

It was no accident that I remained in the West for a further month than planned, though my tribe (an ancient word for family or kin) did not know of my plans. I'd heard rumours in one of the markets, of a tribe deeper into the woodland who elicited a degree of reverence because of its strong connection with the earth and its magic. I'd over-heard a local youngster use their tribe as a fictional set piece in a game. She'd mentioned the tribe's leader, Cazique, several times and he, it appeared, had secured a level of fame amongst the tribes of this region. Without informing my man or my tribe, I set about researching them and eventually understood the land in such a way that I could find their village should I choose to try. I brought the information to my tribe, who collectively proved not only their stubbornness but also their naivety in my vision and scope for the work that I remained committed to.

I was to investigate alone. This prospect was not a new one to me, as any reader of my previous books could attest to. I was more than capable of surviving in the harsh forests of the area. Using my tribesman heritage, my determination and my time-tested survival skills, I would visit this tribe and learn all I could; my readers deserved my dedication and so I would set off against the odds to bring them the knowledge and the truth that they deserved.

It was not a long journey, but had I not diligently researched the area and its lore, I fear I would have found myself impeded or indeed prevented from arriving. As it was, I arrived in the night. I was hungry and bore several wounds from daring escapes from the surrounding wildlife. The Tribe was sceptical at first, but my knowledge of their customs and language bought me acceptance into the tribe, for the time being at least.

The Narako tribe (this ancient word roughly translates to 'pure roots grow') were, on the surface, like any other tribe, they worked the earth and lived as one with the animals which they revered. They were hunters, teachers, Mothers, fathers and offspring; they seemed to live in relative harmony under the watchful eye of their leader, Cazique and his nameless advisors.

It was over a week before Cazique sent for me to meet him in person. This had given me time to gain trust and blend into the village, talk to many of the tribesmen and women, and ascertain what was lurking beneath the surface. My many journeys and adventures have taught me to be ever vigilant and to always read signs put before me, and I knew something was not right in the village. Something bubbled and stank beneath the surface and I made it my task to find out what it was. I only hoped that their leader saw the wisdom in accepting me into the fold so that I could help with whatever ailed this tribe.

Callus
Nightmares
And bonds

"If you lose bits, they don't come back." It was all I could think to say.

Crow'd climbed out the wardrobe and started rubbing at the lump where his finger'd been. He looked better for bein' in the box for a spell, but was still shaken from what had happened.

Wasn't the only one.

She'd snatched me up and put me on a fire's about all I knew. Later, when we left that crazy village behind, Crow told me what'd happened. He told me he'd agreed to bring Osset back to the village; apparently the old woman wanted him worse than I did. I found that hard to believe, but I figured Crow would have promised the moon if it meant he didn't have to set fire to me.

I get shivers just thinkin' about that night. I know how much fire hurts and I know without Laz turnin' up, I'd be gone. He was there when I dragged Crow to the wardrobe, didn't think to ask why or how, didn't really care, just wanted Crow to be safe again.

"She won't be botherin' you now partner, she's long gone to where we all go when were not here, can't say where that is or how long for, but I get the feelin' she's waitin' on you boys deliverin' before she wakes up again." The old man was in a good mood considerin'.

"You're in high spirits for a dead man." I sounded meaner than I felt. The fella had just saved my skin, but I was in a dark mood, just about sick of one thing after another.

"It's all about purpose." He said as he patted me on the shoulder. I just looked and frowned.

"You got a purpose and a job to do there aint no point in bein' an ass about it. Just get ya boots on and get walkin.' Ya hear what I'm sayin partner?" His smilin' was yankin' my crank, but I tried to put on a friendly face, tried to be thankful. I turned to him.

"I thank you, old man,"

He was gone. Damn if that man wasn't a mystery.

I spent the rest o' the time just watchin' over the box, tellin' myself if she came back I'd carve that old woman up good. Truth is, I knew she'd eat us both for breakfast, didn't like the idea that I couldn't protect us. Something dark got inside me in that village, maybe fear, maybe despair, I dunno, but it started eatin' at me and I didn't like it. Far as I was concerned, I wasn't never goin' back to that place.

Chapter 45

Excerpt from "Tribes of the West."
  Book 2 of "The Wise or the Woeful." series
  By Snaaris the Seeker

I had become pig sick of the chores Cazique had given me. My quest to infiltrate his advisors and spread my influence for a better future was temporarily on the back foot. He had me running all around the village, passing messages, feeding beasts, cleaning out the enclosures, anything but guiding his hand or helping with the tribe's dark secrets.

I took matters into my own capable hands. There was an area sacred to the Nakaro where, I was told, outsiders were forbidden. They told me something about this place being an area where the land joined with the animals or some such nonsense. I observed a lot of activity around this area, but nobody would speak of it. Even those that I had garnered trusting relationships with would swiftly move on from the conversation when I ventured to mention it.

One night, after a gruelling day of pointlessly moving soil from one growing plot to another, I risked a closer look. I had heard a sound which, to my sensitive ears, sounded like the cry of a youth in distress. I dressed and crept through the village to the sacred area, known as Navohandros (a term which translates to a place where the roots begin.) Although a few tribesmen and women were bustling around, I could use my skills of stealth and camouflage to blend into the shadows and approach the centre of the activity.

Cazique was there and as I arrived I caught the end of his speech to the gathered few.

"... It is the only way that we can strike a balance with the curse laid upon us *long ago. For this boy to live well, he must share the darkness with the light."*

There was a rumbling of agreement from the gathered people. I believe those present were Cazique's nameless advisors, though they were hooded, and the night was unusually dark.

A silence settled as Cazique and another man worked at a table and others came occasionally to replace items and speak in hushed tones to the elders.

From my position I could see very little, but I observed, at one stage, a thin arm lift from the table, which was then grabbed by Cazique himself and forced back down and out of sight.

The bizarre ritual continued into the night, but I saw little else. I crept back to my hut before the sun rose.

Anonymous Author
Smiling at the enemy

"Fraul Nemiah, how pleasing to see you." Sidian's finely garbed lackey gestured into the chamber with an overzealous flourish. Nemiah joined the assembled guests, dignitaries, ambassadors, and those simply endowed with excessive wealth as they voiced their anxious excitement. The Fraul of the Hive attempted to portray a genuine air of interest, though she could not shake the feeling that she was inspecting the enemy's military advancement. The entire event reeked of power play, and that was not Nemiah's area of expertise. Sadly, Grand Fraul Rachnis had refused to attend and so it fell to Nemiah to represent the Order of the Hive.

"I will not suffer his company with a pained smile while he flaunts his abominable competition to his gathered sycophants." The Grand Fraul had said as Nemiah read aloud the invitation.

"You must go though." Her eyes suddenly wide with curiosity, then instantly apologetic, "I am sorry, Nem; as horrific as it may be, they cannot know we refused his invitation." Rachnis mused with her little finger on the tip of her tongue. "If we do not represent the Hive, then all will presume that Sidian and his Thaumators are making a move against us in plain sight."

"Which they are." Nemiah said dryly. She had a way of cutting to the point whilst Rachnis blurted out poetic musings in her words and then made sense of them. Nemiah was quiet and direct, making her an extremely efficient tool and an excellent sounding board.

After an age of waiting and skillfully avoiding conversation around the room, Nemiah felt relief when the yellow lights flickered and dimmed all around the chamber; she smirked at Sidian's characteristic arrival, always a pinch more drama than necessary.

The Grand Maal of the Reach addressed the room as though he was about to ascend to the sky himself and take on the role of celestial overLord. His silent audience was entirely rapt by his contrived speech. Nemiah had no interest in Sidian's theatrics. Instead, she watched his Thaumators as they scurried around, preparing to let the crowd into their laboratory. He'd uniformly robed them in black with copper orange trims, to Nemiah's eyes a refreshing change from the mostly white with scattered black of Cthonic high society. How annoying for the masked workers to receive such vapid and naïve invaders into their workspace, she mused, wielders of such power yet possessed of such ignorance.

The show continued. Inside the lab, exuberant machinery supplied noise as it hissed and crackled, flashes of electric light quickly illuminating the entire room, then abandoning it to the shadows once more. The chamber was alive with energy, some familiar and some of a more organic nature. Large glass tubes racked against one wall, each of them taller than the average woman and filled with viscous black fluid. Evidence of the use of Magnite technology was everywhere and Nemiah caught sight of Broman, Grand Fraul of the Magnites, as he gazed upon the obvious advancements made to his inventions with a troubled twist to his brow. He would never initiate conflict with Sidian, despite the Grand Maal of the Reach's blatant move against the scientist. It was thanks to Broman and his Magnites' lifelong efforts that Cthonica had advanced so far since the founders took the city. Nemiah made a mental note to visit the old man, a man of peace. He would never condone conflict of any kind, but he would need allies if he was to keep his place on the council should Sidian render him entirely obsolete. The Hive could only benefit from allies with roots as deep as his in Cthonic advancement.

As she circled the strange apparatus and circumvented the more abhorrent guests, Nemiah mentally recorded the scene and its scientific wonders. Grand Fraul Rachnis would want to know everything, although she would almost definitely become enraged and probably take out her frustrations on some poor man from her servant pool.

Just before her slow wandering brought her towards Sidian himself, there was a low boom, and the atmosphere seemed to constrict. Nemiah felt the concealed blade in her thigh pocket pulling towards the centre of the room, and a visible discomfort spread throughout the lab. As it settled, Sidian raised his hands and instantly owned the audience's attention.

"Ladies and gentlemen, it is time." He made his way to a central area where one of the large glass tubes was being slowly lowered to the floor by thick Skelatin arms. A small jet of steam issued from each elbow as the arms straightened and then released their prize. Nemiah was actually a little curious. She edged her way closer, but not so close as to draw attention.

Two Thaumators approached and released locking mechanisms on the strange pod now sitting horizontally in the centre, surrounded by eager and greedy faces. Once the glass door opened and the black fluid slowly drained, the Thaumators retreated at a quick nod from Sidian.

As the lowering liquid revealed a large featureless face, there was an audible hush from the onlookers. Humanoid limbs took form, then the shape of a large human body and the blinking eyes of a newborn creature regarded the crowd.

The silence stretched as the massive thing lifted its arm and scooped up the remaining black goo from its eye socket and flung it aside. Its black eyes then scanned the crowd, eventually settling on Sidian, and it lifted itself from the glass pod. What at first appeared to be clothing remained behind in the pod, obviously some kind of restraint; the being was naked but for black wrappings that covered its groin. It looked human with certain organic modifications, sharp ridges at the elbow and knee and a heavy brow that hung low, shading the black orbs that peered out of deep sockets. The innocence and virginity of the newborn now gone as it climbed free and moved towards Sidian with the grace and balance of an experienced warrior.

The spectacle enthralled even Nemiah, almost forgetting the threat that this being posed to her order. It knelt before Sidian. The Grand Maal of the Reach placed one hand on its shoulder and smiled proudly around the room.

"May I introduce you all to Crawn, the first of my Nephilim."

The crowd erupted in applause.

Chapter 46

Excerpt from "Tribes of the West."
Book 2 of "The Wise or the Woeful." series
By Snaaris the Seeker

The tribe maintained their frustrating silence regarding the strange night ritual I had observed. I was losing faith that I would ever uncover the truth when circumstance, and my own cunning, placed the first piece of the puzzle in my lap.

They had asked me to chaperone a group of youths on a hunt; they were reasonably proficient, but I suspect the elders hoped that some of my talents would pass on to them if I were to take them under my wing.

I had taken the group into a steep-sided ravine where the hunting was bountiful, and I could also pass on my climbing experience. It was on the return up the cliff-side that my fortunes changed.

I crested the top of the climb with rope in hand and before I tied it to a nearby tree, I was able to pass on another jewel of wisdom, 'never let the outsider lead the climb.'

The fear caused by the group's mistake was the perfect tool to ensure they shared their knowledge with me, especially as I had been so generous with them.

They reluctantly told me about a half-breed tribesman who had once lived amongst them in peace until he had taken a liking to Cazique's daughter. The elders had cursed the half-breed and sent him into exile, but not before he had raped the girl.

The youths were deeply angered as I asked about the subject, but I suspect this was because of the despicable actions of this half-breed and the repercussions of his lawless actions. Before I could help them escape the ravine, I discovered that

Cazique and the elders had cursed the half-breed in such a way that he could never be intimate with another human again and he would be eternally shunned by the tribes, leaving him to roam with nothing but the memory of his deeds to fill his mind.

Fascinated, I enquired further into the history of the half-breed and discovered that his forced coupling with Cazique's daughter had given her children; children with... 'problems.'

Crow Hoby

The new world

And a visit from my old one

The distant city seemed to haunt the horizon for longer than expected.

As we picked our way through the landscape and eventually levelled with the plateau, Cthonica became silhouetted against a soft light that spanned as far as our eyes could see. The horizontal corona appeared to move against the spreading fog above the city but failed to permeate, leaving the alien place shrouded in shadow.

"Even the sun don't venture here." Cal said thoughtfully, "good for the likes of us." He gave a quick and sad smile as he picked up his pace. I caught up but got lost in thought as we finally approached the city. What were the likes of us? Two exiles from civilisation, shunned by the sun itself, that had left a trail of bodies and trauma. Laz had made out that we had a purpose, a goal to right the world, that we were to bring the change. How easy it was to find yourself on the opposite side when you were weary. Where was the triumph, the glory for finding this place? I look back on this moment often. It was a crossroads. We were on the verge of defeat with very little spirit left, but we kept walking.

It seemed all my thoughts were turning against me, but I kept walking. I found myself in a bubble of misery and self-loathing. So many memories lurched out of the void to take a bite out of my resolve. My Mother, her face barely remembered, brushed past my mind with a caress but was gone before I could truly picture her. I saw the faces of countless people that had suffered or died at my hands; they asked why, and I knew there was an answer but I was too tired to find it. I kept walking.

Before I could understand why or how, I was on my knees; my Pa was in front of me. He was sliding his blade along his whetstone and talking over his shoulder to his eager boy. That blade kept sliding. The sound sizzled all around us, and it never increased in speed, just kept on going, sharper and sharper as he talked. He flipped his knife over with a practiced hand and the sizzling scrape continued.

"It don't matter anymore, boy." He said as he shook his head. "What you've done is what you've done, can't change it. What you decided then is what you decided then, can't change it." The blade kept moving on the stone, Pa's confidence pushing it forward, then back. The practiced ear could make out the blade's song as it began, that ringing as it lifted from the stone.

"Don't matter what you're gonna do, not right now. That's what you're gonna do." He lifted the blade for the last time and the song rung out, the light catching the sharpened edge, a pure line of white light as he turned and looked at me with pride and satisfaction.

"It's about what you're doin' right now, boy." He smiled then, such a beautiful smile, full of pure joy at that very moment. In that smile, I saw his reunion with my Mother, his integrity in the decisions he'd made in his life, and the pure pride he had in his boy. There was nothing else, just that very moment, and that smile was beautiful.

"It's about what you're doin' right now, boy."

Callus
Gates of Cthonica
Osset's new home

The outskirts were mainly growing plots, patch after patch of out of season beds and abandoned tools. We walked up the main drag, not talkin', just pushin' on. Eventually we started seein' people goin' about their business and eyeing us, not aggressive, we weren't no threat, the state we were in; practically carryin' each other. The shacks and walls got more regular, more people, livestock in cages, people sellin' their wares. Here and there were plates of the black metal that was everywhere in the mine, Skelatin they called it, looked like the inner city got built of it but on the way in, just the odd panel.

I realised Crow was slowin' down, kickin' his legs together more often. He hadn't said a word in a while, but I was keen to get inside the walls and find a place to rest. I put my arm around his waist and gave him a little push to keep goin', but eventually he dropped.

I got in front and put my hands on his shoulders. He was mutterin' something, going through somethin' on his knees. I gave him time, could see he would make it back on his own.

"Do you need help, friend?" I heard a woman askin' behind me, but I kept my eyes on Crow. I heard her get closer. It made me uncomfortable. She crouched bedside me as I held Crow. He was startin' to blink his eyes. She was a ragged worker, had dirt on her face and a couple of teeth missing.

"There is a place to get help." She seemed as nervous as I was; she nodded further into the maze of shacks and low buildings.

Just then, Crow came around.

"It's about what you're doin' right now." He said, lookin' straight at me.

"What's that?" I asked, but he didn't answer, just shook his head and smiled.

"It doesn't matter. Let's go." He stood up then, straight as an arrow, wobbled a bit and looked around.

"You had me worried then." I looked at the crouching woman as we stood; she hesitated and then gestured for us to follow.

"This way." She said. I looked at Crow.

"You good?" I asked, tryin' to keep from soundin' too worried. He smiled again and nodded.

"I'm good."

We followed her through the little town and as we got closer to the inner city, saw the huge black Skelatin gate that led inside. Mariahs stood watching as people entered. They weren't very alert, obviously got little trouble.

"Where are we going?" asked Crow.

"Somewhere safe to get help," I nodded at the local, "apparently."

We followed, and I tried to remember where we were so that we could find our way back to the gate. The streets seemed to have sprouted up randomly, no straight roads to be found. We eventually stopped at a fancy black doorway that seemed to prop up the rest of the building. The woman gestured inside; she didn't talk much, which was fine for me.

We went inside. The place was lit by little faint lights just like the ones we'd seen on the ship so long ago when we'd arrived in this land. She took us through and into an open room full of benches. I already wasn't likin' the look of it. Then she confirmed my suspicions.

"Reverend!" she shouted, and I swallowed hard, fightin' off black memories. I looked at Crow.

"Reverend!" she shouted again. I wanted to get out of there right away; I looked back at Crow again.

"It's a damn Church. Let's go." I grabbed Crow's shoulder and moved him towards the way out when a man stepped in front of us, barring our way. He was smilin' but he was in robes I'd seen before. Memories of Wilf and Osset hit me, and I reached for my hatchet. He was holding out his hand and smilin', had to admit he looked genuine.

"Please don't be alarmed, my friend. You are safe here." Crow stepped forward and took the hand while I watched like a hawk.

"My name is Reverend Joeson."

Chapter 47

Excerpt from "Tribes of the West."
Book 2 of "The Wise or the Woeful." series
By Snaaris the Seeker

The tribe youths I had nurtured were nothing if not loyal. As soon as we returned to the village, they admitted to Cazique that they had revealed the tribe's past to me despite the sacred nature of their secrets.

They punished me unfairly.

They made me enter the Navohandros as a slave to the half-breed's offspring. They were, each of them, disfigured abominations filled with hatred and fury.

They made me fetch and carry, clean and nurture; there was no gratitude, only disdain as I arrived each day to tend to them.

It was common among the Nakaro to name their offspring based on traits that they expressed during childhood. Sidian (meaning echo) was the only child that did not take offence at my presence. He was unconscious throughout my time with the Nakaro. I discovered it was the boy who was the victim of the strange ritual that I had observed. Attempting to calm the boy's spirit, they had adorned half of his entire body in strange, white symbols. Apparently, this was to bring balance and harmony to him. When he awoke, they said that he would no longer be so vengeful.

The boy Crave was another matter altogether. Scuttling around in the corners of his hut covered in his own filth, skittering around like a damn insect, the boy repulsed me. On more than one occasion, I had to discipline him as I entered to deliver his food or change his crib. It became a relief when my duties involved Sidian or the sisters who, compared to Crave, were relatively normal.

Eventually I had my fill of the village and I hesitantly asked for permission to move on, had they not permitted me I would have disappeared into the forest during the night but my extensive knowledge on tribe etiquette told me it was the polite thing to do. Cazique granted me permission to continue with my travels and to continue my work. I must state that the man had little of the bearing I expected from the tales I had heard; he was a man clearly weighed down by the troubles that came hand in hand with responsibility.

On my final day I sensed conflict within his advisors, I suspected that many of them did not want to let me leave, that they still had much that they wished to learn from me, but Cazique held their angry frustrations at bay and bid me farewell.

I was glad to leave the village and its ugly offspring behind, although I still ponder the fates of these malformed children and occasionally I shudder at the memory of the hatred directed at me from the boy, Crave, so unnatural and such a pointless existence.

Anonymous Author

The setting of traps

The Grand Chamber of the Order was itself a depiction of the rise of Cthonic society from the properties of the earth to the majesty of the sky. Essentially, a gargantuan chimney that rose from deep within the ground and opened up like a black metal flower to the choked sky far above. The seats of the Council members positioned around the circular chamber directly across from each other, therefore, connected in one respect but separated by a gulf and bottomless void in another. The Skelatin work on the chamber was sculpted in such a way to allow the council member's voices to travel effortlessly across the expanse. Vorce, Grand Fraul of the Voice, sat at the head, a little higher and so a little louder than the rest of the orders. Cthonic dogma permitted her to host her elite guard around her seat. The Order of the Voice was not considered superior but deigned to carry the voice of the founders and therefore the ultimate word in any balanced votes. They were loyal to the founding principles of Cthonica beyond all other concerns.

Silently, the members of the Grand Council arrived and took their seats, straightened their ceremonial hats and garb, the metallic details sending faint light beams around the chamber as they moved. Their robes were woven from minuscule threads of Skelatin and adorned with minutia of gold, silver, and copper to represent the metals that had given rise to their society from the earth.

"From earth to sky." Grand Fraul Vorce started the proceedings with the standard statement set by the founders.

"From earth to sky." The leaders of the other orders echoed the phrase in a homogenized mumble, Sidian, Grand Maal of the Reach coming last, his voice standing out with practiced oration; beneath her ceremonial hat, Grand Fraul Rachnis rolled her eyes.

The meeting began with a report from each order, an update on the dealings of their particular specialism, each of them twisting their news slightly to further their own goals and shine before the assembled leaders.

Rachnis, in her capacity of Grand Fraul of the Hive, told of the approaching end of winter that would allow her facilities to once again continue production of raw materials to, eventually, send to the Order of Magnites for creating Skelatin. Grand Maal Broman gave a slow grateful nod but a disrespectful snort from Grand Maal Sidian suddenly silenced Rachnis' report.

Rachnis' nostrils flared, but she spoke calmly, almost Motherly.

"Does the Order of the Reach have a pressing point to interject into my report, Grand Maal Sidian?" Every face turned to Sidian, and he sat up straighter. He always seemed to grow an inch when gifted with attention.

"I merely grow weary of the ancient barriers to our success, Grand Fraul Rachnis. With infinite respect I find it difficult to believe that your production must halt to allow for winter, surely a way can be contrived to remedy this?" Rachnis bristled, she knew exactly where he was leading the conversation but before she could speak up Grand Fraul Vorce retorted.

"Grand Maal Sidian, though your point has some validity you would do well to remember that we built this Council upon 'ancient' ways and

251

principles."

"Of course, Grand Fraul Vorce, no disrespect intended. I only aim to hasten our transcendence to the sky, as do we all." Sidian's gaze met Rachnis' briefly before he continued.

"I will soon be in position to provide Grand Fraul Rachnis with the help she needs to maintain production throughout the deep winter, therefore increasing the overall output considerably." Rachnis' cheek muscles strained as she clamped her teeth together, making the blue veins of her face writhe with her fury.

"How kind of the Order of the Reach to look inwards for ways to help, despite its own responsibilities to seek resources from outside Cthonica." Rachnis said with a sweet yet predatory smile before looking at Vishtuum to contribute. The Grand Maal of the Might gave a small cough before speaking up.

"My Mariah's are more than capable of assisting the Order of the Hive with production, Sidian. It is not strength that is lacking but a change in logistics needed through deep winter." Sidian's eyes narrowed, noticing that the old Maal had failed to address him by his full title, an omission that would not have gone unnoticed by the gathered leaders.

"Grand Fraul Rachnis has other concerns to busy her facilities during those weeks, concerns that also assist in our transcendence." Rachnis looked sharply at Vishtuum to silence him, had they not been in the Grand Order's chamber she would have released expletives under her breath.

"And what other concerns does Grand Fraul Rachnis have during these weeks, I wonder?" Sidian smiled as though his trap had sprung and the victory was his. Rachnis raised her head, adjusting her posture to mirror that of Sidian.

"Grand Maal Sidian, although I respect your commitment and interest in the business of other orders, I feel that, as a newcomer to this council, you are lacking the essential knowledge of how the orders work. I do not meddle in the reach's business and it's Thaumators and I expect the same consideration from you; the Hive is mine to command, and I do not need your help to increase my production."

"I had noticed your absence at my event and accepted your disinterest in our success but…"

"Enough!" Grand Fraul Vorce's voice silenced all others, the sound sculpting of the chamber working perfectly.

"Is there any other business to discuss other than the petty squabbling of infants?" The Grand Fraul of the Voice was not angry. She showed no emotion, just an authority that was hard to ignore, particularly when amongst her warriors.

"I… I would like to discuss a promotion within my order." Broman stuttered his way into the discussion, clearly flustered by the conflict in the room. The Grand Maal of the Magnites was a quiet man; he rarely brought anything to discuss other than the unveiling of his inventions. Since they had elevated Sidian to the Grand Order, Broman's voice was repeatedly overpowered. All eyes settled on the small man, his statement an instant relief from the usual bickering.

"I would like to elevate Fraul Bindu as my second." Bindu had reported to the Grand Order before, during an illness that kept Broman in his bedchamber for a time. She seemed a driven and organised woman, an asset to the Magnites.

As was customary, Vorce asked for any objections to be made clear and the surrounding council members offered none.

The Grand Fraul of the Voice slammed her gavel down and pronounced Bindu as Fraul of the Magnites. Sidian gave an almost imperceptible flinch while Rachnis smiled openly.

After the meeting, The Grand Fraul of the Hive returned to her quarters with her smile still in place. Fraul Nemiah was waiting.

"You seem uncharacteristically happy, considering where you've been."

"We have had a victory, Nem, despite the old fool Vishtuum swinging his stupid fists into a fight that wasn't his. We got exactly what we wanted."

"Bindu?"

"Yes, Bindu's elevation is complete." Rachnis rubbed at her aching hands. She'd been squeezing her fists throughout the meeting. Sidian often had that effect on her, sore hands and an aching jaw.

"Whatever Sidian thinks he's doing will soon not matter. The sisters are rising, Fraul Nemiah." Rachnis said fondly as she removed her ceremonial robes with undisguised disdain.

"Finally, women will rule this city and we will force the men where they belong." She lay on her bed and put her hands on an imaginary head between her thighs, then she slammed her legs together in a chomping motion. They both laughed comfortably with hungry eyes.

Chapter 48

Missive to Grand Fraul Rachnis of the Order of the Hive
From Grand Maal Vishtuum of the Might,
Discovered in the archives of the Bravlav family, Cthonica

Dearest Rachnis,

Let me at first assure you that should the seal on this missive become broken before its arrival I have instructed Fraul Brontja to execute the family of the messenger, you may toy with him, and do as you wish but such are Brontja's talents in intimidation it is highly doubtful that he will break his oath.

Although I have agreed not to contact you in this fashion, I felt the circumstances warrant a last communication outside of personal meetings.

You were right, as always, about the resurgence of rebel activity born from the ashes of the Bravlav family. This figure, calling herself 'Mother', has made several threats and has actually stood against my Mariahs during active duty. It is, however, the threats that I have received that present the most pressing concern. In these handwritten letters this 'Mother' explains that she is aware of our project in the Hive mines and that should certain rights not be offered to her, she will endeavour to share her information with the rest of the Cthonic Order.

I know that you have scolded me in the past for giving weight to rebellious rumour and conjecture. I therefore thought it prudent to inform you of these threats before taking any action. The threats also insist that we end our project in the mines, but I do not see how we could oppose Sidian without continuing our work to build the recruits of the future. It is not as if these slave children have a chance at a life any better than the ones we are orchestrating for them.

I trust you will know how to respond to these threats, and I trust that our relationship can continue to blossom once we nullify them. Have no fear. When I receive your thoughts on how to proceed, I will swiftly destroy our enemies and leave no room for future rebellion, such is the strength of the Order of the Might.

I have also heeded your wise council and allowed Fraul Brontja into my confidence regarding our alliances and our future endeavours; she is ruthlessly efficient and has a predator's eye for pathways to advancement; I am confident that she will be a true asset in our joint campaign for power.

Yours, Vishtuum

Crow Hoby
Finding more oppression
The City of Cthonica

"Don't be silly, it's really no trouble to find someone to help; we can't let you wander the city for the first time without a guide, especially as there's a blessing approaching." Cal and I looked at each other. There seemed to be no polite way to avoid having a chaperone.

Despite Cal's instincts, Reverend Joeson seemed to be a good man. He'd insisted that we not carry any weapons in the Church, but he had provided a cupboard to stow them in our shared room. I found the request reasonable. Cal barely spoke in his presence, his body instantly coiling when he was around, but so far there had been no conflict and only kindness on the Churchman's part.

I'd not asked him about it for fear of being impolite, but the Reverend's accent sounded more akin to those back home than the denizens of this new land. Here they spoke more like Dolomon; with brash, stabbing rhythms and seemingly broken sentences, making my voice sound more like a drawl, which insisted on animating my entire face.

We eventually made our way through the ominous black gate as we followed our over eager guide from the Church.

She literally intended to hold my hand as she beckoned us from the Church and into the city itself. Luckily, Cal stepped between us and gently but firmly pushed her hand away from mine; she looked offended and confused for a moment, but then her excitement returned, and she waved us deeper into the towering city.

She spoke non-stop as she pointed out buildings and areas around us at high speed. I eventually stopped listening and just stared in amazement at the place. It was incredible. Most structures were Skelatin and rose like black seashells, twisting as they reached towards the sky, seemingly miles high yet sturdy and proud. These towers interconnected with walkways and ramps everywhere. The city had grown vertically as it had developed, creating layers of vast floors that held courtyards, strange machinery and more twisted structures. Curved and spiralled ramps connected the entire city; not a set of steps to be seen.

It was no surprise that Cal was silent and just as awed as I was. He stared around and above at the marvel of this alien place and occasionally bumped into passing citizens who scurried away, nervous in the presence of newcomers.

As one woman, head to toe in a voluminous black dress with a somehow elitist bright white hat, stepped out of our way, she gave an annoyed shake of her head. The white lace of her head wear flopped around as she stomped away and drew the attention of two nearby Mariahs. I watched them from the corner of my eye as they approached through the crowd. Fear and dark memories from my time in the mines threatened to force me to run or fight. They did not reach for their Bolt Rods but swaggered over with an air of absolute superiority; Cal had not noticed; he was engaged in staring at the brooding black clouds in the sky. Our guide, who, I suddenly realised, was anonymous, stood a few metres ahead and had also noticed them. She had the worry of potential conflict written on her face. Should she intervene and attempt to protect us as our sponsor, or stay out of trouble and remain ahead? She was clearly afraid of the Mariahs.

"It's daytime." Cal said, looking at me with a smirk. His statement completely distracted me from the imminent peril of the Mariahs. I looked at him questioningly, and he pointed at the sky.

"The sun's up but it aint gettin' through those clouds." I realised what he was saying, and I realised we were both out in the middle of the day and were unaffected. Until then, it had seemed that this land was permanently dark, like there was no sun and the people worked and lived as they would in the daytime, despite the light coming from the tall lamps scattered around. Now a faint glimmer of sunlight was visible beyond the enveloping smog above us, desperate to illuminate us but unable to penetrate the clouds. I smiled at what that meant, but with the realisation came confusion, would we still need to sleep, or 'die' as Cal liked to put it?

Suddenly, I snapped out of my musings when a hard shove almost knocked me off my feet. I spun to see that the Mariahs had arrived and greeted me with both hands. Instantly, Cal became alert and poised to launch himself at the two potential assailants.

Our guide had made a brave decision and thrust herself between them and us with her hands held high and her voice panicked and shrill.

"Please, please do not take offence; they mean no harm!" she looked pleadingly at the two silent Mariahs who just stared back, emotionless but for a half-formed snarl on each of their mouths.

"They are from a far place where their language is not so good. Please understand." The woman clasped her hands together desperately as they eyed us all. Then one of them spoke.

"You will explain our ways to your guests before you present them to the city, yes?" The woman nodded wildly.

"Of course! Thank you for your leniency. I am at fault." The Mariah who had spoken just stared at the woman without emotion.

"The blessing siren will ring soon; you will take them from the city and teach them before you return."

"Of course, that is what I should do, thank you!" the woman turned away and grabbed my hand as they left. I shook away her grasp as she attempted to pull me back towards the city gate. Aggression was coursing through my body, and I stood defiantly. The display of dominance had somehow triggered my instincts to stand against this oppression. With the Mariahs now returned into the crowd, I directed my anger at the woman, the poor Church goer who had offered to guide us with innocent generosity.

My entire body clenched, but I fought the impulse to release the mounting fury. Somewhere deep inside me, I knew she was an innocent party, but I could not stop my urges from sliding towards violent intent.

Then Cal stepped between us and smiled at the woman. It was his broad and rare smile, the one that could not hide his fangs as they poked over his bottom lip.

"Thank you for lookin' out for us. My friend just needs a minute. Why don't you go on back to the Church and we'll follow soon enough." The woman was clearly fearful of Cal, but she retorted in her shrill and urgent voice.

"But the blessing! You must come now. If they catch you out during the blessing, it will be the end for you! All of us, we must be in our homes!" her pitch was getting higher and higher. I saw Cal's jaw clench, but he stayed still and silent as she continued.

"Please, you do not know our ways, please come!" the desperation in her had obviously got to Cal too. He lifted the back of his hand.

"Git!" Cal's command did the trick, and the distressed woman scurried away. He turned to me. He also harbored barely contained fury in his eyes.

"Let's eat."

Callus

Hungry

In the city of greed

The Mariahs, and then the tightly strung woman, had riled me good, more than she should've, considerin'. I turned and recognised the look in Crow's eyes. It was daytime, and we'd not fed in some time. I wanted to see what this blessing was all about too, so I figured we'd stick around and stay out of sight.

We moved through the city, now avoiding Mariah's and the locals; they were all in a rush to get home and takin' no notice of us.

We got ourselves higher, better vantage over the city and damn was that city a sight. I'd never seen nothing like it, tower after tower with bridges strewn all over the place, so much black metal everywhere you looked, and the lights, hundreds of 'em peering out from walls and lamps, windows and doors. The place was wild and not in the way I liked it. Still, we were not havin' any trouble from the sun, so things were lookin' up.

We found a place to climb up, in a corner without lights where two bridges joined up. We could see down below and watch as they all started clearing the streets. It was like a damn army was comin'.

Then there was the siren. It started in one place, then spread round the city, a long and screeching noise like nothin' I'd heard before. The people walked faster, even ran, and before long, they were all gone.

Cal started to say somethin', but I put my finger to my lips. 'far as I was concerned, we were stalkin' prey. Might be an unfamiliar land, but huntin' was huntin'. We'd take our time and quietly wait it out.

After a while rain started fallin', not on us, we were under cover but all around us you could see it drop. As we watched, I figured somethin' in my head.

"It's drainin" I whispered to Crow.

"What do you mean?"

"Look at the shapes, everything's pointing down, the rain's all running down."

It was quite somethin' to see if I'm honest. All the ramps and bridges, all the platforms above and below, all had little rivers runnin' down 'em.

"Must be collectin' it all down below." We both watched, amazed, then we saw people movin' about, all robed up in waxed black robes with big hoods. They were walking around in twos and pullin' levers, turnin' wheels, settin' up huge funnels and slidin' out panels on the buildings. Crow was lookin' confused.

"But why do they need so much? Why go to all this trouble?" I was about to offer an idea when an unfamiliar voice piped up. We both jumped.

"To sell it back to us." There was a fella three metres away skulkin' in our spot and we'd not noticed. I reached for my hatchet before I remembered I'd left it in the damn Church.

"Easy, my friends. I am not a threat to you, only to them." He nodded down below to the fellas doin' all the work. He held up one hand, the other was holding him in position up the wall and in the shadows.

"What are you doin' lurkin' in the shadows?" Soon as I'd said it, I saw the joke. He laughed, quietly but comfortably.

"Just like you, friend, yes?" he was smilin' and I couldn't help likin' the man. He'd got the drop on us but wasn't attackin' and meant us no harm; far as I could see.

"Joking aside, you really shouldn't be out here if you don't know where you are; the Mariahs will kill you on sight if you're out during the blessing."

"What's the blessing?" Crow asked.

"I have already told you, when the rain comes, they collect it all and sell it to the people." He was shakin' his head as he spoke.

"They sell the rain?" Crow couldn't believe what he was hearing; I had to gesture for him to keep his voice down.

"Everyone needs water, my friend, and The Cthonic Council are happy to sell it to the people."

"But why do they all have to go home?"

"They couldn't have people collecting their own water, could they? Then there would be no need to buy it from the Council." we both nodded in understanding. This city was a strange and ugly place.

"So, who are you?" I asked our new friend. His clothes were ragged but the perfect shadowy tones to blend into the area. I figured that wasn't no accident. He thought first before he answered, and chewed on his lip.

"We are the ones that stand against the council, all of us. The ones that stand against them." He jabbed his finger down at the two figures passing beneath us. "The Magnites aren't the biggest issue. They're just the workers, the ones with the ideas. It's the Mariahs that cause us all the biggest problems, the Mariahs and their cursed Bolt Rods."

"We aint strangers to them Bolt Rods." I said, and the man smiled as if recognising a brother.

261

"Then you should join us, my friends." He said with a big old smile. "But first you need to get indoors, you are not safe here, not until you know your way around the city, go!" he said as he swung himself round the pipe he was holding up to the level above, then he was gone.

"Perhaps he's right, Cal. This city is strange, and I don't understand the rules, do you?" I shook my head slowly.

"It is one hell of a damned city, and we don't know who to trust."

"We need to find the others if they made it here." I nodded again,

"Strength in numbers." Crow nodded. "But first we got business down there." Crow followed my pointing finger to a lone Magnite as he rotated a creaking wheel that didn't want to be moved.

"I know hunting, whatever city we're in, and I know something else."

"What's that?!

"Sellin' water from the sky aint right."

Chapter 49

My Brother,

    I write to you with the most exciting yet daunting news.

    Before you went into lockdown, they filled the streets with the whispers about this 'Mother' who claimed she could unite the gangs. I, like you, thought her another fool who would stick up her head and get it chopped by the Council! Even the Bravlavs have been quiet of late, and word is they have lost their teeth.

    She organised a meeting, this 'Mother' and again everyone thought her a fool. We agreed to go along, but armed to the teeth, I think everyone was. It was so strange to be in the room with so many rivals. She met us in an old Magnite water plant near the coast. Brother, they came from everywhere! Klinskeys, Street Teeth, even Ronin were there, all eyeing each other, itching to fight over old wrongs. It felt like a Council trap as we waited, me and Gruno stood around like nervous kids, about to get locked in the schoolroom!

    When she arrived, everyone went quiet. I mean everyone! Her soldiers came first, all robed and hooded, then she walked in carrying a sack. She started off by getting a few backs up, said she thought we were all weak, keener to fight amongst ourselves than stand up to the Council. If it hadn't been true, I think they would have had her in pieces, but believe it or not, they listened!

    She went on about how together we could stand and have our way, said something about a plan to find soldiers and start a war. I have to admit she sounded confident, and she kept us all quiet while she spoke. Then, when she'd finished, they started jeering and moaning.

    "How can we dare to fight?"

    "The Mariahs," this and "the Mariahs," that,

"The Council's too powerful,"

Gang members started turning and lost interest, thumbing over their shoulders at the newcomer, shaking their heads at her foolish ambition.

Then it happened. Just like that, she lifted her sack in the air and untied the string.

Something heavy flopped out and rolled amongst the gathered thieves and ruffians. As it rolled, there was a stink that filled the room and a hush as we all held our breath.

"Like it or not, today you have joined my cause. Every one of you has joined the war; it's time to fight or die." She spoke like she could scream, so full of anger and confidence. Her soldiers barely moved as people made their way around the room to see what she had dropped; I was one of the last.

When I finally got through the crowd, I looked down at the severed head of Grand Maal Vishtuum. His dead eyes stared up at me, his mouth slack, his face no longer cruel and his power no longer infallible.

The rebellion has begun, my brother; it's time to come home.

Anonymous Author
Forced hands

It was approaching the end of the first hour of the blessing. The rain had gradually thickened as it fell through the perma-smog and dropped to the hungry ducts and channels of Cthonica, eventually disappearing beneath the city into those realms operated only by the Cthonic Council and their minions.

A black shape nestled between two adjoining Skelatin structures silhouetted by the pale and unnatural light. It unfurled, slowly and steadily lowering towards street level to merge with the myriad shadows that created a deep carpet of blackness that obscured any movement; a sanctuary for the crawling, the skittering and the hungry beings that fed on the leavings of the recently evident populace.

The Blessing's siren had cleared the streets of the cattle, the consumers and the dominated and replaced the citizens with the manipulators, the reapers, the masters, and more recently, the predators.

A lone Magnite, hooded in her long uniform of shining waxed black, methodically checked a series of dials as the rain ran in rivulets from her shoulders. They had set the access panel back from the alley where her complacent Mariah escort awaited the completion of her task. She was alone; the metallic patter of the surrounding and continuous rain masked any sounds she made.

The creeping shadow emerged from the floor behind her as she tapped and adjusted her instruments, oblivious to his proximity.

In one strike, he rendered her unconscious and fed. Just a taste for now. He had the area to secure and the Mariahs to deal with. He bundled her in the corner, stretched his fingers, and took the strap from his weapon's holster.

"When have you finished back there?" The Mariah shouted over his shoulder, clearly impatient standing in the rain as it poured from his tricorn hat, even the conversation with his partner had spluttered into silence.

"I'm all done. Now it's your turn!"

Was the unexpected reply. The obviously deeper, and male voice startled the Mariahs into action. Expecting the female voice of the Magnite, they quickly entered the alley, both reaching for their Bolt Rods.

The first ignited his, which cast a feint blue light over their enemy, who stood in the middle of the alley wearing a menacing grin. The Mariah got close; he urgently swung back his Bolt Rod as he moved forward into an unseen veil of sticky obstruction. He swung his weapon, but his arm and the sizzling rod itself became fast in a strange and invisible substance. His partner was unaware of the trap as he advanced and also ignited his rod. Suddenly a human shape darted out of the alley's shadow and landed upon the first Mariah, pinned and unable to defend himself, the victim merely juddered and spasmed as the assailant's head connected with the Mariah's neck. The second Mariah jumped back startled, but then found his courage and charged, his rod held high.

Though the Mariahs tasted strange and somehow unnatural, their blood still offered an immediate and energising boost. Crave looked up. His legs encircled the midriff of his prey and one hand clung to his own webbed barrier. With his free hand he pulled his revolver and in one smooth motion lifted and fired a shot that passed through the fast-approaching Mariah's cheek and ended his wild charge immediately, his boots lifted as his back hit the floor. The gunshot did not echo; the rain hampered the sound's journey. It was loud, but bounced rather than emanated around the interconnecting parts of the sprawling city.

Crave continued to feed.

When he'd had his fill, he finished wrapping the woman to take back to his lodgings. Brod wouldn't like it, but he wouldn't put up a fight. He knew what had to be done despite his arguing. As Crave hurried from one hiding spot to the next, crossing the city unseen with his bundled trophy, he replayed their last conversation in his head.

"Someone's gotta say it, boss. Are you chasing ghosts again?"

"What did you say to me?"

"You know I don't question you. I've followed you halfway across the damn world, but someone needs to think about what we're doing here. "

"Were going for blood, damn it! Sidian left us in that damn bubble to drown. He won't get away with that, tribe or not."

"Trust me, boss, I want him to suffer as much as anyone, but we just spent the last couple of years tracking..." Crave's second hesitated with the word brother for a moment before continuing. "Callus, across the west, and you know what? We found him! Maybe it's time to put revenge on one side, throw in with this lot for a while, and fight these bastards. What do you think?"

Crave remembered the mix of frustration and fear in his number two's eyes. He knew he was right; they'd followed Callus like desperate wolves for so long that now they'd found him and found out the truth they'd just jumped on to the next desperate hunt. Crave didn't like being questioned; It stuck in his craw and men had died for less, but Brod was different. He'd done what he needed to do since they'd met and never questioned. Hell, he'd kept Crave alive in those early years, dragging in bodies to feed on, keeping his men in line when Crave was sleeping. The man would sure be hard to replace, and this new world was full of surprises. They'd need each other!

Unfortunately for Brod at that moment, Philips came in.

Crave had leapt across the table and slammed Brod's head down onto his face.

"You get one chance Brod!" Crave had said as his mandibles dripped saliva across Brod's short dark hair. "One chance to cross me for all the years you've put in." Brod had not moved; he remained pinned to the table by his head; Philips looked on with a hungry smirk. "You just used that chance, you understand?"

"I got it, boss." Broderick said as his lips smeared across the table's surface. Crave waited a few seconds for the display to sink in and then let go. He reached down and picked up Broderick's hat and passed it to his most loyal friend. He gave an almost imperceptible nod towards Philips and hoped that Brod understood his display, and why he'd had to provide it.

Crave stood up straight and looked at Philips, who quickly made himself busy.

Chapter 50

To Marcin,

Greetings from the Ronin Brotherhood. I only wish this letter held brighter news.

As you are aware, it was one of our Ronin that gathered information that led to the successful infiltration of the Cthonic mine on the southern edge of the Northern Forest. I send my condolences to you and your family regarding the tragic outcome of that campaign. Anton was an inspiration to us all even before our organisations joined in friendship.

Though I am grateful for this chance to show our respects to your family, I do, however, have grave information to share and this is the reason for my letter.

My brother in rebellion, I fear that the situation in the Cthonic mines is far worse than we suspected. Not only are they enslaving our people and the people from the far lands as they discover them, but Rachnis is now stealing our bloodlines! Our one remaining spy on the inside has finally sent word detailing the extent of the operation, and it is horrifying.

The Mariahs are impregnating the women and bringing them to term like farm animals. They then take the children away and send the Mothers back to the mines and, from what I can tell from the coded information we received, they drug the Mothers beyond recognition and when returned they remain entirely lost to their families. The bastard Council is breeding us into their army of tyranny and the poor children will never know. They will be the Mariahs of the future, bred to dominate and persecute the rightful people of their foul city; their own people!!

The Council have no limits to what they can do to dominate.

I beg you, please tread carefully with this information. I have not passed it through our organisation as these times are extremely fragile; My concern is that this knowledge will either enrage my brotherhood into ill-conceived action or it will simply cause many to lose all hope and spirit. Such has become the power of the vile Council and their army of tormentors.

Once again, I apologise for bringing such dark and ill news to your attention. I only hope your family can endure yet another hardship.

Yours faithfully,

Ivar Vaniken, Voice of the Ronin

Anonymous Author
The covering of tracks

Sidian, Grand Maal of the Reach, stood atop his tower on a small Skelatin balcony and watched the roiling Perma-smog above. He stared into the corona of sun behind the black clouds and challenged it to pierce through; marvelling at the power of the machines and infrastructure that dared to hold back the sun itself and smiled a proud and pious smile. By the door behind him stood silently was Crawn, Sidian's proto creation. The huge Nephilim now rarely left Sidian's side; the Grand Maal knew that the games he played left a trail of grudges and enemies in their aftermath.

Sidian's reflective moment ended abruptly as his guardian's head briefly tilted and he immediately announced,

"Somebody wishes to visit with you, Grand Maal."

"See to them, Crawn, I will follow in a moment." The hulking humanoid nodded once and left the balcony to do his master's bidding. Sidian waited a few minutes and then followed, intending to ensure his visitor received the maximum dramatic impact of his arrival.

Sidian sat at a long table across from one of his appointed Thaumators who specialised in matters of sensitivity. Crawn poured them both a drink and retreated to the shadows; Sidian's guest sipped eagerly but did not take his eye off the shadowed Nephilim until Sidian spoke.

"Crawn tells me you have important news?"

"Yes, Grand Maal, news that I think you and only you must know." He glanced again at the silent Nephilim and quickly back. "News that, as you know, I should also share with other council members but, as you also know, I am loyal to you and only ask that I am taken care of in your service." The man was nervous, but brave. Sidian did not react at first to his veiled plead, but his eyes shifted to Crawn and then swiftly to the door. The Nephilim made his way across to stand by the exit. Sidian feigned interest. He shifted forward.

"And what is the nature of this information?" Sidian enquired with zealous curiosity. The Thaumator's eyes simply could not help but follow Crawn across the room before he responded.

"I know where they are." He crossed his arms in victory and sat back in his chair, suddenly assured of his own value.

Sidian's face did not move. He stared into the eyes of his man and awaited the rest of the information; he refused to allow any drama in his own chamber except that which was provided by himself. The Thaumator did not, at first, realise the level of danger he'd put himself in by holding back, then there was a very slight twitch of annoyance that pulsed across the tattooed side of Sidian's jaw; to the Thaumator it was like a physical smack of realisation and he stumbled over his words to fill the silence.

"Church! Osset's Church; the rebels are in Osset's Church!" again, silence. "The rebels who have been attacking the Magnites and Mariahs out in the city have been tracked by my spies to the Church just outside the gates. The one that was kindly offered to Reverend Osset by the Cthonic Council."

Sidian smiled, having finally received all the information and his guest visibly relaxed.

"This is sensitive information indeed, and I thank you for it."

"That is my pleasure Grand Ma..." Sidian held up a finger and stopped the man mid-sentence. He stood and righted his robes before looking to Crawn and then back to the increasingly nervous man. "But I am sure you know that this is the kind of information that I'd like to keep for myself." Sidian's prey was nodding and swallowed loudly. Without a word, Crawn slowly advanced towards the Thaumator, who suddenly stood as Sidian continued nonchalantly.

"That you have kept this information from the Cthonic Council also gives me a dilemma. It forces me to question your loyalty to the order."

"But... but..." Again, Sidian held up a powerful finger; Crawn was almost at the Thaumator, who stepped backwards, almost falling over his own chair.

"I am afraid that I have to think of Cthonic security and the threat that disloyalty implies." Sidian had stepped back to the table and picked up his drink as Crawn arrived at his destination.

"Please Grand Maal, please al..." The hulking Nephilim swung his massive fist and easily crumpled the face of the pleading Thaumator, spraying blood and bone over his own robes as his body spun away and then dropped to the floor of Sidian's chamber.

Crow Hoby
The industrious under belly
City of Cthonica

Thankfully, after our first visit to the inner city, Joeson had not offered us a chaperone again. The man had not spoken to us about the incident, but he obviously had been told. He'd seemed distracted ever since and wanted to say something more, but couldn't quite manage it. Cal and I had discussed that they may ask us to leave the Church, which Cal found a welcome idea, but I couldn't help worrying about where we'd stay if it happened.

It was some days later, but we'd received a message from someone claiming to be 'a friend' that wanted to meet with us in an area near the docks to discuss 'our friendship' we presumed it related to the man we'd met that first day in the city during the blessing, we'd travelled armed just in case we were wrong or our trust misplaced. Of course, we tucked away our hatchets and my sawn down shotgun in our greatcoats. We were not about to head into potential danger without them.

The dock, it transpired, was a large, ramped area that seemed almost as big as the inner city itself. It was within the city walls, but the entire region seemed to be used for industry. From the vantage of the city, we could see the area in its entirety because of the gradual slope it sat upon, leading all the way from the city's plateau down to the sea, which was walled off of course. This area was where the Aileron Dwarf sat; a host of Magnites were working on the ship, which was brought into a lock-like estuary and closed in by gigantic Skelatin doors.

As we approached, we could see a broad and walled street-corridor which led from the ship itself to the inner city, presumably to keep visitors from seeing the filthy and industrious side of Cthonica. The under belly where the marvels created by the rich and lofty were paid for by the poor and desperate.

The area we were directed to was over to the eastern edge of the dock district, a place apparently no longer in use. We had to climb through a small and ragged hole in its wall to enter. This made me nervous as the place nestled against the sea wall and we both had our reservations about its safety.

Once inside the compound, we made our way to a central building, which was barely standing. Here we were told to go 'down' to our meeting place.

"Don't like it, Crow" said Cal as we descended a spiralled ramp which seemed to drill into the land deeper and deeper until it led to a series of corridors. The place was lit by the strange little lights that were everywhere. They seemed dim and forgotten. Thick mould and green tendrils of growth were spreading around the walls and often obscured the lights, leaving dark patches as we moved through the place. At one point we arrived at a junction that was leaking sea water from its ceiling, a few inches covered the floor, but the water was thankfully flowing, otherwise the entire network would have flooded.

We did not see any sign that people inhabited the place. There were plenty of strange and unique insects, but we saw nobody, even as we waited, deep in the bowels of that salty dead and decaying place. We waited at some kind of central open area, dotted with crooked walkways and disjointed pipework but the floor itself was deep with water. We'd arrived halfway up the vast chamber and could only guess how deep the water was below; it could have even fed directly into the sea.

I nervously fingered the nub of my missing finger, then pointed down to the gently rolling black water beneath us. "Is that why this place got abandoned, do you think?" I said to Cal as we waited, neither of us keeping our heads still for very long.

"Could be." Said Cal; obviously not so keen to explore the idea. We waited, and we waited. At one point I was certain that I saw a large tentacle splash out of the water down below and then disappear. I shuddered, remembering the beast that had dragged us down into the sea when we departed the Aileron Dwarf.

"Let's get out of here." I said; we'd waited way past the allotted time, and nobody had met us. I thought maybe we were in the wrong place, but the route they had given us led us to this place and we could go no further. We'd set off back dejectedly when we heard a sudden and loud noise from ahead; we both stopped in our tracks. Cal took out his hatchet and I my gun. I advanced slowly, but Cal had obviously had enough and did not suffer from fear like anyone else. He charged up the corridor ready to swing, but after a search around the place, neither of us could find the source of the sound.

We left that cold wet place and returned to the Church, bringing with us a salted, mouldy stench that was hard to ignore and a sense that we were alone in this strange and perilous place.

Chapter 51

Grand Fraul, I must first apologise profusely for my lack of contact since my last report, My duties have forced me to spend all my time in Sidian's lab with my fellow Thaumators, I am forbidden to leave the chamber because of the infectious nature of the project that the Grand Maal of the Reach is having us work on. The man is insatiable in his experimentation and often disregards all safety protocols in search of a fast track to the answers he seeks.

I pose substantial risk to myself in sending this report, but I feel it is imperative that the Council know what he is doing. The Grand Maal, in my mind, is unstable and can only bring chaos to our great city. If this is to be my final report, I only hope that it helps to bring this man down from the Council and stops his diabolical experimentation as soon as possible.

He has not visited the lab in some weeks and I have continually enquired about his absence, but discovered nothing until a few days ago.

Apparently, he has been spending his time in the company of a captive deep in the subterranean foundations of the Tower of the Reach. This captive is apparently some kind of priest from across the sea and the Grand Maal visits him daily to learn more of his ways. Apparently the prisoner's screams are heard in the higher levels of the tower but nobody except Crawn, the horrible abomination, may accompany the Grand Maal and so they know very little amongst the Thaumators of Grand Maal Sidian's motivations or outcomes from his latest project.

I only wish that I could offer more insight into this situation, but I am confined to the lab indefinitely.

Please, Grand Fraul, I would ask that, should the chance arise, I transfer to a different location; I feel my time is ending; I have heard talk of using surrogate human wombs in experimentation for the birth of Nephilim and I am one of only ten female Thaumators in this facility. Before the distraction of his latest project, it disappointed the Grand Maal extremely that we had not replicated the success we had with Crawn. He was very keen to find a solution to this problem and his desperation often fuels bold and extreme measures. His Thaumators live in fear of failing him and have not resisted in the past when human elements have been introduced to further his scientific goals.

Yours faithfully,

M

Anonymous Author
Where there is will...

Fraul Brontja left the cremation chamber with an indifferent air; she strode alone from the dome-like structure with a relaxed swagger that belied the funereal pageantry she had left behind. She had played her part well, even made an elegant speech about how she could never fill the void left by Vishtuum's death. It was partly true; she would never command the Order of the Might in such a bombastic and ineffective way. Memories of the previous year's necessary sycophantic facade made her shudder as she strode from the facility.

As two Female Mariahs joined her, one on each side, she made amends with what she'd had to do, what she'd had to become to gain her own seat of power.

"Fraul Nemiah regrets she must change the location of the meeting, Grand Fraul." One of the Mariahs said as they both formed up behind her; both patched heavily in white, a sign of their experience and loyalty to the Order of the Might. Brontja smiled hungrily. It was the first time they had addressed her by her new title.

"Lead the way, Mariah." She gestured for them to move in front, which they did without question. The extra power she now commanded felt palpable; these women would gladly lay down their lives for her. The idea flooded her body with vigour and she quickened her pace towards the meeting with her conspiratorial sister. Her two Mariahs instantly matched her speed.

Dolomon slammed his fist onto the desk and stood, his chair squealing as it skidded and fell behind him.

"They are innocent!" he shouted at the gathered rebels, who did not seem surprised at his outburst. Several shook their heads at the large man as his red face grew angrier.

A silence fell across the meeting, broken only by the soft dripping of sea water as it landed on a moss-covered extraction pipe in a dank corner. The meeting was, as all their business, conducted in an abandoned industrial unit that was left to perish by the council after they discovered the benefits of building higher than sea level. Slowly becoming sodden as it decayed, the entire district gave way to the damp flora that thrived in the new conditions. The rebels kept moving around the area, finding new subterranean camps all the time, but the inevitability of the sinking district was constantly shrinking their operation. They'd lost hope before the Mother had arrived and revitalized their passion to oppose the council.

"Dolomon, with greatest respect, you know we don't have the resources to keep going up against the Mariahs." The bravest of them attempted to nullify the raging man.

"No! Not with respect, never respect for Dolomon. You only think of yourselves." His furious face swept the room, meeting the eyes of as many as he could. "I will speak with her. She will understand and kick your asses, yes?" he stomped from the room and slammed a door already hanging from its hinges in his wake. They remained to think over his proposal, though many of them were unsure what it entailed, as he was furious before they'd actually arrived in the room.

"What's got you so worked up?" The Mother said as the large man came crashing into her room. His white suit and red face was a stark contrast to the greys and greens of the mouldering and mostly book-less library she had taken as her latest base of operations.

"These rebels, they sit and talk and talk." He clapped his hands together loudly, "There is no action with them!" he continued to growl incoherently until she stood from her map and engaged with him.

"What is it you want them to do, Dolomon? Look at this place." She gestured around the room at the crumbling furniture and the leaking ceiling. "We need to move on, set up a proper place to fight from; we can't go running to the aid of everyone that crosses the Council, not until we are better prepared to fight them." Dolomon was already shaking his head.

"You don't understand. The Mariahs are moving in to take these people because they think they are us! The fools think they have found the heart of the rebellion and they are ready to swoop!" his fury was slowly turning to desperation to explain his thinking. The Mother's eyes showed concern but still a reluctance to put her people at risk.

"I don't like that anymore than you do but…" Dolomon shook his head, his face flushed again, and he opened his mouth to interrupt. This enraged the Mother, who stood up straight and pointed into his face, her eyes blazing.

"Enough!" she commanded. "I understand your anger but I command here and I will not have you question me, Bravlav or not!" the raising of her voice had summoned her guards; they had slipped into the room behind Dolomon and removed their hoods. Dolomon showed the leader his hands and spoke in a subdued voice.

"The ones in the Church, there are two of them, an old tribesman and a younger lad. They both wear long coats and have just arrived in the city."

Sudden realisation dawned on her and her eyes went wide.

Chapter 52

Dear Reverend Joeson,

I write to you with both positive and disappointingly sensitive news.

I am led to believe that you understand the complicated situation regarding your religion as its presence takes shape here in Cthonica.

It is this rather delicate matter that I would like to clarify.

As you know, I gifted your religion a Church through the Cthonic Council. An arrangement brokered between your Reverend Osset and myself, Grand Maal of the Reach. I have not only agreed to further fund this Church but have also secured backing for several new premises within the city's walls. I am sure you will delight in this news and I look forward to receiving your gratitude in person when I visit the Church.

This brings me to the sensitive matter that I wished to share with you.

I have spent considerable time with Reverend Osset and have dedicated myself to learning the intricacies and history of your religion. I find the premise both fascinating and extremely productive, and I have embraced this religion here in Cthonica.

Sadly, I have found that Reverend Osset, although very knowledgeable, has a considerable lack of vision in terms of development in this area. As I have already stated, I have learned the details of the religion and concluded my studies to a level which will allow me to take this belief structure to the next level and entwine its roots in that of Cthonic culture. During this process, Reverend Osset has proved somewhat obstructive and has attempted to oppose me to a heretical degree. I have awarded the man the respect he deserves as a high-ranking member of this religion, but he has sadly wasted the opportunity in this case.

The situation insists I take control of this matter immediately and as from this moment, I will take control of this religion and its presence in our city. I will appoint new Reverends within the city and ask that you support me in this endeavour. I look forward to hearing your ideas when I visit, which I intend to do as soon as my schedule allows.

My role, as it is for all those who sit on the Cthonic Council, is to ensure the city's ascension towards the sky; in order to do that, I have plotted a course through religion and technology to ascend myself towards Godhood, so that I may shepherd our citizens to their new and productive lives beyond the constraints of the earth.

Yours sincerely,

Sidian
Grand Maal of the Reach
Cthonic Council
Cthonica

Crow Hoby
Exploring my surroundings
City of Cthonica

I had decided not to venture into town; the crowds were a vexation, so much urgency, so much chaos. For a thriving city full of hundreds, maybe thousands of people, it was so quiet, nobody seemed to talk, especially not to me, an outsider. The days were dragging. Tiredness crept up on me and often I longed to rest in the day whilst Cal did. The night seemed to energize me. Even in that strange and unfamiliar city, the darkness seemed to invite me while the daytime hung on me like a weight around my soul.

Cal usually had a few minor requests for me while he was out of action, but today there was nothing. I wandered around the Church and observed as it slowly took shape. Rev. Joeson had told me he had only just started the congregation some weeks back and people were still working on the building. I got the feeling that he was still molding his own role, too. He often seemed uncertain of what he should be doing. Directing Skelatin workers and pipe engineers did not suit him but when he talked to his people in hushed and calming tones, advising about his God and his ways, he seemed to thrive and his eyes became brighter.

Id woken up later than usual. Each day it seemed to creep up on me and I woke feeling tired and somehow unnatural. I'd helped Rev. Joeson put out some chairs and helped him sweep the entrance, but I'd then ran out of motivation. I wandered aimlessly, looking for areas inside the Church I'd not seen before. Without trying very hard, I'd found a slope down into a cellar. I descended as I mused about how I'd seen no steps in Cthonica, only ramps and slopes. My mind clearly craved something of interest, some nourishment, as did my body. In the day, I had to fight the urge to just lay down and rest, or 'die' as Cal would describe it. At night time, I was constantly fighting an inner demand to attack and feed. My body was twice as strong and just as fast, and predatory instincts made me feel sharp and capable.

The cellar was bigger than I'd expected and seemed to open the length and breadth of the entire plot of the Church. Black Skelatin pillars propped up the floor and kept it from touching the slightly moist ground. I could see almost as well as in the daylight, though I knew there was very little light until I rounded a corner to find an ornate door marked by two small candles; almost burnt out. I wondered who it was that had kept them aflame.

Just as the thought came to my mind, I heard footsteps on the cellar slope. Somebody approached. Their own candlelight danced around the cellar walls, illuminating the thick pillars. Then an elderly lady appeared before the strange door. She jumped and almost dropped her candle as she saw me, holding one hand up to protect herself.

"It's OK, it's me." I said stupidly. I don't think she knew who I was. I'd certainly never seen her before. "I live here. Rev. Joeson gave me sanctuary." The poor woman's eyes seemed about to bulge from her sockets as she straightened herself and cleared her throat.

"You shouldn't be down here." She said with a croak, "you'll have an accident without a light." I could still see fear on her brow as she shook her head. She moved around to the door without taking her eyes off me. I hoped my curiosity would ease her.

"What's through the door?" I said, sounding somewhat like a cheeky child.

"Nothing for you!" she returned, clearly gathering her stoic composure. "Rev. Joeson has asked me to relight the candles." She said proudly, then as she swapped out the candles one by one and her voice took on a more comfortable tone, she looked at me as if she intended to gossip. "The Reverend has a very important visitor."

"Who's that?" I answered. I didn't really care, but I felt bad for scaring the old woman.

"Never you mind." she scolded, "and stay away from this door, Reverends only." With that she disappeared, her glowing candle swaggered away and left me in the dark.

I heard a loud crash and raised voices as I made my way back to the upper floor, then a scream; the unmistakable voice of my recent acquaintance. I ran to the main body of the Church towards the sound which emanated from the Reverend's quarters.

Callus

Acceptance

And regrets

Dammit, Crow's I' restless. I knew it was happenin', but wanted to hide it away. He needs to be restin' when I do. He's not a kid no more. Seen it in his eyes when I leave him for the day; he's been lookin' more tired each day. I wanted to protect him from so much, but in the end, he's just followin' my path. At least he still has a good soul, that's if we have souls, still can't be sure.

I've not left him any jobs for the mornin' figured he deserves a last day for himself. I'll bite the bullet, have a talk with him tomorrow night. From now on, we'll die together. I'm sure Joeson'll keep us safe in the daytime.

Not entirely sure what to do next, that's the problem, can't seem to find anyone in this crazy place. Figure we'll have to creep into the city one night, see if we can find anyone else hidin' out again. I'm sure they're out there watchin' us!

Thought I'd be much happier without no sun, but this place is slowly sendin' me crazy! Sometimes I feel like writing this stuff is the only thing keepin' me goin'. I've been writin' some other stuff, just for Crow, for whenever he ends up on his own. Don't like to think about it but I can't go on forever, even though it seems like I already have. Been through damn wars, fires, riots an' now I'm across the sea, dammit, it feels like the world keeps turnin' into some place different while I'm still standing here; can't last forever. Hell, I don't even know if I want to.

I still miss her, dammit, was her that got me on this road, but I'd give it all up for her. People say 'it'll be alright in the morning.' Dammit, it's still not alright and I've died a thousand times.

Thank whatever Gods or Goddesses sent me Crow.

Crow Hoby
The new world
Torn asunder

I arrived in the room as the Mariahs were leaving it. My stomach flipped upside down and back as I took in the bloody scene. Rev. Joeson, or what remained of him, splattered into one corner. His dark blood shamed me by making my nose twitch and a low growl emanate from my stomach. The old lady was close to his body. She was still breathing slowly, the electric burn of a Bolt Rod still settling in the air.

I followed a raised voice through the building, wondering who would want to attack a Church. Then I heard a loud crunching sound, a destructive crash of furniture, and my mind raced instantly to Cal in his upturned wardrobe.

I sprinted towards the sound, wishing I was armed, but my weapons were in the room I was approaching.

I heard Cal roar.

More crashing furniture.

I arrived at our room; luckily the show inside engrossed the two Mariah door guards who didn't notice me arrive. Beyond them was an enormous

282

monster of a man, if it was a man. It was much bigger than a person and bulged with excessive muscle. Its skin was blemished and gave the impression someone had painted it to look human. It's black robes littered with dust, blood and bits of wrecked furniture. As I watched, it swung Cal around with one arm and slammed him into the wall with a catastrophic crash. Out of sight, another man nonchalantly spoke. I didn't catch what he was saying.

My fury and instinct to protect Cal drove me past the turned backs of the Mariahs and into the room; I was unarmed and unable to stop the beast that was swinging him around like a child's doll. Behind me, I heard Bolt Rods igniting.

"Noooo!" Cal had seen me from his crumpled position and screamed in defiance as the behemoth stepped towards him. My mentor, my partner, my everything looked more defeated than I had ever known, but he summoned a last burst of strength and spent it on me.

He quickly got his feet back on the ground and charged at me, wrapping my body in his arms and charging towards the two Mariahs. As we barged through and beyond them, I heard and smelled the rods connect with him and he ejected me out beyond into the corridor as his body fell. I matched his momentum and kept running; he had offered me this chance to get away before they took him.

I bolted from the Church, past an ornate goath drawn coach outside. My mind was raging, but my legs took Cal's gift thankfully and I did not stop.

As I eventually slowed, I found myself exhausted in the dock district, where we'd failed to meet the rebels a few days earlier. It was the only place I knew. I crumpled against an alley wall and let my screaming thoughts settle. My hands gripped and squeezed my head in frustration and fury. It felt like I'd been there for hours when I heard approaching footsteps. I looked up with a snarl, ready to tear apart an approaching Mariah.

"I am sorry my friend, I am here now also, soon it will be night, yes?" to my absolute surprise there stood Dolomon, he smiled at me like a kindly grandfather in contrast to the two massive revolvers that gleamed on his hips.

Chapter 53

To Gralfur Honnim, Chairman of the Society of Scientific Exploration

I hope this finds you well

It is with significant excitement that I contact you, and with great hope this letter finds its way to the society.

As you know, I have found accommodation in a small encampment near the Western edge of the Helmire Valley, where I am fortunate enough to observe the abandoned city of Haalflife.

Here I have become moderately comfortable and have learned to survive as the locals do, but I have, in no way, abandoned my position for the society. Quite the opposite, in fact, and therefore I feel it is so incredibly necessary to contact you.

Until now, my observations have been distant and blighted with a lack of occurrence. I have included in this letter my findings over the last year, but, as you will find, there is little to confirm that life is possible in the poisoned city.

However, during the past two months, I have seen evidence that the city is indeed habitable. I have observed from closer distances and record my increments as I gradually approach the boundaries of the city itself. Not only have I seen an increase in indigenous fauna, but also I have witnessed scavenging groups from the Helmire encroach on the region and leave during the following days, apparently unharmed and in good health.

We were right! The poisonous air that has afflicted the city since the communion is slowly dissipating and therefore creating a habitable treasure trove of pre-communion culture and technology for the taking of those prepared to explore it.

I would be grateful if you could prepare an expedition and meet me at the included coordinates. I will barter with the Helmire locals for safe passage for the society's men and eagerly await our success.

Randulf Penum

Scientific Scout

Society of scientific exploration

Anonymous Author

Reflections

Callus disdained the irony as they dumped him into yet another dank cell. Since he had attempted to balance his moral debts and inch his way towards personal redemption, he had found himself in a similar predicament, on occasions too frequent for his liking. Yet again unable to resist his arrest as two simultaneous blows from ignited Bolt Rods had rendered him unconscious. As he awoke, he learned that he had suffered multiple blows from less technological weapons also whilst unable to defend himself; the result was a sore body and a somewhat bitter mind.

The former Tribesman, once again, shared his cell with one other, another crumpled form in the far corner. His quiet muttering suggested his mind was fragile.

Callus climbed to his feet and assessed his wounds, which were mostly superficial. He heaved against the iron bars of the cell to find them as sturdy as they looked. His instant motivation was to get to Crow, an undeniably parental calling had replaced his desire to survive.

"You will not leave this place, not until Sidian decrees it." Said the ageing man in the corner, as he turned to sit upright and see who had joined him. His voice was still powerful despite the rasp in his throat, a sign of his ill health from these poor conditions. "Better to make your peace with God." The old man's head flopped down in resignation, then silence reigned once more. Callus stared hard at the man's face. He felt as though he recognised something in the way his mouth curled; a small scar traced a short white line across his lip and into the grey whiskers that had grown around it.

The old man suddenly laughed aloud. He cackled until his eyes watered and his breath caught in his throat, causing a bout of dry coughing.

"What's so funny?" asked Cal, frowning at the man's mirth.

"It's not funny." he replied, his face suddenly serious. "I have devoted my life to the word of God and now he has chosen a different word." he continued to stare at Cal, almost daring him to mock his misfortune. His wide eyes bulged and shuddered with his conviction. Cal looked away and sat down dejectedly.

"It seems we are both victims of injustice, friend. The world has turned and put us where it thinks we belong."

Crow Hoby
Amongst friends
Charging blind

Our reunion did not seem to be a priority. Dolomon had introduced me to some of his friends and offered to help me rescue Cal. We'd then gone to the Church to collect my weapons, Cal's diary, and a handful of his effects. It all happened so fast that I hardly knew what was going on. The one thing that I knew was that Dolomon would not be helping me if he didn't think there was any hope of saving Cal. There was hope, and I was clinging to it desperately.

The big man was kind and protective, even snapping at his friends if they got in my way. He was like an enormous dog with its pup. I didn't mind. I felt like a small pup in an enormous world. Something inside me was threatening to break.

Dolomon kept talking about the rebellion and I wanted to interrupt with complaints about our supposed meeting, but he was a hard man to interrupt and I did not have the spirit to face that challenge. I saved all my energy for the fight ahead.

There were six of us. We hid around a shadowed corner across from the tower of the reach, whilst Dolomon gave them his orders. I didn't take any notice. All I could think about was seeing Cal again. The grief lodged in my chest. It wouldn't slide down or come back up until I saw him again and knew what had happened. I loaded my shotgun, and I felt Dolomon's massive hand on my shoulder.

"I have gift for you." He said with a grin and a wink. "The Mother, she sends her regards, yes?" He was holding a Bolt Rod which was attached to a metal box, obviously the source of its power. He helped to strap it around my waist and under my great coat; it felt good and powerful in my hand.

"Remember, charge is not quick, yes? 'Takes time to build up again." I nodded, wishing I could fire it up there and then, but that would bring unwanted attention before the attack began. While the rebels were preparing, I swung it around. The cable was a little unwieldy, but I felt I would get used to it.

"You ready, little Crow?" Dolomon said, I didn't like the nickname but then most people were little to Dolomon and if it hadn't been for him I would still be slumped in an alley trying desperately, but physically unable, to cry.

Dolomon insisted I stay back during the initial attack. I tried to refuse, but he'd already explained that they needed to get me inside with my Bolt Rod. If that meant losing men at the front door, then so be it. I couldn't really argue with his commitment to my cause.

The tower itself was guarded but not heavily. It seemed very few people thought it wise to attack the tower of the Reach, despite its many enemies.

The charge was brutal. One woman and a man I'd never even spoken to went down to Boltrods before their allies went in with blades and took the Mariahs down. Dolomon had tried to keep his guns out of the fight until the alarm went up but couldn't help himself when three unexpected Mariahs came rushing to help their colleagues, their rods blazing. Dolomon pumped four shots into them with his two revolvers, the loud thump and flash of light illuminating his gleefully sadistic face with each shot. All three went down cold.

Myself, Dolomon and two other rebels made our way inside the tower. There were no Mariahs in the vast foyer, just three spiralled slopes, two leading upwards and one down.

The rebels instinctively went to ascend the tower, but something stopped me from following, something in the air, a faint but definite taste and smell.

"Ill go down." I said and ran for the descending slope. Dolomon followed me but I was unsure what the others did, such was my reckless devotion to finding Cal.

We made our way past many arched doorways as we descended, but my instincts and the familiar smell in the air told me to go deeper within the earth. At one entrance I almost ran straight into a Mariah as she stepped out. As surprised as I was, she was not holding her Bolt Rod uncharged. I ignited for the first time and swept low as my momentum took me past her. There was a sudden flash and a harsh vibration as the rod connected with her left knee. Her face instantly contorted, and she collapsed to the floor; the rod went dead in my hand. Dolomon then arrived and patted his huge hand on my shoulder while he took an exhausted breath.

"Best to switch off, yes? Or get a nasty surprise!" he gasped for air with his hands on his knees. I switched the Bolt Rod's handle to the off position as the understanding dawned on me. When it charged up again, it would ignite when it was able, not when I told it to. We carried on running.

"How long do they take to charge?" I asked as we ran. Dolomon had to stop to answer breathlessly.

"Not long, but enough time for someone to slip past the defences, yes?"

We appeared to have reached the lowest level. We went around a corner and through a double door, slowing to reduce the noise we were making. It appeared nobody knew we were there.

Suddenly, there was a loud bang, like a gunshot on the other side of another door, then another, followed by an unmistakably familiar whoop of success. I opened the door and the waft of burning hair that had led us down to the depths of the tower assaulted my nostrils. Right in front of us, ducking behind an upturned desk, was Laz. He was peering down the sights of a long rifle whilst he held his acrid cigarette at bay in his twisted mouth.

He fired and whooped again, clearly a successful shot down a long corridor.

"Well, crease my britches. How long you gonna take next time, boy? Here, hold my cigarette. Damn things goin' burn my face off." he gestured with his head and I took the stinking roll-up from his lip and watched him shoot. The corridor was a long one; I could see cell doors on either side as it stretched into the distance. Mariahs were poking their heads out and shouting to each other, trying to coordinate an advance. The corridor already displayed a few black-clad failed attempts.

"Listen here boy, I aint gonna be here for long but I got to impress on you the importance of Rezidrual purpose." Laz fired again, then glanced at me to make sure I was listening.

"Rezid what?" I asked. It seemed a very surreal place to be having the conversation, but nothing was ever typical where Laz was involved.

"Rezidrual purpose!" he snapped, "Like I've kept tellin' you all this time. When things've all run out of purpose, don't be mistakin' that they's all done, you get me boy?" he reloaded and took out an advancing Mariah near enough between the eyes. Dolomon laughed heartily at Laz' shot. The big man did not like the Mariahs. My only concern was to get past them to Cal, who I felt sure was down that corridor. I tried to think back to any of the cryptic conversations I'd had with Laz since we'd met, and then something clicked. I remembered the glass bubble they'd trapped us in. Laz was gathering useless items; we were floating in the sea in a glass bubble completely at the mercy of the local creatures. I suspected many thought him mad, but they'd coughed up spent casings, old coins and other trash.

"Residual purpose!" I said aloud. Laz looked at me and shook his head like I wasn't getting it. "No, I get it!" I looked up at Dolomon, who was pulling his guns out with a concerned look on his face. I turned to Laz, who was no longer there. Dolomon's guns started blazing down the corridor and he moved forward; I followed in his wake.

One, two, three Mariahs span onto the floor, painting the walls red, then Dolomon stopped and had to reload. There were more Mariahs now advancing. They could clearly see that he'd had to stop firing. That was my chance; I pushed past Dolomon and ignited the Bolt Rod.

Three of them came at me. They were all swinging crackling blue rods, but luckily the corridor only allowed for two at once. I waited for the first to swing and blocked with my own. There was a shower of violent sparks, but the block succeeded. I kicked at the First Mariah's knee and felt a satisfactory pop as both our rods died and returned to black. I swung the smoking but dead rod around to block the second attack, unsure if it would hold without power.

It did. I knocked the second swing off its trajectory and swung at the open area in the Mariah's left side. Just before it connected, the rod burst back into life. It cast blue sparks across the Mariah's face as the ignited rod made contact and sent the man sprawling to lay faced down. I stepped over the body to face the third who was already swinging. I went to block, but he was wise to my moves; he swept lower and somehow connected with my Bolt Rod's cable. The sparks flew again and this time it was me who came out worse; the Bolt Rod completely severed the cable; my rod would not be recharging. There was a moment of panic when I realised the best I could do was defend, but I could not attack. I'd failed Cal. I would wake next to him in a cell with an impending death sentence.

Dolomon's revolver sounded again. Two shots, hastily reloaded, were all it took. My current attacker and the one screaming as he held his own knee suddenly fell silent.

Chapter 54

Anonymous Author

Face to face with the devil

"OSSET!" the name woke Callus from his reflective stupor and instantly conjured bitter aggression. He took a moment to clarify where he was and how badly he hurt. There was gunfire and the sounds of combat beyond the cell door. The tiniest glimmer of excitement made him stand as two black-robed men appeared from around the corner and began unlocking the door.

As they stepped in, the huge monstrosity that had captured Callus back at the Church joined them. He carried a wide, ornate blade that looked somewhere between sword and axe. It was nighttime and Callus could feel its gifted energy within him, despite the pain of his wounds and mistreatment.

The cursed tribesman was about to strike. First, he'd take out the underlings and then face the beast. He had the night on his side and a desperation to fight his way through to Crow. He crouched, about to pounce, when they spoke the name again, the power of its heritage stopping Callus in his tracks.

"Osset!" one of the robed Cthonicans accompanied his announcement with a kick to the old man, who was pitifully attempting to deny his own existence. He kicked again, and the man twisted on the floor to look up at his assailants. Fear replaced desperation and misery.

Immobilised by what he was witnessing, Callus' mind flashed back to so many years before, so much anger, so much hate and desire for vengeance.

He stared at the wizened old man as the two guards brought him to his feet with a click of old bones and a whimper of the doomed. This was the object of his calling, his crusade across the world, the final chapter of his redemption. Callus' mind flicked to the image of the small bottle, gifted to him by his dear friend and saviour; the words etched to last forever. He'd given the bottle to Crow and gladly. He'd surrendered this treasure, this icon to a being who deserved it. Realisation dawned on him that his redemption was already complete. This pitiful wretch was no longer his to destroy. Wilf's kindness had followed him into his new life and into Crow's.

As he looked on, Callus' mind came back to the present as the wide blade fell; the gigantic man had swung it through one side of Osset's neck and out the opposite side just below his rib cage. Blood erupted and Callus leapt.

Crow Hoby
Hell's gateway
Full circle

More Mariahs came, but miraculously I remained out of the reach of their Bolt Rods. Dolomon was fumbling and dropping bullets with each reload as I pressed on, forcing him to fire, reload and repeat as more and more bodies fell to his barrage. I wondered how many reloads the big man had left, but dismissed the thought as a distraction. I was nearing Cal and would free him as he had me in those black and poisonous mines.

Nearing the end of the corridor, I noticed a rebel who had arrived with Dolomon; he was struggling with a Mariah, his rod was black but as I glanced over another appeared and took him down with his own sparking blue weapon.

It seemed like a desperate dream. I was running as fast as I could, but the corridor advanced painfully slowly and the surrounding carnage unfolded as if under water.

It was that dreamlike moment that haunts me to this day, that moment that weighs my judgments and fires my blood; the moment that set a course for my existence and graced it with infinite and enduring pain.

The immense man that I'd last seen swinging Cal into the Church wall emerged from the last cell. Behind him were two black-robed men carrying an enormous sword between them. As I ran on and watched them, the muscular beast lifted his hand slowly to reveal what he held so triumphantly.

The severed head of Callus, my partner, my friend, my brother and my father, stared blankly at me and the world finally changed into the cruel and agonizing place that I had hoped it was not.

Anonymous Author
Fools cavalry

More rebels arrived to assault the tower of the Reach, accompanied by the Mother herself. The foyer choked with combat and the electric sounds of Bolt Rods as they immobilised and recharged to swing again, mingled with the screams of the wounded. They'd mostly armed the rebels with blades and spears, but the occasional gunshot would signal the end of one of the many Mariahs.

It was the first time that an actual tower had ever faced attack, and The Mother knew it was a futile and expensive move, as soon as she reached her aim she would call a retreat and hope that there were still people alive and able to fall back. Her personal guard surrounded her and defended her with spears but occasionally one would fall and she relished the chance to swing her sword, the way she moved made her untouchable and she dealt death to any Mariah within her reach until her loyal guards could refill the defensive gap.

Eventually, the way to the lower levels cleared as most of the Mariahs were appearing from above. She made her way down below ground with a handful of guards. The corridors, already strewn with bodies, were slick with blood. Some were stirring into consciousness after Bolt Rod strikes and they stopped to help them up and orientate the confused rebels before moving on.

Crow Hoby
Nothing left to fear
Finding a new purpose

I could not look into those dead eyes. The pain was too massive to be contained in my small body. I clenched my eyes closed and ran as if my legs were the only things that could still function. In the blackness, there was a strange solace, and my mind transported to a memory of a conversation with Laz. It was like trying to recall a dream. Only my body was hurtling blindly towards the most deadly being I'd ever witnessed.

Laz was pouring out his usual rhetoric, but somehow my mind was ordering and rearranging his lines. He was trying to tell me something as a last-ditch attempt to keep me alive as I ran on. I knew faintly that I was running full pelt with my head down past the bodies of fallen Mariahs, but I did not care. Another part of my mind whispered encouragement. This was the only way I could join Cal and be safe from torment.

I felt as though I'd opened my eyes, but only in my mind's eye. Laz's face was right there, too close for comfort and I squirmed as I ran, luckily I did not trip, I later felt as though Laz had also been guiding my feet, how else could I have traversed the body strewn corridor without seeing. Laz was whispering to me about his 'rezidrual purpose' and how the only way to finish the mission was to learn.

"Learn what?" I'd spoken out loud, and that somehow brought me to my senses. I stopped running and opened my eyes.

The immense man was before me, flanked by his robed entourage. He was speaking, but I could not hear his voice; he had lowered Cal's head. I could still make out Laz' whispered instructions, but could not understand them. It was like he was speaking to someone else inside my mind.

I looked down to see I still held the severed Bolt Rod and Laz whispered. "Yes!"

Without commanding it to, my body then turned, ready to fight. All the while, Laz was instructing, and I was observing. The Grand Maal of the Reach's gargantuan pet snarled an attempt at a smile, which his colleagues shared. Though utterly occupied by my own thoughts and those of Laz, I could understand the comical scenario that I was in. This creature had already taken Cal's life, and probably countless others, with ease. His shoulders alone gave the impression that he could crush rocks without breaking a sweat, and I was squaring up for one-on-one combat with a broken and lifeless weapon.

"Aint no such thing as lifeless." Laz interrupted my musing again, and everything came together. As if my thoughts, the mind of a senile old man who thought himself a wizard and my subconscious had an agreement while I was out of the room grieving, and now it was time to deliver.

I took the dead Bolt Rod in both hands and somehow felt for its missing purpose, its reason to exist. Built to channel electricity from its source and send it through the bodies of its wielder's enemies. I had all the pieces, and I had an abundance of new purpose for the weapon. I was brimming with it. Every part of my body suddenly felt ready to burst. A vision of Cal's lifeless face presented itself in my mind, and the energy within me doubled. My thoughts went to the people of this brutal city and its tyrannical ways, and it doubled again. My time in the Cthonic mines created a small leak of this residual energy as it built and swelled within me; the leak reached my Bolt Rod and there was a brief crackle.

The brute before me saw the rod's ineffectual splutter; he raised his head and laughed.

The energy exploded from me like a torrent as it burst its dam. Bright blue electricity fired from my Bolt Rod and arced across into his body. Another surge joined the first, then another and another. The released energy was nothing short of pure lightning. It arced across to the stiffened body of my enemy, tongue after tongue of blue power lashing him as he convulsed. Eventually, his body wasn't enough to channel the amount of purpose I was releasing, and the tongues of lightning spread over to his men. They quickly became overwhelmed by the intense discharge. Unable even to scream, the three bodies smoked and flames climbed as the lightning subsided. As the intense light diminished, the bodies blackened and the growing flames beckoned them to crumble and fall to the floor as piles of ash.

A soft hand eventually settled on my shoulder and I turned from the scene of destruction I'd wrought. Behind me stood several rebels; their mouths hung in disbelief and reverence. Dolomon approached, stepping over and between scattered Mariah's bodies.

Though I did not have the energy for astonishment, it surprised me to see that it was Silk who held my shoulder; her Mother reached from her sleeve to wrap around the top of my arm reassuringly.

"You're the 'Mother?'" I asked in a pitiful voice, and she nodded. Blood speckled her face.

Chapter 55

Dear Crow,

I don't expect you'll be reading this soon, but I know there's a few things that I've never said, and I know I never will. I want to apologise for sharing the curse that was meant for me. I've thought about this long and hard. It wasn't right to share it. Back then, I thought I was helpin' you, but I've realised that sharing my blood was more to help me than you, even if I did convince myself otherwise so many times.

What Laz says is right; crazy as he is, that guy knows more than he should! They created this curse for one, me. By sharing it, we split the benefits and the costs and that means that when I go; I believe it will all come to you. I'm sorry for that and hope that the full weight of my deeds does not do to you what it did to me; you are better than that, Crow; you are so much better than I ever was.

In the early days, you once asked me if I had any friends and I said your father, your real father. That stranger was the best friend any man could ask for. I know he had his own reasons for giving his life and I know he missed your momma more than anyone else can ever understand, but he put you in my care. He gave me responsibility and purpose; he gave me a reason to put one foot in front of the other. Not only did your poppa give me a chance at redemption, but he gave me the best and greatest gift of my long, long existence.

He gave me you.

Silk

Twining the threads

Understandably, Crow had spoken very little since we returned to camp. We'd set up an area to patch up as many as we could; Daroch was a fine healer, but I feared many were well beyond his talents. The death toll had been high, and I knew I would somehow have to answer to the others and defend my decision to intervene. Luckily, most of the survivors had witnessed Crow's power and I could use that to offset the heavy cost of our losses. I closed my eyes as I stood at the entrance to my room. A single tear, easily disguised as one of the many leaks that dripped around me, dropped from my chin. Beneath my armour I felt you settle supportively around my chest.

"Heard what happened." Crave had a habit of unintentionally sneaking up on people. It was his nature.

"Damn foolish to get involved if you ask me." his voice sounded strained; he'd taken to not wearing his mask at camp and as I turned, I saw his mandibles could not keep still, a sign of the tension warring within him.

"What I did is done. Time to move on." I said, as I looked around at the derelict wreck that we currently occupied. You deftly appeared from inside my collar to wipe away the tear, and I stood taller, and sniffed.

"We also need an army." He said, I could tell he wrestled with the word 'we.'

"Funny you should say that." I replied, glad to think about the future and swallow the loss for a moment. "Magan has an idea where we can get one."

"Not more damn prophecies!" The Outlaw lifted his arms in frustration and turned to stalk away.

"Crave!" I called after him. He stopped and looked over his shoulder.

"The question is, are you and yours with me?" his mandibles stretched, it almost looked as if they were about to stroke his beard in thought. He squeezed his fists, turned, and stepped closer.

"You promise me Sidian, and we go where you go."

Crow

An empty shell

Only vengeance mattered

There was a soft knock on the doorframe of my new quarters; I glanced up to see one of Silk's druids peering around the corner. He took me noticing him as a signal for him to enter. Grief still trapped me in my own mind, chasing off memories and testing my threshold for inner torment. He approached and checked my body for wounds, like me he had not spoken. I ignored his prodding and probing, even allowing him to open my mouth to look inside. He showed no surprise at my fangs or at the pallor of my skin. I could almost feel the changes happening as Cal faded away, and I received the full weight of his curse.

I could feel the daytime as it begun, the ever-present smog still hindering the sun in the Cthonic sky, but I could feel its rise behind the brown-grey veil above. Behind my weariness and my black thoughts I could feel the dormant strength as it waited for night like a crouching monster.

"You cannot heal me." My cracked voice was barely discernible in the commotion of the adjoining room. A make-shift hospital for the wounded rebels that had fallen to help me.

I had failed. Not only had I been unable to stand against the corruption of Callus' curse, but also I had failed to deliver his redemption, and now it was too late.

The druid spoke in equally quiet tones. "Magan says that I am to check on you, anyway. We have a long journey ahead."

"Who is Magan?"

"He is my chieftain, my leader."

"I thought that Silk, The Mother." I corrected myself. "Was your leader." He piqued my interest. My desire for conversation gave me a brief reprieve from self-torment. The druid smiled a warm and caring smile. He looked as though he knew everything there was to know; it was a strange sensation.

"The Mother is the one that we must follow; she will help us right the world, as will you." I looked at him properly for the first time. His face was serene and his smile was that of pure satisfaction despite the bloodshed and trauma that he'd laboured to repair. Just as I was about to speak, Silk walked into the room. The druid nodded, but continued his work silently. The rebel's leader smiled at me but did not speak. I think she understood there was very little to say in the presence of such shared grief.

"I think there is little you can help with, Daroch, but I thank you for trying." The druid nodded, smiled and left the room. The silence continued between us for some time before she eventually spoke to me.

"We have to leave this city to rebuild." She sounded regretful, but decisive.

"It looks like a lot has happened to the both of us since we parted." I replied without agreement. I was too weak for decision making. She nodded.

"There will be time to tell my story on the journey, if you'll come?" There was a very slight plead in her eyes. "Magan says there's an army awaiting a leader to the north in a city long dead."

"Who is this Magan?"

"It may sound strange but he follows a prophecy. He brought his people across the mountains just to find me. He believes I will fix the world." I raised a cynical eyebrow, reminding myself of Cal.

"Do you believe him?"

"He found me, he brought me here, and he has helped me to forge this rebellion. He has said that when the time comes, we will need to travel to the dead city to find our allies."

"When the time comes?" I queried. She thought for a second before deciding how to answer. She quoted Magan.

"When our brother commands lightning, our hour has come; to find allies in the dead city and return with a forgotten army to right the world."

I scratched my head, unsure of what to say.

"Will you come?" I got the feeling that Silk rarely had to ask anything of anyone twice.

"Together we'll bring them down and avenge our fallen. Where you go I will follow, sister!"

Sidian, Grand Maal of the Reach
 Lord of the Thaumators
 Cthonic Council

We were furious beyond measure! How dare they enter our home and destroy our creation. We knelt beside the ashen pile that had once been our Nephilim, our child. We touched the black and grey soot with our gloved hand and fought off the pain and urge to roar with frustration. One of us needed to be pragmatic. Enemies beset us. One could grieve while the other made plans for vengeance and domination. The rebellion had to be crushed; severe action taken to end their unfortunate streak of success and ensure they never spoke of rebellion again.

And all the while, the fool Rachnis thought herself wise, her machinations hidden even from us. Her little matriarchal coup was gathering momentum, but she too would perish beneath our boot as we ascend to Godhood. We'd taken the first Church and more would bloom across the city. The people would succumb to the ways of God, the fear, the desperation to appease and the reverence. We would climb towards the sky, not only through domination of the Council, but with guile and superiority. We would supplant the foreign God and reign over Cthonica. From there, our power and dominion would spread across the world and our enemies would collapse in regret and shame.

We stood sharply and turned on the amassed Mariahs.

"Bring Thaumators; we need more Nephilim."

The End

About the Author

DB Rook lives in the North of England with his wife and two beautiful children. He is a drummer, a gamer, and a dreamer who loves to spend time in other worlds, as well as this one. He has spent the last 10 years working in the charity sector whilst occasionally visiting the Wayward World to stretch his legs and feed his soul.

This book is dedicated to the memory of Eric Perkins, may he rest in peace.

Keep an eye open for more books from the
  Wayward World Chronicles…

DB.Rook@outlook.com

If you enjoyed this book, please consider posting a review and spreading the word. The world is blissfully full of books. Please help people to find this one!

You can connect with me on:

- 🌐 http://dbrookbooks.com
- 🐦 https://twitter.com/DB_Rook
- 📘 https://facebook.com/DBRookBooks

Subscribe to my newsletter:

- ✉ https://db-rook.mailchimpsites.com

Printed in Great Britain
by Amazon

11670539R00181